Radiance

Diamonds of the First Water
Book Four

SYDNEY JANE BAILY

cat whisker press

Boston

Second Paperback Edition, 2024
ISBN 978-1-957421-62-9

Published by Cat Whisker Press

Cover: Dar Albert, Wicked Smart Designs
Book Design: Cat Whisker Studio
Editor: Chris Hall

DIAMONDS OF THE FIRST WATER

A Diamond for Christmas

Clarity

Purity

Adam

Radiance

Brilliance

OTHER WORKS

The RAKES ON THE RUN Series
Last Dance in London
Pursued in Paris
Banished to Brighton
Gretna Green by Sunset
The Lady Who Stole Christmas

The RARE CONFECTIONERY Series
The Duchess of Chocolate
The Toffee Heiress
My Lady Marzipan
The Gingerbread Lady

The DEFIANT HEARTS Series
An Improper Situation
An Irresistible Temptation
An Inescapable Attraction
An Inconceivable Deception
An Intriguing Proposition
An Impassioned Redemption

The BEASTLY LORDS Series
Lord Despair
Lord Anguish
Lord Vile
Lord Darkness
Lord Misery
Lord Wrath
Lord Corsair
Eleanor

PRESENTING LADY GUS

THE BLACK KNIGHT'S REWARD
with Marliss Melton

DEDICATION

Dedicated to Queen Elizabeth II, who went to her well-deserved rest while I was writing this book. She shared a birthday with my late father, April 21, although she was a few years older. I often gave her a respectful nod on his birthday. It must be a blessed date, indeed, to have produced two such extraordinary people.

And while not wishing to be irreverent by following that dedication with this one, I also dedicate this story to a gentle soul, Sabrina "Sabby" McFlabby, my beloved 16-year-old tuxedo cat who departed this earth on November 26, 2022 while I was finishing up the final chapters. Her passing has left a large hole in my heart, and in the hearts of those who knew and loved her.

ACKNOWLEDGMENTS

I want to make mention of (*i.e.*, acknowledge) my own family on my mother's side, the Garrards. I don't know if we are related to Queen Victoria's Crown Jeweler, Sebastian Garrard, who plays a large role in this book, but I now have an interest in finding out.

My grandfather, Cyril George Garrard, worked as a tool and die maker somewhere in or around London and was a highly skilled craftsman. I recall from childhood how he seemed able to make anything with his capable hands and was also an avid gardener and winemaker.

Also, I want to acknowledge the help I received from my dear sister. My deepest gratitude to Toni Young, who read Radiance's long story and made it so much better with her suggestions.

INTRODUCTION TO
DIAMONDS OF THE FIRST WATER

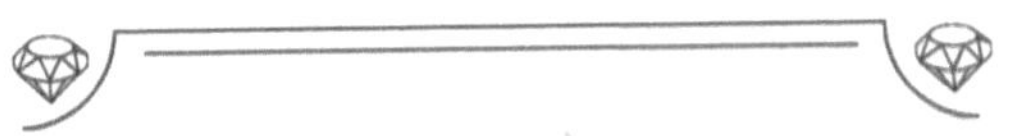

Once upon a time, an Irish family by the name of O'Diamáin emigrated to England from the north of Ireland, from County Doire to be specific. You may know the area as Derry or even Londonderry, if you are thinking of it after King James I granted the city a royal charter.

Felim O'Diamáin, who was the youngest son, sailed across the Irish Sea to make his fortune, bringing his pretty wife and two young children with him. As the story goes, they stopped over on the Isle of Man for a perfectly peaceful night before landing at Ravenglass the next day and traipsing through the Lake District.

Another version swears they took the shorter but far more dangerous route north across the sea to Portpatrick, finding themselves in the southernmost part of Scotland. From there, if they indeed came that way, they headed east toward Gretna Green. Not for any quick anvil marriage, mind you, but to traverse the border to England.

No one knows for sure the veracity of either tale, nor particularly cares. Once they arrived in England, Felim did very well for himself, as did his descendants.

At some point during the twelve-year reign of George I, another O'Diamáin by the name of Liam was made an earl for his devoted service to the Crown. During those years in the early eighteenth century, King George also created a few dukes, at least one marquess, some barons, a single viscount, and other earls. But we're not interested in any of them, although some may have helped to quell the riots that ensued when Hanoverian George outmaneuvered any pesky residual Stuarts hoping to claim the English throne.

Nevertheless, our interest lies with Liam. With his new earldom came much wealth and land, specifically in Derbyshire. And naturally, a title. However, George I, being of Germanic descent, didn't find the Celtic name of O'Diamáin tripped easily off his tongue. Neither did he master Gaelic or Manx, for that matter. In any case, with a little persuasion and an extra thousand acres, Liam became William, the Earl Diamond, as his male descendants have been known ever since.

Over the years, the earls have enlarged the original house to be an impressive manor, always named Oak Grove Hall, which is the translation of their long-ago home of County *Doire*.

Generations later, while inheriting the earldom and all its assets, Geoffrey, Lord Diamond and his beloved wife, Caroline, have wealth of a different nature as well—five healthy children: Clarity, Purity, Adam, Radiance, and Brilliance. They are known as the Diamonds of the First Water, at least by their parents.

This is Radiance's story . . .

PROLOGUE

London, 1852

Radiance Diamond lowered her favorite pen with its lunar-shaped steel nib, setting it beside the recessed inkwell that she'd already filled in preparation for the lecture. The afternoon's lecturer had just entered through the door at the right front of the main theater in the Royal Polytechnic Institution on Regent Street. And the sight of him was enough to halt her squiggling with pretty, albeit expensive, blue ink while the rest of the audience were still taking their seats.

Radiance's attention was riveted. Although she'd attended a variety of lectures all across London, both interesting and dull, she'd never set eyes upon the geologist, Mr. Edward Lockwood, before.

Her breath caught. Now, she never wanted to take her gaze from him.

What a rum duke! All broad shoulders and thick, unruly brown hair. Tall but not gangly. Attractive eyes that, from a distance, appeared to be an unusual shade of golden-brown.

Sighing, she sat up straighter, coughed slightly to gain his attention, and waited for him to notice her.

As expected, his head turned in her direction. Most men, at this point, saw her bright red hair, a natural inheritance from her mother, Carolyn, the Countess Diamond, and their interest piqued. Not that everyone liked red hair, but everyone usually *noticed* it.

Usually, some reaction would follow, especially when she wore it partly up and partly down in the current fashion. Curled, but not too tightly, to drape across one shoulder.

Some lively lady had named these soft curls as "follow-me boys." A delicious description since she and all her friends liked nothing so much as being followed by eager, attentive gentlemen.

To her astonishment, Mr. Lockwood, reportedly an advisor to the Queen and Prince Albert regarding gemstones, barely acknowledged her, if he did at all. His glance went over her and on to the next person and then the one beside him. No raised brow, no smile, not even a sneer of derision to indicate he was one of those who didn't care for coppery curls.

The gall! She would not cough again. If he didn't have the sense to see a female of her quality, so be it. Still, when this man of science began his discourse, a captivating lecture, she was entranced. And if she missed a few words here and there because she was watching his attractive mouth, or if her thoughts strayed to the fantasy of dancing with him, no one could blame her.

At the lecture's end, the entire audience broke into an enthusiastic round of applause, slightly muffled by all the men's and women's gloves. Radiance assumed now he would look at her. After all, he'd had over an hour to notice her in the third row, directly centered in front of him.

Again, she was disappointed by how he attended to the gems he'd used as examples. Carefully, he put his collection back in their velvet pouches and wooden cases.

Not looking up at anyone, barely acknowledging the appreciation of his listeners, Mr. Lockwood paid all his attention to his exhibits. By the time he was finished, most of the people around Radiance had risen and left. She hadn't meant to stay but had been mesmerized by his movements, the way his hair fell over his forehead while he looked down, the way his hands were quick and sure.

Finally, he glanced up and met her gaze. Her heartbeat quickened. Then he gave the briefest nod, collected his specimen cases, and walked out.

EDWARD DROPPED HIS COAT on the bench in his front hall, assuming his housekeeper would retrieve it and tidy it away as she tidied up every other aspect of his life, from newspapers left on his sofa to cat fur on his counterpane. The mess was there one minute and, thanks to Mrs. McSabby, gone the next.

He headed directly along the passageway to what should be a dining room, which he used as his workroom. Nearly dinnertime, the fading rays of light came in through the windows that went almost up to the crown molding. They were the reason he used that room.

Those fingers of light played across the large table where he placed his specimen containers and his sheaf of notes.

"Rather a successful afternoon," he said to Monty, his gray striped cat, lying atop the table, catching the last sunbeams. It stretched out a paw, patting one of the wooden boxes.

If Edward opened the lid, the cat would undoubtedly exert himself enough to knock a gemstone out of one of the trays and send it skittering to the floor.

But Edward didn't intend to sort through the specimens or put them away in the drawers of his gem cabinet. He still had work to do, a professional courtesy for the Queen's Crown Jeweler. Sebastian Garrard had asked him to examine a rare blue tiger's eye for its cleavage traits. The Queen wished to turn it into a ring for Prince Albert, but Garrard was uncertain of its stability.

As Edward drew up a chair and donned his magnifying spectacles, a sudden flash of fiery-red hair and a pert, confident smile flitted across his thoughts.

He frowned at the memory of the minx from the auditorium. *Why would he think of her?* True, she was lovely, but he doubted she'd been there to learn. Many people went to his lectures hoping he would bring out samples of rare jewels, which he often did, or gaudy jewelry, which he never would.

She probably had a penchant for sparkling baubles and was in possession of less brains than Monty, although her green eyes were a more vivid hue.

"Can you believe she had brighter eyes than you?" he asked his cat, who yawned broadly.

Then Edward banished the chit from his mind, pushed the magnifiers up the bridge of his nose, and got to work.

CHAPTER ONE

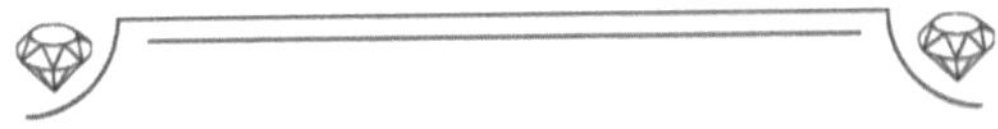

Radiance Diamond thought nothing in her young life would compare to the displays and inventions she'd seen the previous summer at the Great Exhibition, or the Grand International Exhibition, depending upon which newspaper one read. The impression made upon her of the various wonderful items produced by the nations of the world had been so huge, she'd been sorely tested as to which path to take.

Ultimately, after multiple visits to the Crystal Palace in Hyde Park, it was the fine jewelry that called her to return more than to the paintings or the sculptures or even the weaving, for all of which she had an aptitude.

Radiance had decided to dedicate herself to jewelry-making.

Indeed, almost the moment she'd arrived back at her family's home on Piccadilly, she had made arrangements to set herself up a place to study and work. Thus, Radiance transformed her eldest sister's former bedroom, empty since Clarity had moved out years earlier upon marrying.

With a spacious table, a comfortable chair, and good lamps, Radiance read books, studied illustrations, and tried her hand at designing jewelry.

Her parents had encouraged this new interest, believing all their children should follow wherever their minds and passions took them. Moreover, with Lord and Lady Diamond's generous support, she had everything at her disposal, including a lapidary's mill and a tripoli stone for polishing, a pair of magnifying spectacles, and some semi-precious stones with which she could practice gem cutting, as well as carving wax and tools for making molds.

After a few months of diligence, she had secured herself a place in a master jeweler's establishment in the Hatton Garden area, the very heart of London's jewelry-making community.

In Mr. Bonwit's Greville Street shop, she showed the jeweler what she accomplished on her own.

"You have an eye for this," he told her after she showed him her designs. "But whether you can bring your creation to fruition is another matter. If you will allow me and my apprentice to make your jewelry, we will do so gladly."

"I wish to learn," she'd asserted.

Thus, under Mr. Bonwit's tutelage, she learned how to tame gold and silver to match her designs and how to fashion rough gems into glittering jewels. Whenever she had a plan in mind, carefully drawn, she went to the workroom behind his shop and spent hours perfecting her skills.

He let her don a heavy apron and work alongside him, learning not only to cut gems on the lap's mill, or scaif as Mr. Bonwit called it, but to work with the noble metals, hammering them into intricate designs, creating wax molds that were then cast in molten gold and silver. Lately, she'd learned the delicate art of filigree.

She knew she was like a pet to Mr. Bonwit—an oddity whom he liked to show off. Occasionally, he brought customers into the workshop. *This is Lady Radiance, an earl's daughter, come to learn from me.*

Nevertheless, she took her instruction seriously.

"I wish to learn niello," she told him, having been impressed by a manchette bracelet she'd seen with a likeness of the Queen and the Prince of Wales.

Mr. Bonwit frowned. "It is not as simple as setting a stone in gold or silver."

"I know," Radiance said. She wanted to know how to use the black mixture of sulphur, copper, silver, and lead to create unique black designs fired onto silver.

"Don't tell me I should have apprenticed myself to S. H. & D. Gass, who made those pieces I saw at the exhibition."

Mr. Bonwit's furrowed brow deepened. "*I* shall teach you the art of niello," he said. "But you must walk before you run."

Radiance hid her smile. She intended to learn everything and started soaking up his knowledge as a flower took in sunlight.

Yet her interests led her further than making jewelry. She was fascinated by the gemstones she'd seen, particularly those in the Great Exhibition's India exhibit. Almost as talked about as the famed Koh-i-Noor, or "Mountain of Light," which people had lined up to see, was the Darya-i-Noor, or "Sea of Light," a massive pink diamond surrounded by ten smaller diamonds set in an armlet.

Radiance had spent many minutes sketching it while hearing other viewers exclaim over its gaudy setting.

In its own display area, apart from all the other jewelry, was the famed Koh-i-Noor diamond, which had belonged to Queen Victoria ever since Her Majesty became the ruler of India. The year before the Great Exhibition, it had been ceremonially presented to her by the eleven-year-old King of India, although the boy and the Queen were separated by thousands of miles.

When Radiance first saw the diamond, exhibited in what looked for all the world like a bird cage, she was not impressed. Supposedly, the display was really an elaborate safe. If one attempted to open the cage, the diamond, along with the other two smaller diamonds that had been part of the armlet worn by the orphaned king, would drop into a secure compartment below.

Unfortunately, the Koh-i-Noor was displayed poorly. Radiance could see at once that it was an imperfect diamond and, to her western sensibilities of beauty, cut badly.

"It's large but not at all a shining 'Mountain of Light'," she said to her best friend Diana.

Almost unanimously, the public expressed their disappointment in the "egg-shaped lump of glass," as one newspaper called it.

The next time Radiance went to the Crystal Palace, the diamond had been moved into a secure tent and shown more openly, surrounded by six gas lamps and twelve small mirrors. The Queen, Prince Albert, and their two oldest sons had gone to the reopening, hoping to sway public opinion.

Most deemed it only mildly improved and even blamed the diamond for the nearly unbearably hot temperature inside the tent. Thus, it was still unpopular.

"Slightly improved," Radiance had said to her mother, who accompanied her to see the Koh-i-Noor for the second time. However, it wasn't a sparkling first-water diamond, and she would swear she could see yellow flaws.

Although smaller in size, the Hope Diamond, also exhibited at the Crystal Palace, was far lovelier to Radiance's eye. "The blue shimmer is remarkable."

"Isn't it, though?" agreed her mother. "Almost as rich a blue as the rest of our family's eyes," Lady Diamond added. She and Radiance were the only two who shared the same verdant-green eyes and rich red hair from her Grandmother Chimes's side of the family.

"Let's look at some rubies and emeralds to better match our features, shall we?" Radiance suggested, and they had done so. Going around the Great Exhibition with her mother was one of her fondest recollections. Although watching her youngest sister queue up to use a public toilet—*"Because it's a novelty,"* Bri *had declared excitedly*—was another memorable moment.

On a breezy, rainy spring day, the sunny summer exhibition of the year before was merely a distant memory. Seated at the table in her private workspace, Radiance read over her notes from months earlier, written during Mr. Lockwood's lecture at the Royal Polytechnic Institution.

Despite how stern and disinterested the geologist had been months earlier, not responding to her playful glance, she couldn't help but appreciate the information he'd imparted, albeit on the shallow side due to the mixed audience—men and women who were not particularly science-minded. She'd watched the newspapers for a more in-depth lecture but hadn't seen one until recently.

Since it was being held at the Geological Society in Somerset House, Radiance was certain the lecture would be both comprehensive and to the point. The former seventeenth-century palace on the Strand had been rebuilt to house governmental offices as well as various artistic and scientific societies.

Unfortunately, she could not attend except as a guest of a member either of the Geological Society or one of the other societies that made up the north wing of Somerset House. And thus, after spending the prior week finding such a person, she strolled along the Strand with Lord Benedict Woolley, a friend of her brother-in-law, Lord Hollidge. Her maid, Sarah, had been left behind in the carriage with an exciting penny dreadful.

Up the grand stairs to one of the lecture halls, she walked beside Lord Woolley, whom she'd only met once previously at a dinner party thrown by her eldest sister, Clarity. He was stocky, self-assured, and a little loud, but he had been only too happy to do her this *favor*.

"Anything for my friend. After all, Hollidge married your sister, so your family must be good folks. Why, if I married you, he and I would be family. *Wot wot.*"

Hoping he didn't get any ideas as to her having an interest in him, Radiance kept her conversation solidly on the day's topic of the earth's hardest substance.

"Not my usual line of interest," Lord Woolley said after she mentioned how a good cut could change a gemstone entirely. "I am a member of the Royal Society that meets next door to the Geological Society because of my fascination with the small animal populations."

"Truly?" she asked.

"Yes, indeed. Foxes, rabbits, squirrels, birds." He waggled his eyebrows. "Rabbits."

"You said rabbits twice," she pointed out.

"Did I?" he asked before grinning at her.

"Mm," she replied and directed her attention to the still-empty front of the lecture hall.

"Maybe that's because they are the most prevalent due to their mating habits. *Coupling* all the time," Lord Woolley outrageously began. *"Procreating* quickly and often. *Breeding* like . . . like rabbits," he finished before loudly laughing.

Radiance sighed, positive his discourse was improper for her ears. Besides, Mr. Lockwood had entered, a little late, through a door at the front of the room and was even then looking up toward the source of the hilarity.

For the briefest instant, their eyes met. Radiance was thrilled to see her imagination had not embellished the geologist's attractive face and figure. He was, as she'd remembered, exceedingly handsome, with his broad shoulders filling out his frock coat and his long legs shown to muscular perfection under his tan trousers.

Moreover, by his long glance, Radiance was certain he recalled seeing her previously. Then his gaze moved on to Lord Woolley, still laughing over nothing. Mr. Lockwood scowled slightly.

"Will you hush, please," Radiance hissed, embarrassed to be associated with the man while he was braying.

"I offer my apologies, dear lady," Lord Woolley said, sounding suitably chastised. "I intended no harm or offense." He withdrew a hinged, silver snuff box, opened it, and sniffed a pinch of tobacco into each nostril.

About to turn away when he closed it with a snap, she spied an engraving on its top. It was the Crystal Palace, complete with flags flying.

She softened, thinking of the favor he'd done her by taking time out of his own life to attend the lecture.

"That's quite all right," Radiance assured him. "I simply don't want to miss anything Professor Lockwood has to say." In the lecture announcement, she'd read he was now teaching at King's College, directly next to Somerset House. "I greatly admire your snuff box, by the way, as I adored the Great Exhibition beyond all events I have ever attended."

She smiled at Lord Woolley, stopping short of leaning on his arm or batting her lashes, yet still seeing the instant he took the hint. Despite having a shelf full of mementos from the exhibit, she was thrilled when he handed it to her.

"Take it, please. It is an honor to give it to you, Lady Radiance." He twirled his sandy-brown moustache while she examined the gift in her palm.

"Thank you, my lord." She slid it into the small hidden pocket of her skirt's waistband. Sighing happily at how life seemed to work out for the best, Radiance turned her attention once more to the present.

Opening her satchel, she drew out a clothbound notebook, her pen, and her inelegant but portable pewter inkwell.

"It appears you are serious," Lord Woolley said.

"Indeed, I am. I have a keen interest in diamonds and gemstones, both precious and semi-precious, in their natural state, as well as after they've been turned into jewelry."

"I see." He paused. "And why?"

"Why what?" she asked, realizing she was already doodling a design onto the blank page under where she'd written *"2ⁿᵈ lecture by Mr. E. Lockwood, April 28, 1852."*

"Why are you interested in such things?" Lord Woolley asked. "I fail to understand how it can benefit you, nor what you would do with the knowledge. As the daughter of one lord and, potentially, the future wife of another."

Radiance considered. "Why are *you* interested in small animals?"

His placid face broke into a smile. "That is a simple answer. I enjoy hunting, and thus I need to know how the population of foxes is doing. And the animal life is symbiotic. Do you know what that means?"

She narrowed her gaze. "Of course I do." Counseling herself to ignore his condescension, she said, "In other words, you want to make sure the animals are healthy in order for you to kill them. Is that right?"

"Yes," he said, sounding a tad confused. "Strange when you put it that way."

"Good afternoon, gentlemen," Mr. Lockwood began. Then his gaze fell upon Radiance, making her sit up straighter, and he added, "and lady."

This engendered muffled laughter, with many heads— all male—turning her way. She didn't particularly mind the attention, nor had she realized until that instant that she was the only female present.

Lifting her chin, Radiance fixed Mr. Lockwood with the most imperial stare she'd learned from her mother. While she still thought him a rum duke, she wouldn't tolerate being made sport of. Not while the master jeweler Mr. Bonwit had called her *talented.*

After a moment, Mr. Lockwood blinked and looked down at his notes.

"Today, I shall speak to you about diamonds," he said, "starting with that which has come to be called the Hope Diamond. A nice enough name for an extraordinary stone. I hope you don't mind if I begin with a history of this magnificent gem since I know only some of you belong to the Geological Society. The rest of you, I assume, are laymen."

He glanced at her again. "And laywoman."

Radiance spoke without thinking. "I assure you, Mr. Lockwood, I am not uneducated nor an amateur, so you may remove me from such classification."

The entire audience fell silent, and Mr. Lockwood, too. Then he cleared his throat.

"And do you have any objection to my beginning with a history, or do you perhaps wish to dive in and dazzle us with your own knowledge?"

She felt her cheeks warm. He was mocking her when all she wanted was to take in what he could teach and, of course, get a close look at the Hope Diamond. Radiance believed Mr. Lockwood would show them the actual gem, for she'd read a newspaper account of him doing that very thing the year before, delighting his audience. But it wouldn't happen until the end of his lecture. Thus, she certainly would not let him drive her away.

"I am content for you to proceed," she said, before adding, "without patronizing your avid listeners, not even the female ones."

Again, silence descended upon the auditorium.

CHAPTER TWO

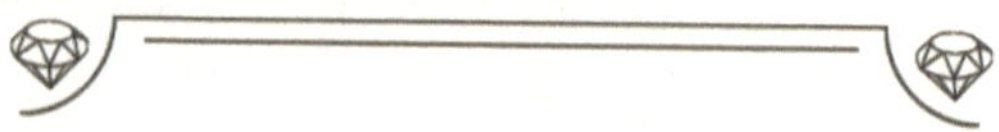

After a strangely combative encounter with the sole female in his audience, Edward began his talk with a tutorial on diamond cutting. "Let's speak briefly of the earliest crude polishing and then the introduction of grinding facets."

He went through the developments of the fifteenth and sixteenth centuries.

"And then came the first true *rose* cut." He discussed other popular cuts, including Hogbacks, which became the *baguette* cut and showed semi-precious stones of the *table* and *point* cuts, before explaining how the Baroque period gave birth to the *brilliant* cut, which in turn brought about the *marquise* cut.

While knowing most were there to get a close view of the famed Hope Diamond, he wanted them to truly appreciate the spectacular structure of all diamonds.

Diamonds were uppermost in his mind as it was his first lecture since returning from visiting mines in India. He'd traveled as far as Kollur on the Krishna River and down to the jungles of Ceylon for other precious stones, only to nearly meet a sticky end the night before he got on the boat to return home.

Despite an unwelcome souvenir, an itchy scar across his side that stretched around to his lower back, he had lived another day to study gems, and his thirst for travel hadn't been dimmed even a little by that nasty encounter with a knife-wielding native.

Next year, he hoped to travel to Africa once again, as far as the Cape Colony. And having been to Brazil in 1847, his first extended voyage, he had witnessed when the earth yielded the cache of diamonds known as the *Chapada Diamantina*. A return trip was a necessity.

And then, of course, there was Australia, on his list for some day in the not-too-distant future. He shook his head to stop wool-gathering. London was as exciting a city as any.

"Some of you may be familiar with the term *cleavage*."

Even as the word left his lips, he recalled the lady amongst them. Some rude dogs used the word as often as the term *beard-splitter* and for the same mysterious and tantalizing female part.

Glancing at the red-haired lady, being struck again by her unusual beauty, he assumed she had never heard either of those insulting words.

"Diamonds have perfect cleavage—that is, their crystal structure allows for smooth facets when cut. Thus, lapidaries have been cleaving diamonds successfully since at least the sixteenth century."

After explaining a little more about their molecular makeup, he discussed *sawing*, the last of the gemstone-shaping methods.

"And now," he said, "let us delve into the history of the Hope Diamond, from when the French gem merchant Jean-Baptiste Tavernier acquired the stone in the 1660s while in India."

The lady raised her hand.

"There will be time for questions at the end," he told her. "And yes, I have the Hope with me if that is what you wish to know."

"No, sir," she said. "I merely wanted to point out that you neglected to mention the Mughal cut."

Startled by her knowing the term, he nodded. "I had thought to discuss it when we get to the most well-known of all the Mughal cut diamonds."

"The Koh-i-Noor," she said.

"Yes, exactly. If that is all right with you," he added, wondering if she would hear the sarcasm lacing his tone.

"That is a good idea," she said jovially, "although for organized notes, it might have been better mentioned during your talk about the cuts." She tilted her head. "Please, carry on."

A few of the audience members chuckled at her regal directive. Edward cleared his throat.

"The Hope Diamond is thought to have been originally mined from the Kollur mine in the Gunter district of Andhra Pradesh. How Tavernier acquired it has been lost to the annals of time." He didn't mention his almost religious-like trek to see the area.

"Perhaps Tavernier stole it from a statue of the goddess Sita, wife of Rama. In any case, he returned to Paris with a somewhat triangular stone, reported to have weighed 112 carats. He soon sold his 'Tavernier Blue' to King Louis XIV."

Edward held up a large poster showing the diamond's original shape.

"And that's the first time we learn of it being cut," he said. "In 1673, the Royal Jeweler, Monsieur Pitau, was charged with making 'a piece to remember,' and he did exactly that over a period of two years. It's hard to believe the king was so patient."

His audience chuckled appreciatively.

He held up another large drawing, this one showing the cut diamond. This time, the listeners murmured their approval, but the fiery-haired female shook her head. She offered an expression of such disapproval that he couldn't help engaging with her again.

"Is there a problem?" he asked.

She seemed surprised to be addressed, but Edward didn't doubt for a moment that she would speak her mind and respond.

"I could have sketched a better, more realistic-looking stone, sir."

"Is that right?" he shot back, annoyed since he had done his best. Sketching had never been a skill he'd mastered. "Do you fancy yourself an artist?"

"Oh, she is very good," the man beside her spoke up. "You should see what she's drawn here. Your very likeness."

She had drawn him! Edward watched her cheeks bloom with color at the disclosure. He had never had such a distraction in one of his talks before, but he was only half annoyed. She was too lovely to be angry with. What's more, he now longed to see her drawing.

Nonetheless, he had to regain control of his lecture.

"If you wish to see quality art, then I suggest you go down the hall to the Royal Academy. Fortunately, it is in this same wing."

"Thank you, sir, but this is the lecture I wish to hear," she returned evenly. They stared at one another for a long moment, and then he continued.

"This cut gemstone, now only sixty-seven carats, was newly christened 'the Blue Diamond of the Crown of France,' or more simply, the 'French Blue.' And it is considered one of the finest examples of a blue diamond."

Rapidly, he went through how Louis XV had the diamond set in a pendant in 1749 by another court jeweler, Andre Jacquemin, and how the unfortunate Louis XVI was rumored to gift the diamond to his equally unfortunate queen.

"That last statement may be entirely fanciful," Edward added, "since the diamond was meant to be reserved for kings. However, Queen Marie Antoinette *may* have worn it. We believe it was smuggled to England with her other jewelry before she was beheaded, or it was simply stolen after many of the crown jewels of the French Royal Treasury were turned over to the government. We know for certain that there was a great deal of looting, including of the crown jewels, in September of 1792. And then some halfwit decided to launch the unfounded notion that the diamond is cursed."

Another wave of mumblings went through the audience. These men of science were unlikely to believe in a curse. Besides, all the other victims of the French Revolution certainly couldn't blame their fate on a blue diamond of exquisite beauty.

He found himself looking again at the radiant redhead scribbling notes. Or he assumed she was and not sketching his likeness again. *How strange . . . and flattering!*

Scanning his page of notes to make sure he wasn't forgetting anything, he continued, "We lose track of the diamond again until 1812, when it is already cut in its current shape, although not yet owned by Mr. Hope. A London diamond merchant, Mr. Eliason, speaks of a 'massive blue stone of 45.54 carats,' thus another twenty-two carats smaller than the French Blue, but we assume it is the same one . . . In the ensuing years, until 1839, common opinion believes our own George IV owned it, yet I have thoroughly consulted the Royal Archives at Windsor and can find no confirmation."

At this point, Edward paced the front of the room, warming to his tale as they approached modern times.

"In any case, King George had debts, and if he did own it, he sold it to pay them. Finally, in 1839, it came into the hands of London banker Henry Philip Hope as recorded in an entry of the gem collection catalog. At that time, it became known as the 'Hope Diamond.'"

RADIANCE KNEW ALL THIS, yet found herself hanging upon Mr. Lockwood's every word. Her note-taking had dwindled in favor of simply watching the man presenting information that he clearly knew as well as he knew his own name.

"When Mr. Hope died in 1839, his heirs fought an extended legal battle over the stone. Henry Thomas Hope, his nephew, eventually inherited it. And we are fortunate that he displayed it in the Great Exhibition of London last year, when many of you had the treat of seeing it in person, some for the first time."

The way he said it made Radiance certain Mr. Lockwood had seen it and even held it many times. And then, as she'd hoped, he withdrew a wooden box from under the table, placed it on top, and opened it. Inside was a black velvet cloth, bunched up haphazardly. One could almost hear the collective holding of breath.

Lifting this out, he unfurled the velvet, smoothing it and straightening it until the blue diamond was directly in the center, on display. Then he positioned a lamp on either side.

The room erupted in applause. Finally, Mr. Lockwood held up his hands.

"I am fortunate to be upon close acquaintance with Mr. Hope, who intends to keep the diamond in his family and also to keep it in its current cut without losing any further weight. I will allow you all to walk past it and view it at the lecture's end, as long as you don't attempt to touch it. In which case, I will have to shoot you."

Radiance started to laugh, as did a few other people, but Mr. Lockwood's stern expression quelled their mirth. He appeared to be serious. In the next instant, he withdrew a pistol from his satchel and placed it upon the edge of the table before him.

While a stunned audience stared silently, he resumed the lecture as if there was nothing out of the ordinary.

"Does anyone know why the diamond has a distinctly bluish hue?" Mr. Lockwood asked while they were all still gaping either at the stone or at the gun.

Radiance put up her hand, thinking many would join her. Surely, it was a rhetorical question. Yet only a few of the hundred or so listeners raised their hands. Beside her, Lord Woolley merely crossed his arms.

"I didn't realize there would be an oral examination along with this lecture," he quipped. Then he saw her arm lifted in the air. "Don't say you actually know the answer."

Before she could lower her arm, Mr. Lockwood said, "You there. Can you tell us why?"

Radiance couldn't credit that he was truly addressing her out of all those in attendance. Perhaps there was someone behind her to whom he might be directing his question. She would hate to speak out of turn.

"I am speaking to you, the singular lady in our midst. Or did you raise your hand simply to stretch?"

Radiance nearly gasped at such an insult and, leaning forward, blurted, "The coloring is due to the amount of boron within the carbon that makes up a diamond. I hope I said that simply enough in *laywoman's* terms."

Then she sat back, satisfied with his surprised expression.

"A very succinct and accurate explanation. Thank you." He finished with a nod. "And that explains why, unlike the Hope Diamond, the Koh-i-Noor was something of a disappointment to those who saw it at the exhibition. It isn't a sparkling clear gem, nor of a particularly attractive hue."

"Agreed," she said, despite knowing he was speaking to everyone.

Regardless, he directed his next remark to her.

"Since you gave the correct answer, would you like to come to the front and view the diamond up close?"

Radiance's heart skipped a beat. *Yes, she would!* Mr. Lockwood didn't have to ask twice.

Standing, she threaded her way quickly along the row, her path made easier by the fact that every man in the entire lecture hall rose to his feet. Hastening down the aisle to the front of the room, she nodded to their esteemed lecturer before peering down at the blue diamond. It was the absolute best view she could imagine short of holding it up to the light.

"Have you seen it before?" he asked.

"Yes, sir," she answered, not taking her gaze from the magnificent stone. "At the Great Exhibition. Thrice, in fact." After a few moments of examining it, seeing the perfection of the cuts to which it had been subjected in its long existence, she glanced at him.

Her initial notion of him being a handsome man had been correct. Close up, he had dash-fire to spare, with rich brown hair and eyes the color of golden topaz with an intriguing glimmer.

"What other gems did you see at the exhibition?" he asked.

"The Koh-i-Noor." Her cheeks warmed, realizing she was standing in front of a room full of men while gawking at Mr. Lockwood. She cleared her throat.

"Do you have that with you, too?"

"Alas, no." He appeared amused. "Queen Victoria doesn't lend that out for lectures, even to this prestigious institution. I believe it is safely with the other royal jewels at the Tower."

"I see. But you do have access to it, do you not?"

He clamped his lips closed.

"You may return to your seat now."

Hm. She was dismissed but didn't mind. The experience had been singularly thrilling nonetheless, and she bent over to see the stone more closely for one last look.

Would Mr. Lockwood pick up his gun if she stuck out her gloved finger toward the diamond?

And then, all thought fell away as she saw what looked like a small fissure. Her mouth fell open while she stared in disbelief. Most certainly, she hadn't seen any such flaw upon viewing the diamond at the exhibition the year before. Of course, she'd been at a distance, but no one, not even during this lecture, had ever made mention of such an inclusion in the Hope, either.

"Mr. Lockwood," she began.

"Please return to your seat. We have more diamonds to discuss."

Radiance hesitated, looking from the stone to the now stony-faced man. Then she leaned closer and blew, in case it was simply a hair that had floated gently onto it.

"Excuse me! What are you doing?" He raised his voice, and the audience gasped.

CHAPTER THREE

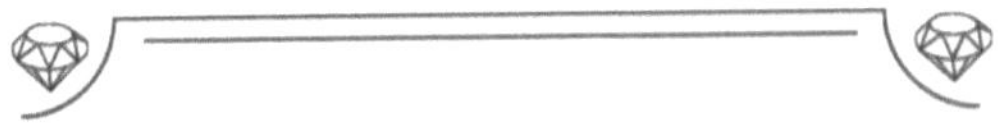

Radiance ignored him and examined the diamond again. Perhaps a hair was underneath the gem, between it and the velvet.

"Might I touch the stone?"

"Absolutely not," Mr. Lockwood shot back. "I have already made that clear. Now please take your seat so we may continue."

She did as he asked. After all, if she was incorrect, then she would make a fool of herself. It might have been a trick of the light. She needed her magnifying spectacles to be certain.

Back in her chair, she started to muse upon what she thought she'd seen while Mr. Lockwood discussed the far more famous Koh-i-Noor gem. Since she had read so much about the Indian diamond, it was as though he were retelling a favorite story. However, when he began his discourse upon the Dresden and continued with the Florentine, the Nassak, and the Sancy, Radiance paid close attention. As these were less known to her, she took many notes, filling her pages until the lecture was over.

At its conclusion, the audience rushed to the front, filing past the Hope Diamond in an unruly fashion. Although Lord Woolley tried to push her into the surging throng, she held back until they could bring up the rear.

Radiance wanted to take one last lingering look, to try to confirm what she'd seen. Mr. Lockwood had pulled the diamond back toward him, perhaps concerned by the enthusiastic viewers. At the new angle, she saw nothing out of the ordinary and decided it had been mere over-excitement on her part.

When she raised her glance to apologize for her odd behavior, Mr. Lockwood looked as though he might ask her a question. His perfect lips actually opened slightly, but then his mouth closed, and he merely nodded. She did the same, amenable to saying nothing more.

At her elbow, however, Lord Woolley wasn't finished. "A jolly good talk," he said jovially, addressing the geologist.

Mr. Lockwood startled as if he hadn't expected any sort of praise.

"I am glad you found it enjoyable," he replied stiffly.

Radiance thought he could not more plainly indicate that he didn't give a rat's arse if anyone liked it or not.

"It was interesting in places if a jot long-winded," Lord Woolley added, ruining his prior praise, "and not nearly as good as the talk I went to last week on the invasion of our country by the Muntjac."

"The what?" Mr. Lockwood asked, his golden-brown eyes widening as he looked from Lord Woolley to her and back again.

Radiance wondered if barricades were being set up at all major ports against the mysterious invasion of which she hadn't heard a word.

"The Muntjac," Lord Woolley repeated. "Those little deer from the Orient. Mr. Reeves brought them to his Woburn Park estate in Bedfordshire back in 1838. Very naughty of him."

"I've never heard of him or his deer," she admitted, looking abashedly at Mr. Lockwood. Undoubtedly, the man wished to be rid of pesky audience members who wouldn't go away.

Lord Woolley shrugged and continued on without noticing whether anyone was heeding him.

"John Russell Reeves is the East India Company Chief Inspector of Teas. I say he has no business bringing off-island deer to Britain. I swear some have escaped their enclosure. A new species as large as they are—"

"You said they were little," Mr. Lockwood pointed out.

"*Hm*?" Lord Woolley frowned. "Oh yes, little *deer*. But they aren't squirrels, are they? Besides, they don't even look like our deer. And since they graze, there can be serious consequences. Why, they may clear shrubs in our woodlands. Only imagine what that might do to the birds and butterflies."

Radiance tried to imagine but couldn't. It appeared to her as if Mr. Lockwood wasn't even trying at all. He glanced back and forth between her and Lord Woolley with a somewhat judgmental expression.

All at once, embarrassed at the notion this intelligent, attractive man thought her to be coupled with Woolley, Radiance wished to depart as quickly as possible.

"Thank you again, Mr. Lockwood." Radiance turned away, sorry the lecture was over. She could listen to the man all day long, not to mention gaze at him.

"Shouldn't we make proper introductions?" Lord Woolley asked, making her halt sharply.

"That isn't necessary," she began, feeling certain they'd overstayed their welcome.

"Good manners are always necessary. *Wot wot!*" he insisted. "Whether at a ball or here at a Somerset lecture, it is my duty to introduce you to this gentleman with whom you converse so freely."

Radiance thought that sounded even more as though they were engaged.

"Not *your* duty, exactly," she protested.

"Mr. Lockwood, I present Lady Radiance."

She sighed. In all her young years, she'd only minded her given name a few times. It certainly wasn't pretentious on her part, as one young lady had declared during Radiance's presentation to the Queen at court.

"How can *I* be pretentious?" she had asked the other debutante. "I did not choose it."

Her mother had hurried her away from the sneering girl. "She is jealous, that's all," Carolyn Diamond had insisted.

In any case, her family and friends called her "Ray," which was short and easy. But now, in front of the impossibly attractive Mr. Lockwood, Radiance could only wish Lord Woolley hadn't spoken her name with such flourish that he managed to turn the three syllables—"*Radi-ance!*"—into a long, drawn-out, sing-song of a word.

"Excuse me?" Mr. Lockwood queried, looking at her directly.

"I am Lady Radiance," she said softly. "Pleased to meet you."

He blinked. "Are you making a joke?"

Lord Woolley laughed. "That's not the best of it, sir. She is Lady Radiance Diamond. Isn't that a delightful mouthful?"

Radiance nearly covered her heated face with her gloved hands but managed to square her shoulders and keep her composure.

"Is he speaking in jest?" Mr. Lockwood asked. Still, he was addressing *her*, not Lord Woolley. Moreover, she thought his expression to be a tad peeved.

"No, of course not," she said.

The geologist crossed his arms. "Really? If I were a butcher, would you and your . . . your friend think it amusing to approach me and introduce yourself as Lady Succulent Lambchop?"

Radiance was stunned into silence, but Lord Woolley laughed long and loudly.

"That's very good, sir."

"And what is your name?" Mr. Lockwood asked. "Lord Dull Stones?"

Although it was unkind, Radiance wanted to laugh at the remark, but clearly, Lord Woolley didn't. Instead, he bristled.

"Here now. Did you insult me, sir?"

"I haven't time for this," Mr. Lockwood said. He'd already stuffed his notes into a leather satchel along with the pistol. Now, quick as a hummingbird, he rolled the Hope Diamond in its velvet and dropped it back into the wooden box. Snapping the lid shut, he tucked it under his arm and preceded them from the hall.

"Strange, uncouth fellow," Lord Woolley said as they followed slowly.

Radiance did not agree, so she said nothing. On the street, she allowed Lord Woolley to assist her into her father's carriage where Sarah was now dozing in the corner, her serialized magazine open on her lap.

Before Lord Hollidge's friend could ask her whether he might escort her again at a later date, she yanked on the bellpull. Her father's driver started forward.

"Thank you," she called out the window, then settled back against the squabs. Soft but firm, not too worn but broken in, and smelling of her father's familiar cologne and her mother's pretty perfume.

Lady Lambchop! Radiance could not crack a smile because Mr. Lockwood clearly considered her real name equally as ridiculous. For her own part, her thoughts remained firmly on the Hope Diamond for the duration of the ride home to Piccadilly. She ought to have told him her concern and risked his derision.

That evening, looking at her drawings both of him and of her sketches of the diamond from the Great Exhibition, she knew she must follow her conscience.

EDWARD KEPT THE CLEVER female in his head for far too long, still musing upon her while eating a late supper of roasted chicken and potatoes, which Mrs. McSabby set before him.

He'd been surprised to see the woman again, even more amazed to have remembered her from months earlier. Quickly, he'd realized why she was so memorable. It wasn't merely her flaming red hair, nor her emerald-colored eyes, but also her forthright manner.

Interested, intelligent, confident.

He reminded himself the intriguing woman had a beau, one who thought himself quite the issuer of a humorous dry bob.

What had he called her? *Radiant Diamond!* It wasn't in the least witty, either, almost sounding like a woman of pleasure. Not the hedge-whore variety, but an expensive courtesan like his own Miss Maura.

In reality, the man was a bore!

Yet having his interest captured and held made Edward's thoughts wander back to when he last had a long-term connection with a female. While still at university, there'd been a lively girl he'd imagined he might marry. However, he'd lost her due to neglect.

Fortunately, he couldn't claim to feeling particularly distraught when a more attentive swell had stolen her out from under his nose.

That had been six years earlier. Since then, he'd escorted a few pretty women hither and yon when the fancy took him. Usually, they were some friend's sister or cousin. He'd never felt the urge to pursue them beyond a single dance or one excruciatingly long evening at the theater. When it came to the fair sex, Edward feared he was becoming more persnickety each year.

Luckily, he lived in London, and there was no shortage of paramours, beautiful and educated for those times when he felt the urge and could pull himself away from his work.

The following morning over coffee, the redhead came back unbidden into his thoughts. She fell into none of the categories he was used to. Thus, he mentally tucked her into a compartment in his brain similarly to how he sorted the precious stones in his collection cabinet.

Not yet in his thirties but growing painfully close, Edward wondered if he was destined to be a bachelor. Then he wondered no more about such nonsense when a missive arrived from the Queen, summoning him to Buckingham Palace in two days' time.

Now *there* was an astute and interesting female. And her husband was an equally good egg. Edward had met them on numerous occasions, after their Crown Jeweler, Mr. Garrard, told them what a "discerning eye" he had for quality gemstones.

The royal couple had consulted with him when they were presented with choices that few were offered. The Queen, in particular, had hoped for something prettier than the armlet in which the Koh-i-Noor was now set with two other smaller stones. And her disappointment was keenly felt by the Prince Consort.

Moreover, after the gem's disappointing reception at the Great Exhibition, they'd asked his opinion on keeping the diamond as it was or cutting it.

Size mattered in gemstones, but so did the refraction of light, something the Koh-i-Noor sorely lacked. Edward had offered them his opinion—either live with the knowledge that one's famed diamond was less than spectacular or risk cutting it. Poorly done and the Koh-i-Noor would lose value. Well executed and its popularity would soar even as its carat weight—and thus, its size—shrank.

The summons from the Palace, in fact, requested he attend a meeting to decide upon which jeweler would do the cutting. Edward shook his head. Most of the jewelers were at least a decade older than he was, some two decades. Moreover, he was a geologist, not a skilled cutter or polisher. Still, he was honored to be asked to advise.

Meanwhile, he had to keep the Hope Diamond safe. Edward had been accused of a slight tendency toward absent-mindedness. That was fine with a shoe or a glove, even his favorite hat had occasionally gone missing before disappearing altogether, but such a trait would not do with one of the most precious gems in the world.

However, Mr. Hope would not return for a few days, and Edward had been instructed to return it only to him. Thus, he had stashed it in the back of his sample cabinet.

A knock at his front door interrupted him as he packed his satchel in preparation for heading to King's College. After a minute, he heard another knock and realized his housekeeper wasn't going to attend to the person on his doorstep.

"Blast!" he muttered, striding along the passageway toward the front of his home.

"Mrs. McSabby!" Edward called into the silence. However, a maid whose name he didn't recall poked her head from the small salon just as he went by.

"Where is she?" he asked.

"On the third floor, I believe, sir."

"But someone is at my door on *this* floor."

"Shall I—?"

"I'm nearly there already," he pointed out, shutting the door as he passed, barely a second after she withdrew her kerchiefed head.

Then he paused. Tugging on the ends of his sleeves, reassuring himself he was wearing a coat, Edward opened the front door.

"It's you," he said to the red-haired female from his lecture.

"You answered your own door!" she said, sounding equally surprised before she immediately clamped a gloved hand to her mouth. "My apologies, sir. That was dreadfully rude of me."

He felt tongue-tied. A female on his doorstep. This particular pretty one. *Insulting him.* How could *she* be at the door of his Berkeley Square townhouse? He cleared his throat.

"I suppose you have never opened your own front door."

"No, actually, I have not." After that admittance, she simply stood there.

"Are you alone?" he asked. "Or is your bore—I mean, your *beau* with you?"

Her lovely face, which was all creamy skin and pink cheeks, with a dusting of freckles over her nose that he hadn't noticed prior but now charmed him—that face took on an expression of confusion. Then she smiled in comprehension.

"Oh, you mean Lord Woolley from the lecture. He is *not* my beau. He is not my anything."

"I see." Although he did not. *What did she want? How could a single lady knock upon his door?*

"I have a maid accompanying me, sir," she added when he hesitated. Gesturing behind herself to an expensive-looking carriage parked a few feet away. Another female, presumably the maid, peered from the window.

"I am not certain you grasp the meaning of accompanying, but it is all the same to me." And it was. Not that Edward didn't know society's rules, but he hadn't time to worry over them. It wasn't his problem if this lady wished to flaunt the customs of her class.

His class, too, since his father was a middle son of a viscount. Although since he wasn't titled, Edward felt he could more easily be allowed to forget the extreme niceties.

"May I come in?" she asked. "It is about the Hope Diamond."

Ah! Now her visit made sense.

"No, you may not see it again, nor may you hold it. That is out of the question. I bid you a good day."

She didn't back up an inch. "Is it still in your possession?"

"That is none of your business. Good day."

He went to close the door, but she didn't move. Despite thinking her a bothersome chit, he couldn't close the door in her face. Not in any female's face.

"Will you please step back and turn away?"

"No." The lady's hands went to her hips. "As a geologist, you should be interested in what I have to say."

"Very well. Say it."

"You wish me to conduct a conversation on your doorstep?"

Edward nearly snapped a resounding *yes*. Instead, he told her the truth because she was ruffling him in ways he hadn't been ruffled in a while.

"I don't wish to conduct a conversation at all."

"It is important, sir. I believe the stone you have is not the Hope Diamond."

"I don't have time for such foolishness. It was given to my care by Mr. Hope himself. Good day."

And this time, he did close the door, somewhat firmly.

He hated to think her a scam artist who was pretending to be a lady. What other explanation was there? She had wanted to hold it in her hand during the lecture. Coming to his home, she probably thought to flirt with him so savagely that he didn't notice if she slipped it into her pocket.

He might be a tad distracted by her, but he would definitely notice that.

"You may be sorry," she said from the other side of the door.

"Doubtful," he muttered and returned to his workroom.

CHAPTER FOUR

Edward didn't usually attend dinner parties, belatedly touching his necktie to make sure he was wearing one as he entered his parents' blue and gold drawing room. If he discovered himself lacking neckwear, it wouldn't be the first time he'd arrived partially undressed. Once he'd gone to a party without gloves. He had kept his arms folded until they sat down at the table, waited for the other guests to remove their gloves, and then relaxed while he ate.

A lack of neckwear would be harder to hide.

However, this evening, he had been summoned to Park Lane. In their villa-style house with its balconies and spacious rear veranda, reminding him of Brighton, his parents were the hosts. His formidable, long-suffering mother had specifically requested his presence.

Edward was already wary of her matchmaking interference since she made it known she longed for grandchildren. He was relying upon his sister to handle that duty if only she would hurry up and find herself a husband.

"Thank God you came," his father said, "or I would never have heard the end of it. My life, such as it is, would be ruined." The senior Lockwood was nearly as dramatic as his wife.

Edward was so unlike them in that regard as to make him wonder if he was even a fruit of his father's loins.

"I am certain you would have survived," he said, "and had many happy years to come."

His father laughed uproariously.

"There you are!" his mother said, echoing his father's sentiment.

He kissed her cheek. "Here I am. As summoned."

"You speak as if I am Her Majesty and not simply a loving mother who misses her only son."

His mother sounded entirely reasonable until she added, "And who intends to find that son the perfect wife if he's too lackadaisical to do it for himself."

What could he say? "Thank you, Mother. I'm going to get myself a glass of wine. Unless you're already serving brandy. Are you?"

She fixed him with a hard stare. "You didn't even tell me how lovely our home looks. And after I went to such an effort."

Naturally, she meant she'd driven her staff probably to Bedlam with her demands. Yet he hadn't noticed that the house in which he'd been born and reared on the outskirts of Mayfair appeared any differently from any other time he'd gone to a party there.

As usual, it displayed all the lavish niceties. His father had done very well for himself as a man of many interests, as a commissioned soldier, and then as an investor in the East India Company while also importing tea and silk and even the coffee of which Edward was so fond.

"It looks magnificent. Is there any brandy?" he asked again.

"No. We are serving wines from Burgundy and from Champagne. If by the evening's end, you have asked some lady for permission to call upon her in the upcoming days, then I shall make sure you have a glass of brandy."

Edward was of two minds—one, he ought not to have come at all, which was nearly what happened because he'd forgotten about the dinner until Mrs. McSabby had saved his bacon by entering his workroom and giving him a tongue-lashing.

While he was deciding whether it was worth the effort, she'd laid out the terrible consequences. If he didn't attend, his parents would coat him with a layer of guilt so thick he would have had to cut his way through it with a carving knife. More than that, his mother's disappointment would be made known to him every day for the rest of the year.

His second choice, if he had remembered the party, was to have come early and taken up a clandestine place in the corner of the drawing room. It was only by arriving fashionably late that his parents had noticed him. And then he spotted Lillian, his sister, and crossed the room through the two dozen or so guests.

"Well met," he said fondly.

"Greetings, Brother dear. You came to keep me company at last."

"Hardly necessary. I know you attract suitors like—"

"Please don't say flies. That's not a very nice comparison."

"Like bees, then, to honey," he said.

"And how would you know?" she scoffed but with her usual good nature. "You haven't been at the same assembly as me in months. Not since last Christmas."

"I know you are much admired because you are Miss Lillian Lockwood, pretty and—"

"There's Lord St. John," she interrupted. "I have been hoping to meet him. Excuse me, Edward."

"Pretty and a devoted sister who would *never* choose a handsome face over her own brother," he finished after she hurried toward their mother in order to gain an introduction.

He cast his gaze around the room, and that was when he saw her—a head of flame-red hair, mostly swept up with some curls down around her ears. What's more, she was staring at him. *How on earth had she secured an invitation?*

It was painfully obvious she would do anything to get into his good graces. Without hesitation, he strode toward her, watching while her green eyes widened.

"What are you doing here?" Edward demanded, barely restraining himself from grabbing her arm and hauling her out. There was something entirely galling about her boldly breaching his parents' house, using their hospitality for whatever plan she had hatched.

"I was invited," she said, without an ounce of shame.

"Were you? Shall I ask my mother if there is a Lady Lambchop on her guest list?"

The infernal female smiled at him, a smile as dazzling as a stone that had received the most perfect cut, a brilliant, not a table cut.

"I doubt you will find such, sir, but you might try asking about—"

"Edward," interrupted his mother's voice. "You cannot defy all grace and civility and start introducing yourself to my guests. You must await either myself or your father. Regardless, I am glad you noticed *this* particular young lady. I have only recently begun a friendship with her mother, the Countess Diamond."

Edward let that sink in. *The Countess Diamond. Lady Diamond.* A daughter would be—

"Lady Radiance Diamond," his mother continued, "may I present my only son, Edward Lockwood." He wished her tone didn't have that hint of disappointment whenever she spoke of him. She thought little of his line of interest, regardless of his success in the field. *Playing with rocks*, she called it.

In any case, the redheaded lady now had the upper hand. Lady Radiance raised an eyebrow, while his humiliation colored his cheeks a deep-ruby shade.

"Thank you for the introduction, Mrs. Lockwood," she said, "but we are already acquainted. I have attended two of your son's informative lectures."

"Have you?" His mother glanced at him and then slowly back at Lady Radiance, without the least subtlety.

"Imagine that, Edward. A beautiful lady who also has a brain."

"Just like your own mother," his father added, having come upon them. "I apologize for interrupting, but I need you, Wife, on the other side of the room."

"Nothing grave, I hope."

Edward's father shrugged. "That remains to be determined. A matter of seating preference."

"Gracious!" Edward's mother exclaimed. "Now that you two are properly introduced, we shall leave you to get better acquainted. I'm sure you had little opportunity to chat during one of those dusty lectures on rocks."

Edward sighed. His mother had no idea what he did, nor did she understand his passion. On the other hand, she would be shocked to learn how much discourse had already occurred between him and the interesting Lady Radiance.

As soon as his parents moved away, Edward took a deep breath and looked directly into the lady's verdant eyes, peridot in the lamplight. Luckily, he saw mirth rather than malevolence dancing in their depths, reminding him of Monty when he was being his most mischievous.

"I offer my profound apology," he said.

"For calling me Lady Succulent Lambchop?"

"I apologize for my assumptions and accusations," he said. He'd made an arse of himself, without doubt.

"Your apology is accepted, sir. I have no interest in making you squirm."

"But you do have an interest in gemstones, do you not?" he surmised. "And it is genuine?"

"It is. Practically from the moment I saw what was presented at the Great Exhibition, the jewelry and the gems, I knew I had to learn about both. I also know a bit about how to make precious metals moldable."

"Do you?" He was surprised.

"Watching hard gold turn to liquid," she began, then sighed. "I find metalworking to be almost as fascinating as gem work."

She was the oddest female he'd ever met.

"I suppose I must now ask why you ill-advisedly came to my home."

"Why was it ill-advised?" she asked.

Edward wasn't sure if she was being serious, so he answered.

"Obviously a single lady cannot stop at a man's home willy-nilly. We hadn't even been properly introduced as we have now."

"I admit I have a tendency to flout certain restrictions put upon my sex, but I always take along a maid, at the very least. Moreover, my decision to visit you was not made lightly." Then she offered him a saucy smile, and he thought her lips looked succulent indeed.

"Besides if you recall, we *were* suitably introduced, and by a titled lord, no less! Just because you didn't believe my name in no way lessens the fact that I was, in fact, presented to you."

Well! She had him there, and objecting would only lead to a fiddlestick's end.

"Regardless, sir, you haven't asked me why I came knocking upon your door, which you answered yourself."

His cheeks warmed again. She was teasing him as if they were friends.

"I assumed you were there to get your hands upon the Hope Diamond."

She nodded. "Then you are correct. I do wish to look at it again. Am I too late? Have you already returned it to Mr. Hope?"

"I still have it. He is out of town and instructed me to hold on to it until he comes back."

"Then it is not too late," she mused.

At that moment, his parents summoned all the guests into their large dining room, made larger by two great doors being opened into the smaller salon beside it. Seating, as usual, was assigned.

To Edward's dismay, he found his name card before a place setting that was too distant from Lady Radiance to continue their conversation. Thus, for the next two hours, he was left to wonder about her reason for wanting to look more closely at the diamond. He had deduced it was something beyond mere curiosity.

Tucking into his meal, he busied his brain with considering the combined weight of all the gems on the men and women currently in his parents' home. However, the young woman to his right interrupted his summing of carats.

After determining what he did for a living, she had little interest beyond asking if he could get a discounted price on jewelry for her. His curt response—"No!"—had her turning to the guest on her right and ignoring him from the pottage to the pudding course.

On his other side, a lady wondered if he knew the best way to clean her jewelry. He nearly gave the same response. Yet since she'd asked nicely, he replied, "I suggest you send it to a jeweler to have it professionally cleaned. Barring that, you may ask your maid to let your gold and silver soak in vinegar or gin."

"Gin!" she exclaimed. "I never have that wicked liquor in the house."

Not caring about her moral view upon gin, he continued, "For gemstones, however, it's best to use diluted soap and then rinse with warm water. Vinegar can get into porous stones and damage them."

He was warming to the discussion. "Always dry with a soft badger's hair brush and polish with a fine cloth or soft leather. Did you know you can keep your silver from tarnishing by storing it completely covered in sifted arrowroot?"

Her response, a long blink, followed by, "No, I did not," ended the conversation, apparently satisfying her enough that he could return to his own contemplations. But he found his mind and his glance wandering down the long table to Lady Radiance. He could scarce believe he'd made fun of her name and been rude to her. *Twice!*

If his mother hadn't approached, he might have gone too far.

Not that Edward gave a fig about her being an earl's daughter, but he tried not to be discourteous. Sadly, he'd been accused of such before, when his mind had wandered during someone's discourse. It was usually inadvertent, *not* intentional, disregard. Most people simply could not keep his attention the way crystalline corundum, which made up both sapphires and rubies, or pondering Dr. Hutton's geological theory of the igneous origin of everything could keep him enthralled.

Catching Lady Radiance's gaze, he received a smile from her which surprised him into returning the expression. After that, he kept his gaze on his plate, thinking this dinner party was as interminable as every other one, worse because the courses were keeping him from the only interesting thing at the party—finding out why she'd shown up at his door.

Finally, they reached the moment when the guests *oohed* and *aahhed* over the raspberry summer sponge cakes doused in thick, creamy syllabub. His mother's staff presented them along the center of the table like pink and white buttons before each was taken away again to be sliced, served, and devoured. Then his mother rose, and his father and all the men followed suit.

"We shall have coffee, sherry, or brandy, to each their preference, in the drawing room," she announced.

"Thank God," Edward muttered. When silence ensued, he realized he'd spoken aloud . . . and loudly.

On his feet, drawing out the chair for the lady on his right, he added, "For I know the quality of both the coffee and the brandy under this roof, and we are all in for a treat."

That seemed to satisfy. But when he glanced again at Lady Radiance being escorted by Lord Chippens, she looked amused. He had a feeling she knew of his impatience, perhaps even relishing it.

CHAPTER FIVE

Once more in the Lockwoods' blue and gold drawing room, Radiance selected a glass of sherry from a tray and waited, knowing Mr. Lockwood's interest had been piqued. As predicted, he approached as soon as he saw her standing with Diana and her dining escort, Lord Chippens.

Upon seeing his determined expression, she took a step toward him, wishing they could speak privately.

"Lady Radiance," he began, "will you now explain your mysterious visit to my home?"

Upon hearing Diana's barely audible gasp, Radiance knew she ought to have moved even farther away. The man acted as if he didn't even notice anyone else around them.

With a quick verbal parry to his idiotic remark, she sought to remove the image of her being on his doorstep from the minds of those who had overheard.

"I sent my *footman* to your door, sir, in order to ask when your next lecture would be held and where. Hardly a mystery."

She shrugged dismissively, as he deserved. "You can provide the information now if you wish, so we may all be kept apprised of your fascinating talks." Radiance gestured around to include the others and to lessen any hint of impropriety.

Finally, his eyes took in the others, and she saw the dawning realization that he'd put her reputation in peril.

"Yes!" he said loudly. "I am sorry to have missed you. I mean, missed *your footman*. I was out."

At his stilted tone, Radiance turned to Diana, hoping she was otherwise engaged in conversation, but her friend's eyebrows were raised with interest. She turned to glare at Mr. Lockwood. He would have to do better.

"I was out at a place," he continued lamely. "At . . . my club."

"Which club do you belong to?" asked Lord Chippens with mild curiosity, obviously also overhearing the conversation.

Drats! Radiance hoped Mr. Lockwood had a good answer.

"You wouldn't know it," he assured him. "Not White's or Boodle's or any of those. Just a small establishment. A place where . . . where geologists gather."

"I had no idea there was such a place," Lord Chippens said. Nor did Radiance think there truly was one.

"We don't have many members," Mr. Lockwood continued in what, to her, was clearly a prevarication, "and we like it that way."

"What is its name?" Lord Chippens asked.

Radiance nearly groaned on Mr. Lockwood's behalf, for his lordship was like a foxhound on a vixen's scent.

"I am not at liberty to tell you unless you are a geologist," Mr. Lockwood said somberly. "Are you, in fact, a studier of the earth? Do you know the differences among igneous, sedimentary, and metamorphic rock?"

Lord Chippens appeared startled. "Why, no."

"I didn't think so," Mr. Lockwood said, his tone supercilious indeed. And now Radiance wished to tug the carpet of arrogance out from under him.

"But I do," she said. "I won't bore everyone here with the differences, but does that afford me entrance to your club?"

"My apologies," he said. "Men only."

Radiance had expected as much. "Maybe when I am a famous geologist," she teased, "then I shall change that rule or start my own club."

Unexpectedly, Lord Chippens laughed heartily. "A famous *female* geologist!" he said when he could speak. "*And* a club allowing women. What next? Flying elephants?"

Although Mr. Lockwood's expression indicated he thought Lord Chippens a tedious dolt, he could not possibly feel the insult on her behalf. And she did feel it quite keenly.

Whirling upon the still cackling Lord Chippens, Radiance demanded, "Do *you* know why the Hope Diamond is blue?"

His face reddened. "No," he confessed. "Why should I? Why should *you*, for that matter? What use is it?"

"What use?" she repeated, incredulous. Glancing at Diana and Mr. Lockwood, Radiance couldn't credit the question. "What is the use of knowing the earth is round or how far away the stars are or that the ocean is salty? What use is a Shakespearean sonnet or knowing that flowers need sunlight? In other words, my lord, what use is knowledge? Sometimes it is simply for the knowing. Sometimes the knowledge can be put to practice. And other times, it is merely to keep one's brain from turning to mush and oozing out of one's ears."

With that, she stared at his left ear as if expecting to see the mush of which she'd spoken.

Mr. Lockwood's satisfied smile indicated he understood her set-down and approved of it, even when Chippens unthinkingly put his hand up to his ear. Diana, too, was grinning behind her glass of sherry.

Finally, Lord Chippens mumbled an excuse and wandered away, probably to scrape his pride together in a horse bucket. And Radiance calmed her temper and decided to return to civility.

"Have you two been introduced?"

When her petite, brown-haired friend shook her head, Radiance said, "This is Mr. Lockwood." Then she turned to him. "Miss Stepney is my dear friend."

"I am honored to make your acquaintance," he said. And Radiance hoped the geologist was finished with his faux pas for the evening. It seemed he might be when he added, "Your father, Mr. Stepney, has a reputation for a discerning eye as a collector of exquisite art."

As Radiance relaxed, still wondering how they would speak privately about the Hope Diamond, he leaned forward, staring at Diana's necklace, a silver chain holding a highly polished brown stone with a long history in her friend's family.

He gestured to her throat. "A curiously ugly pendant for a young woman to wear."

Mortified gasps, hers and Diana's, met his words. Radiance would gladly throttle him if she could, especially when she saw tears well in her friend's eyes.

"My grandmother gave it to me," Diana said, her lower lip trembling, "just before she shed her mortal coils. It is a toadstone, and she vowed it would keep me safe."

If the man knew any sense of decency, he would now drop the matter.

"What a strangely twisted promise," Edward said. "The correct term is *bufonite*, *bufo* being the Latin word for toad. Toads are poisonous and thus, as the story goes, the toadstone from a . . . ," he chuckled, "from a live, elderly toad's head, harvested by putting said toad on a piece of . . . of . . ." He dissolved into laughter before shaking his head, trying to rein in his mirth.

Radiance curled her fingers into fists. She and Diana shared twin expressions of dismay, which he seemed to take for disbelief because he continued his lecture.

"You could only harvest the stone from the toad's head by putting the living toad on a piece of red cloth. A magical red cloth!" He chuckled again at the absurdity. "Wearing it near one's skin purportedly has the power of an antidote to poison!"

He sipped his brandy calmly. If he was waiting for them to smile or laugh, he would have a long wait. Diana had been an accident-prone child, and whether coincidence or not, the gift of the mythological toadstone had much improved her outlook, if not her balance.

With confidence of its protection, Diana seemed to have stopped tripping and falling.

Mr. Lockwood, apparently wanting some reaction, said, "Don't you see how ludicrous it is, even if it were a stone from a toad's head? However, it is no more that than it is a piece of shiny dung, which it resembles." He pointed to the pendant. "And it cannot protect you from any ill happenstances any more than it can save you from poison."

Radiance rolled her eyes. Yet with Diana looking downright distraught, she had to stop him.

"Regardless of your opinion, sir, on its efficacy or beauty, the stone is cherished by Miss Stepney and her family."

He nodded, seeming to understand. "Was your grandmother from Oxfordshire, by chance?"

Diana's eyes widened. "Why, yes!"

"I had a feeling," he said. "Because your toadstone is really a fossilized tooth."

This time, Radiance did smack her own forehead with her gloved hand.

"A tooth!" Diana snatched the pendant lying upon her chest and craned her neck to look down at it.

All Radiance could do was shake her head to deter him, but he plunged onward.

"Yes. From an extinct fish of the genus *Lepidotes*. Basically, a very scaly carp-like fish about a foot long from thousands of years ago. Many of their fossilized teeth have been found in Oxfordshire sediment, which is why I surmised your grandmother's area of residence."

Diana's lips formed an *O*, then with her face flushing red, she clamped a hand over her mouth and hurried away.

Mr. Lockwood watched her go, looking acutely puzzled by her reaction.

"How odd," he said.

Radiance sighed deeply. "Not really, sir. My friend was apt to accidental falls, and her grandmother gave her the toadstone to keep her safe."

"But it cannot do that," he protested. "Surely, she should know the truth, especially if she is going to wear such a thing around her neck like a savage. Besides, it reminded me of one of my cat's messes on the rug when my housekeeper forgets to let him out into the back garden. A woman of your intelligence, you must have known what it was."

Radiance sighed again, half appreciating his compliment while wishing he hadn't felt the need to drive Diana to tears.

"Things are not always what they seem, sir." Radiance thought of the Hope Diamond again, but it would have to wait. "In the case of my friend's belief in the stone—it was not such a bad thing. I must go find her and make sure she is not unduly suffering."

"Better she should wear spectacles," he called after her.

THE EVENING WAS NOT yet over, but Diana had left after excusing herself to Mrs. Lockwood. Radiance had thought her friend admirable in claiming a headache rather than denouncing their hostess's son as a ninnyhammer.

A dunce of a man to whom she would try once again to tell what she thought she had seen at his lecture.

Unfortunately, after watching Diana leave, Mrs. Lockwood remained by Radiance's side, and thus, when she approached Mr. Lockwood again, his mother was at her elbow.

"Edward, have you spoken with your Aunt Gertie yet? She just bumped in to me in the hall and said she hadn't realized you were here."

"Then you have your answer," he said. "I have not spoken to her yet, or she would have known I was here. Although how she could have missed seeing her only nephew over the dining room table is beyond me."

"Impertinence!" his mother exclaimed. "And before this nice young lady, too. That won't win over Lady Radiance. If you can be rude to your own mother, then you shall be rude to a wife."

A wife! Radiance peered at him more closely, despite feeling a little embarrassed. *Was he on the lookout for a life partner?* While she thought him heavenly to look at and admired his mind, his manner of plain-speaking to the point of rudeness and his disregard for civility were hardly desirable. She ought to keep her hat set at Lord John Castille whom she'd met at the first ball of the Season. A viscount with all the social graces, an excellent dancer, and a man who'd plainly shown an interest in her in return.

But Lord Castille was not present, and Mr. Lockwood now looked peevish.

"Mother," he warned.

Perhaps realizing she had gone too far, Mrs. Lockwood made a face of contrition. After all, the man wasn't a child to be reprimanded in front of a guest. Mrs. Lockwood might be able to wrap her husband around her finger from what Radiance had seen that evening, but one didn't usually hold the same sway with one's offspring.

"Come with me, please, Edward," Mrs. Lockwood said more politely. "And we shall try to soothe your elderly Aunt Gertrude. Otherwise, she may cut us out of her will."

"Mother," he said again, yet with less heat. "Stop teasing, or people will think you to be on the edge of poverty, and Father will not appreciate such an insult to his financial acumen. Besides, Aunt Gertie is a kind soul who would never cut anyone out of anything. Not even a cut indirect."

His mother did, in fact, turn to Lady Radiance.

"Truly, I am speaking in jest. My sister-in-law has a touch of the gout. She was the one seated to my husband's right. Currently, she has taken the chair by the hearth, and if my son has any sense, he'll go greet her and admire the large, ugly stone around her neck."

Radiance saw his interest grow. Perhaps he intended to insult another female's beloved necklace that evening.

"What type of stone?" he asked with a childlike curiosity before glancing at Radiance. "Would you care to meet my father's eldest sister and see what gemstone she's sporting this evening?"

"Yes, of course," she said.

Mrs. Lockwood presented a satisfied smile.

"Then I shall leave you two young people to make the visit," she said. "After all, I have other guests with whom I've barely spoken half a sentence."

CHAPTER SIX

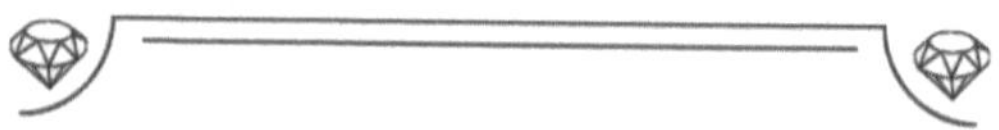

Radiance watched the party's hostess walk away.
"Your mother is nice."

"Is she?" Mr. Lockwood asked. "If you say so, but she can test one's patience," he said with a complete lack of self-awareness as to his own faults in that regard.

"Anyway, let us go take a look at my aunt's necklace."

"You mean introduce me to her while doing your duty as a loving nephew."

He shot her a wry grin, a little crooked and producing a dimple on one side. Her breath caught. *My, what a rum duke when he smiled.*

"That's precisely what I meant," he agreed and offered her his arm.

They approached a lady perhaps ten years older than Mr. Lockwood's father.

"There's my Ned. I missed you earlier by my arriving more than fashionably late and being whisked directly into the dining room."

"I am glad to see you, Auntie," Mr. Lockwood said. He pressed her proffered hand between his before leaning forward to kiss her cheek. When he drew away, Radiance could tell he was examining the necklace she wore.

His mother had been correct in the stone being large and ugly. What's more, Radiance was stumped as to what the pendant was. Not onyx, yet it was dark. It had a sheen to it, but it revolted her. Truly, it was far worse than an old fish's tooth that Diana wore.

Before she could tidy up her expression, Mr. Lockwood introduced them, and she knew his aunt had plainly seen her distaste.

"I am pleased to meet you," Radiance said, rearranging her features into a smile.

"And I, you. What an unusual and lovely name if I may say. And I noted you were admiring my necklace?"

Was the lady teasing? With no way to know, Radiance had to say something.

"It is . . . interesting. An unusual piece, to be sure. Why, I don't even recognize the stone."

The older lady laughed, and Edward joined in.

"Not a stone," his aunt said. "And absolutely hideous. I only wore it to annoy my sister-in-law. I bet she made remark of it."

While Radiance digested this bit of inter-familial teasing, Mr. Lockwood gave the answer. "It's gutta-percha."

When Radiance could do no more than shrug, he added, "Mostly a resin compound from Malaysian trees. Like rubber."

She nodded. "I did see a great deal of rubber at the exhibition, including an ingenious little boat, like a rowboat, made out of it. Entirely unsinkable, but I didn't see rubber jewelry."

"Perhaps you missed Mr. Goodyear's booth," he suggested.

"Indeed, I had my attention elsewhere," she agreed. "But why would someone use it in place of a gemstone?"

"Why indeed?" the aunt replied. "But I saw it and had to buy it. It wasn't as cheap as such ugliness warrants but not nearly the cost of a pretty gem."

Radiance looked to Mr. Lockwood for his opinion.

"I suppose the material is something of a rarity, and thus a jeweler felt the need to display it. I've seen a few rings set with a blob of gutta-percha. Even better, I saw a walking cane made from it recently. It won't rot in the rain the way a wooden cane might."

"A cane seems like a very good use for it," Radiance said. "Or perhaps for the soles of shoes." Then she gasped, realizing the insult.

"Do not worry," Aunt Gertrude said. "I take no offense." She gave them a curious stare. "Do the two of you have an arrangement yet?"

Yet? Radiance's glance shot to Mr. Lockwood's surprised face while her own cheeks warmed.

"No, Auntie. We are merely . . . that is, Lady Radiance came to a couple of my lectures. She has a keen interest in gemstones."

"Does she?" his aunt asked, her tone utterly amused. Then she gestured for a footman to come over. After accepting a glass of port, she let the man take her empty one. "Isn't that charming? But the obvious is apparent as my father used to say."

"My interest in gemstones is true," Radiance told her. "I even study the craft under a master jeweler."

This clearly shocked the woman who sat up straighter. "At a jewelry shop? But you are Lord Diamond's daughter."

"I am not working there for payment," she assured Mr. Lockwood's aunt, "but for what I can learn."

His aunt's eyebrows rose nearly to her hairline. "You are a rarity, indeed, but not such a kind as my ugly pendant."

"Thank you," Radiance said, although she wasn't entirely sure whether she'd been complimented.

"The party is nearly over," the older woman added. "Thank goodness." And she swallowed down the rest of her drink before holding the glass out to Radiance, who took it, and her other hand out to her nephew, who grasped it.

"Help me up, Ned, and get me to my carriage."

Radiance still hadn't had a chance to speak privately to Mr. Lockwood and feared she wouldn't.

"Of course," he said, offering Radiance a rueful look. "I shall see you in a few—"

"For goodness' sake, Ned, the girl won't melt away while you're outside." And she seemed to be the one leading him as the two walked away.

However, by the time he returned, his parents were already saying goodbye to their guests. Radiance offered them her gratitude for the invitation to the interesting evening. Then she slid on her gloves and accepted her mantle. Mr. Lockwood lingered nearby.

"Shall I walk you to your carriage?"

"That would be lovely," she said, relieved for the opportunity.

Thus finally, as her father's barouche pulled up out front, she could speak plainly.

"I need to see the Hope Diamond again. May I come to your home tomorrow? I promise to bring my maid and have her come inside instead of awaiting me in the carriage."

He hesitated. "I could bring it to your home."

Radiance thought about that. Her mother would be intrigued, and her father might wish to speak to Mr. Lockwood in his study.

"Won't it appear to the world as if you are courting me?"

Mr. Lockwood took a step backward.

Radiance added, "Only because your parents invited me here tonight. And if you come calling the very next day…" She ended with a shrug.

He considered. "Perhaps you are correct. I would hate for your family to be misled."

And thus, Radiance arrived at eleven o'clock the following day for the second time at Mr. Lockwood's home on the southeast side of Berkeley Square. As promised, she had Sarah beside her and even allowed her to use the knocker.

This time, a round-cheeked housekeeper opened the door, her face a picture of surprise when she beheld a lady and her maid.

"I believe I am expected," Radiance said.

"Oh, no," the woman retorted. "I believe *you* are at the wrong house."

Radiance was tickled, glad to know Mr. Lockwood didn't have a stream of female callers.

"I assure you I am not. I am here to see Mr. Lockwood. Didn't he mention my visit?"

"No," the housekeeper said, but she quickly swung the door open. "The man is as absent-minded as a March hare," she muttered.

More loudly, she added, "It's only that Mr. Lockwood doesn't have much company." Another mutter came out, "None at all, in fact."

Radiance and her maid followed the woman into a moderate-sized parlor that was spotless but seemed neglected nonetheless, at least regarding furnishings.

"Excuse the lack of a wife's touch, but this is the home of a bachelor who goes out for his entertainment."

As if realizing she'd said something to dishonor her employer, she added, "May I bring you some tea or coffee while I tell Mr. Lockwood of your arrival?"

"Nothing, thank you."

The housekeeper spent another moment looking her up and down. "To think he forgot the likes of you," she said. "Don't that beat all. And with a maid as well! My word!"

Then the woman ambled out. Half a minute later, Radiance would swear she heard an oath uttered loudly, twice, followed by hurried footsteps. Mr. Lockwood appeared in the doorway.

"My sincere apologies," he stated, running a hand through his hair until it stood on end. "I was working last night, rather late, and forgot about . . . I mean, your visit slipped my mind." He groaned. "There is no way to say that without it sounding dreadfully . . ." He shrugged.

Radiance wasn't used to being forgotten, but he was so charmingly aware of his flaw, she didn't mind.

"Your apology is accepted, sir."

"Thank you." He glanced at the maid and nodded to her. "Would you both come to my workroom?"

"That's all right. Sarah may stay here. She has some reading material with her."

As soon as she said it, the young woman took a seat on the sofa without being asked, pulled a thin book out of her pocket, and settled in.

Radiance trusted that would suffice. Having Sarah come into each room like a shadow or a pet had never appealed to her. Moreover, it showed a level of distrust that might insult the geologist. "I promise I have no qualms that you will turn into a desperate marauder the moment we are alone."

More's the pity, she thought. For she'd been unable to rid herself of the notion that he had a passion running deep, like an underground river in a diamond mine.

Nodding as if he hadn't really heard her, he gestured for her to accompany him. They went no farther than the doorway at the end of the hall.

Radiance wandered in, and something warm and furry brushed her skirts as it entered with them.

"Oh!" she exclaimed. "Where did the cat come from?"

"That's Monty, and he's always around. He was probably watching from the top of the stairs. I hope you don't mind cats or are afraid of them."

"Cats are fine by me," she said, even as Monty jumped onto one of the tables filled with a variety of clutter. "So wild and yet domesticated, too."

And then, there they were, alone finally except for his cat, who stretched and rubbed its face on a purple and white geode. She glanced around, taking in his workroom, as he'd called it. From the placement of the chandelier, Radiance assumed it was meant to be a dining room.

However, in place of a single polished table and tidy chairs, there were cases and shelves, two smaller tables covered in bric-a-brac, and a desk strewn with papers and maps. Large split geodes displaying their crystal interiors rested upon stacks of books, and gemstones, shining in the lamplight, were in evidence, dotted here and there around the room as if mislaid and forgotten.

She half expected to see the Hope Diamond simply abandoned on one of the surfaces.

"Do not worry," he said, watching her scrutiny of his workspace. "The Hope is safely tucked away."

"I didn't doubt it," she said, although she had.

"Mr. Hope returned last night and sent a message this morning. Therefore, today, I must take him his diamond."

Nodding, Radiance wandered around to the far end of the room, still examining the curiosities. "I would wager Mr. Hope wouldn't want it out of his sight for too long, especially not with a man who conducts important discussions on his front step."

For her remark, she received a small smile as Mr. Lockwood undoubtedly remembered trying to make her tell her purpose while keeping her at bay.

He did recall, for suddenly, he stood straighter. "You've gone to a great deal of trouble to speak privately with me."

"And to see the diamond again," she reminded him, for Radiance wouldn't know the truth until she did.

"Tell me what is your concern with the diamond?" he demanded.

"May I see it first?"

"No," he said, surprising her. "Not until you tell me. I have spent too many hours wondering."

Radiance took a deep breath. She would have to explain, it seemed, before he would allow her the satisfaction of seeing the stone again to be sure she was correct.

"Does the Hope Diamond have a flaw?"

At once, he shook his head. "No. It is as close to flawless as one can . . . well . . . *hope* for."

"Then if what I saw is real, the diamond you presented at your lecture is not the Hope Diamond."

CHAPTER SEVEN

"**P**reposterous! I collected it from Mr. Hope myself." Edward was quick to take the velvet pouch from a drawer in his cabinet.

"Did you examine the diamond at that time?" she asked.

He shook his head. "You sound like a police inspector. But *no* is my answer. I had no reason to. I doubt Mr. Hope would dupe me with his own stone."

"I cannot think why he would," she agreed. "And it has been in no one else's possession?"

Edward answered without hesitation. "Absolutely not."

Except for Monty. He recalled the cat's interest in the big stone before realizing he was letting his fancy take over.

"What is this about?"

Lady Radiance took a deep breath. "I had read it was a perfect stone. I've seen it myself at the exhibition, although never before close up as at your lecture. And you have just confirmed that it is flawless."

It was difficult to concentrate on her words now that he was watching her mouth. She had soft, plump lips of a pretty rose quartz color. He could easily imagine covering them with his own before taking the lush lower one gently between his teeth.

"Thus, I was surprised to see a fissure in the stone."

Suddenly, she had all Edward's attention.

"A fissure!" He tore open the velvet and grabbed for one of the magnifying spectacles he had on his table, which he quickly thrust onto his nose, tucking the arms behind his ears.

"Yes," she said, coming to stand beside him. "Small, a hairsbreadth is all. Or perhaps it was merely a hair. That is my expectation, and why I wished to see it again."

Edward didn't answer. Instead, he did something he almost never did. He held the gem with his bare hands and walked over to the window. An unusually cloudless London day gave him a good view as he held the Hope diamond up to the light.

"Are you speaking of an inclusion?" he asked, looking at it from underneath. "For the notion that you had spotted one no other person has ever seen before is impossible."

"Perhaps an inclusion," she said, "or merely a surface crack."

"Merely," he muttered. "There is nothing 'mere' about a flaw appearing *in* or even *on* the Hope Diamond." And yet, he knew she was right. While delaying looking at the diamond from the top down, he could already see something that could not possibly be there.

Suddenly, her warmth seeped through the sleeve of his coat, and he realized she had followed to stand close beside him. She was leaning against his arm to better see, and he caught the aroma of a delicate floral scent.

Neither lavender nor rose. He lowered the diamond as he tried to identify the soft aroma.

"There!" she exclaimed.

Edward looked at her, not at the diamond, and through the magnifying lenses, her eyes were enormous emeralds. Pulling off the spectacles, he locked his gaze upon her once more, knowing the insane urge to kiss her.

"I saw it again!" Lady Radiance declared.

"Did you?" *What had she seen?* Then he recalled what they'd been looking at.

"Sadly, yes," she said. "Even without magnification. And I hate to be correct in this particular instance."

With abject dread, Edward tore his glance away from the lovely woman filling his senses and put it back where it belonged. She was correct. Not a surface crack but a flaw, an inclusion deep in the heart of the Hope Diamond. *How extraordinary and utterly impossible!*

"What a shame," she murmured, peering at the diamond while leaning on him, distracting him with her lush curves.

"Does such a thing ever occur spontaneously?" she asked while Edward peered at the gem again through his magnifying glasses despite being able to see the flaw with his naked eyes.

Finally, he lowered the stone, knowing it was not the real Hope Diamond. It couldn't be.

"May I?" she asked.

Wordlessly, he handed her both the gem and the magnifying spectacles. As she put them on and looked, he walked away. He was ruined.

"What do you make of it?" she asked.

Edward sat down at his desk as if he were alone. Resting his head in his hands, wondering if he would end up in leg irons, he comforted himself with the notion that he'd wanted to see Australia and find his own opal, like the German geologist, Johannes Menge.

A moment later, Monty brushed his furry cheek against Edward's forehead.

"Stop it." *Who would look after Monty? Would he be allowed to take him on the convict ship?*

Then Edward heard footsteps and looked up. Barely a foot away, Lady Radiance had rested her ruffled rear against the large-grain oak top, leaning directly beside him. She observed him as keenly as she'd been studying the diamond.

Edward blinked. His reputation would be shattered. His livelihood gone. Had someone in the audience at the lecture managed to make the switch? Or had it happened before he'd even taken it to Somerset House?

She placed the stone back onto the black velvet and laid the glasses beside it. While her face was solemn, he doubted she understood the import. He had in his possession something that should not exist.

"It's not the Hope Diamond," he told her in case she was thinking anything else. "It is a fake."

"Truly?" she crossed her arms. "Are you certain?"

He nodded, not taking offense. "I know the Hope as well as I know my own hand."

At that moment, Monty was rubbing across his knuckles. When she reached down and stroked the cat's head at the same time, her delicate fingers sinking into Monty's fur, the sight made his stomach clench. Or perhaps it was the knowledge that Mr. Hope could sue him for everything he had or ever would have.

Whatever it was, something was making him feel like he was on a rope swing, the one he'd played on as a boy at the estate of his grandfather, the viscount.

"How can that be?" Lady Radiance asked finally when he said nothing more.

"I don't know." For the first time in his adult life, Edward had no answer.

"What will you do?"

"What I was going to do before you arrived and destroyed my sanity."

"I beg your pardon."

"My apologies," he said, feeling his throat closing up as he watched Monty, purring as loudly as a steam engine, stretch out, seemingly boneless.

Then Edward thought about the chance encounter of Lady Radiance coming to his class.

"I am grateful for what you noticed, but I cannot fathom how this could have happened, nor when it was switched. How could I have been so careless? Regardless, I must go to Mr. Hope's residence today as planned."

"You sound as if you are going to your execution."

He ran a hand through his hair. "I cannot imagine what he will say or how I will ever be trusted in my field—indeed, in this country—ever again."

"May I accompany you?" she asked unexpectedly.

With his brain throbbing, not to mention his neck aching from looking up at her, Edward suddenly realized the disgracefulness of his behavior. Shoving back the chair, he rose to his feet.

"Please, again, accept my deepest apologies, this time for the rudeness of my behavior. I am not myself. Would you care to sit?"

RADIANCE HADN'T MINDED his casual manner and understood it had been brought about by the shock of what she'd brought to his attention. Moreover, not standing on ceremony or civility indicated he considered her an equal and not a prissy, sensitive female.

"Thank you, no. I would like you to let me go with you to see Mr. Hope."

He shook his head. "I shall not hide behind your skirts."

Despite knowing the seriousness of the situation, laughter burst out of her before she could stifle it. Naturally, his expression darkened.

"It is my turn to offer an apology, sir, but I don't see it the same way. If Mr. Hope accuses you of some duplicity, then I can assure him that you had no idea you were in possession of a fake stone."

He nodded thoughtfully before tilting his head and fixing her with such an intense look, her stomach fluttered. "How do you know I'm not lying?" he asked.

"It never occurred to me that you would." But she had to ask, "Are you?"

He offered a wry smile, and his dimple showed. "No."

"Then let me come and vouch for you. Besides, I would very much appreciate an introduction to Mr. Hope."

"Why? In fact, what is your interest in gemstones? Why were you at my lectures?"

Because you are the most intriguing man I have ever encountered.

Obviously, those were not words she could say. But her cheeks heated before she regained her composure. In any case, that wasn't the true answer.

"I have an eye for jewelry design, or so I've been told. I sometimes work under the tutelage of Mr. Bonwit, but I wish to know much more than how to set a ruby or create filagree."

"You are unique," he declared, "and a kindred spirit. If you work with Mr. Bonwit, whom I know to be a master jeweler, then I shall gladly introduce you to Mr. Hope."

He finished packing up the stone and slipped it into a satchel.

"How do you know *I'm* not the one lying?" Radiance couldn't believe she was flirting.

"About your interest in gems? Are you?" he asked, echoing her words.

"Not at all. Are we going now?"

"If you have no prior engagement, then yes."

She felt the thrill of an unexpected escapade. "Then we should take my carriage as it is available and waiting outside your door."

He grimaced. "Just because I sometimes answer my own door, that doesn't mean I don't have my own carriage."

"Do you?"

Mr. Lockwood sighed. "No, but by choice. When I travel out of the city, I take the train. And in London, it is far easier to hail a hansom cab than to bother maintaining a horse and vehicle."

"Perfectly understandable, sir. Consider my father's carriage the same as hailing a cab since I am already here. And I have my maid as a chaperone."

He slung his satchel over his shoulder and gestured for her to precede him from the room.

"I don't know much about your world of being a titled young, single lady, but I believe a maid is not considered a true chaperone. After all, you could order her to close her eyes or bribe her not to tell anyone of your behavior."

Radiance was charmed by his concern for her reputation.

"Might something occur that would necessitate my giving her such an order or bribe?" Her continued flirtation was met with silence, and she glanced over her shoulder.

His face was a picture of . . . *desire, perhaps?* Not knowing any differently, she would vow he was thinking about something inappropriate. *Regarding her!*

When a little shiver tickled along her spine, she let herself imagine being in his arms and, if she wished, being kissed by him. She'd been kissed before—in the first case, not more than a quick peck, and the second time, a wet and sloppy attempt with the only excitement being that they might be caught in a garden.

Sadly, neither gentleman had enticed her to a second kiss, although both had been very good dancers. Lately, her only burgeoning interest was Lord Castille, a spirited man with whom she'd already shared a few dances. Unfortunately, there had, as yet, been no opportunity for him to kiss her.

Then Mr. Lockwood shook his head as if clearing an untoward thought.

"I will restrain myself, Lady Radiance, if you will."

She nearly tripped over the hallway carpet. *Could he read her mind?*

CHAPTER EIGHT

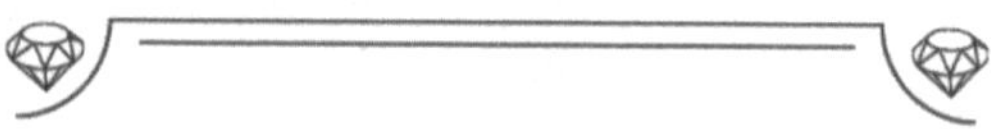

Unbelievably, Edward was going to keep company with Lady Radiance as he went to his assured demise. After donning his hat, he reached for his gloves, finding only one on the hallstand. Glancing up, he saw her taking in his every movement. She stared at the single glove he held with a measured gaze.

In some ways, she was an annoying woman. Having called for her maid to rejoin them, Lady Radiance stood in his entrance hall, scrutinizing his life. She glanced at the runner on the main stairs, up at his hanging lamp, and even at the hall mirror at her own reflection.

Their eyes met, for he was looking over her shoulder. When they did, she whirled around to face him. In the morning light, her eyes were more of a beryl green than the dark emerald he'd noticed previously in the lamplight of his parents' dinner party.

Shaking his head, he shoved his hands into his coat pocket, only to come up with the other glove.

"*Ah-ha!*" he said aloud and tugged both on before opening his front door and gesturing for her to precede him.

However, when he saw the luxurious carriage with the coat of arms, he stopped.

"Is something wrong?" she asked.

"Just admiring your father's carriage."

The lady looked at it as if seeing it for the first time.

"That is quite an insignia," he said, staring past her at the Diamond crest.

Lady Radiance shrugged. "My father is the Earl Diamond, after all. Do you know I have a brother and three sisters whose names would also amuse you? Shall I tell you?"

Speechless, Edward could only nod. For while he'd belatedly recalled the existence of Lord Diamond the evening before, he knew nothing of the man's offspring, except for Lady Radiance.

She went toward the carriage, where a footman held open the door.

"Mr. Lockwood will give you the address," she told the man before climbing in. Her maid followed.

Edward told the driver Mr. Hope's address on the corner of Piccadilly and Down Street and then joined them, making himself comfortable on the buttery soft seat.

"Do you know he is our neighbor?" Lady Radiance asked.

"I did not. Your home is . . . ?"

"Farther along the park," she said as the carriage lurched into motion, "toward Bolton Street."

He had gone past it a hundred times, not realizing a family of Diamonds were inside.

With a steady hand, she checked her pale-yellow hat and smoothed her skirts with the other.

"My eldest sister is Clarity. She is married to Lord Hollidge."

Edward could think of no response except to nod, waiting for her to continue.

"The next eldest is Purity. She is married to Lord Foxford."

Edward had heard of him, considered something of a rake a few years earlier.

"My brother's name is Adam, which you may recognize comes from *adamas*, as being derived from—"

"From Latin for hard stone," he finished.

"Exactly. Then in birth order, I come next, followed by my younger sister, Brilliance."

"Unusual names for an unusual family," he offered, almost ashamed to tell her his only sister's ordinary name.

Lady Radiance shrugged delicately. "I am not sure we are unusual except for our names, but I dearly love my brother and sisters."

"I have only the one sister with whom you may have become acquainted at the dinner party. Her given name is Lillian."

"Indeed, I did. Miss Lockwood has your same hair and unusual eye color. She was clever and fun, too."

He wondered if Lady Radiance was thinking of the correct female. And then, as they were swiftly approaching Hope's new mansion, what everyone called Hope House, his brain dismissed anything but thoughts of the diamond. Edward was deep in the suds and no mistake.

He could not possibly have imagined when he awakened that morning, looking forward to a cup of coffee and some buttered toast, that he would be riding in an earl's carriage with an earl's daughter, no less.

Yet here he was, and there she was—across from him!

Moreover, he never would have dreamed he could be responsible for having lost the famous diamond belonging to a parliamentary statesman, who was not only formerly the Groom of the Bedchamber for both King George IV and his successor, William IV, but had also aided Prince Albert in organizing the Great Exhibition the year before.

Beyond that, Mr. Hope had been something of a mentor to Edward.

"Do not worry," Lady Radiance said. "Although, I confess, it feels as though we have entered the pages of one of Sarah's adored *penny dreadfuls*."

The maid flinched, and her eyes grew as large as saucers, staring at him. He had never read one but knew they held all sorts of criminal activity and even supernatural and monstrous beings, such as vampires. The illustrations that drew people to give up their pennies revolted him with their callous disregard for decency and human life. They always seemed to drip blood or show someone being hanged.

Still, as the Bard said, to each his own, and he sent the maid a nervous smile. Unlike him, she and her mistress had nothing to worry about.

"Do you know Mr. Hope?" Edward asked Lady Radiance.

"My parents have dined with him, but I have never had the pleasure."

"A fascinating man," Edward mused, "from a successful and industrious family. Dutch bankers, interior designers on a grand scale, financiers of the Dutch East India Company, travelers of the globe, art collectors, and of course, diamond and gem dealers, too."

"And this Mr. Hope has been a member of Parliament, if I'm not mistaken," she added, "although not in the same House as my father."

Almost too quickly they turned onto Piccadilly, heading west toward the mansion that Henry Thomas Hope had commissioned a mere two years earlier to house his father's and his own vast art collection. Everyone agreed the beautiful stone and metal exterior, created in the contemporary French style, was a magnificent edifice.

If not exactly friends, Edward and Henry Hope were mutual admirers, who enjoyed talking about rare stones and gems. Besides the famed blue diamond, Hope had also inherited from his uncle several other valuable jewels.

Thinking of how little sentimentality the man had displayed over his boyhood London home near Cavendish Square—ordering it demolished without even preserving its memory in oil paint—Edward wondered what his own fate would be, having somehow lost the precious stone.

In no time, as if traffic parted for a wealthy man's carriage, they were at their destination, Hope's new mansion. Edward didn't even bother to protest when Lady

Radiance told her maid to wait in the carriage. For an instant, he felt sorry for the young woman until she pulled a magazine with a lurid illustration on its cover from her pocket and buried her nose in it. Not a bad way to earn a living, he supposed. At that moment, with the task ahead, he would gladly trade places.

They were shown directly to Mr. Hope's welcoming and well-lit reception room, in which Edward had been a dozen times. Exquisitely furnished with Hope's own family-designed furniture and pieces from his art collection, including Old Masters as well as a few pieces of ancient Greek sculpture, the room was a model of understated taste and wealth. Moreover, its cream-and-gold walls and tawny carpet with the most muted of patterns let the furnishings make the room's statement.

"Lady Radiance, this is Mr. Hope," Edward introduced, giving her the honor of both her sex and her title, rather than presenting her to the great renaissance man, as Edward thought of him.

In his early forties, Hope was currently a member of Parliament and greatly respected, although everyone knew he had attempted yet failed more than once to obtain a title of his own. He bowed to Lady Radiance.

In return, she offered him a sweet smile.

"Lady Radiance trains with the jeweler Mr. Bonwit," he added to avoid any misunderstanding as to why he was accompanied by this particular female.

"Is that so?" Mr. Hope looked dumbstruck. "The Earl Diamond's daughter is an apprentice."

"Not really an apprentice, sir," Lady Radiance answered, taking the seat she'd been offered, "although I am learning the craft."

"Indeed." Then he turned his attention to Edward. "I assume you have my precious stone."

"To tell you the truth, sir, I don't believe I do."

"What do you mean?" Mr. Hope relaxed against the wingback chair and crossed his legs.

Edward wondered at the man's calm manner. After all, they weren't speaking about some pea-sized gem.

"I have seen the Hope Diamond enough times to be certain it has no inclusion. And yet, the stone I currently have in my possession has one. I cannot explain it, sir. I swear to you that I never let the diamond out of my sight."

To Edward's amazement, Mr. Hope's face broke into a broad smile.

"Well done, young man. I am sorry to have perpetrated a deceit upon you, but I needed to be certain I could trust you."

Edward's heart, which had been racing with worry, thudded uncomfortably in his chest. "You knew I had a fake."

"Indeed, I did. I gave it to you myself. Yet you not only discerned that it wasn't my diamond, you didn't try to return it to me without mentioning it."

"How could I?" Edward asked. It had never crossed his mind to do so. "That would endanger my reputation, not to mention open me to an accusation of thievery."

"True. Thus, you have exceeded my expectations on both fronts."

Edward had to tell the entire truth. "To be honest, sir, I hardly looked at the diamond. As per usual, it remained secure until I drew it out to show those in the lecture hall, and then I returned it to its pouch and box." He drew it out of his satchel and placed it on the table between them. "It was Lady Radiance who spotted the flaw and did so after a remarkably quick scrutiny."

"Did she?" Mr. Hope turned to her. "And how did you come to be so close to the stone that you could see the inclusion?"

"I attended Mr. Lockwood's lecture, sir. And when I answered a geology question correctly, he gave me the privilege of taking a closer look at the diamond. I was shocked to see the flaw."

"How clever of you! I am only glad to hear you didn't have access to the diamond because you are Mr. Lockwood's *special* friend."

"Indeed not, sir," Edward exclaimed. "I would never do such a thing."

"Simmer down, Mr. Lockwood. I was teasing. My trust in you is obviously well-placed. Now, do you wish to hear why I did it?"

"I do," Lady Radiance said before Edward could answer. "And how did you create such a near-perfect replica?"

Mr. Hope smiled, then said to Edward, "I like this lady. She's beautiful *and* intelligent. You should keep her around."

Edward glanced at Lady Radiance, hoping she wasn't offended, but she returned his look with utter placidity.

Then Mr. Hope snagged his attention again. "A skilled jeweler who had previously worked for Rundell and Bridge before it dissolved—*such a loss!*—he made it at my request and created the flaw precisely as I asked because Queen Victoria has a problem. And when the Queen has a problem, then we all have a problem."

"The inclusion was put in as a trap?" Edward asked, not too happy about being doubted.

Mr. Hope tilted his head. "Honestly, it was a test. And you passed. Or more precisely, your lady-friend did by noticing it, but you passed with your forthrightness. I would say the two of you make a solid team, one who may solve the Queen's dilemma."

"Which is?" Edward prodded, ignoring Hope's implication that he and Lady Radiance were joined in any way.

"Someone is switching the royal jewels for fakes."

Lady Radiance's gasp sounded extraordinarily loud in the vaulted room.

Mr. Hope nodded. "Some trusted jeweler, and currently the royal family uses only two firms, has a thief working in its midst."

"Or the trusted jeweler himself is a thief, perhaps," Lady Radiance mused.

"Absolutely not!" Mr. Hope said. "I know both of the master jewelers personally. But someone who works for one of them, someone with access to the jewelry when it is being cleaned or repaired and who has the necessary skill. It has happened twice that we know of."

"Did you think I might have been the thief?" Edward couldn't help asking.

"No one is above suspicion, and you have access."

Edward shrugged. "Access, perhaps, but not the skill. I couldn't make such a forgery as you created."

"I could," Lady Radiance said softly.

Edward watched Mr. Hope's head turn slowly toward her.

"Could you?"

"I have a knack for exacting detail, although I prefer to create original pieces. Mr. Bonwit trains his apprentice, and myself, by having us recreate his finer works. And with learning to cut a gemstone, he has us substitute, for example, a garnet for a ruby, a blue topaz for a sapphire, and so on. If the apprentice ruins the gem with a poor cut, it is not so costly. Once we can cut and polish well enough to sell our work, then we set it in a ring or as a pendant necklace for a customer who cannot afford the more expensive stones."

Edward remained silent. He had nothing to add as he knew little of how a jeweler trained. He was more interested in why Hope had involved him.

"Sir, are you tasking me with something?" Edward asked.

Mr. Hope steepled his fingers together and considered for a moment.

"No, Mr. Lockwood. I believe I am tasking *both* of you with discovering who has stolen two of the Queen's jewels. In fact, with Lady Radiance's help, you may have this all wrapped up by the time the Lammas bread is baked."

"Sir," Lady Radiance interrupted. "I do not understand. How can I help?"

"At the very least, two pairs of eyes are better than one, and no one will suspect you of knowing anything about gemstones. Pretend you are there merely as an interested observer, as Mr. Lockwood's lady-friend."

"Where, sir?" she asked.

"At the Palace. If you are willing, you may accompany Mr. Lockwood to an upcoming meeting of those involved in recutting the Koh-i-Noor." Then he looked at Edward again. "You may have already received the summons, yes?"

Edward nodded, still thinking about taking Lady Radiance with him as his "lady-friend."

"The Queen and Prince Consort wish to speak with you prior to the meeting. One man, Mr. Minton, an employee of the Crown Jeweler himself, is already in jail. Will you help?"

"We shall do our best," Edward said, glancing at the lady and receiving a nod of agreement. "Are you directing the investigation, sir?"

"No, on the contrary," Mr. Hope said. "There is *no* investigation, and I am in charge of absolutely nothing. Almost no one, not even those involved in improving the Koh-i-Noor, knows that anything is amiss. Yet the three of us and the Crown Jeweler, Mr. Garrard, know differently. The community of goldsmiths and jewelers in London is relatively small, so you cannot tell a soul. But we must help the Queen."

Lady Radiance rose to her feet, and Edward followed.

"We shall help Her Majesty," she declared. "Won't we, Mr. Lockwood?"

"We shall," he agreed.

CHAPTER NINE

Radiance was humming softly to herself. *How wonderful to have fallen into such an adventure!* And all because she knew why a diamond was blue and, thus, got to see the Hope up close. Except it turned out that it wasn't the Hope after all.

Perhaps, if she helped Mr. Lockwood, then she would get to see the real one, maybe hold it in her hand. And then, there was the Koh-i-Noor!

Besides the gemstones, she was forming an association with the dashing geologist. Clearly, he was held in high esteem by Mr. Hope. And if he'd been invited to Buckingham Palace, then he was also admired by the royal family.

Unable to calm her heartbeat the morning of the meeting, Radiance had donned one of her finest day dresses. Nothing that smacked of vulgarity or pretentiousness in case she really did see Queen Victoria, although she could hardly credit such a thing. A demure pale-jade gown, with cream-colored piping and buttons, and a matching jade felt and satin bonnet.

In the drawing room, she awaited Mr. Lockwood, who insisted on picking her up. Another exciting novelty—riding in a public cab!

"You must take Sarah with you," her mother had reminded her earlier before taking a seat on the sofa to help her pass the time.

Radiance smiled. Their maid had more opportunity to relax and read than even she herself did.

Then she heard the sound of carriage wheels, just as she had all morning, and ran to the window like a youngster awaiting a promised gift. This time, however, she wasn't disappointed.

"He's here!" she exclaimed as a hansom cab drew up out front, and she darted toward the door.

"Ray, please calm yourself," Carolyn Diamond said, halting her daughter's unseemly rush.

Rising to her feet at the same moment that Mr. Dunley crossed the foyer beyond the open drawing-room door, the countess called out to their butler, "He must come in and be introduced."

"We are not going out together upon a social occasion," Radiance protested. "It isn't as if Mr. Lockwood is escorting me to the theater."

Her mother laughed—a lovely familiar sound. "Not yet, anyway."

Radiance shook her head, then she heard Mr. Lockwood's voice. A moment later, his handsome face and his tall, well-formed physique appeared in the doorway.

"Good day," he greeted.

"Indeed, it *is* a good day," Radiance gushed, unable to contain her eagerness a moment longer. "I am looking forward to our mission. Mother, this is Mr. Lockwood."

Coming in, the geologist gave a smooth and appropriate bow. "I am honored to meet you, Lady Diamond. Your daughter has a keen eye for gems."

"Yes," her mother said, taking Mr. Lockwood's measure. "She certainly does."

Radiance knew her mother was insinuating she had an interest in the man that wasn't merely professional. Maybe that was because all she could speak of for the past twenty-four hours had been Mr. Lockwood this and Mr. Lockwood that.

He cleared his throat, perhaps uncertain what to say to her mother's quip. Then he asked, "Does Lady Radiance take after you in her interests as she does in her features?"

"Oh, no," Lady Diamond said. "My daughter is one of a kind in our family. I tend to enjoy reading poetry more than studying gemstones. But my husband has an interest in gold, particularly owning it, so perhaps she takes after him."

With that topic exhausted, Radiance hoped to herd Mr. Lockwood toward the door.

"As soon as I send for Sarah," Radiance said, "then we can set out."

"I shall await you on the doorstep. It was a pleasure to meet you, my lady," he said to her mother before retreating.

Her mother called after him. "I trust you will keep my daughter safe and take fine care of her."

After a pause in the doorway, Mr. Lockwood nodded, sent Radiance a wary look, and departed the drawing room.

She rounded upon her mother. "What are you doing?"

"I like that young man," the countess said with a satisfied nod.

"May I remind you that you have only just met him?"

"Regardless, I can appreciate his fine appearance, obviously appealing to you. Moreover, he looked me directly in the eye, spoke well, dressed tidily, and thinks you are wonderful."

"He never said any such thing." Radiance thrust her head around the doorway and into the hall. "Mr. Dunley, please tell Sarah we are ready to leave."

Then she glanced back at her mother. "Don't start matchmaking. But I'm glad you like him."

"*Ah ha!* You *are* interested in him in a romantic way."

Radiance's cheeks warmed. "There isn't much not to like about him, I admit."

"And he is unattached," the countess added.

"How do you know that?"

Her mother shrugged. "Your father and I would never let you interact closely with a man without first doing our due diligence and having him investigated."

Radiance had to close her mouth and breathe in some patience. "When did you have time to do that?"

"Before you went to a second lecture."

She shook her head in disbelief. "That was absurdly premature."

"Maybe so," her mother said unconcerned, "but at least we weren't caught out when you said you had accompanied him to Mr. Hope's home and intended to be his guest at the Palace. Imagine if we'd had to hire someone to investigate him on such short notice."

Radiance supposed her parents were used to marriageable daughters and the men who caught their eye. She was the third, after all. By the time Bri found someone who interested her, Lord and Lady Diamond would probably already have the man's shoe size.

"Do not keep him waiting," her mother said, "or the Queen."

Radiance nodded and joined Sarah in the foyer. Examining her bonnet in the hallway mirror and seeing it perfectly situated, she smoothed her hands down the front of her dress before allowing her maid to drape her mantle in the matching shade of pale green around her shoulders.

After tugging on her gloves in the blink of an eye, she and Sarah were out the door and aided into the awaiting carriage by Mr. Lockwood himself.

He'd secured a four-seater cab, with plenty of room for Radiance and her maid on the forward-facing side.

"Have you been to Buckingham Palace before?" Mr. Lockwood asked when they were underway.

"Yes," she said, "but not without my mother and sisters."

He nodded. "You are probably more knowledgeable of the ways and customs of court life. I fear I am always putting my foot in it."

She liked his self-effacing manner. But after his conversation with Diana, she could well believe it. Still, she decided to be encouraging. "You have seemed entirely capable in any situation in which I've seen you so far."

"I am in my element in a lecture hall or with a straightforward individual such as Mr. Hope."

Radiance considered whether he was speaking in jest and decided he was serious.

"If I catch you doing anything inappropriate, I shall . . . I shall tap my chin with my pointer finger, like so." Radiance did precisely that. Her sister Purity would surely approve of her attempting to help someone in a social situation.

"Very well," Mr. Lockwood said distractedly, looking out the window as they rode into the Palace's central courtyard and under the cover of the West Portico's entrance.

In the next instant, he hopped out while the carriage was still rocking and, before the driver could descend from the dickey, assisted first Radiance and then her maid.

"M'lady," Sarah whispered, halting and staring at the awaiting footman and then up at the royal residence's façade of creamy golden Bath stone. "I cannot go in there."

"She is *your* Queen, too," Radiance reminded her. "Don't forget, you are every bit a subject of the Crown as I am."

"Yes, m'lady, but—"

"I shall allow no buts," Radiance interrupted. "If you cannot bring yourself to look upon the face of Her Majesty or have her look upon yours in return, then you may stop just outside the chamber. But you will come inside with me."

Radiance didn't know where her fortitude was coming from, but she was giving herself the same orders as she gave to Sarah, except she wouldn't be allowed to remain in the hallway of the Queen's drawing room.

"This way," said the footman, who had obviously been awaiting them. "Our Lord Chamberlain requested I take you and her ladyship directly to Her Majesty upon your arrival."

Radiance's nervousness blossomed like a rose in June. This was no ceremonial situation, such as being presented to the Queen at the tender age of sixteen. She was going to see her as an adult female with thoughts in her head, not as a vacuous debutante who had eagerly accepted the monarch's kiss upon her forehead, the same as was offered to every daughter of the peerage.

Her stomach did a queer flip when they walked up the gilded grand staircase, craning their necks at the larger-than-life paintings.

Luckily, before Radiance could think too much more about what she was doing there, it was too late. The footman invited them to enter Queen Victoria's drawing room overlooking the Palace gardens. As suggested, Sarah stopped at the double doors, practically melting into the wallpaper.

With a nod to her, Radiance continued into the magnificent room where more of the Queen's footmen stood next to a door at the far right. In between was a floor-to-ceiling window of more panes than she had time to count. There was a tapestry-covered wall and another with an equally massive painting of an ancient battle. Under their feet was a richly weaved carpet, and overhead hung a vastly oversized chandelier that Radiance knew she could swing from without doing it any damage whatsoever.

Without a bevy of white-clad young ladies whose mothers fussed with their long trains, as well as their honored relatives and sponsors looking on, the room seemed even larger than she recalled.

Through the entire time from the cab to the reception room, Mr. Lockwood had walked silently beside her.

"Here we are," he said unnecessarily.

"Yes," she agreed.

Thankfully, they weren't in the intimidating throne room, in which formal balls were held and dignitaries were hosted, although there were two thrones in this room as well. Radiance wondered if the Queen always needed one for when she decided to sit in the presence of visitors.

"You have been here before?" she asked, as they strolled to the other end, halting a few feet before the golden thrones with the red velvet seats, one ever so slightly smaller than the other. "To this room, I mean?"

"Yes," Mr. Lockwood said. "The few times I've been summoned, it has been to this room."

"I have been here, too," she said.

He didn't ask her about it but merely nodded.

Radiance thought he looked nearly as discomfited as she felt. *Who could blame them?* There was something awe-inspiring simply about being in the Palace, let alone speaking with the Queen.

"What are you doing?" he asked.

"Pardon?" Radiance jumped at his tone. "What am I doing?"

"You were humming."

"I wasn't. Was I?"

"You were," he sounded uneasy. "I would not if I were you."

"I shall not," she promised. "I didn't realize . . ." Radiance trailed off as a ripple went through the room—of seriousness and grandeur and gravitas. Each liveried footman stood straighter and seemed to hold his breath.

Somehow, they knew Her Majesty was approaching.

CHAPTER TEN

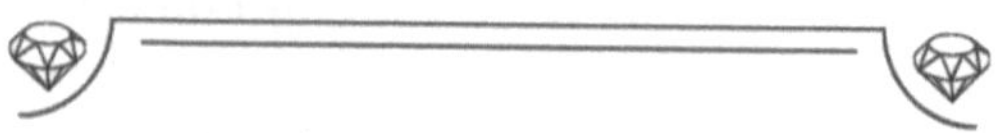

Queen Victoria entered, arriving via the door behind the thrones, with two royal guards following. Radiance immediately dropped into a low curtsy, seeing Mr. Lockwood's equally deep bow out of the corner of her eye. They awaited permission to straighten and to speak.

"Good day, Mr. Lockwood," the Queen said. "I understand you have brought with you a new treasure."

Being addressed, Mr. Lockwood could rise and look upon his Queen. "Your Majesty, I am honored to see you again. May I introduce to you Lady Radiance, a daughter of the Earl Diamond."

"You may," Queen Victoria said. "In fact, you just did. Rise, Lady Radiance, so I may see if your name suits your face."

With her heart pounding so loudly she was certain both Mr. Lockwood and the Queen could hear it, Radiance rose from the deep curtsy for which she'd rehearsed many times during the past twenty-four hours.

Radiance couldn't help taking the Queen's measure. When she'd been presented to Her Majesty a few years earlier, she'd been so nervous with her knees knocking together, Radiance could hardly recall any details. And when it was her turn, she had hurried to approach the throne and then back away while not even seeing the Queen's face—not that she could remember, anyway.

Other times, at the Palace with her parents, she'd been too far back in the throng to see more than an impression of the Queen's crowned head of light-brown hair and her ermine cloak.

Trying not to stare, Radiance now took in Her Majesty from foot to head as she raised her eyes. A short woman of thirty-three, a wife and mother, Queen Victoria had been their ruler already for fifteen years.

Radiance thought her splendid. Her eyes sparkled with intelligence, her hair shone, and she had a pleasant face.

"Your Majesty, I am honored to be in your presence."

"I thought you'd left your tongue in the antechamber," the Queen quipped.

Mr. Lockwood started to laugh. Radiance saw the moment Queen Victoria's face went from approving to annoyance with the smallest of frowns. He was laughing too long and hard at nothing, probably due to nervousness. It would be considered a mocking insult.

Swiftly, Radiance coughed to get his attention and then tapped her chin. To her relief, he stopped at once and regained his sensible manner.

"Has the Crown Jeweler arrived?" he asked.

The Queen shook her head. "To my knowledge, no. I wanted to speak with you first. As Mr. Hope has probably informed you, we have more than one issue at hand. First, there is the matter of—"

The door behind her opened, and Prince Albert entered.

Radiance dropped into her practiced curtsy again and saw in her peripheral sight that Mr. Lockwood was once more bowing low.

"Please rise," His Royal Highness said before he addressed his wife. First, he bowed to her and then took the hand she offered. "My love, I hope you don't mind my tardiness. I was making sure Sir Ellis had brought the model and that the original is nowhere nearby. With a nefarious individual determined to perpetuate such monstrous deception, we must be equally determined not to let anyone get near the Koh-i-Noor."

"As always, I welcome your thoughtfulness, dearest Husband," Queen Victoria answered. "I was just about to tell Mr. Lockwood and Lady Radiance about our problem, but I am happy to have you take over."

With that, Queen Victoria wandered toward the thrones and sat upon the larger one.

Radiance nearly laughed at the way the Queen plopped herself down, as if she were any female enjoying getting off her feet rather than the most important ruler in the world.

Unable to take her gaze from their pretty monarch, Radiance only half listened to Prince Albert discuss something manly and uninteresting about a recent incident at Tattersall's horse auction. From what she'd gleaned of Mr. Lockwood, he probably wasn't interested, either.

Then suddenly, the prince switched topics, mentioning the two stones that had already been pilfered, one from a coronet and one from a brooch. He had Radiance and Mr. Lockwood's full attention.

"We would never have discovered the forgery if Her Majesty hadn't dropped the brooch—"

"It slipped off," Queen Victoria corrected.

"Indeed," Prince Albert said. "Unfortunately—or as it turned out, fortunately—the brooch happened to fall onto a marble floor, and the main stone, a large sapphire, popped out."

"My husband gave it to me as a wedding gift," the Queen said, obviously irritated.

The Prince Consort went to her side and patted her hand.

"When we gave the brooch to Mr. Garrard to repair, since it was his shop that made it for me twelve years ago after he became the Crown Jeweler, he came in person at once to say the sapphire was not the original. It wasn't even a sapphire, but a—"

"A blue spinel," Mr. Lockwood said.

Radiance began to tap her chin again to stop any further offensiveness such as interrupting royalty. Not heeding her, he continued, "As is the Black Prince's Ruby or the Timur Ruby, both red spinels."

The royal couple stared at him for a long moment. Radiance wanted to slap a hand to her forehead and another over Mr. Lockwood's mouth.

"Have I yet expressed my appreciation for your pointing out *during* the Exhibition that the Timur Ruby was actually a spinel?" the Queen asked.

Radiance cringed at Queen Victoria's tone, which was anything but appreciative. It must have been a shock to learn that the ruby sent over with the Koh-i-Noor was not a precious stone.

By bringing it up, she feared Mr. Lockwood, despite his best intentions, had put his oar in where it wasn't wanted. This was proven a correct assessment when the Prince Consort folded his arms, leveling a glare at the enthusiastic geologist.

"While we are grateful for your discerning eye, the *so-called* Black Prince's Ruby is currently in Her Majesty's crown, set there by Rundell and Bridge," Prince Albert stated, "and we shall continue to call the stone thusly."

Clearly, he wished to drop that avenue of discussion. "Regarding the sapphire, you are correct in thinking it was switched for a spinel."

"Did Mr. Garrard take responsibility?" Mr. Lockwood asked.

"No," the Prince Consort said. "He has been our trusted Crown Jeweler for years. The brooch had been cleaned at his shop a mere month earlier. That was now three months ago."

"Then Your Royal Highness has discovered the culprit?" Mr. Lockwood asked. Radiance thought that a sensible conclusion.

"We thought so, and thus, sent a constable directly," Prince Albert said. "The man who had worked on the brooch was arrested."

Radiance felt a measure of relief. But it was short-lived.

"That was not the end of it," Queen Victoria chimed in. "Not even the beginning of the end."

"The Queen is correct," the Prince Consort said, looking fondly at his diminutive wife. "The sapphire has not been recovered. Moreover, the fake gem caused a bit of a ruckus around here. We had an inventory done, and each piece was examined by Mr. Garrard and his employees."

"Yes, I remember," Mr. Lockwood said. "I was invited by him to watch two jewelers while they worked, but he didn't tell me why."

"What did you observe?" Queen Victoria asked.

"Your Majesty, I saw nothing out of the ordinary. The men dutifully examined and recorded each stone."

Prince Albert nodded and crossed his arms. "That is true. But you were not here when an emerald popped from a coronet, which had been recently cleaned by a different jeweler, the House of Neble. As feared, it too turned out to be a fake stone."

The Prince Consort drew the two stones from his trouser pocket and held them out to Mr. Lockwood. He picked up and studied the blue spinel first. Then he looked at the green stone.

Drawing out magnifying spectacles from his pocket, Mr. Lockwood held the stone up to light. "A tourmaline, I believe."

"That's what Mr. Garrard said," Prince Albert confirmed.

"May I ask, Your Majesty," Radiance began, having finally found her voice, "had the same man who was already under arrest also cleaned the coronet?"

"A good question," the Prince Consort said. "Unfortunately, the answer is no. Mr. Minton, the forger of the sapphire, was already at Newgate. Thus, we suddenly had a riddle. Moreover, they were not even cleaned at the same time."

"One might have been altered months earlier, if not years," Mr. Lockwood said.

"Unlikely," Radiance put forth her opinion. "While it sounds as though the forger is an excellent jeweler, substituting a stone, especially when done with haste, without altering the setting at all causes problems of durability. Thus, the stone only remains in place for a short period of time until some duress is put upon the piece."

Prince Albert glanced at the Queen. "She does have a good head," he remarked, and Radiance felt a surge of happiness clear down to her toes.

"It would seem so," Queen Victoria agreed.

Radiance could hardly believe she was chatting with the Queen and the Prince Consort, nor that they were praising her.

"In any case," Prince Albert said, "Minton never worked for the House of Neble, which handled the coronet."

"I suppose the matter of transportation from Buckingham Palace to the jeweler and back again has been thoroughly investigated," Mr. Lockwood wondered.

"If the piece is with the royal jewels at the Tower, like the Koh-i-Noor," Prince Albert explained, "then our Master of the Jewels handles it."

"Mr. Swifte," the Queen said. "He's had the position since before I was born. A very capable custodian."

Prince Albert cleared his throat. "He retired this year. Now, the post is held by Lieutenant-Colonel Wyndham."

"I say," the Queen looked put out for a moment. Then she brightened. "I suppose a military man is a good choice."

"Indeed," said the Prince Consort.

Radiance thought their conversation, as if they were any couple sharing news, was charming.

However, Mr. Lockwood was focused on their task. "If the jewelry comes from the Palace," he prompted, "as the brooch did, then who handles it?"

"The Lord Chamberlain's office," Prince Albert said. "Lord Exeter has only been serving the household since the end of February, but he is above suspicion."

With a nod to Radiance, the Queen added, "However, suspecting the courier is a clever thought. It certainly makes more sense than to think one of the royal jewelers, present or past, has betrayed us. And even stranger to think that it has happened more than once."

"More than strange, Your Majesty," Mr. Lockwood said. "I think it unlikely. The jewelers of London, as Mr. Hope recently reminded me, are a relatively small community. There is probably only one forger."

"Exactly," the Prince Consort said. "Which is why we asked you to come. The meeting today is regarding the delicate task of cutting the Koh-i-Noor, but under these circumstances, we are naturally wary."

"May I ask why Your Majesty wishes to recut the Koh-i-Noor?" Radiance asked.

"You may," the Queen said. Yet instead of answering, she narrowed her eyes. "Have you seen it?"

The full awareness that she was having an audience with the Queen of the United Kingdom of Great Britain and Ireland, Ruler of India, daughter of a prince and princess, granddaughter of a king, and one in the long lineage that came before her, weighed upon Radiance's shoulders.

At that moment, with her heartbeat speeding up, wondering if Queen Victoria was going to bring it out for her to view and perhaps even to hold, Radiance thought she might collapse at Her Majesty's feet.

CHAPTER ELEVEN

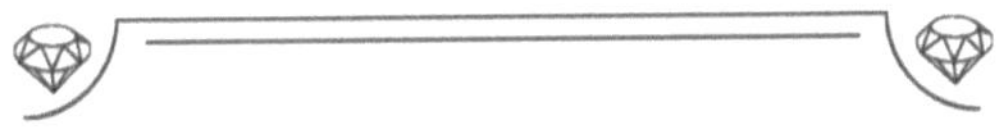

Edward felt concern slice through him as Lady Radiance appeared momentarily tongue-tied. Moreover, she seemed to sway slightly. He took a step toward her. Being overcome by the importance of the situation was understandable. While he'd been in the presence of the Queen and the Prince Consort twice now, he, too, felt it was a momentous occasion.

Finally, Lady Radiance answered.

"Yes, Your Majesty. I saw it a few times when it was on display. If I may say so, the entire exhibition was a grand treat for which I am certain all your subjects are grateful."

"My husband is the one to thank," the Queen said, brushing aside the lady's gratitude. "Do you know what *The Times* said about my diamond when it was first unveiled?" Her Majesty asked.

Another hesitation, and then Lady Radiance said in a quiet voice, "I do, Your Majesty."

"Can you repeat it for us? If not, then I shall have to ask that a copy be brought here." Queen Victoria sounded tweaguey.

Edward winced. He knew exactly what it said, and he would wager Lady Radiance did, too. Anyone interested in gems would have read it and felt a pinch of shame for whomever wrote the nasty opinion that upset the Queen.

As expected, Lady Radiance nodded. Speaking softly, she said, "The review was something along the lines of the Koh-i-Noor being unsatisfactory."

"Much worse than that," the Queen said swiftly.

And then, to Edward's surprise, Queen Victoria cleared her throat and recited from memory, "'Either from the imperfect cutting, the difficulty of placing the lights advantageously, or the immovability of the stone itself, which should be made to revolve on its axis, few catch any of the brilliant rays it reflects when viewed at a particular angle.'"

The Prince Consort coughed. "That's why we moved it, my Queen."

"Imperfect cutting!" the Queen exclaimed, bringing her fist down upon the arm of her throne. Then she took a breath. "Yet *The Times* was correct. No matter that they were rudely impudent."

When next she spoke, she addressed him and Lady Radiance at the same time.

"Lord Dalhousie, my trusted Governor-General who was instrumental in bringing the diamond to Great Britain, has said as much. He, too, criticized the first exhibit, saying our beloved Mountain of Light shows poorly for being a rose and not a brilliant cut."

"It cannot sparkle like the latter," Lady Radiance pointed out. "It isn't the diamond's fault, Your Majesty. A new cut shall make all the difference."

Edward thought it ironic that Lady Radiance had a sister whose name was close to the best cut but didn't think it something he should share. No matter one's enthusiasm for the topic at hand, one simply didn't treat these two royals as regular people and start chatting about incidentals.

"Mr. Dalhousie was also correct in saying we ought to have displayed it on a table covered with a black velvet cloth," the Prince Consort said. "Nor should it have been attended on either side by the other two diamonds that came with my wife's armlet. Never mind. With the help of our specialist in light, Sir David Brewster, our Crown Jeweler, Mr. Garrard, and our geologist from King's College"—he nodded at Edward—"we shall not muck it up again."

Briefly shocked at being included among the stellar gentlemen who would steer the diamond's cutting, Edward said, "I am acquainted with Sir Brewster." A mere week earlier, they'd discussed the singular iridescence of opals.

"I have attended one of his lectures," Lady Radiance spoke up, surprising him. "Sir Brewster knows everything about reflection and refraction, and if anyone can direct a jeweler to bring out the best in the Koh-i-Noor, it will be him."

The prince looked impressed. "Unfortunately, Sir Brewster thinks the diamond is flawed at its very heart. It has yellow speckles in its core, and one of these has marred its ability to refract light."

"That is one of the reasons, Mr. Lockwood, we want you to take another look at it."

Edward nearly took a step back. He doubted he would come up with a different conclusion than the esteemed Sir Brewster. His concern must have shown upon his face, for the Prince Consort added, "He thinks cutting it presents a very high risk of destroying the diamond entirely."

The Queen made an exclamation of apprehension, but Prince Albert continued, "Sir Brewster believes, if it survives the cutting intact, then the Koh-i-Noor will, at the very least, lose so much of its size as to make it . . . no longer the impressive stone it is."

All at once, the Queen rose to her feet. "I find the whole situation incredibly draining. There are too many matters going awry, from the loss of two jewels to how best we can improve the Koh-i-Noor without ruining it and, most importantly, without someone exchanging it for a fake!"

"I shan't let that happen, my love, and I am confident that, with the help of Mr. Lockwood, we shall not only recover what has been stolen but determine the best course for your diamond."

Edward wasn't so certain but offered a nod of agreement anyway.

The Queen was clearly finished with the discussion.

"I know you shall consult with Mr. Garrard and come up with the best solution for everything. Thank you for coming," she said. Then their diminutive monarch turned and left the way she had come, as Edward bowed low and Lady Radiance dropped into a curtsy beside him.

The Prince Consort watched her go. "This has become an extreme annoyance to Her Majesty," he said softly as if it pained him. "And thus, a thorn in my side as well."

"Are we only to speak of the Koh-i-Noor today, Your Royal Highness?" Edward asked. "During the meeting, I mean?"

Prince Albert continued to stare after his wife. "Gutes Fräuchen," he murmured softly.

Edward exchanged a glance with Lady Radiance, suddenly feeling as if they were intruding upon something private. She raised a shoulder in return, looking equally uncomfortable at the Prince Consort exposing them to a private nickname, *my little wife*.

Finally, Prince Albert turned.

"Most of the men in that room today do not know about the fake jewels. Thus, please keep the discussion solely on whether the Koh-i-Noor can be cut without losing its physical integrity."

Prince Albert gestured toward Lady Radiance. "If you and Lady Radiance are able to figure out how the royal jewels were meticulously copied and switched, then we shall be forever in your debt. I don't know if you can, nor if anyone can."

"Your Royal Highness, Mr. Hope told us about Mr. Minton from Garrard's," Edward said, "but he didn't mention precisely the coronet nor the House of Neble."

Prince Albert offered a wry smile. "He doesn't like to speak of it because of a familial connection through Mr. Neble's deceased wife."

"Did someone from the House of Neble also go to jail, Your Highness?" Lady Radiance asked. "And was Mr. Minton released since another forgery happened *after* he was convicted?"

Edward thought her as thorough as anyone from the Metropolitan Police.

"As far as we know," the Prince Consort answered her first question, "Mr. Neble works alone, and his trustworthiness is beyond doubt. Nonetheless, he was interrogated, just as Mr. Minton was, but we refrained from casting charges against him. Which brings me to your second question, and the answer is no. Mr. Minton is the only suspect we have. He had a trial and was judged guilty."

Edward could see by Lady Radiance's face that she was going to start a debate with the Prince Consort. Something about stubborn redheads came to mind, but he had believed it was merely an old wives' tale—until that moment. One did not argue with His Royal Highness. He began tapping his chin, but she wasn't looking at him.

However, the Prince Consort sighed. "Nothing but a mystery. We know it wasn't Mr. Neble. He is wealthier than Midas, with no reason to do anything so egregious this late in his career. Yet he cleaned the coronet himself, swearing they were all the genuine, original gems when he had finished."

And then, Prince Albert bid them good day, and they each sank into their respective postures of courtesy while he followed the Queen, leaving Edward and Lady Radiance still looking at the floor.

They straightened at the same moment. Hardly a breath later, the door at the other end of the room opened, and the same footman who'd led them there returned.

"This way, please," he said.

As soon as they entered the hallway, Lady Radiance's maid fell in step behind them, and they walked in silence. Edward began pondering what they'd been told. It seemed inconceivable that two different people could get away with the same type of crime—forgery—on two separate occasions.

He nearly walked into a porcelain vase as he considered and dismissed the possibility that there was more than one master forger of gemstones.

"Careful," Lady Radiance advised, somehow setting her hand upon the vase and steadying it before it toppled.

The footman turned with a raised eyebrow.

"Please, my lady, do not touch any of the royal collection."

Lady Radiance snatched her hand from the porcelain before giving Edward an exasperated glance.

Just when he would have apologized, the footman added, "There may be many temptations along the way to the corner Yellow Drawing Room, as we call it."

Edward could only shrug his apology as she gritted her teeth beside him.

They followed the liveried man along one of the palace's extensions. Thus, without going outside, they crossed the width of the central courtyard and entered the famed architect Edward Blore's new east wing. The Queen's request for more space, including guest rooms and nurseries, had necessitated moving the Marble Arch that previously fronted Buckingham Palace so the new wing could be built.

Briefly, Edward wondered how anyone living in a palace could need space. And then they entered a light-filled room down the center of which was a long table.

Many of the furnishings had been brought from the Royal Pavilion at Brighton when the Queen sold the seaside palace to pay for the addition. Thus, the room wore a festive Oriental appearance.

Around a long, polished table sat men he knew, and some he didn't. As soon as they registered the fact that there was now a lady present, all five rose to their feet en masse.

"Mr. Lockwood and Lady Radiance," announced the footman as if they were entering a ballroom at Devonshire House.

Not that Edward had ever been to a ball there, but he could imagine.

"Gentlemen," Lady Radiance said, "please resume your seats."

Quick as a whip, she took the closest chair to put them at ease and allow them to do as she bid.

The next empty chair was on the other side of the table, and Edward strolled around to it, nodding to the Crown Jeweler, Sebastian Garrard, bowing low to the Duke of Wellington as well as to Lord Cawdor, Director of the British Museum. They nodded back, and then he introduced each one to Lady Radiance, as well as Mr. Chapman, the man who removed the Koh-i-Noor from the armlet under Mr. Garrard's supervision, and Lord Exeter, the Queen's current Lord Chamberlain, whom the lady knew through her father, and lastly, the distinguished mineralogist Professor Tennant, who'd already studied the diamond and written about it extensively. More nodding occurred.

There was a stranger who was introduced by Garrard as Mr. Rathmond, and Edward knew him by name to be a gem broker.

"My apologies for keeping you waiting, gentlemen," Edward said.

"Not to worry," Garrard returned. "Obviously, this lovely lady was worth our patience."

The men all chuckled politely, but Lady Radiance didn't look pleased at being blamed for their tardiness. Yet the Crown Jeweler could not disclose to the rest of those gathered that Edward had been summoned to speak with the Queen and Prince Albert before the meeting. Moreover, he had no idea of Lady Radiance's involvement. Thus, Edward was forced to let the little jest stand.

"I shall get you caught up," Garrard said. "We were discussing the best way to cut the Koh-i-Noor with the least loss of weight." Then he nodded to Lord Cawdor. "Show them."

To Edward's amazement, Cawdor flipped over a folded cloth in front of him and exposed the Koh-i-Noor to the gaze of all those gathered. Lady Radiance gasped. Even more surprising, the museum director picked it up and tossed it toward Edward, who caught it midair.

At once, he realized what it was.

"Apsley Pellatt's flint glass model," Edward said.

Having seen it before, he took only a brief glance, then said, "Lady Radiance, would you like to examine it?"

Despite a general muttering, which he ignored, Edward sent it skittering across the table toward her. As he'd expected, she set her gloved hand upon it easily before it could fall over the edge onto her lap.

Raising an auburn eyebrow, she lifted her hand off the stone and took a look as every head turned to watch her. However, she didn't pick it up. Rather, she reached under the table and drew up her reticule, opened it, and in the next instant, fished out a pair of magnifying spectacles.

After slipping these on, only then did she pick up the stone and study it. When her gaze next found Edward's, he nearly laughed at how her eyes appeared like two magnificently large emeralds.

"I saw this reproduction at the exhibition, too," she said. "If it had been in a more prominent display, I vow people would have flocked to the glass model in equal number as they did to the diamond. Despite having the same irregular cut as the Koh-i-Noor, its clarity is superior, far more like water than the real jewel. Far more even than most glass due to Mr. Pellatt's manganese oxide blend."

In the silence that followed, she put it back onto the table. Edward wondered if Lady Radiance realized she had awed the others into silence.

"Alas," she added, "with its inferior refraction index, it can never have a diamond's dispersion. No matter the cut, glass merely looks like ... well, like glass. No internal reflection, thus no sparkle."

"You are correct," said Chapman, taking up the model. "I haven't seen the Koh-i-Noor since I removed it for Mr. Pellatt to copy, but even a diamond thusly flawed in both core and cut is more pleasing than this glass, no matter how well made."

"Speaking of cut," said Garrard, "let us return to the discussion of how the Koh-i-Noor shall be improved. I greatly admire Sir Brewster, and I am aware his examination of the diamond led him to inform Her Majesty and His Royal Highness that it cannot be improved. Or, if it is, then it will be at the sacrifice of much of its size."

He let that sink in for any who hadn't pondered the grave decision.

"However, I have examined it carefully, as has my brother." Garrard took a breath. "We believe it can be done and have told the Queen such."

"Agreed," said the jeweler Chapman, but a fellow geologist, James Tennant, caught Edward's eye. They shared a professional moment of doubt.

"However," continued Garrard, "we must consult diamond cutters from Amsterdam. My brother and our partner, Mr. Spilsbury, concur. They are the best for handling this delicate task."

A general outcry ensued. Lady Radiance appeared clearly surprised by the uproar. But these men were as British as they came. To admit to the world that they hadn't a cutter in all the United Kingdom who could match the skills of a foreign jeweler was an affront. And perhaps their pride was even more wounded by the fact that a beautiful lady was in the room.

Edward decided to speak up. "I don't think Mr. Garrard is being unfair. We know British jewelers are unsurpassed with design and with goldwork. One need only look at Rundell and Bridge's famed punch bowl, which the Queen adores, to be in absolute agreement on that fact. Yet we've seen the diamond cutting from the Continent. Moreover, we can all understand why the Queen would wish for only the most skilled."

The others turned their boiling pots to simmer.

"As long as it is all overseen by *our* Crown Jeweler," the Duke of Wellington said, nodding to Garrard.

"Certainly *not* left in the care of the Dutch," suggested the museum director.

The discussion continued in earnest, seemingly going around the same points, until Edward longed for a cup of coffee and the peace of his workroom.

Lady Radiance, who had listened attentively, seemed fairly bursting to say something. He didn't have to wonder long what it was. In the masculine atmosphere of one man interrupting or speaking over another, her lilting voice smoothed the rough tenor at the table the way a lap's mill smoothed a ruby.

"Is the intent to retain as much size as possible, balancing that against the number of facets?" she asked.

"Some think the weight alone is the Koh-i-Noor's glory," Garrard said. "It is, after all, one of the largest in the world."

"But if it is ugly, what is its value?" asked Professor Tennant, now holding the model up to the light. "If we prefer the clarity of this glass model, then the diamond may as well be as big as a rock from my garden."

Rathmond, the gem dealer, perhaps invited for his vast knowledge of gemstones and also of jewelers worldwide, nodded in agreement. He took notes, remaining silent instead of vying to be an integral part of the process that would make Queen Victoria love her precious diamond as she should.

Edward was about to ask him his opinion on the Dutch but was halted by the Lord Chamberlain's next question.
"No offense intended, my lady, but why are you here?"

CHAPTER TWELVE

"I have a . . . a keen interest," Radiance trailed off and sent Edward a nervous glance as a mumbling of questions went around the table.

"You are not a guild member, I presume," the Lord Chamberlain added, "nor are you in the goldsmith's company."

"No, my lord, I am not."

Edward cleared his throat. "Is there a man here who wishes to ask the Queen or the Prince Consort why they invited *us?*" Purposefully, he included himself. "I am not in the goldsmith's company, either."

The muttering ceased.

"Everyone in this room is here to assist," Edward reminded them.

The meeting ended with the grudging agreement to send an inquiry to Coster Diamonds in Amsterdam, suggested by Garrard as being the best cutters in Europe. They would have to agree to send their two most skilled polishers to England for the Koh-i-Noor was not to leave British soil.

When they all stood to leave, Professor Tennant approached Edward to converse upon the recent developments in Australia. Not only had Menge discovered an opal two years earlier but recently, sapphires were discovered during gold mining on the Cudgegong and Macquarie rivers in New South Wales.

Neither of them had yet laid eyes or fingers upon one of the Australian opals.

"They say they are dark blue, yet with a strong green dichroism," Edward repeated what he knew.

"Some say they are more green than blue," countered Tennant. "If one falls into my hands, I shall let you know immediately. Or at least, the very moment *after* I am finished examining it."

Edward grinned, then promised to do the same. Their discussion continued on opals since he had a fascination with them. Upon the conversation's conclusion, he was out the door and halfway along the hallway when he recalled he'd arrived with Lady Radiance.

As he turned, he saw her hurrying after him with her maid in tow.

RADIANCE WAS SURE HE'D forgotten her. The way Mr. Lockwood strode along the Palace corridor, without looking right or left, perhaps lost in thought. She couldn't recall ever having been neglected in such a fashion.

However, he suddenly halted, turned, and waited.

"There you are, Lady Radiance," he said, but she had an idea he was only saying that to cover himself.

"Yes," she said. "Here I am, where you forgot me, trailing in your wake."

His cheeks flushed slightly.

"Nonsense. I am just clearing the way for you."

"Truly? As if I am the Queen? Goodness, I cannot have people looking upon my face as I pass."

He coughed. "Yes, well." When he said nothing more, they continued in silence, leaving by the east frontage exit under the balcony the Queen had specifically requested be built. From it, she could watch parades or bid her troops farewell and later welcome them back. Or she could simply allow her subjects to catch a glimpse of her growing family on its second-story perch.

When Mr. Lockwood went to hail a cab, however, Radiance stopped him.

"I would prefer to walk, sir."

Thus, they strolled through Green Park toward Piccadilly, with many other pedestrians enjoying the temperate weather.

"Did that go as you had hoped?" Radiance asked.

"Truthfully, I had no expectations, although the plan to consult the Dutch is a sound one. If Mr. Garrard hadn't suggested it, then I or Professor Tennant would have. Nevertheless, it was better coming from the Crown Jeweler."

"A pity the model was more pleasing than the real stone," she mused.

"It will take a skilled hand to cut around the Koh-i-Noor's yellow inclusions," he said. "Obviously, the diamond will lose carat weight, but if it greatly increases in clarity, then it will be worth it."

Of course, that was important, but the Koh-i-Noor hadn't been Radiance's primary reason for going to the Palace.

"The meeting with the Queen and Prince Albert gave me a lot to think about. Do you have any notion where we should begin our investigation?"

He sighed. "I do not."

Keenly aware that he hadn't asked her whether *she* had any ideas, she would share hers anyway.

"We ought to speak privately with Mr. Garrard as soon as possible and then with poor Mr. Minton."

"*Poor* Mr. Minton?" Mr. Lockwood repeated. "How so?"

"It seems he has become a scapegoat."

"A *scapegoat?* An interesting word," he mused, "as are *scapegrace* and *scapethrift*. But let's hope Mr. Minton isn't a *scapegallows!*"

Mr. Lockwood had an interesting brain, what some might call irksome, though. Radiance was trying not to be annoyed by the way his mind caught on something that engrossed him, making him dive in up to his eyeballs, forgetting what was on the shore.

To divert him from etymology and back to the business at hand, she said, "The man to my left, with the dark hair and eyes, I believe his name was Mr. Rathmond. He was quiet. Do you know him?"

"Only that he is a gem dealer. But I had never met him before today."

"He was fidgeting with his pen, except when you gave me the glass model. I thank you for that, by the way. Even though it wasn't the real stone, it was thrilling nonetheless."

"You're welcome. Anything else about Mr. Rathmond?" he asked her.

"He stared very hard at it as if he wished he could snatch it from me. And he took notes about who would be handling the Koh-i-Noor."

When Mr. Lockwood shrugged, she decided to disclose why the man had actually made an impression upon her.

"He also rubbed my leg with his ankle. I thought it an accident until he did it again. Rather disconcerting and most unpleasant."

She had Mr. Lockwood's full attention. He looked appalled. "You should have said something."

"I couldn't, really. The blame would have fallen upon me, as if I had no place in a meeting of men who were discussing anything important, without inciting one to a lust so deep he had to rub against me like a randy dog. I would have instantly become the object of pity and ridicule."

Apparently embarrassed, he glanced behind them at her maid, but she was deaf to their conversation. Even while walking, Sarah had her nose buried in a book again as Radiance had known she would. After all, when they reached home, her maid's duties would call her from the gripping tale.

"Never mind, sir. I only wish I could have helped in some way."

"Perhaps you still shall," Mr. Lockwood said kindly, "and I shall, too."

"How?" she asked.

"I honestly have no idea. But we will do as you suggest and speak with those involved." They reached her front steps. "And we shall keep our eyes open, mine and your pretty green ones."

His unexpected compliment had her mumbling her farewell before she slipped inside, momentarily leaving Sarah on the step until she remembered her.

Opening the door again, Radiance urged the maid inside, nodded to an amused Mr. Lockwood, and closed the door. A lovely warmth spread through her at the idea of a continuing entanglement with the attractive geologist. He had a calming way about him, yet at the same time, he made her insides tingle excitedly.

The following day, Radiance returned to Mr. Bonwit's in Hatton Garden. Before she'd even taken a seat at her usual table, he approached her to ask questions about the important gathering at the Palace.

"How did you know?" she asked.

"There is a jeweler's grapevine as strong as any servant's one. An hour after you and the others dispersed, I doubt there was a gem worker or goldsmith in London who hadn't heard of the meeting and knew everyone who was at the table, including you. Why were you there, by the way?"

Although she couldn't speak of the fake stones that had been set in the Queen's jewelry, she could discuss the topic of the second meeting.

"The Queen and Prince Consort are dissatisfied with the appearance of the Koh-i-Noor. And I have a good eye," she said, then smiled since he was the one who always said it.

"You do, as do others," he pointed out. "Myself, for instance."

"True, but I have a friend who is a geologist. He was invited to give his opinion on the diamond, and he kindly invited me. I was honored."

"Most assuredly so. Are they inviting the Dutch over?"

"They are," she said. "What is your opinion?"

He sighed. "I think that is the correct decision, but not because there isn't a man in England who could cut the diamond just as well. However, should something go wrong, it only makes sense that those in charge, the Royal Keeper of the Jewels and the Lord Chamberlain, can blame the Dutch. And if it goes well, those same men will take credit for choosing the best cutters and directing the entire process."

She hadn't considered that it was a calculated decision to protect the Crown Jeweler. Knowing Mr. Bonwit for an honest man, she wished she could tell him about the fake jewels. But she could ask him a question.

"Do you know Mr. Rathmond, the gem dealer?"

Mr. Bonwit nodded. "In the past, I purchased some stones from him but not anymore."

"Why not, if I may ask?"

Mr. Bonwit shrugged. "I thought his price to be too high for the quality of what he was selling."

"Is that all?" she asked.

"What do you mean?"

"He didn't try to sell you any stones that weren't genuine?"

Mr. Bonwit bristled. "He wouldn't dare insult me in such a manner. I would know upon examination at once if a stone was fake."

After that, he showed her how to make prongs so strong they would not let slip a precious stone, then allowed her to set a single ruby in a ring.

Before she left, she asked, "I would very much like to make my own earbobs."

He nodded. "What stone? Emeralds to match your eyes, perhaps. The Prince made them even more popular with his engagement ring to the Queen."

Prince Albert's gift of a ring featuring a serpent with an emerald set in its head had spurred an entire decade of the popular motif as symbols of eternal love. Radiance didn't care for snakes and couldn't imagine why they represented the deepest emotion, with pretty emerald eyes or otherwise. When the Royal couple purchased their Balmoral home, she'd much preferred the jewelry with delicate Scottish designs that had quickly come into fashion.

"Actually, I very much like the golden topaz stones you purchased last week. I think there are two of a similar size."

"Indeed. A good choice for your coloring." Then Mr. Bonwit smiled. "If you make them, I will sell them to you at a fair price."

"I trust you will," she said. "And then you will be able to tell everyone in London you have an earl's daughter as your special patron."

The man chortled. "Believe me, I already do."

At home that afternoon, Radiance was surprised to receive a note from Mr. Lockwood.

Dear Lady Radiance,

I have made arrangements to speak with Mr. Minton mid-morning tomorrow. I will spare your tender sensibilities and go to Newgate alone. Never fear, however. I shall keep you updated.

Yours sincerely,

Lockwood

Keep her updated! Radiance wasn't going to be left out of meeting the man who might hold the key to such a magnificent deceit as well as be a master jeweler on a scale to commit a forgery upon the Royal family.

She could write back to Mr. Lockwood and risk being denied, or she could show up at his home the following day.

Naturally, she would have to go early so as not to miss his departure.

CHAPTER THIRTEEN

A knock sounded as Edward drank coffee in his parlor. Setting down the newspaper, he wandered into the front hall, looking along the passageway and up the staircase, but his housekeeper wasn't anywhere to be seen. *Again!*

With a shrug, he opened the door.

"Lady Radiance!" He wished his tone hadn't been so welcoming. He also would have preferred Mrs. McSabby had answered the door in his place.

"If you ever decide to stop being a geologist," the lady said, "you will make an exceptional butler. So very prompt. Although I've never had a butler, nor anyone for that matter, come to the door with a cup in hand."

Edward nearly sloshed his coffee over the rim. He had forgotten entirely about it. Even as he backed up a step to allow her entrance, he couldn't help admonishing her.

"Where is your useless, book-reading maid? And why have you come uninvited? Again!"

"I wish to go with you to meet the man in jail. Why wouldn't I? It's not often one meets a master forger. And Sarah is in my carriage."

"I thought he was 'poor Mr. Minton,' the scapegoat." Edward let her follow him into his parlor, where he refilled his cup from a silver coffee pot. Then belatedly recalled how one treated a guest.

"Would you like a cup of coffee? Or tea?" If he found Mrs. McSabby, she could brew a good pot of tea, couldn't she? He had no idea since he never drank it.

"No, thank you. I am simply glad I caught you before you left."

"*Hm.*" Edward supposed there was no harm in her going. "I did tell you I would let you know if I learned anything."

"Indeed, but that is not nearly as efficient as using my own ears and eyes."

Monty appeared and ambled over to brush around her legs. To Edward's surprise, Lady Radiance stripped off one glove. When she bent low to stroke him, her bare hand running through his cat's fur, Edward had a visceral reaction that caught him by surprise.

With his groin pulsing and his blood coursing swiftly enough to make him perspire, he was ready to forbid her to accompany him. Yet his words came out as acquiescence.

"Very well. You may come, and yes, before you ask, I suppose we can take your carriage." He set down his cup, still shocked by his body's sudden awakening.

Lady Radiance nodded. "Thank you. But you must put on a coat, or we shall look an odd pair. I imagine my father wouldn't be pleased to know I accompanied a man in such a state of undress."

Edward glanced down. "Good God!" He had conversed with her in only his shirt-sleeves, as if they were lovers. "Give me five minutes."

With that, he sprinted from the room and up the stairs. If he was going to start entertaining callers, he had better get entirely dressed in the mornings before he left his bedroom. He was letting himself become a little too slovenly in his own home.

Lady Radiance had seen him in such a casual state without need of smelling salts. He smiled to himself, imagining what it would be like if they were a couple. So far, he had thoroughly enjoyed their interactions, and each time he saw her, he felt his interest growing.

But the physical part of him that had also grown in her proximity gave him pause until he considered how long it had been since he'd paid for an evening with Miss Maura. Normally, if he was in London, no more than a fortnight at the longest went by between visits with his favorite courtesan. By the second week, she kept popping into his thoughts until he hailed a cab and headed over to where she kept an expensive suite at Brown's Hotel on Dover Street.

In truth, he was slaking his lust above his means, for she counted the Duke of Argyll among her admirers. But Maura charged him the knave's rate. As she explained it, she enjoyed Edward's company both in and out of bed. Due to all that was going on in his life, he hadn't even missed the pleasure of his paramour.

With Lady Radiance below, Edward shrugged into the first jacket that he pulled from his armoire. Realizing it was an evening tailcoat, he yanked it off and threw it onto the bed before finding a more suitable replacement. A worsted-wool, gray frock coat.

As he descended the stairs, he hoped his appearance met with her approval. He could easily picture her on his arm, promenading around Hyde Park—or under him on his white sheets, her hair like a shower of rubies around her. He shook his head.

"Steady, man," he muttered.

"Perfect," Lady Radiance pronounced when he reentered his parlor, still trying not to think of her naked in his bed. Blinking up at him, she asked, "Is it time to go?"

Again, he felt the sensation of being on a swing as a child. He would swear his stomach flipped.

"I am expected any time before noon," he told her.

"That's grand. I am so very glad I caught you."

He nearly said, "As am I." In truth, he would have been as content to go by himself, merely for the reason he could maintain more focus without the distraction that a beautiful woman caused, particularly one who smelled like sunshine.

Where had that stupidly fanciful notion come from?

"Shall we go, my lady?" And feeling a little foolish, he opened his front door precisely like a butler and gestured for her to lead the way to her father's carriage.

When they entered, her maid didn't even look up. Didn't Lady Radiance's parents know how inadequate the maid Sarah was as a protector of their daughter's innocence?

"How is it that you are allowed such freedom?" he asked.

"Freedom, sir?" Lady Radiance parroted, looking bemused. "What can you mean?"

"To be out and about with merely a maid, who is not considered an adequate defender of your virtue in the best of cases. And this one . . ." Edward didn't finish his sentence despite thinking he could say anything concerning the young woman in question without her even noticing he was speaking about her.

"What are you reading?" he asked, feeling irritated on Lady Radiance's behalf.

The maid didn't answer but simply turned another page.

Lady Radiance sighed. "Sarah is blazing her way through Mr. Reynold's *The Mysteries of London*. Thus, I'm sure you can understand why she is so absorbed."

"I haven't read it," he confessed.

"Not even when it was serialized?" Lady Radiance asked.

"Not even then."

When the maid gasped, Edward felt as if he'd committed a sin. "Why is that so hard to believe?"

At this, the previously silent Sarah finally uttered a few choice words. "Because it's bloody wonderful!"

As Lady Radiance began to laugh, the maid hunched over the book once again and returned to ignoring the outside world. Perhaps if his lot in life were to follow around someone without participating in anything that person did, then he would lose himself in a novel, too.

Fortunately, he usually found his life stimulating enough that a fictional world held no interest.

"Sarah is correct," Lady Radiance said, "albeit a little crudely expressed. It is an intriguing collection of stories."

"I shall get to it one day." When he was old and gray and no longer had vision enough to see deep inside the crystalline structure of a stone, then he would have Reynolds read to him to keep his mind active.

For a moment or two, he imagined Lady Radiance in that position, seated beside him on a comfortable sofa, reading to him while he watched her lovely mouth form the words and listened to her lilting tones tell him a story.

Yes, that was a nice old age to which he wouldn't mind looking forward.

"Did you, sir?"

Edward realized she had asked him something. Should he pretend he'd been listening and not fantasizing about her as his mate, or should he admit to not knowing the question?

"I beg your pardon, but I was thinking about our errand and missed your last query."

"That's quite all right," she said. "I confess I, too, have been preoccupied by the notion of a skillful counterfeiter stealing the Queen's jewels. What I asked before was whether you knew Mr. Minton beforehand or ever had dealings with him. After all, everyone keeps saying the jewelers' community is a small one."

"His name is unfamiliar to me."

Lady Radiance was so full of surprises that Edward half expected her to say she knew the man. However, she simply gave a ladylike lift to one shoulder and a tilt of her head.

And then the earl's comfortable carriage came to a halt.

"I guess we shall meet the man together," he said and exited the carriage. Yet when he turned to offer his hand, she paused and looked up. The forbidding granite edifice stretched in either direction from the corner of Newgate and Old Bailey Streets and rose over their heads with three stories of heavy stonework.

"I confess this is not a place I ever thought to come," she said softly. "While I understand the deterrence factor of a public execution, personally, I do not need such spectacle in order to maintain an honest life."

Edward was glad Lady Radiance was with him after all when the chief warder treated them civilly upon finding out he was in the presence of Lord Diamond's daughter. Moreover, instead of having to meet Minton in the common room where most of the male prisoners lived and ate together, they were told they could await him in a room near the prison's entrance.

"Does everything go smoothly for you?" Edward couldn't help asking her while they waited.

"I have no idea what you mean," she responded, but her small, satisfied smile indicated she did know.

And then the door opened, and a most unlikely perpetrator entered. Older than Edward had expected, James Minton was escorted by a guard, who after a look around the room, stepped back outside.

"You've come from the Palace," the man said.

Edward shook his head. "Why, no. What makes you think so?"

Mr. Minton shrugged. "'Tis always the Palace. Cajoling or bribing or threatening me. But they've never sent a woman before."

"Good day, Mr. Minton. I am Lady Radiance."

"Are you, now?" But Minton's tone was flat.

Edward hoped the man wasn't going to be rude. But the jeweler cocked his head and said, "A fitting name for a radiant young lady. What can I do for you? If I had my work bench and tools, I would make you a pretty necklace, indeed."

Then Mr. Minton started to cough and looked longingly at the chairs.

"Please, sit," Lady Radiance invited and took a seat, so the older man could, too. Edward remained standing where he was.

"Are you ill?" she asked.

Mr. Minton shrugged. "I have felt better."

Edward didn't want Lady Radiance to start feeling pity for the man who may have ruined the royal brooch and still had in his possession a precious sapphire, squirreled away somewhere.

"Do you still maintain you are innocent?" Edward demanded.

"I *knew* you were from the Palace," Mr. Minton grumbled. "I maintain I am innocent and shall do so until Kingdom-come because I am! I would scold you both for wasting my time, but it is better to be in here than out there. I don't suppose you could ask the guard for a pint of ale." He folded his hands on the table and looked hopeful.

Edward sighed. "I think that is highly unlikely." Wanting to return the conversation to the matter at hand, he asked, "What was your defense in court?"

"Young man, it is extremely difficult to prove one did *not* do a thing. I could only say that I cleaned the brooch, which I did. No one disputes that fact. They said the sapphire was no longer a sapphire. I wasn't allowed to examine it. Again, all I know is that I cleaned Her Majesty's brooch. For doing so, I was convicted of falsifying a gemstone. How does one prove the absence of an action?"

"May I ask a question?" Lady Radiance began.

Edward liked her polite yet firm way of speaking and nodded to her to begin.

CHAPTER FOURTEEN

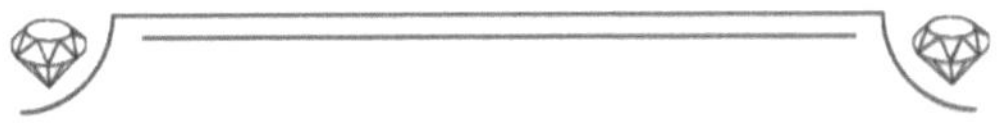

Radiance had actually been asking Mr. Minton whether he minded her interrogating him, but Mr. Lockwood had intercepted her request. Nevertheless, she wanted to show the older jeweler, a man of enough age that he must have spent decades working his craft, the respect he deserved.

Even if he was a forger and a thief!

"Mr. Minton, I am sorry we cannot procure you a pint of ale."

Mr. Lockwood made a sound of exasperation, but she ignored him.

"When the gemstone was switched, was that the first time you had cleaned the Queen's brooch?"

"Young lady, I did not switch the stone. And no, at my age, there is not a first time left for much, except being put in jail. I have cleaned the brooch before upon occasion."

Her heart pained for the man. "Are you married?"

Mr. Minton nodded. "I am. My wife visits regularly. Luckily, I have been employed long enough that she shall not become a watercress-seller or, worse, a matchstick beggar." Then he sighed loudly.

"They never let Mrs. Minton bring in any lokum or Pontefract cakes, my two favorite sweets. She tries, but they take it from her. The blackguards!"

Radiance glanced at Mr. Lockwood. Seeing his golden eyes already locked on her, she experienced a shivery tingle along her spine. Straightening, she directed her words at him rather than at the jeweler.

"If Mr. Minton has cleaned the brooch before without mishap, why would anyone believe he suddenly acted out of character?"

"I don't know," Mr. Lockwood replied. "The Palace must have had reason and some proof."

"They had no proof," the old jeweler insisted, "because I didn't do anything apart from clean the blessed piece, and now I wish I had never touched it."

"Who asked you to perform the cleaning?" she asked.

"My employer, Mr. Garrard. Often, he or Mr. Robert Garrard would have done it personally, but they had other business."

"Other business?" Radiance considered the task. "What could have been more important than handling the Queen's jewels?"

"Indeed, I have no idea."

She looked again at Mr. Lockwood, seeing he also thought it strange. Surely, being asked to clean Queen Victoria's jewelry was an honor.

"How did you get the brooch?"

Mr. Minton stared at her. "I don't take your meaning, my lady."

"Who gave it to you?"

"Mr. Garrard directly. He's the Crown Jeweler, after all."

Mr. Lockwood unfolded his arms. "Were you the only one in the room when you cleaned it?"

"I feel as if I'm on trial again," Mr. Minton complained.

"The Crown Jeweler is considered above reproach," Mr. Lockwood said to the unfortunate jeweler. "That leaves only you."

"Only me." Mr. Minton had a coughing fit before adding, "I have never done anything remotely against the law, except record a dodgy number of windows in order to lessen my city tax."

Radiance felt sorry for the man and for Mrs. Minton. And she had no doubt as to his innocence. No one had ever seemed less like an arch rogue who had time to—

She caught herself. *Time!*

"Even if Mr. Minton did replace the sapphire with a spinel," she began.

"Which I didn't," Mr. Minton insisted under his breath.

"That does not explain how he had the means to make a perfect replication of it. Did the judge believe he had produced a perfect fake from memory?"

Mr. Lockwood shook his head. "I believe the court thought Mr. Minton would give up the name of someone else who did have the means. Someone who would have given him the replica already made with the instructions to replace it during the cleaning and return the real one to the counterfeiter."

"I could snitch on no one," the old jeweler said, "since I have no knowledge of any crime. Thus, they had only me to convict."

"And no one else put hands upon the brooch apart from you and the Crown Jeweler?" Mr. Lockwood asked.

"And the footman," Mr. Minton added.

"Which footman?" Mr. Lockwood asked.

"The one who picked up the brooch."

"Lord Exeter didn't collect it himself?" Radiance asked, thinking it strange that the Lord Chamberlain would send someone.

"Exeter? You mean Lord Breadalbane, my lady. And he always sent a footman."

She ignored his mistake over who the current Lord Chamberlain was. "By chance do you know the footman's name?" Radiance asked.

"Absolutely no chance at all."

At her astonished look, Mr. Minton added, "He was sent by the Lord Chamberlain, and he had a paper with the royal seal. '*By the grace of God, Queen of the Britains, Defender of the Faith,*' and all such. That was good enough for me."

A brief knock heralded the return of the guard an instant before the door swung open.

"That's all the time you have," the tall, stern man said, eyeing Radiance before looking at the prisoner. "Come along, Minton."

In a few minutes, she was outside again with Mr. Lockwood, breathing the sooty air of London.

"He's not guilty," Radiance said.

Her companion stopped in his tracks as they reached her carriage. "How can you say that with such certainty?"

She had no proof, only a feeling. "I simply believe he's innocent. Did you think him a man of cunning?"

They settled into her father's comfortable carriage before he answered.

"Honestly, no. I wouldn't have thought him to be anything but a slightly grumpy old man."

"I would be grumpy, too, if I was put in jail unjustly. But the absence of guilt is hard to prove."

She glanced at the book Sarah was consuming, with all its deception, dirty deeds, and machinations.

"Perhaps someone wanted Mr. Minton to be blamed. Someone who knew he wouldn't be able to clear his name since there were no witnesses to him *not* doing the crime."

Mr. Lockwood looked thoughtful, and Radiance couldn't deny she liked *everything* about him so far. Every lock of chestnut brown hair, every well-shaped muscle she'd glimpsed through his white shirt when he'd answered his door in a state of wonderfully enlightening undress, and every flash of his topaz-colored eyes. She even appreciated his current pensive expression.

"A limited number of people have access to the Queen's jewels. And each one would have been thoroughly questioned."

Radiance wasn't satisfied. "We must speak privately to Mr. Garrard."

Her handsome geologist gave her his first dimpled smile of the day, and her body tingled with awareness.

"You have a good head for this," he remarked.

And you have an extremely attractive one, she thought.

"Thank you," Radiance said demurely. "I understand the matter is serious, but I confess to finding the whole thing if not entertaining, then a welcome diversion. The notion of investigating such an important theft, and perhaps resolving it, is better than what I would normally be doing."

"Which is?"

Radiance squirmed. He already knew she attended lectures and dabbled in the craft of jewelry-making at Mr. Bonwit's. *What else could she tell him?*

"Everyday life, I suppose. I sometimes look after my elder siblings' children. I keep a journal of the day's events. I ride. I go to parties and to dances." She left it at that, unable to admit how lately she had found herself lost in pleasant daydreams of becoming his wife or, at the very least, being his partner at a ball. She would very much like to be encircled by his strong arms and feel his hands upon her.

"Is traipsing along, even to Buckingham Palace, and meeting with musty old jewelers in prison more to your liking, my lady?" he asked. "You won't find a suitable husband hanging around with me."

That stung a little. *Was he purposefully warning her off?*

"Did I say I was in search of a husband? Or even in need of one, for that matter?" Radiance wished her tone hadn't gone from jovial to waspish. Mr. Lockwood would know he had struck a chord she didn't wish him to play. Or more precisely, a chord she did wish he would think about playing. Sadly, so far, he hadn't shown a modicum of interest in her as a female.

He put up his gloved hands to ward off her words.

"No need to get in a tweague, Lady Radiance. My sister always has a man on her mind, and she is about your age, I warrant. I wrongly assumed you, too, had an interest in marrying. If you are happy as a single lady, perhaps living your life in an independent fashion like a blue-stocking, then that is your choice. And I no more judge it to be a bad one than I applaud it as a good one."

Radiance cringed. Now he thought her a prude who didn't want to be with a man. She decided to set him straight at once.

"I do wish to be a wife someday. And not in the far-distant future, either. I have seen my two elder sisters and my brother make successful marriages."

He nodded. "A strange topic we have strayed upon. Undoubtedly too intimate for our association."

She looked at her hands in her lap, feeling a little dejected. And they were almost at her door. Then she had an idea.

"I am attending a ball at the end of the week. Perhaps you are going as well, sir?"

"Unlikely," he said, "since I have not been invited to any upcoming events." He laughed. "Not for the rest of the year."

Gracious! She eyed him. No invitations at all. Why, he was practically a pariah. Radiance brightened as an idea came to her.

"Then I shall invite you to come as my escort."

He frowned, and the carriage rocked to a halt. "Why would you do that?"

Oh dear! Didn't he have the smallest inclination to spend time with her apart from their common interest in gemstones?

"In order for us to . . . to spend time discussing Mr. Minton." Radiance nearly rolled her eyes at her own nonsense. "It seems you think the prosecutors were hoping for him to give them the real forger on a platter. Maybe we can come up with a few ideas of whom that might be."

To her amazement, he nodded. "Very well. Shall I collect you at your home? And will the attentive Sarah come, too?"

Radiance wasn't certain of the answer to either of those questions. But her heart was pounding with excitement. She was going to a ball with Mr. Lockwood as her escort. *How delightful!*

"I will send the details to your home tomorrow," she said, just before the driver opened the carriage door.

Mr. Lockwood descended. "I look forward to it, my lady."

"And you won't go conducting any investigating in the meantime without me?" she asked.

He tilted his head. "I cannot promise that. Something may arise—"

"Then send word, and I shall accompany you."

"We'll see," he said. "In any case, I am glad you came. Always better to have another pair of eyes and ears, even if we didn't learn much."

"We should go see his former employer next," Radiance reminded him. Hating to beg, yet desperately wanting to remain a part of whatever was unfolding, she added, "Please do not go without me."

He shrugged. "I shall endeavor to keep you involved."

She supposed that was as good a promise as she was going to receive from him.

CHAPTER FIFTEEN

Edward wished he could say he had no idea how he'd got himself into the unusual circumstances of attending a ball with the upper ten thousand. It was so far out of his normal sphere of social interaction, he could hardly credit that he'd agreed to it.

Yet he had. And he had purposefully put himself into a tailed evening coat for the singular reason of taking her in his arms for a dance, hopefully a waltz. If the sizzling sparkle died off after that, then he would know what he was feeling was only a fanciful whim. He had never been associated with an earl's daughter before. She was someone new, clever, and beautiful, and that must be why he felt randy as that wretch Rathmond who had rubbed her leg.

Moreover, Edward's edginess was his own fault for neglecting to enjoy even a single evening lately with Miss Maura. It wasn't as if he couldn't afford her.

However, ever since Lady Radiance had come to his front door with the startling claim that the Hope Diamond was fake, he hadn't desired his flash mollisher.

Ultimately, the lady had decided to arrive at the ball with her chaperone in her own conveyance. Edward couldn't help wondering if she didn't wish to be collected in a hansom cab. For his part, he didn't want to be picked up in her father's carriage, either. It hinted of emasculation and subservience.

Thus, he found himself at Cobble House, a private home—*an impressive one at that!*—on the Duke of York Street in St. James's, surrounded by people he didn't know, awaiting her arrival.

And there was no mistaking when Lady Radiance arrived. Her name was mentioned but not before her parents were announced.

Edward swallowed. Her chaperones were the Earl *and* Countess Diamond! He hadn't expected Sarah, the disinterested maid, but he certainly hadn't expected Lord and Lady Diamond.

They were dressed as befitting their station at the top tier of Mayfair society. And behind them, standing alone while surveying the ballroom, was their copper-haired daughter. A breathtaking sight in amethyst satin. Hearing himself gasp, he knew, for the first time, what a breathtaking woman looked like.

His feet were carrying him forward before his brain realized it. Edward saw the instant Lady Radiance spotted him. She smiled. The effect was dazzling, to rival the room's crystal chandeliers.

"Father, this is Mr. Lockwood, the geologist."

The geologist who desperately wants to kiss your daughter. Edward was shocked at the irreverent thought that came winging into his head.

"Lockwood," Lord Diamond returned. "My daughter speaks most highly of you. I understand you have previously met my wife, Lady Diamond."

"Indeed, I am happy to see you again," Edward told her ladyship. It was easy to see where Radiance came by all her fiery-haired, green-eyed stunning appearance. "Your daughter is an unusual addition to the field of jewelry and gemstones."

"Unusual and welcome, I hope," Lady Diamond said, eyeing him astutely. "Ray," she said over her shoulder, "I believe this gentleman wishes to claim a dance."

Edward should have been embarrassed, but he wasn't. He was simply enchanted when "Ray" stepped toward him.

"Good evening, my lady." He had the insane wish to claim her for himself for the rest of the evening.

"Good evening, sir. I am glad to see you. And look, they have provided us with such adorably illustrated quires. Elsewise, with so many dances tonight, we should all quickly lose track of our promised partners."

She held out a sheet of folded paper attached to a ribbon.

Edward stared at it. After an awkwardly long moment, he reached out and took the proffered item. She also handed him a pencil, for which he was grateful since he would never have thought to bring a writing implement to a dance.

"Please choose any *two*," she instructed.

Her parents exchanged a look while his insides warmed at her request.

Lady Radiance ignored them. "We have much to discuss."

"Perhaps Mr. Lockwood will take the dance before dinner and be your dining partner," Lady Diamond suggested. "Then you can have an opportunity for a long chat."

"That would be most agreeable," Lady Radiance said.

Edward was barely listening because she was so utterly . . . *radiant*. From her upswept crown of ruby hair, shining with peridot stones threaded onto golden wire and woven through it, to her eyes catching the candlelight, becoming emeralds on fire, she gleamed like a precious gem.

"Would you?" she asked, and he was further distracted looking at her blush-red lips.

"Would I?" he asked softly.

Her father coughed, and Edward realized he'd better gather his wits lest he be caught drooling over the earl's daughter and tossed out of the ballroom before the dancing even began.

Glancing at the small paper in his hand, he did as suggested, writing his name next to the dance prior to the midnight dinner. However, he hesitated in choosing the next one.

"Hurry along, Mr. Lockwood," said the Countess Diamond. "Other gentlemen are waiting."

Edward looked around. Sure enough, a small group of eligible men were standing only a few feet away, awaiting their turn. Their presence made him want to fill in the entire schedule with his own name. He chose the last dance.

"Thank you," he said, as he returned the card, watching Lady Radiance slip it over her slender, white-gloved hand.

"And I thank you, sir," she said.

Her father coughed again, and Edward realized he needed to move along and let the rest of the men—undeserving wretches, though they may be—have their turn. He'd barely nodded and retreated a step before another took his place.

"Lady Radiance, may I have the honor of a dance?" the man asked.

Edward ought to have asked her thusly but had forgotten his etiquette in her presence. Never mind, he had secured two dances and a dinner partner. Feeling momentarily satisfied, he encountered the lout from his lecture. The man recognized him at the same instant.

To Edward's amazement, Lord Woolley ignored him and continued past without acknowledgment. No doubt he, too, was going to request a dance.

At once, it hit him squarely. He was supposed to ask *other* ladies to dance. Edward couldn't simply lurk by the curtains or the terrace doors and await his turn with Lady Radiance, all the while trying to find flaw with her other partners.

What a nuisance! He'd imagined as her escort, he would be with her all evening, until she said, "Two dances." The old rhyme from university had come back to him:

One dance and you might fancy a bedding.
Two dances and you'll be at your wedding.

Nevertheless, he had penciled in for two without hesitation. And now he ought to put his name on some other willing females' quires.

RADIANCE KEPT HER GAZE on Mr. Lockwood while she danced with other men. Some, she had met before. Most in fact. And they had all been of little interest except for Lord Castille.

But her geologist, despite not being titled nor behaving in the least like the gentlemen to whom she was accustomed, had captured her attention. On the other hand, her dance with Lord Castille was also yet to come, and she greatly enjoyed his company.

Meanwhile, she noted with whom Mr. Lockwood danced, wondering if he would take a fancy to Lady Terrence or Miss Stark, or any of the others.

Finally, it was the dance before dinner. Mr. Lockwood's gaze found and held hers as he approached. Radiance couldn't help the silly smile that sprang to her lips. He looked so unlike his normal self, which was understated and often a little scruffy. That evening, he was downright dashing in a charcoal gray suit with a dark-blue satin necktie and black gloves. His hair was even tidy.

With a start, she realized he probably dressed and combed his hair himself, rather than employing a valet as her father did. As many of the gentlemen attending the ball did, too.

Strangely, it made Mr. Lockwood even more attractive.

"What are you thinking?" he asked when they stood facing one another while the other dancers got into place.

Radiance felt her cheeks warm. She couldn't tell him. Instead, she admitted, "Only that I have been looking forward to dancing with you."

"As I have with you," he said, sending a thrilling shiver along her spine.

With that, the music started. One of his hands took hold of hers while he rested his other on the small of her back. Her body's instant and heated reaction, sizzling under his touch, was something that hadn't happened all evening with any other man. The evening took on a rosy new appearance.

When the dance ended, she nodded to her parents and accompanied Mr. Lockwood into the grand dining room where a buffet meal was spread out. People began at one end where a footman handed them a plate and then made their way down the expanse of a twenty-foot table. After wending their way up the other side, guests found a place to dine in one of the public rooms that had been opened for just such a purpose with extra chairs.

"How lovely," she said, thinking the garlands of fresh flowers on the chandeliers and the swaths of roses on the mirrors and sconces around the room transformed the usually stark chamber. "Hasn't Cobble House been decorated beautifully for tonight?"

Mr. Lockwood released her arm in front of the footman with the plate and took his place in line behind her.

"Honestly, I wouldn't know, having never been here before. But it appears satisfyingly festooned."

She nodded at his description while removing her lace gloves and putting them in the small satin reticule hanging from her wrist alongside the slightly curled and crumpled dance quire. To keep from insulting him with any other question that might bring up his inexperience with the world of the nobility, Radiance concentrated on the dishes laid out before her.

There were so many to choose from, she wouldn't taste even half. Sticking to those which were easiest to eat while standing in case they didn't secure a seat, Radiance placed a savory cheese roll, a small-cut sandwich of tongue and another of sliced cucumber on her plate, then caught herself humming with happiness. Mr. Lockwood was making his choices behind her, exclaiming at the selection.

At the far end of the table were iced wafers, sweet biscuits, and little squares of lavender sponge cake, which her mother loved. Radiance hoped her parents were having a good time and finding old friends, but when she glanced around, she didn't see them.

"I am famished," Mr. Lockwood said.

They each accepted a glass of wine from a server's tray before making their way through the large crop of single people searching for a lifelong mate that evening. Just as fervently, Radiance would now search for a secluded spot to eat and chat.

"How the deuce am I supposed to eat with both hands full of plate and glass?" Mr. Lockwood asked, sounding truly baffled and even a little annoyed.

She couldn't help chuckling softly. "We are meant to find a table, an alcove, or even a hearth mantel to rest our glass upon while we eat. Let us try in the library or the music room." From her experience, those often remained empty.

As expected, guests were taking up places all over the upper chambers. There were far fewer on the ground floor where she led Mr. Lockwood. In fact, the library was empty and with a table and chairs for their convenience. Although not entirely sure they ought to have strayed so far from the throng or from her parents, she could see no harm in eating privately.

Yet she hadn't expected Mr. Lockwood to shut the door behind them.

Radiance opened her mouth to advise him of the impropriety, but he sprinted forward to set his plate and glass down so he could pull out a chair for her.

"This is unexpected," he said. "I wonder if the hosts would be annoyed to know we ate sandwiches near their book collection. It seems they have maps, too." He ran a hand over the map cupboard and then peered down to see what newspapers were in a stack by the window.

Radiance imagined the learned geologist might start perusing the shelves and examining the books rather than eating. At last, he took the seat opposite and raised his glass.

"To your health and to our first meal together," he said, then winced at his own odd toast intimating there might be more to come. She didn't mind his presumption one bit.

"To your health, Mr. Lockwood." She sipped the wine before giving in to the hunger pangs after a long day and a couple of hours spent dancing. They ate in silence for a few minutes.

And then he surprised her. "I feel as if I have you at a disadvantage."

Her heart picked up its pace, and her imagination ran wild. *Was he going to press his advantage of strength by taking her in his arms?*

"How so?" she whispered.

"I know *your* first name, and it's not 'Succulent' as I first thought. Yet you don't know mine."

Radiance let the prickling tension dissipate, while feeling a little disappointed. His advantage was nothing as fun as an embrace or a kiss.

Besides, 0f course she knew his name. She had made it a point to discover it months ago, even before his mother had formally introduced them. Moreover, Radiance thought it manly and fitting. He seemed eminently like an *Edward*.

"I do know your given name. It is Edward."

"It is George," he corrected.

"No, it isn't," she immediately retorted.

His eyes widened. "Isn't it?" It was his turn to chuckle. He sipped his wine and cocked his head. "Then tell me my own name."

Oh dear! She ought to have thanked him for telling her and said it was a fine name. But she had thought of him as Edward for a while now and could not possibly think of him as George, although it was also a fine name.

Looking at him from under her lashes, she shrugged and mumbled, "I thought your name was Edward."

"Did you?"

Her gaze shot to his. He was teasing her. She could tell by his crooked smile with his single dimple—one that made her pulse race and sent a feeling of excited expectation sizzling through her.

"Well, isn't it? Even your mother introduced you thusly." Radiance waited, popping another bite of an iced wafer between her lips while staring at his handsome mouth, still hoping he had a notion to kiss her.

After all, they were scandalously alone. They might as well make use of the shocking situation.

CHAPTER SIXTEEN

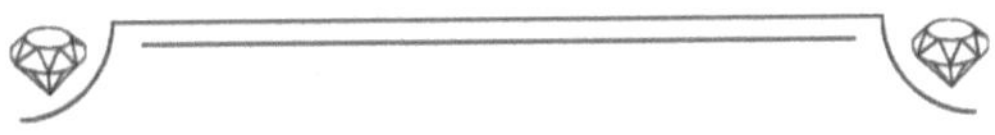

Edward was flattered that Lady Radiance had an interest in him.

"I was born George Edward Lockwood, II," he explained. "My grandparents were all in favor of royal names, it appears. Yet my parents seemed to regret it almost at once since they have never called me anything except Edward. I have never used George, although I assume it is scrawled upon my birth notice and a university diploma tucked away somewhere."

"I suppose it is of little consequence to me presently, sir. I cannot go around calling you either Edward or George, while you are free to call me by my name."

"As long as there is a 'lady' in front of it."

"Obviously," she agreed without irony. After all, she'd been called a lady from the day she was born, and being addressed thusly must be as natural to her as breathing.

Another rude saying from his university days came to mind. More than one young man upon meeting a titled lady would then tell his chums about the encounter. As a group, they would recite: "The lady behind the 'lady' may not be a lady underneath." To which the young man would exclaim, "I pray to Venus, *not* underneath!"

It was juvenile. Yet many a man would report that Venus had answered his prayer, and a lady was as likely to let a man explore beneath her skirts as an untitled one.

Edward would wager his own life that Lady Radiance was a lady through and through, as well as under her skirts.

But he still wanted to kiss her. It wouldn't make her any less a true lady. Then again, if she didn't want to be kissed and he insulted her tender sensibilities, it would ruin their blossoming association.

He was willing to risk their joint jewel investigation in order to finally satisfy his desire to taste her lips.

"I am glad we can speak freely," she said, her voice a little breathy.

His curiosity was piqued. "Are you?" He hoped she wanted to murmur words of yearning.

"Yes." Radiance finished her wine and set the glass down. "I keep thinking about Mr. Minton."

Mr. Minton! He barked out a short laugh without thinking. They were entirely alone, for which he ought to be shot or made to offer for her hand at the very least, yet all she was thinking about was the wretched Newgate bird.

Edward wished to hear her thoughts, but he also wanted to claim her mouth under his, which would greatly impede her ability to speak. Rising to his feet, he held out his hand. When she took it, sliding her bare fingers against his, he had an inkling he would get his way.

Drawing her up beside him, Edward fell into her luminous eyes, which seemed to catch and reflect every particle of light in the room. If they were true emeralds, he didn't think they could be any more beautiful.

"If you recall," she added, "Mr. Minton said it was really Mr. Garrard's duty to—"

Edward ran his thumb over her lower lip, and she stopped speaking. Then he leaned in close and nuzzled her left ear, wanting to place a kiss just below it, but he refrained. Instead, he whispered, "You smell . . . sparkly."

In a husky tone, Radiance asked, "How does one smell like a sparkle?"

"You do," he insisted. Something about her fragrance reminded him of gemstones glittering on a bed of luxuriously soft velvet. And then Edward could wait no longer. Covering her mouth with his own, he experienced the moment she gasped, opening her mouth under his.

Sliding his fingers into her hair and cradling her face, he tilted his head and deepened the kiss. When she relaxed against him, Edward dove into her wet softness, his tongue plundering her mouth like a diamond miner.

Her hands clasped the lapels of his coat and held on to him before she drew back a mere whisker's width.

"You mustn't do that," she whispered against his lips.

He couldn't imagine why not. It felt right. His bare fingers were finally touching the silky softness of her fiery tresses. And the sensation of pressing close to her while starting to nibble on her lower lip was as intoxicating as any glass of brandy.

Letting loose her lip from between his teeth, he trailed a path of kisses along her jaw and down the slender column of her neck.

"I want you," he confessed in a voice that didn't sound like his own, surprisingly full of passion and longing. He certainly hadn't meant to say any such thing.

She stiffened, and he hoped his raw confession hadn't sounded too crude. Relinquishing the silken skeins of her hair, his hands roamed down her back, across the satin gown until they rested at her waist.

Rather than push him away as she had every right to do, Radiance threaded her hands up and around the back of his neck. Edward wished he could sweep her away somewhere truly private.

Blazing a trail of kisses along her exposed collar bone, he reached the upper swell of her left breast. Her fingers slipped into his hair, gripping him tightly. And he knew he had to stop, just as he knew she would let him continue because she was an utter innocent.

"*Mm,*" she moaned, her head arched back to give him access.

His answering groan was torn from deep inside, where his body throbbed for her. He was like a university student again, ready to toss her skirts up and take her on the library table in the midst of the fancy foodstuffs. Cucumber sandwiches be damned!

But even though he found himself gripping the soft globes of her bottom, and despite feeling her hips tilt toward him as if she couldn't help herself, he restrained from treating her like a light-skirt.

He couldn't yet tear himself away, however. Their second kiss was heady and hot, raw and intense, as if they were two people who already shared a relationship and had been kept from one another for an eon. His soul relaxed as if coming home, while his body sizzled with pent-up lust.

Edward would swear it was the most satisfying kiss he'd ever given or taken. *And from a proper lady at that!*

Even when he released her mouth, they remained pressed front-to-front for a long moment, her full breasts crushed against him. Then slowly, he stepped back, drawing in long breaths while she did the same, silently eyeing one another and wearing—he was certain—equal expressions of surprise.

Radiance spoke first.

"Not my first kiss, but the best one, I don't mind telling you."

His heart was still thumping so hard, he could hear it in his ears. But he caught her extraordinary words and felt a twinge of jealousy over the man who had kissed her before, followed swiftly by pride that his was better.

"I shall be honest, too, for I have kissed a few females. That one rocked me to my core."

"Well," she said, and nothing more, simply looking pleased as Punchinello.

Edward wasn't sure of the etiquette after ravishing a lady in a library. Before the moment turned awkward, however, he ought to think of her virtue, no matter how belated, no matter how passionate the woman.

Running a hand through his hair, hoping he was tidying it and not messing it further, he said, "I suppose we ought to return to the party before we are missed and your parents set a date for our wedding."

Her lovely face clouded over like London skies in the spring or the fall, winter or summer, for that matter. Clearly, it was the wrong thing to say.

"I'm sorry," he blurted at once. "I meant no disrespect. But obviously, a kiss, no matter how extraordinary, doesn't warrant being leg-shackled. I would hate for your father to feel as though he had to force the issue."

He laughed, hoping she would, too. She was upper nobility and could not possibly have an interest in an untitled geologist without a butler. *Could she?*

"You are right," Radiance said, her tone cool. Picking up her plate and empty glass, she went toward the door.

He had to hurry to reach it first, yanking it inward just before she reached it. Radiance sailed gracefully, albeit swiftly, out of the room without hesitation as if she would have marched right through the blasted door if he hadn't opened it for her.

Damn! He had cocked that up, and no mistake, although he wasn't sure how.

Not bothering to retrieve his own plate and glass, he followed her, making sure she got safely to the dining room where she wordlessly set her service down on a table cluttered with other dirty dishes.

Then she turned and offered him her usual small smile, except it was devoid of warmth, and her emerald eyes were most definitely glittering with anger.

"Will you escort me back to the ballroom? I believe the dancing will begin again soon. My card is full," she added sharply.

Of course it was! She was the most beautiful, desirable woman in London. And he had insulted her.

Edward wasn't certain to what degree he had erred until he went to claim her for the last dance of the evening, their second one, only to witness Radiance and her parents leaving through the open double doors of the great chamber.

Including Woolley, it was his second cut direct of the night. A few minutes earlier, as the clock struck half past one, he'd seen Radiance on the dance floor, smiling and laughing with some other lucky chap. Thus, there could be no claim of a head or stomachache—no necessity for leaving except to avoid him.

He hoped she didn't tell her parents why she wished to escape his presence, or he could expect a terse visit from the earl later that day.

Edward left directly, walking for a few minutes in the damp and chill night air before he hailed a cab. It was just as well. His life, while touching the edges of hers, was decidedly different. He hired public transport, and she rode in the luxurious comfort of her father's town carriage. Similarly, Edward's home was too modest to welcome a lady into it, as his life was too small and boring. Radiance deserved to shine at private balls and exclusive dinner parties with those of her echelon.

And then Edward wondered why he was thinking of their lives joined at all.

THE FOLLOWING AFTERNOON, Radiance went to take tea with her two older sisters at Clarity's home on Grosvenor Square. She had decided she needed guidance, and there was no one better. Except perhaps their mother, but she was unsure if Carolyn Diamond would be thrilled to learn of her daughter's behavior under her own nose.

Her sisters would offer counsel without the parental condemnation. Or so she hoped.

"You kissed him? After your first dance and at your first ball together?" Clarity sounded beyond surprised.

Expecting her oldest sister's next words to be those of censure, Radiance waited. Yet Clarity gave small clap. "How fun! Was it a good kiss?"

"I don't have much to compare it to," she said. "But of the few I have experienced—"

"How few?" Purity interjected, not appearing nearly as amused as their sister.

"Two," Radiance said, despite thinking it wasn't really any of her sister's business. "That's not really the point. Besides, Mr. Lockwood and I have already been to a dinner party together, so this was our second social interaction. Also, I've attended two of his lectures and accompanied him to a meeting at Buckingham Palace."

She nearly added "and to Newgate jail" before she recalled she couldn't speak about the fake stones.

"What on earth did you go to the Palace for?" Purity demanded.

"To speak with some very important people about helping the Queen with her diamond problem."

"Her diamond problem!" Clarity laughed heartily, tickled for some reason. "I have never heard of such a thing," she said finally. "It is beyond anything. Tell us all about it."

"The Koh-i-Noor is lumpy and flawed. Prince Albert and the Queen want it improved. Mr. Garrard thinks it can be done while Sir Brewster thinks it risky."

Silence met her words, and Radiance fidgeted, twisting her hands in her lap.

"Again, that is beside the point except to let you know I didn't kiss a man upon first meeting him at a ball and sharing a plate of sandwiches."

"What *is* the point?" Purity asked more softly.

Radiance couldn't help the great sigh that escaped her. "The kiss transported me to a realm of pure sensation without thought or worry. It was absolute bliss."

Her sisters glanced at one another.

"And then what happened?" Clarity asked.

"Mr. Lockwood ruined it by making a joke about Father demanding we marry, and then he wanted to hurry me back to the ballroom."

"What a dunce!" Purity said. "He ought to have got down on one knee and thanked his lucky stars for sending such a glorious girl his way. Ungrateful, ungracious clod! Civility would demand he behave as if marrying you was uppermost in his thoughts and his most avid wish."

Radiance hadn't expected such a vehement declaration.

Maybe Clarity hadn't either, for her eyes widened. She leaned forward, staring into Radiance's eyes with her beautiful blue gaze.

"I think your gentleman friend was most likely overcome by his own emotions. When they get that way, they tend to say silly things. He was giving you an escape as much as himself. How did you end the evening with him?"

Radiance considered her sister's words. Maybe Mr. Lockwood—*Edward*—had felt the depth of the kiss as keenly as she had. She hoped so. In truth, she had wished for him to say as much instead of his skittish words about being forced into marriage with her.

"He used the term *leg-shackled*," she said softly, instantly wishing she hadn't because Purity reared back, and even Clarity, who usually thought the best of everyone, raised her eyebrows. Now, her sisters would think him a scoundrel.

"Unfortunately, we didn't speak again," Radiance continued. "I told him I had many other men to dance with—which I did—and then I left before the final dance, which would have been our second one."

She'd come off the floor and told her parents that her ankle hurt. They'd taken her swiftly from the ballroom without a backward glance. It would have been too awkward to dance with Edward again.

"Oh dear," Purity exclaimed. "You left him without explanation nor apology." She appeared truly distraught by the breach of manners.

"I am shocked Mother allowed you to do so," Clarity added.

"I fibbed and told her I'd already let him know I was leaving before I left the dance floor with my previous partner. Really, I just wanted to make Mr. Lockwood feel insulted as I had."

Purity shook her head. "You must send him an apology at once and tell him you were overcome with . . . with . . ."

"With the vapors," Clarity added helpfully.

"The vapors!" Radiance repeated. "I hope he knows I am made of sturdier stuff than that. I shall tell him what I told our parents—that my ankle hurt. I hated lying to them, and I don't wish to create yet another one for him."

She paused and sipped her sister's fine tea blend.

"Must I really apologize?" Radiance knew Purity would think it the proper thing to do, but Clarity might say differently. "After all, he was audacious and then hurtful."

"If you left him waiting without a dance partner and without even saying goodbye after a fabulous kiss, then, yes, I think you owe him an apology. Not only for your bad manners but for the childish behavior. If you are grown up enough to receive a kiss from a gentleman, then you ought to be mature enough to handle the consequences."

Radiance stared at Clarity. Her words seemed so unlike her usual self who soothed and left one feeling pleased that even Purity was staring at their eldest sister.

Clarity shrugged. "I simply cannot bear to think of poor Mr. Lockwood, whom you said earlier doesn't normally mingle in ballrooms, made to feel awkward or out of place. And if he was overcome with profound emotions for you, he might have been waiting all evening for that second chance to express himself—only to be thwarted by your abrupt departure."

When Radiance looked at it that way, she did feel a wee bit sorry, imagining him standing on the edge of the dance floor, having looked hither and yonder for her. She should and would send him a note.

"I shall do as you suggest, but it is irksome nonetheless, to be in the wrong after . . . never mind. Now, do you have any cream cake, perhaps with raspberry syrup?"

Radiance changed the subject. Every once in a while, she thought about Mr. Minton, not only the unfairness of his situation but also something he had said which bothered her. Unfortunately, she couldn't figure out what precisely it was—yet the irksome notion played about the edges of her mind nonetheless. She would dearly love to tell her sisters everything and perhaps suss out the niggling issue. But she could not.

Thus, determined not to slip up and say a word about the forged and stolen gems, she happily told her sisters all they wished to hear about her involvement with the Koh-i-Noor.

"Your name will go down in history as the woman who helped," Clarity declared.

Radiance wrinkled her nose. "I would prefer being the woman who cut the diamond to make it sparkle, but that is out of the question. I am only now practicing on semi-precious garnets."

As soon as she got home, she wrote to Mr. Lockwood.

Dear Sir,

I made the egregious error of not letting you know about my departure from the Cobble House ball. With a bruised ankle, I had no choice but to withdraw from the dance floor. I hope you were able to find a replacement partner upon noticing my absence.

Sincerely,

Lady Radiance Diamond

That seemed utterly suitable. But then she thought about their investigation. Despite the kiss, she still wanted to help solve the crime and was ever more certain of Mr. Minton's innocence. The best thing to do was discover who was involved with the second fake gemstone.

Thus, she added:

PS. I believe our next step ought to be to speak with Mr. Garrard.

Satisfied, she folded her letter, sealed it, and addressed it before finding Sarah. Once her short missive had been dispatched, there was nothing Radiance could do but wait.

CHAPTER SEVENTEEN

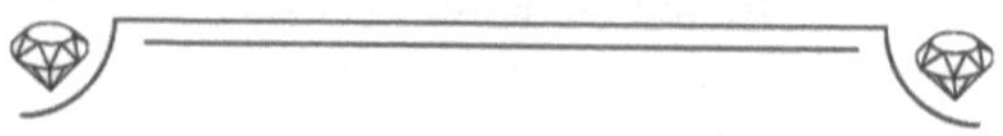

Radiance did not have long to cool her heels. Moreover, since Mr. Lockwood apparently didn't employ a fleet of footmen, he brought the answer in person.

While seated on the drawing room sofa, she plainly heard him in the front hall.

"Is Lady Radiance at home?" he asked Mr. Dunley.

She smiled. Not exactly what Purity would deem the correct question from an uninvited guest. He ought to have asked if she was seeing visitors. It was none of his business whether she was at home or not.

As expected, their proper butler didn't give him a direct answer. Moreover, since she was in the drawing room, he didn't invite Mr. Lockwood in. Instead, Mr. Dunley told him to wait in the foyer.

Radiance went to the drawing room door, still holding the newspaper she'd been perusing. There was much to be gleaned about the state of the jewelry industry and its current trends by looking at the shop advertisements. She also read the stock prices for diamonds, gold, and silver, as well as the general business news about who was now working where, who had closed up shop, and who had opened a new one.

"Good day, Mr. Lockwood." She nearly called him Edward. She only thought of him as Edward now that his mouth had been upon hers, not to mention his hands.

"What a pleasant surprise," she said.

"I have come to apologize."

Oh dear! "No," she warned. "Say no more." Then after glancing at Mr. Dunley, she beckoned Edward into the drawing room. When he stepped over the threshold, she asked, "Would you care for any refreshments? Tea, perhaps?"

"Thank you, no. I shan't stay long. As I said, I came only to tender an apology."

Radiance shut the door with a polite shake of her head to the butler who had awaited any request for her guest.

"You really must stop saying that," she beseeched. "I accept your apology."

"But you cannot since I haven't said it properly or expressed why I was apologizing."

"I know why. Because of . . . your actions." She lowered her voice to a whisper. "In the library."

"No," he blurted.

At her expression, somewhere between stunned and shocked—*for how else could she look?*—he hurriedly added, "I mean, yes, I suppose. *Not* my actions exactly because I don't regret our kiss for an instant."

She winced that he'd said it aloud under her parents' roof. *Had he never heard the expression of the walls having ears?* The ears belonged to any number of their staff.

However, since he wouldn't stop apologizing or mentioning the regrettable behavior, she repeated herself.

"I accept your apology and don't blame you at all, sir. If you will only stop mentioning it."

"I am apologizing for cheapening the delightful experience by talking of possible recriminations. Were there to be any, I would greet them with dutiful acceptance."

Dutiful acceptance? Worse and worse! Radiance couldn't help shaking her head.

Mr. Lockwood appeared concerned. "It is you who would suffer from being tied to someone who answers his own doors."

That made her laugh despite herself. "Indeed. The benefit would all be on your side."

His face fell. Men had pride. And while *he* could joke about it, plainly, she could not. She had well and truly put her slippered foot in it. Deeply, too.

They couldn't seem to get on an even keel.

"Mr. Lockwood, if you will not accept a refreshment, will you at least take a seat?"

"No," he said stubbornly. "Since you have accepted my apology for almost inadvertently saddling you with the likes of me, then I shall be on my way."

Radiance sighed. "Do you accept my apology for leaving you without a dance partner?"

"Yes, of course." He waved it away as if he hadn't known what a terrible offense she'd committed.

"Good. Do you know who was involved with the second forged gemstone?"

He appeared caught off guard. After a moment, he took a seat after all.

She sighed again since he failed to notice he'd committed an egregious error. Quickly, she sat beside him.

He frowned. "Mr. Neble is a notoriously reticent man. As far as I know, he doesn't leave his workroom for the floor of his shop and never speaks with customers."

"He spoke with someone from Buckingham Palace, and he shall speak with us. Why should Mr. Minton rot in jail while someone else goes free?"

"You are determined to become Minton's champion."

"Indeed, I am."

Edward had regained his good humor. He smiled at her, showing his single dimple, and her heart twinged. "Then, my lady, I shall find out how we can gain an audience with the slippery fellow."

"Meanwhile, we must visit with Mr. Garrard, agreed?"

"If you say so," he began, sounding amused by her enthusiasm. "When?"

"If you are free, then why not now?"

Thus, within a very few minutes, Radiance was in a hansom cab with her maid and Edward. Traffic was its usual nightmare, and they ended up departing the carriage at the corner of Haymarket and Panton Street, walking the rest of the way to R. & S. Garrard & Company.

"WE MUST BE CAREFUL," Edward reminded her. "We cannot insult Mr. Garrard. His shop has a royal appointment, after all."

Whereas Edward had nothing but his reputation, which he would like to keep.

"I shall be careful," Lady Radiance promised.

But he feared her idea of *careful* might not be the same as someone more prudent.

Who was he to talk, after the library entanglement? Moreover, in his head, having had his tongue in her mouth, he thought of her as simply Radiance. Edward also recognized a new sensation of propriety and protection. Neither had ever been needed nor felt regarding Miss Maura.

They entered Garrard's establishment to the sound of a bell on the door announcing them. With her maid immediately taking up a place in the corner and pulling out a penny dreadful from her coat pocket, Edward waited for a shopgirl to approach.

"Please tell Mr. Garrard that Mr. Lockwood and Lady Radiance are here to speak with him."

"Which one, sir?" asked the young woman wearing a starched white apron over a striped gray dress.

"*Sebastian* Garrard."

In short order, they were taken from the main floor of the shop up the stairs to an office. It was a spacious one, staid and elegant, with not only an immaculate, uncluttered desk positioned so that Mr. Garrard's back was to the window, but also a seating area placed before it around a mahogany tea table. The furnishings were all in shades of dark blue, gray, and white—a nicer workspace, Edward thought with a pang of embarrassment, than his own home.

"You recall Lady Radiance from the meeting," Edward said.

"Of course," the Crown Jeweler gestured for them to sit. "A pleasure to see you again, my lady. I hope your parents are well."

"Yes, sir. Thank you for asking." And she took the blue velvet chair offered her.

"Shall I send for some refreshments?" Garrard asked, as if they were visiting at his home.

"Thank you, no," she said as Edward and the jeweler also sat.

Before Edward could dive in with their questions, Garrard leaned forward with a beatific smile.

"What brings you both here today? A nuptials ring, perhaps?"

Edward coughed, somehow choking on air, while Lady Radiance simply smiled before offering a smooth response.

"If and when, Mr. Garrard, then I shall certainly consider your fine establishment. I cannot speak for Mr. Lockwood."

"Jolly good!" Garrard said.

Edward decided they had best move on to the topic at hand.

"We don't wish to take up too much of your time, but we have some questions about the situation to which few are privy."

"But I am?" Mr. Garrard asked.

"Indeed, as Royal Keeper of the Jewels—"

"Actually, since 1843, I am the Crown Jeweler, a slightly different title." He preened, but Edward could not blame him. It was an honor, indeed.

When Edward hesitated, Radiance added, "And as such, you more than anyone know the importance of keeping safe the royal jewel collection. We were told that there have been two imitations passed off as gemstones."

Mr. Garrard eyebrows rose. "You know about the forgeries, do you? It's a sad situation since they are still unrecovered. I have the best detectives in London keeping their eyes and ears open for any possible sale of the stones."

"We didn't know that," Edward confessed. "I imagine it is like looking for a grain of sand on Brighton Beach."

"Just so," Mr. Garrard agreed. "Two grains! The stones themselves, as I am sure you're aware, are not particularly memorable except for having been used in two pieces of jewelry worn by the Queen. It's not as though either stone is the Koh-i-Noor." Then he paused.

"That explains your inclusion in our little committee. Because you're searching for the lost jewels."

Radiance glanced at Edward who looked back at her and nodded.

"We are trying to determine the perpetrator of the replications," she confessed. "And that is why we wished to speak with you."

"Me?" Garrard shook his head. "I assure you I had nothing to do with it."

"Perhaps you could speak to us about Mr. Minton, sir," Radiance persisted.

The Crown Jeweler turned somber at once. "A bad apple amongst us, and what a dreadful thing to do to our Queen."

"Indeed," Edward agreed. "And, as you say, even worse since the stones were never recovered."

"If the sapphire and emerald are still in Britain, then they are most likely safely hidden away." Mr. Garrard shook his head in dismay. "And to think I hired Minton myself, although he was trained long before. He worked for Rundell and Bridge prior to coming here. And you cannot ask for a better reference."

"But why would he steal the stone if he couldn't sell it?" Radiance asked.

"Who said he couldn't? He could sell it easily *outside* of Britain," Mr. Garrard insisted. "Some collectors would pay more, in fact, because it belonged to the Queen of the United Kingdom of Great Britain and Ireland."

Edward hadn't thought of that. Someone would pay dearly for the thrill of owning something Her Majesty had worn.

"Then it may never be recovered," Radiance said morosely.

"Not unless someone is very foolish," Garrard said, "and wears it in a recognizable setting amongst those who know the Queen's jewels. And anyone who did what was done to procure the sapphire is certainly *not* a fool."

"You are no longer speaking of Mr. Minton, are you?" Radiance asked. "Is everyone else who works for you above suspicion?"

Edward cringed. It certainly was a question that might raise the ire of the Crown Jeweler.

"Mr. Minton could very well have worked alone. We have sketches in our archives of all the royal pieces we've created, and he had access to them. In any case, no one else was anywhere near the brooch."

Edward watched Radiance frown, clearly thinking up more questions, but when she chewed her luscious lower lip, he felt a tugging ache in his groin.

Finally, she spoke again.

"May I ask why Mr. Minton was given the brooch to clean rather than doing it yourself?"

Edward gaped. She was all but implying Garrard had been derelict in his duty.

She was lucky to be both beautiful and an earl's daughter. Still, Mr. Garrard's jaw worked as if he were chewing bread, and he gritted his teeth. Finally, he answered her.

"I had important business with a gem dealer. You met Mr. Rathmond at the Palace." Then he cleared his throat. "And my entire company is on the royal warrant, my lady, and thus all those who work for me, including Mr. Minton at the time."

Radiance looked as if she was satisfied by his response, but Edward wanted to know more about the ankle rubber.

"I had never met Rathmond before, but I understand he buys and sells all over the world."

Garrard nodded. "Indeed. He often has interesting stones. His prices are high, though." He looked at Radiance. "I wouldn't try to purchase your engagement stone from him. He'll lead you on an expensive dance before you knew what was happening." He winked at Lady Radiance.

Edward was embarrassed for his sex and their condescending ways.

Luckily, before Garrard could do something equally belittling, such as pat her on the head, he rose to his feet, and Edward understood their meeting had come to an end.

However, as Radiance stood, she had another question. "Do you have any idea how the emerald might have been switched out of the Queen's coronet?"

Mr. Garrard stiffened. "You must try to speak with Mr. Neble, and in that endeavor, I wish you good luck. He has become somewhat . . . difficult in his later years."

"Then why was he given the coronet to look after in the first place?" Radiance asked.

Mr. Garrard wore an expression of chagrin. "He created it many years ago for the Queen's mother, and thus, he was sent the coronet because the House of Neble has always been sent the coronet. That is how these situations are handled."

"Thank you for your time," Edward said. With that, he put a hand on Radiance's arm and steered her from the establishment, making sure to retrieve her maid on the way out.

"Everyone knows the task of creating each article of jewelry for the royal family is protected and fought over," he said. "You can only stir up hard feelings by asking about another jeweler's piece."

"I had no idea it was such a touchy subject," Radiance said. "I would think Mr. Garrard ought to be satisfied at having made Prince Albert's wedding gift for the Queen and being the Crown Jeweler. In any case, he seems to think the matter of Mr. Minton is done and dusted."

"And you do not?" He knew the answer.

"No. I believe the discovery of the second counterfeit stone should have cleared Mr. Minton."

"Not necessarily. Even if he was incarcerated at the time it was discovered, he could have done it beforehand."

"But he never worked on the coronet," Radiance protested. "Mr. Garrard made that clear. It is time we pay a visit to the House of Neble."

Edward smiled at her take-charge tone. "As I've said, he is quite the recluse now. I have never met him."

She shrugged, and it was the prettiest thing he'd seen.

"Mr. Neble will undoubtedly see me if I say I wish to have something created especially for the House of Diamond."

Her tone left no doubt she was entirely serious.

"Moreover, if the esteemed geologist, Edward Lockwood, were the one to send him my request acting as my personal consultant for jewelry, I am sure we will be invited rather swiftly."

"We can but try," he agreed. She was probably correct, although Edward liked to think he could see the man even without subterfuge or using the impressive name of Diamond.

"I shall send word to Mr. Neble's establishment that Lady Radiance Diamond wishes to have a consultation."

"Thank you," she said. "Now, would you care to come home with me to tea?"

Edward stopped in his tracks, his arm raised to hail a passing cab.

"I prefer coffee, but why are you inviting me to your home?" Edward had the sudden notion all the talk of nuptial rings and of her being his *lady-friend* was going to her head.

For his part, he had decided to pay a visit to Maura on the weekend and relieve the pent-up frustration in his loins. If Radiance had some pent-up emotions of her own, he didn't know what she was supposed to do about them. As far as he knew, nice young ladies hadn't much choice of release.

"We have the finest coffee," she interrupted his salacious thoughts with more mundane ones. "And I wish to oversee the letter we're sending to Mr. Neble. After all, you are writing it on my behalf."

"I assure you I am capable of composing a missive that will gain us entry."

She gave him a long stare.

Edward was almost certain there was some pressing reason he ought not to go off with the pretty lady, but for the life of him, while looking into her intelligent eyes, he couldn't recall what it was.

CHAPTER EIGHTEEN

"I will accept the offer of your help and the coffee." Edward found himself wanting to get along congenially with her. And not only because of the astounding kiss or the notion they might enjoy another one at some opportune moment, but because she truly was helpful.

And while he had no idea why the Prince Consort had put his faith in him over a London inspector or constable, Edward knew letting His Highness down was not an option.

Thus, he directed the driver to the Earl Diamond's home on Piccadilly and soon found himself ensconced, not in the drawing room but in a library. *Had she brought him there to remind him of their previous encounter?*

With the door remaining innocently ajar and Sarah in a small chair in the corner, they locked gazes. A lightning bolt of heat shot through him. He saw its answering sizzle behind her glorious green eyes.

Indeed, her cheeks turned a sweet pink color, as if all the freckles had joined together.

Drawing out a chair for her at the rectangular reading table, he happily breathed in her fragrance while she took the seat. When he pushed it in, the urge to lean in and trail his lips down her neck nearly overwhelmed him. Instead, he took the chair opposite her.

As soon as the coffee and tea service had been brought in by a capable footman, Radiance pulled open a cleverly concealed, shallow drawer from under the table. Withdrawing a sheet of thick cream-colored paper and a pen, she slid both over to him. Then set an ink pot at his elbow.

As he stirred sugar into his coffee, Edward considered what to write. Suddenly nervous, he hoped he could craft the perfect letter and not disappoint her. Besides, it was more interesting to watch her splash milk into her cup and then pour in the steeped tea.

"Not particularly a lover of coffee?" he asked.

She sent him her brilliant Diamond smile.

"No, not really, although I adore the smell of it."

He couldn't help laughing for sometimes he, too, enjoyed the aroma more than the taste. "Shall we begin?"

Together, they had written the short, impressive missive before the coffee cooled.

"I hope you will let me know as soon as you hear back from the House of Neble," she said.

"I shall. I would hate to receive a stern lecture from—" Edward stopped himself and looked at the ticking clock on the mantel. "Dear God. I am supposed to be at King's College giving a lecture in fifteen minutes."

Radiance, to his surprise, didn't look as alarmed as he felt.

"Do you ride, Mr. Lockwood?"

"Of course."

She rose quickly to her feet and bypassed the bellpull to go into the hallway. Unlike his own staff, the Diamonds' servants were attentive. Almost instantly, he heard her giving instructions for a horse to be saddled and brought around from the mews behind their home.

"Hurry," she urged.

When she re-entered, Edward had already folded the single sheet and stuffed it into his pocket and was tugging on his gloves.

"You'll find that one of our mounts will get you to your appointed talk faster than a hired carriage."

"I'm sure it will, my lady. I thank you."

"You're most welcome." She led him back to the front door where the butler was already waiting to open it.

"It was an interesting day," she said.

"Indubitably, it was." He gave her a shallow bow, which seemed odd considering he'd nibbled her soft skin and touched her delectable posterior.

Perhaps Radiance, too, thought it a little formal, for she raised a dark ginger eyebrow.

Shrugging, he turned to the sound of horse's hooves.

"I shall return it anon," he promised.

EDWARD HAD BEEN ONLY a little late for his lecture. Afterward, he went out for wine and beef with a few of the other professors who'd been lingering in the hallway, including Mr. Maurice, their esteemed professor of theology as well as of English literature and history. The year prior, he'd been accused of heterodoxy and asked to resign, which he'd refused to do.

Apparently, he was hard at work upon more theological essays, and the others were trying to tame his views with little success.

Thus, after a brief disagreement over whether to go as far as Dick's on Fleet Street while ultimately settling for Simpson's Divan nearby on the Strand, Edward was roped into the fascinating theology discussion. He stayed long after they switched from wine to brandy.

It was late when he returned to Lord and Lady Diamond's home with the borrowed steed. Rather than interrupting the earl's household, Edward rode around to the mews, awakened the lowest member of the groom's staff, and made sure the horse was safely stabled.

He couldn't help looking up at the back of the house, wondering which bedroom held the mesmerizing Radiance. To his shock, she was standing in the window. To his further astonishment, she opened the sash and leaned out, her red hair hanging before her shoulder in a thick braid, easily seen in the moonlight.

He sent up thanks for the unusually cloudless sky.

"Greetings, my lady. I hope I didn't awaken you."

"Oh no, sir. I was reading while awaiting your return."

"I should have told you not to wait." He felt badly thinking of her struggling to keep her eyes open.

She laughed. "I assure you I was so thoroughly engaged by a fascinating book that the time flew by. How was your lecture?"

"A goodly one. And thanks be to you, I didn't disappoint a room full of burgeoning geologists. But I did miss having you there." Edward clamped his mouth closed. *Why on earth did he say that?*

Even though it wasn't bright lamplight, he still thought he could see her smile.

"How kind of you, sir. However, I could not simply walk into the hallowed halls of King's College as if it was a public lecture hall."

"What about Lord . . . I'm sorry, his name has escaped me. That forward chap from the lecture at Somerset House. I saw him again at the ball."

Edward had a nasty habit of letting names slip from his memory if the person wasn't important to him. A bad trait, indeed. Almost as bad as forgetting he was supposed to lecture. There were probably any number of other things he'd already forgotten that he had forgot.

"You mean Lord Woolley, sir. He is a friend of my brother-in-law, and I didn't wish to ask his lordship again to sponsor me as I wouldn't want to give him the wrong impression."

Edward stood a little taller, glad she had said that, although it wasn't his business whether she liked Woolley or not. Then he had an idea.

"I can sponsor you the next time you wish to go to a lecture at the Geological Society." Another surprising utterance from his own mouth. Maybe he'd had more brandy than he realized.

To his alarm, she leaned farther across the window sill.

"Would you truly?" she asked.

Only then did he realize she was undressed and wearing a nightgown. *The minx!*

The moonlight caught a collar of frilly white lace, making it glow, while the delicate pink satin of her gown shimmered. His breath caught in his throat.

For a few seconds, he looked at the brick wall before him, wondering if it were scalable. Then he came to his senses.

"Yes, truly. With your interest in gemstones and your apprenticeship at Bonwit's, there is no reason you shouldn't be admitted to the society on your own merit."

"Oh, Edward!" she exclaimed before clamping a hand over her own mouth.

ALL EVENING, WHILE TRYING to focus on a book about spinels, the spectacular mineral which had been confused with rubies and sapphires for over a thousand years and was now causing such trouble for the Queen, Radiance had been keeping her ears perked for horse's hooves.

Edward would either forget he had their horse and leave it at the King's College stable or be a good sport and return it to their mews. If he remembered it, he was the type of man who wouldn't leave a horse out front tied to the railing, nor knock on their door at a late hour.

As soon as she laid eyes on him, Radiance had been flirting shamelessly, hoping he would notice her state of undress and maybe even spy the curve of her bosom.

But she certainly hadn't meant to blurt out his name like a tawdry harlot. Although leaning out the window, trying to show him her wares, she was halfway to behaving like one.

Immediately, Radiance drew back inside.

"My apology for being forward, Mr. Lockwood," she said, now barely able to see him.

"Please, think nothing of it, my lady. We have arrived at a state of mutual regard, I think, when we can occasionally, in private I mean, address one another by our given names."

Radiance felt warmed by his remark, while wondering how they might enjoy the privacy that was reserved for the married. However, in the tidbits she'd heard from her sisters, one could sometimes arrange for it.

"I agree wholeheartedly," she said. But not wishing to appear eager, she added, "And now, I must go to sleep. I am expected at Mr. Bonwit's first thing tomorrow for a lesson on working gold and silver in the repoussé technique."

"Very good," came Edward's voice. "I am impressed indeed. Good night, my lady."

"Good night, sir."

RADIANCE HAD FALLEN ASLEEP almost at once. Feeling full of hopeful exuberance, she entered Mr. Bonwit's tidy shop the following day. Two customers were at the glass case, attended by young Miss Rachel Bonwit, who had no interest in making jewelry, only in wearing it and selling it.

"Good day, Lady Radiance," the jeweler's daughter said as she always did when there were patrons in the store. "This is the Earl Diamond's daughter," Miss Bonwit added, earning Radiance a long glance from both customers.

"Good day," she said to each before continuing her way toward the back where stairs led up to the jewelry maker's room. Mr. Bonwit's daughter's words reached her.

"That lady, an *earl's* daughter, mind you, works alongside my father because she thinks our jewelry to be so very, very fine. And she wears it herself, of course."

Radiance smiled, not minding being used in the least if it helped. After all, she wouldn't have approached Mr. Bonwit if she hadn't thought him a skilled artisan. Although, the term "work" still rubbed her the wrong way. It wasn't as if she would be caught dead behind the counter showing rings and necklaces or taking money from customers.

Upstairs, she nodded to Mr. Carmichael, who was an actual apprentice. He had no other means of support and stayed with Mr. Bonwit's family in their upper-middle-class residence north of Russell Square. Radiance had the notion if he played his cards correctly, then he might find himself wed to the pretty Miss Bonwit one day and inheriting the entire business.

The young man cleared his throat as he always did before speaking.

"Mr. Bonwit left you something on your table, my lady. He was called away and promised to instruct you in the *repoussé* technique next time you come."

"Thank you," Radiance told him as a wave of disappointment crashed over her. Hoping Mr. Bonwit had left her something interesting to practice, she slid open the envelope and drew out a single page as well as a gold ring with finely detailed leaves supporting a single sapphire.

My Dear Lady,

Sorry to disappoint you. We shall have a lesson in repoussé the next time you come. If you would use the talent you already have and create a replica of the sapphire ring, I will be much obliged. Don't let Carmichael try to pull seniority over you or take the project away. Sadly, he is still behind you in cutting stones, although his en tremblant *brooches are second to none.*

Sincerely,
Bonwit

Radiance glanced up at the man who earnestly watched her to see what she would be doing. After sliding the ring on her finger, she rose to her feet and went to the safe box where raw stones were kept. From the drawer of rough sapphires, divided into smaller compartments by size, she lifted out one stone and then another, comparing each to the one in the ring on her left hand.

Choosing a comparable size, she signed out the stone, writing her name as well as the carat size on the small ledger before closing the drawer.

Back at her worktable, after putting on her magnifying spectacles, she felt the pure joy of polishing the planes with the scaif. And then she forgot about Mr. Carmichael and lost all track of time.

"I am leaving for the day, my lady," the apprentice said, and Radiance finally looked around. She had risen from her seat only once in the past few hours to get the molding wax so she could copy the gold band.

"You are exceptionally skilled at both design and at polishing," he added.

"You only need more practice," she told him, immediately realizing it was an insult.

Sure enough, he reddened. After all, he'd been at the craft of jewelry-making for a year and a half already. And she'd had far less training. However, she had spent endless hours learning about each stone's distinct planes of least bonds in order to create cleanly cut cleavages. Once committing those to memory, she could "see" where to make the correct cut, almost without thinking.

Mr. Carmichael still erred by trying to polish a facet that lay parallel to the cleavage plane. His polishing led to flaking and a rough surface. But that was for Mr. Bonwit to discuss with his apprentice. Not her.

"As for me," Radiance added to soothe him, "I have tried for many hours and cannot affix the little springs for *en tremblant* the way you do so effortlessly."

He nodded, seemingly appeased.

"Perhaps, if Mr. Bonwit lacks the time," the apprentice suggested, "then I could give you a lesson at your convenience."

Unsure whether he was being genuine, condescending, or flirtatious, she neither accepted nor turned him down.

"That is very kind of you to offer. Thank you. I bid you good afternoon."

"Aren't you coming now?" He approached her work station. "I would be honored to walk you to your carriage."

Oh dear. Maybe he was flirting with her. Footsteps on the stairs distracted them both. Miss Bonwit appeared and looked at Mr. Carmichael, standing close to her table, then at Radiance and back again.

As if guilty, Radiance felt her cheeks heat. A curse of her red-headed, creamy-skinned Irish ancestors, causing her to blush with anger, happiness, guilt, or for just about any thought that crossed her mind.

Miss Bonwit pressed her lips into a flat line of disapproval. She nearly turned to leave, then seemingly recalled she'd come upstairs for a reason.

"You," she said with annoyance, looking at Radiance, "have a visitor."

"Excuse me. Do you mean a customer?"

"No." With that, and a last glare at Mr. Carmichael, Miss Bonwit turned heel and left.

Radiance exchanged an awkward glance with the man as she rose to her feet, and he gestured for her to precede him.

To Radiance's surprise, when she entered the shop, the ankle rubber from the Palace meeting awaited her.

"Mr. Rathmond," she declared, greeting the man with his shock of black hair, dark eyes, and patrician nose. "How on earth did you know I was here?"

As if an echo of Mr. Hope, he said, "The jeweler's community is a small one."

She ought to have expected the predictable answer.

"I suppose you're right." Still, she knew he would have had to ask more than one person about her in order to find out she was at Mr. Bonwit's. "However," she pointed out, "I am *not* a jeweler."

"Your interest in it and that you study with Mr. Bonwit are becoming well known. In fact, I barely had to mention you to another jeweler, and here I am."

He looked her up and down.

The situation was most unusual. Normally, only men who were hopeful suitors visited Radiance, and they came to the safety of her home. At Bonwit's, she was not under the protection of her parents.

Conversely, since they had been introduced at the Palace, she supposed there was nothing untoward in speaking with him in a public place, as long as they were not left alone.

Before she could make sure of that, Mr. Carmichael interrupted to bid her good afternoon and strode out of the store. Moreover, Miss Bonwit was suddenly nowhere to be found.

A feather of fear tickled her spine as she faced Mr. Rathmond.

CHAPTER NINETEEN

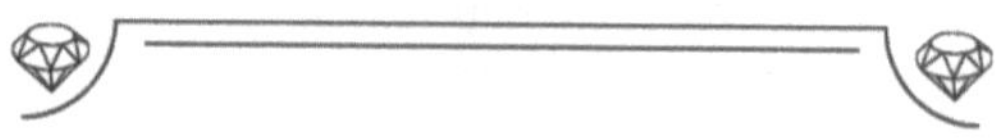

Squaring her shoulders, Radiance crossed her arms. "Why did you find it necessary to locate my whereabouts?"

Mr. Rathmond tilted his head, taking so long to answer she grew wary, her skin prickling. "I want to ask you a question," he said at last. "Why were you at the meeting?"

Radiance frowned. She certainly didn't have to answer him. "You ought to have dropped your card at my home. If I wanted to speak with you, then I would have returned an invitation."

"My mistake," he said. "However, since I am here, perhaps you will do me the honor of a response." Strangely, he managed to crowd her without moving an inch closer.

Disconcerted, she answered, simply to get him to leave. "I was there as Mr. Lockwood's guest and with the full approval of Her Majesty."

"Her *Majesty*," he repeated, giving the slightest shake of his head. "Can you imagine our little Queen is the ruler of India?"

Radiance wasn't sure what to make of that. "I can easily imagine it, sir, because Queen Victoria is, indeed, the ruler of India."

"*Hm.* Why did the Queen want you in the meeting?"

Radiance was ready for his impudent question. "I have a good eye," giving him no further explanation. "What is *your* part in ensuring the Koh-i-Noor is improved for the Queen?"

"Do you know who I am?" he countered.

She nearly laughed. It was the kind of question better asked by a titled man of importance, a duke, or even her own father.

"You are Mr. Rathmond, a gem dealer, and that is all I know."

"Then allow me to enlighten you. I have traveled the world and met with heads of state. I have bought and sold many fortunes while not yet making my own, and I have procured the best *for* the best, or at least those who think they are."

"Whatever do you mean?" she asked, a little flummoxed by his poetic way of speaking.

"The best gemstones for the best people. Royalty, nobility, patrons of the arts if the 'art' in question is jewelry."

"How did *you* come to be at the meeting?" she asked for he hadn't answered her question any better than she had answered his.

"I was invited because of my extensive knowledge of gemstones and also having seen the work of many jewelers around the globe."

If that was the case, then she would respect his opinion. "Do you believe inviting the Dutch to recut the Koh-i-Noor is the correct decision?"

Mr. Rathmond stared a long moment in utter silence, making her fervently wish Miss Bonwit would reappear.

"Lady Radiance Diamond," he whispered her name, and she shivered. "I am not sure that is the correct question we should be asking ourselves."

Then he looked around himself, perhaps realizing they were alone.

Radiance was no shrinking violet. Nevertheless, having been told by her father from a young age to listen to the little voice inside her—one that was telling her she was in danger—she considered her options. Either run for the back door, the stairs, or the front. She moved toward the entrance.

Luckily, the door was still unlocked and yielded to her tugging its handle. In the next instant, she was on the street amongst the many passersby. Some held packages, baskets, and bags, or strolled along unencumbered. Those nearby gawked when she burst from Bonwit's shop without her coat and gloves as if she didn't know the rules of civility, charging out onto the sidewalk half dressed, impeding people, nearly treading upon someone's toe.

"Lady Radiance," Mr. Rathmond said directly behind her having followed closely, "did I upset you in some way? I only meant I wasn't sure the famed and historic diamond should be cut at all, regardless be it by the Dutch or the British."

"Of course, I merely needed some air. I've been cooped up for hours."

"Doing what, may I ask?"

"Polishing a sapphire," she said without thinking.

His face remained passive except for the smallest tick in the muscle of his jaw. "Do you seek to be a better lapidary than the Dutch?"

She raised her chin. "Maybe I already am, Mr. Rathmond. And now, I bid you good afternoon." Walking around him, she entered the shop and locked the door behind her before drawing down the shade over the glass. Radiance wasn't usually one to tremble, but her fingers had a definite shake as she did so.

"Maybe I am," she repeated. *What a ridiculous, prideful thing to say to a man who had seen the best!* She had no idea why she'd said it, either.

Recalling the sapphire at her table, she hoped it had turned out as well as she'd imagined and climbed the stairs to tidy away her work. She was more than ready to go home.

RADIANCE RAPPED ON MR. Lockwood's door two mornings later. Another day had passed with no word from him regarding the House of Neble, and she couldn't contain her impatience. *When would they meet with the jeweler?*

If Edward wasn't at home, it would not have been a wasted trip for she would go to Neble's by herself, pry Sarah from the carriage, and at least take a look at the inventory of his shop.

Luckily, Mr. Lockwood's housekeeper opened the door, looking far less surprised than the previous time.

"He's in his workroom," Mrs. McSabby said. "If you'll follow me."

Radiance did as invited and was promptly shown into Edward's private study. His back was to the door, and he was bent over, examining something.

When he didn't immediately turn around at their footsteps, the housekeeper said, "Mr. Lockwood, you have company."

"I have no time for company," he replied. "Send whoever it is away. Say that I'm out."

The housekeeper looked at Radiance and shrugged.

"He's out, m'lady."

Radiance smiled. "I can see that you are in, Mr. Lockwood."

Indeed, she could also see the fine shape of his buttocks and his thighs, for again, he wore no coat, but simply had his shirt tucked into his trousers and a waistcoat over it.

The view disappeared when he whirled around at the sound of her voice.

"The deuce!" he exclaimed. Then frowned. "Mrs. McSabby, I didn't mean for you to say any such thing *if* the visitor is in the same room with me."

"Yes, sir," said the housekeeper. "Shall I send her away regardless?"

"No, thank you. That won't be necessary." His expression relaxed as he looked at Radiance. "But please bring us some coffee."

"Yes, sir, but I think you left the last pot full." She went to a table where the cat was stretched out. "Shoo, you moggie."

Monty did not move a whisker. Mrs. McSabby picked up the silver decanter, tall like a chocolate pot. She gave it a little shake.

"As I suspected, you haven't drunk a drop."

"Then reheat it, please," Edward said.

Radiance wrinkled her nose. It would taste even worse than fresh coffee, and she already didn't love that.

"Please don't go to any trouble on my account," she said. "I don't need anything at all."

Edward sighed. "Very well. Leave it, then, Mrs. McSabby. If I want some, I'll drink it cold."

"You'll forget, and I'll be clearing that away and tossing it down the kitchen drain in another few hours," the woman scoffed before she left.

Radiance had never heard a member of staff, not even a head of household, speak to her employer in such a tone. Ignoring the impudence, she went over to the cat and stroked its head. Monty seemed to like her, or at least, he didn't show an ounce of animosity, which might not be the same thing as liking.

"Do you often forget to drink your coffee?" she asked Edward.

"I didn't realize it, but I guess I do. I must exasperate my staff with my requests for such things as coffee and . . ." He looked around.

Radiance spied a plate with a sandwich on it at the same time as he did.

"And sandwiches," he added. "Although I don't recall asking for one today. It must be from yesterday. I wondered why I was so hungry by dinner. Quite famished last night."

Radiance nearly laughed. "There's also a plate with sliced apple, bread, and cheese."

"Ah, yes," he said. "Now that *is* from today. My stomach was rumbling, having skipped breakfast."

"I can see why Mrs. McSabby might balk at bringing you anything more."

He shrugged. "What can I do for you, my lady? Perhaps a piece of cheese?"

The dried-out chunks were entirely unappealing, unlike the man who stood before her.

"No, I came because I was having trouble waiting any longer to hear from you."

He cocked his head, making her insides melt. Edward Lockwood was attractive without knowing, which made him yet more so.

"Waiting to hear from me?" Absently, he popped a piece of cheese into his mouth, making a slight face of distaste before he chewed and swallowed.

Radiance wondered when he would realize his current state of undress and don his coat. Not soon, she hoped, unwilling to tell him it was slung over the back of a chair pushed against the wall.

"Yes," she said. "I hoped you would send word."

"Did you?" He appeared flummoxed. "Whatever for?"

Radiance had no answer except to wonder why he was toying with her. A small flame of anger flickered to life inside of her.

"Mr. Neble," she reminded him, watching as understanding crossed his face.

It was plain to see he had forgotten his promise. His expression would be comical if she hadn't been on tenterhooks awaiting a missive from him practically each hour.

"The deuce," he said again.

Twice swearing before her—Radiance knew Purity would be appalled. And he was still in only shirt and waistcoat.

"How could you forget when we had a plan? All you had to do was tell me when you heard back from him. I am most disappointed." Radiance crossed her arms. "However, now that I'm here, you can tell me his response in person."

CHAPTER TWENTY

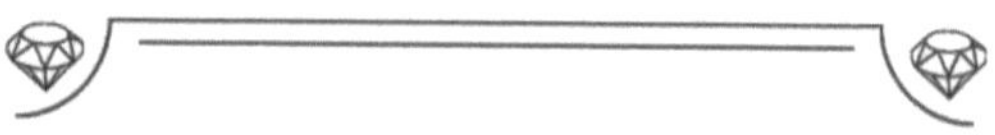

Edward felt like a dunce. Everything had slipped his mind when he'd been brought a magnificent find, opals from Australia, gifted by a fellow geologist who knew of his great interest. He had devoted the better part of the past two days to studying them, dissecting a few, and even trying to set one on fire.

"Fascinating," he wrote in his notes. "A silica-based mineral that is non-crystalline. Rather the opal is made up of gelatinous blobs less than a micron in diameter." And he hadn't finished examining them yet.

"I haven't heard back," he confessed. *Dare he tell her?* He had to, although he hated to lose her good favor.

Striding over to his coat, he slid his hand into the pocket and withdrew the single sheet. "Because I haven't yet sent the letter we worked on together."

Even wearing a gaping expression, she was a stunning beauty.

"How could you forget to send it?"

"I had opals . . . ," he began.

"But the Queen," she countered. "And Mr. Hope and poor Mr. Minton."

Edward hung his head, feeling like a naughty child. In truth, he was simply a distracted one. He had ever been thusly. When something caught his attention, everything else seemed to lose any importance. He'd often thought he should employ a secretary, but he kept forgetting to look in the paper.

Why, he even needed a helpful person to remind him to look for another helpful person! He didn't say that, as he had an idea Lady Radiance wouldn't find the humor in it.

Embarrassed, wishing he'd at least sent off the damn missive, even if he had subsequently forgotten to heed the answer, he grabbed for a slice of stale bread and bit into it.

Another bad idea. It was monstrously dry. While he chewed manfully, the beautiful woman before him seemed to be reddening with annoyance.

It took him another few moments to swallow before he poured himself a cupful of coffee. Cold and bitter as expected, but it did the trick of washing the last crumbs down his sorry gullet.

Then he spied the milk in its miniature pitcher. "Mrs. McSabby is always trying to get me to put milk in my coffee, the way she takes her tea. I argued with her for months, and then came to find out it's the Austrian method, and even farther away, how they prepare it in the Orient, too. Although my housekeeper has never been in a coffeehouse in her life, she was spot on. And I have come to appreciate her dubious wisdom."

Radiance said nothing as he poured all the milk into the inky black coffee.

"Probably putting in the sugar is a fool's errand," he remarked into the silence while Radiance glared at him. He put in a single teaspoon, anyway.

"The sugar crystals won't melt, as you know, and the coffee will be crunchy." He smiled, trying to soothe her with some levity. Then he took a sip. "Crunchy cold coffee. Could there be anything worse?"

"Yes," she hissed. "Waiting for two days for an important message that never came, only to find out it never will."

"Ah, well, I suppose that *is* worse." *What could he do besides apologize?* "I am terribly sorry."

Noticing her hands were balled into sweet feminine fists at her sides, he set the cup down. Radiance was adorable. She also had every right to be furious with him.

"Since you have been waiting and since I've made a muck of it, why don't we go to the House of Neble directly. We shall skip the letter altogether and take our chances. Would that satisfy you, my lady?"

She relaxed her hands. "But you said he doesn't see anyone, and Mr. Garrard implied the same."

While it was the truth, Edward hoped Neble's reticence didn't apply to the nobility, after all.

"Let us try. If he refuses to see us, then I'll send the letter, and we'll add something about your father particularly wanting to patronize his establishment."

That earned him a tight smile.

"We can but try," she said. "Your coat."

"The deuce!" he exclaimed and hurried into it. "You should have said something."

She held up her hand. "I was not offended."

With a backward glance at his opals, Edward could scarcely believe how dreadfully slipshod he'd been recently. And it wasn't only Radiance whom he'd let down. The Queen needed his help. And he'd been selfishly categorizing his latest interest while those who depended on him awaited his better self.

Once again, he took a seat in the Earl Diamond's carriage with Radiance and the silently reading Sarah. They passed through the jewelry neighborhood of Hatton Garden to the eastern-most section and stopped at Neble's establishment on Saffron Hill.

"You may remain here," Radiance said to her maid.

Edward didn't protest but simply pushed open the door to the shop, stepped aside, and let the lady precede him.

Not bright and busy as a jewelry store on Bond Street, nor steeped in dark wood and history like Garrard's, Neble's was tucked away, small, and—*dare he say it?*—dingy.

Nevertheless, a clerk in a starched apron approached when they entered.

"May I help you?" the man asked.

"My name is Lockwood. This is Lady Radiance Diamond. We were hoping to . . . ," but he trailed off when the clerk gawked at Radiance, probably because of her name. In any case, he had plainly stopped listening.

Edward coughed to regain the man's attention. "We wish to speak to Mr. Neble."

Without hesitation, the clerk responded, "I am sorry, sir, but that is impossible."

Radiance spoke before Edward had a chance to argue. "Is Mr. Neble here?"

"Yes, my lady."

"Then how can it be impossible to see him?" she asked.

The clerk shot Edward a look as if it were his fault that he'd brought a difficult female to the shop.

"Because he is working. He remains in his workroom most all hours of the day and sometimes into the night, too. That is why he hires people like me to meet with customers."

"What if the customer wishes to order something specially designed by Mr. Neble?" Edward asked.

The clerk shrugged. "I am well versed in all types of jewelry. You can show me something here in the store and tell me how you want it altered. Then I impart your wishes to Mr. Neble. Or I can sketch what you wish if you can describe it."

"There's no need for that," Radiance said. "Please give this to Mr. Neble." She reached into her reticule and handed the clerk a folded piece of paper.

Unfolding it, the man spared a quick glance before frowning.

Radiance put her gloved finger on the drawing. "Tell him I have the central stone in that armlet. I want to know if he can recut it to make it sparkle."

"It seems to be a large stone," the clerk remarked. "In need of cutting—or polishing as we call it. What type of stone is it, please?"

Edward was looking at the sketch upside down but recognized it at once. Surprised, he glanced at Radiance. Her expression was a study in boredom.

"It is a diamond, of course. But I do not wish to discuss this with you. I intend to discuss it with Mr. Neble."

"As I told you, my lady, you cannot," the man said again.

"Take him the drawing," Radiance insisted. "We shall await his response."

"Very well, but I tell you, it will do you no good."

"We'll see. Won't we?" She looked past the clerk. The discussion was finished.

Edward thought her marvelous.

When they were alone, listening to the clerk's footsteps on the stairs, he whispered, "That was the Koh-i-Noor."

"Indeed, it was."

"You are an excellent artist. And your plan is a good one, trying to lure Neble out of his den."

Her smile was genuine this time. "Thank you. I am hoping he shan't be able to resist."

In a very brief time, the clerk returned. Alone. Edward wondered if even the Queen herself could get the man out of his workshop.

"Mr. Neble will see you upstairs," the man said, his tone subdued.

"Isn't that accommodating of him?" Radiance remarked evenly.

Without hesitation, not waiting for the clerk to lead her, she simply headed to the stairs. Edward watched the sway of her full, flounced skirt, a mesmerizing movement, and had to prod himself to follow.

With a backward glance at the clerk, who'd also been watching her attractive swinging way of walking, Edward hurried after her.

He had never met Mr. Neble before, but his reputation as a goldsmith was legendary. However, his demeanor as a recluse was becoming more so. The clerk caught up to them halfway along the passage and led them to his employer's office.

He knocked, waited, heard the beckoning call of "enter" before opening the door.

"Sir, these are the people I told you about. Lady Radiance, Mr. Lockwood, this is Mr. Neble."

"Come in," the older gentleman said. Then he demanded, "Who is manning my shop?"

The clerk scurried back the way they had come.

Edward followed Radiance, expecting a dark and gloomy room to match the dinginess of the downstairs and the purported mood of the master jeweler. Instead, there were more lamps than would normally be found in a space thrice its modest size. The window curtains were open, too, letting in the watery London sun. He nearly had to squint at the room's brightness.

Before him, seated at a large worktable was a hunched older man who'd retained a full head of hair, which was exceedingly white. Perhaps it looked so snowy because of the lamps, both those on the table beside Mr. Neble as well as those hanging above him and the rest that stood on the floor around him.

The jeweler was wearing not one but two pairs of spectacles and still held Radiance's drawing in his hands close to his face. He didn't rise, despite the entrance of a lady, which made him seem a low individual until he spoke.

"Forgive me for not standing." He addressed Radiance. "My knees are not good at all. By the time I rose for courtesy's sake, the sun would have set." He actually chuckled to himself.

Thus far, he was not at all what Edward expected.

"Please, take a seat." Mr. Neble waved his hand that held the paper toward the vacant space on the other side of his table, as if chairs were there.

Edward looked around. Sure enough, a few small, ladder-back chairs were lined up against the wall behind them, on either side of the closed door.

"I rarely have visitors, so it seemed best to push them out of the way," Mr. Neble explained. "With such an arrangement, my canes don't get caught upon them when I walk."

Radiance hadn't yet said a word. Edward admired the way she purposefully waited and watched and didn't blurt out silly things, nor had she taken offense at not having a chair awaiting her.

Quickly, he drew two of them across the room. As he and Radiance seated themselves, Edward looked at the man's worktable. It reminded him of his own, except there were also instruments for working with gold and silver and an abundance of magnifying spectacles.

"It was good of you to see us," Radiance finally spoke.

"I wanted to see the Queen," Mr. Neble said. "It's been many years since I have looked upon your face, Your Majesty, but you appear quite unlike yourself."

Edward exchanged a glance with Radiance. *Was he speaking seriously, a confused old man, or in jest?*

Again, Mr. Neble chuckled, seeming less and less like the reclusive, crotchety curmudgeon Edward had expected.

"But you are obviously *not* Queen Victoria, so why did you send me a drawing of the Koh-i-Noor as if it was in your possession?"

CHAPTER TWENTY-ONE

Radiance hoped Edward didn't start spouting forth a lie about her wanting him to make her a piece of jewelry and, thus, bringing her own personal geologist with her. She could tell at once that Mr. Neble was sharp as a tack, and such unnecessary deceit would be disrespectful.

"Sir, we wish to speak with you about a matter of extreme importance relating to the Queen." She considered how best to approach the delicate matter.

"We were recently visiting Mr. Minton," she added, seeing Edward startle out of the corner of her eye. "He was found guilty of replicating one of the Queen's sapphires and stealing the real one. Do you know him?"

Mr. Neble hesitated. "I do not know him personally. However, I know *of* him. The jeweler's community is a small one. If you were visiting with him, then you were at Newgate."

"Indeed, we were."

The old man nodded. "A very strange thing to think an old jeweler like him would want to risk everything on such a scurrilous endeavor."

Mr. Neble could have been speaking about himself.

"Forgive my boldness, sir, but there was another forgery."

Edward shook his head. Radiance shrugged one shoulder. She probably ought not to have spoken of it outright. But how else would they learn the truth?

"There was, indeed," Mr. Neble said, and nothing more.

Edward leaned forward and said, "We won't insult you by pretending not to know that the other piece with the fake stone, the coronet, was cleaned—"

"Originally made, occasionally cleaned, and rarely, if needed, repaired," Mr. Neble declared, "by me!"

"And that is why we're here," Radiance said, keeping her tone so mild she might have been speaking about how many spoonsful of sugar were best in tea, rather than a terrible crime perpetrated against Queen Victoria.

"Did you make the sketch?" Mr. Neble asked.

"I did, sir."

"Then you've seen the diamond, haven't you?"

"I have," she agreed.

"May I ask how? Was it at the Great Exhibition?"

"Yes, sir. I saw it there."

He paused. "I didn't go."

She thought he sounded sad and wondered if his poor knees had kept him from enjoying one of the wonders of the ages. There was also the matter of the many lamps and spectacles.

"I didn't need to go to a crowded, badly lit place like that," Mr. Neble continued. "I've seen the best jewelry in Britain and made some of it myself. Probably nothing else of any interest at the so-called Crystal Palace."

Radiance decided to leave off her usual raving over the exhibits. It would be like rubbing salt in a wound.

"We cannot help wondering how you managed to clear your name, sir," Edward interjected, surprising Radiance with his directness, "when Mr. Minton was unsuccessful."

"I didn't need to clear it because I didn't do anything wrong," the jeweler said.

"Mr. Minton said the same thing," Radiance told him. "Yet he was not believed."

Mr. Neble sat up a little straighter, only long enough to sniff loudly and proclaim, "But I *own* the House of Neble." Then he hunched over again with a sigh.

Edward spoke again, "May we ask how the circumstances differed?"

Mr. Neble picked up a magnifying glass and looked again at the drawing he still held. Then he set both down.

"I cannot know how they differed because I have never spoken to Mr. Minton."

"Don't you wish to find out who tampered with the coronet you created?" Radiance asked. "Aren't you curious as to who took the emerald and replaced it with a tourmaline?"

The older man shrugged. "It has nothing to do with me."

Radiance sighed. They were getting nowhere.

"Would you at least tell us whether the Lord Chamberlain brought the coronet from the Palace, or did you collect it?"

"It has been a long time since last I was at Buckingham Palace or at the royal family's prior residence of St. James's, although I enjoyed more than one meeting with the king there. It would be difficult now," Mr. Neble said.

As if embarrassed by his failing legs and eyesight, he added, "Even if summoned, I wouldn't go to the Palace like a lackey. My father was a master jeweler. I am a master jeweler. My son, had he lived, would be, too."

"I am sorry for your loss," Radiance said softly.

She glanced at Edward. "Who last brought the coronet to you for cleaning?" he persisted.

"A Lord Chamberlain, as you surmised."

"There is only one, isn't there?" Radiance asked.

Mr. Neble frowned. "There have been many," he said. "Sometimes they retire, sometimes they die, you know. We all die." His tone became brusque. "I have work to do, so you must leave. Unless that is, the two of you need a wedding ring."

She shot Edward a look. *What was it with these jewelers and their desire to create a ring for her nuptials?* She decided to be frank.

"By the time I marry, sir, I may be skilled enough to make my own wedding ring."

"How can that be?" Mr. Neble asked.

"I am learning from Mr. Bonwit."

"Is that so? Bonwit? A good jeweler," he declared.

Without another word, he donned two pairs of spectacles, one over the other. Surely there was a better way to get more magnification than that. She'd seen some impressive magnifying lenses at the exhibit.

Mr. Neble seemed unbothered by the extra weight on the bridge of his nose or around his ears. Picking up what appeared to be a blue topaz with pincers, he brought it close to his face, squinted, and shook his head.

Setting it down, he next captured a sapphire in the tiny metal points. Again bringing it close to his face, he nodded with satisfaction.

Radiance was about to rise, feeling defeated when Edward pressed their case.

"Did you perform the coronet's last cleaning here in your workshop?"

Nearly dropping the gemstone, Mr. Neble bristled. "Of course I did it. Who else?"

"There is no need to raise your voice," Edward said. "I am simply asking if you are the only jeweler here. Do you have apprentices? If not, how will the House of Neble continue?"

Mr. Neble started to sputter. "That is none of your business."

"I believe we should go," Radiance said, fearing the older man would become apoplectic should they continue to aggravate him.

"Very well. You cleaned the Queen's coronet yourself," Edward persisted. "Who better since you made it? And then you handed it back to the Lord Chamberlain?"

"No, to a footman," Mr. Neble said. "I saw his livery, plain as day."

"Thank you," Radiance said, thinking there was nothing the poor man saw plain as day anymore. He was no help as far as she could tell. He might have seen the livery, but he probably could not make out the footman's face, nor identify him.

Rising to her feet, she waited for Edward to do the same. Then they bid Mr. Neble good day and left. Radiance didn't think her geologist realized how the jeweler's pride over his failing health was trapping him in his workroom.

About to tell him her thoughts, there, on a crowded street in full daylight, Radiance was shoved sideways into the brick building. She didn't even see the person who knocked her over. Her shoulder struck first and then the side of her head before she crumpled to the ground in pain.

WHEN RADIANCE OPENED her eyes after having squeezed them shut against the discomfort, Edward was beside her. Crouching low, he took hold of her hand.

"Can you stand, my lady?"

"Yes." Although her head was throbbing, and her shoulder ached.

When he helped her to her feet, she wobbled alarmingly, feeling as if the pavement were swaying like a ship's deck. She gripped his hand more tightly until the sensation passed.

"Let's get you into the carriage." Like a docile lamb, she let him lead her to her father's brougham.

After he assisted her inside, Radiance couldn't help collapsing onto the squabs beside her maid. By the time Edward had instructed the driver to take them back to her home and climbed in, Sarah had dropped her penny dreadful onto her lap.

"Blimey!" she exclaimed with an unladylike curse.

"Don't swear," Radiance admonished in a soft tone.

However, her normally silent maid was in grand form.

"What monstrous misfortune has befallen m'lady?"

Edward rolled his eyes. "She sounds like a Covent Garden actress. Probably those histrionic tales she's always reading have fueled her dramatic speech." He leaned forward and touched Radiance's hand. "Are you injured?"

"I think not. At least, not greatly and nothing of a permanent nature." She touched the side of her head then looked at her glove. *The barest smear of blood.* "I have an abrasion on my temple."

Instantly, Edward took her chin in hand, despite Sarah looking on. Tenderly, he turned her head before touching the scrape. Again, she saw a little blood.

"The shallowest of grazes," he assured her. And she did, in fact, find him a reassuring person, regretting the instant he released his gentle hold of her. Then she touched her own shoulder just as gingerly.

"I was momentarily stunned," she recalled. "Did you see him?"

"I caught a glimpse. Nothing out of the ordinary about him, a man with a black cap pulled down low and wearing a baggy brown coat. Not a gentleman, I warrant."

"With that, I would agree," Radiance muttered wryly.

"Are we going to Scotland Yard?" Sarah asked, her eyes like saucers.

Radiance frowned, then winced at the twinge on her temple. "Whatever for?"

"To give your statement to a sergeant or a detective," her maid said. "Someone attacked you, m'lady, probably hoping to crush your head, shatter your skull, and let your brains ooze out. Or at least leave you senseless, maybe even dead."

"Sarah!" Radiance admonished. "Those stories have addled your mind."

"Not at all, m'lady. But you and Mr. Lockwood are investigating a crime, aren't you? Just like in some of those stories. The criminal always tries to stop anyone from discovering his wicked behavior."

Radiance locked her gaze with Edward's golden-brown one and, at the same time, feeling the hair on the back of her neck rise. She knew he was thinking the same thing. Sarah might be right.

"We don't even know who the forger is," Radiance said. "My maid's idea is absurd, isn't it, sir?"

She wanted him to say it was a preposterous notion. Edward didn't.

"We've asked questions of a number of people," he pointed out.

She nodded slowly. "And even though we don't know much more than we did before, the forger doesn't know that. We might be missing something obvious."

"I do not know if there is an *obvious* perpetrator," he said, "but I am beginning to believe Mr. Neble was given favorable treatment over Mr. Minton."

"At last!" Radiance said. "Then this wasn't an utter waste of time, although close to it." Not to mention having cost her a pair of soiled gloves and an unsightly scrape.

"On the contrary," Edward said, "I think we learned a great deal."

She was rubbing her shoulder with her other hand and paused. "How? What do you mean?"

"Mr. Neble is nearly blind, don't you think?" he asked.

"Yes, I do," she agreed.

"I wonder who else knows his vision is so greatly impaired?" Edward mused. "Someone might have taken advantage of his situation. After all, Neble was extremely defensive about the cleaning and who might have done it."

"He was, but the poor man's son died."

"I fail to see why that fact has any relevance. Still, someone else must be doing the work for the House of Neble. Even with two pairs of spectacles, he mistook a topaz for a sapphire."

"What if he mistook the man who collected the piece for a royal footman when he wasn't any such person?"

Edward nodded. "I was wondering that, too, but another jeweler would still have had to make the fake stone and set it in the coronet. And the little crown made it safely back to the Palace. If a stranger had returned it, wouldn't someone have noticed?"

They sat in silence for the remainder of the journey to her home. In a minute, they would part, and they would have no reason to be close again until the next meeting of the Koh-i-Noor committee.

If only he would invite her to a concert or perhaps to the Cremorne Gardens in Chelsea. They were all the fashion, now that Vauxhall had gained a reputation for seediness, although many still thought the latter to be greatly amusing.

"Mr. Lockwood, do you enjoy music?"

"I would be a savage if I didn't. Why do you ask?"

"London has many good venues for listening to music, don't you think?"

"It does," he agreed affably, but his brain was clearly still focused upon the stolen gemstones. "Do you have any further suggestions for continuing our investigation?"

Radiance decided to try again. "We could discuss that very topic during a walk at Cremorne Gardens. Have you been there?"

He appeared surprised. "Once or twice. Hasn't everyone? Haven't you?"

"No," she admitted. "Yet I should very much like to."

"I recommend you see a balloon ascent if you go," he said. Then he frowned. "I think our next discussion should be with the Lord Chamberlain."

Radiance sighed. Perhaps the man simply wasn't interested in her despite the fabulous kiss, which she had hoped to repeat at the earliest possibility. Yet it was seemingly more and more impossible.

"Yes," she snapped. "We must go see Lord Exeter."

CHAPTER TWENTY-TWO

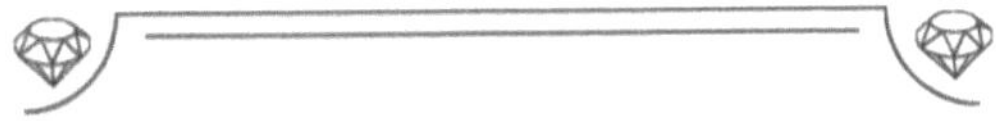

Edward wondered why Radiance sounded frustrated. Almost tweaguey. Perhaps she was still shaken from the incident. For his part, he had never been so frightened for someone else in his entire life.

He hadn't had time to react to the individual who careened into her and kept moving. The cad hadn't even paused to determine if he'd injured her. In any case, one of the most important people in his life—as he'd quickly realized—was upright one moment, then down upon the filthy street at his feet, the next.

Moreover, when her glorious eyes had opened in her pale face, he'd sent up a silent prayer of gratitude.

And now, plainly, she wanted a little fun. Oddly, she seemed to want it with him. Or maybe she was merely discontent due to the unsatisfactory meeting with Mr. Neble.

"I would wager Mr. Neble is not really reticent at all," he said into the carriage's silence. "He obviously cannot see well outside that illuminated workroom, and maybe he doesn't want anyone to know. After all, a jeweler losing his sight will also lose his business. I would also wager against him having done the cleaning of the coronet himself."

After a brief hesitation, during which he imagined Radiance was still dreaming of a visit to the Cremorne Gardens, she nodded.

"Perhaps there is someone working for him," she mused, "whom he wishes to keep secret."

"Someone who might have done something unlawful. Yet he cannot speak of it without admitting he is no longer capable of jewelry-making himself."

"More loose ends," Radiance said, crossing her arms under her splendid bosom.

Edward would love to take her to the pleasure gardens, but that would be akin to a declaration of intent, or the possibility of some future declaration at the very least. *Was he prepared for such?*

Then again, he didn't like to think of her exploring the gardens with some thundering buck. She didn't deserve to be pawed or slobbered upon.

In fact, with her sparkling, jewel-tone eyes staring back at him, he realized he couldn't *not* ask her. Obviously, she wished to experience the pleasure gardens. Just as plainly, he wanted to share the experience with her.

He could at least ask if she would like to go under his protection.

"Lady Radiance," he began, "as soon as you have healed from the brute who ran into you, would you be amenable to my accompanying you to the gardens in Chelsea?"

"Oh, yes, sir. That would be most agreeable." Then he was treated to a smile of her lovely bowed lips.

"You wish to go at night, I assume." Cremorne opened some days at three o'clock, but most days at five.

"Indeed, I do. I wish to avail myself of the full enjoyment of the gardens."

Good lord! He hoped she didn't say such a statement to another man.

"Such as the ballooning you mentioned. Also, the marionette show and the crystal grotto."

"Very well." He was growing excited at the thought of accompanying her and pleased to see the anticipation of such an outing had brought the color back into her face. She looked to have forgotten the shock of a few minutes earlier.

"As long as you don't insist we take the slow, three-penny steamer to Cremorne Pier," he teased, "for I think I would tear my hair out during the interminable and crowded voyage. We shall go at the desirable hour of eight. Will the fair Sarah attend with us?"

"I shall see if one of my married sisters will go," Radiance replied. "I think that would be more appropriate."

He felt a sliver of nervousness snake through him. First the parents, now the sisters. He thought of Lillian, not knowing if she had been to Cremorne or Vauxhall, for that matter. He would welcome having someone in his corner.

"Perhaps I should invite my own sister."

Radiance beamed at him. "Miss Lockwood is most welcome, sir."

And thus, not sure why he'd been compelled to invite Radiance, he would once more escort her out in public. Yet the previous time, at the Cobble House ball, they had not arrived together, so he doubted tongues had wagged or anyone had noticed their single dance. Arriving at Cremorne, their association would be obvious to anyone.

Two nights later, along with his sister who'd been thrilled with the invitation, Edward collected Radiance at her home. Her parents allowed him to whisk her away since Lillian was in their midst, with the understanding they would soon be under the watchful eye of her older sister, Lady Foxford.

"I wanted Clarity to come," Radiance explained, "but she was otherwise engaged."

Then she sighed and added, "Purity is perfectly lovely, and I am certain you will enjoy her company."

Edward couldn't help narrowing his eyes.

"Why did you speak thusly?"

"What do you mean?" Radiance asked innocently.

"You said I would like your sister as if you were trying to convince me or yourself."

She gave a little laugh. "She is known for being rather exacting, persnickety some might say."

"What do *you* say?" he asked.

"That she has a big heart and always does her best to make sure every civility is exercised in order for those around her to be at ease. She dislikes indecorous or uncontrolled behavior."

"Yet she married a rake."

Radiance gasped and looked at Lillian. Perhaps she wondered if his sister would be judgmental. He would like to assure her that she wasn't.

"How did you know about Lord Foxford?" Radiance asked.

"Once I found out I was becoming associated with one of the Diamonds, then I did a little investigating."

Her expression came over shocked. He couldn't help laughing.

"I promise you, I found out nothing more than whom your sisters and your brother married and that your parents are powerful and well liked."

"I see." She sounded uncertain.

"You aren't angry, are you?"

She hesitated. "No, I suppose I am not. Merely surprised. I would have told you anything you wanted to know."

Edward hadn't wished to ply her with questions. She might have got the wrong idea about his intentions. Besides digging into a subject, putting it under the magnifying glass as it were, was simply his nature.

"You shouldn't have been a sneaky nosey-poke," Lillian suddenly chimed in.

"What? A nosey-poke!" He wished he hadn't invited her if she were going to slander him.

Radiance raised a lovely auburn eyebrow as if to say, *See, even your own kin does not approve.*

"In the future, should I wish to know anything," he promised, "I shall ask you forthwith."

"The future," Lillian echoed. But she knew better than to ask outright whether the two people seated opposite one another were thinking of forming an attachment.

Radiance offered a small smile. "I shall endeavor to answer anything as openly and honestly as possible."

"Then tell me, how is your shoulder? As to your forehead, I cannot even see a blemish."

"Both have satisfactorily healed," she assured him.

"We've arrived," Lillian declared excitedly.

"I cannot believe I am here," Radiance said, her green eyes flashing.

Edward felt the same way. For him, he couldn't believe he was there with this particular female, an earl's daughter, instead of simply going with male chums as he had before.

"I want to see everything," Lillian said as they passed through the grand entrance to the gardens, located on King's Road. A large star-shaped lantern illuminated the ticket box, and then they were strolling the well-lit grounds.

And, indeed, they did see everything. Edward found it amusing, even heartening, to witness the two young ladies experience the pleasures of Cremorne for the first time. While still indubitably a garden—much more so than Vauxhall—there was every manner of show going on all over. There were side shows, shooting galleries, a fringe of ancient trees and a spacious avenue on which to promenade. There were also fountains and statuary; refreshment-bars, dining boxes, and tables.

"We can eat outside later or go into the hotel dining room," Edward said. "We can decide once we meet up with your family."

"A bowling saloon!" came her excited response, nothing to do with something as banal as eating. "I wish to try it. Don't you, Miss Lockwood?"

"Oh yes," Lillian agreed before lowering her voice. "I understand they have American-style drinks."

Edward smiled. "Then we shall bowl and drink. But I don't think we can do everything in one outing. There is a maze, too, don't forget, and some type of show in the south garden theater."

"I would like to see the marionettes in the smaller theater in the north garden," Radiance said, when suddenly she pivoted. "There they are."

"Sister!" she called out before hurrying across the lawn toward a dark-haired female accompanied by a brown-haired man. After embracing the former and touching the arm of the latter, Radiance turned and escorted them back to where he and Lillian waited.

"May I present Mr. Lockwood. He is a geologist. And his delightful sister, Miss Lockwood. This is Lord and Lady Foxford. But I'm sure you may call them by their—"

"Ray," Lady Foxford interrupted her sister. And that was all she needed to do to make Radiance stop the too-familiar offer she was about to make.

"It is a pleasure to meet you both," Edward said. "Have you been here before?"

As it turned out, they had. Lady Foxford, while looking nothing like Radiance, was intelligent and welcoming. Lord Foxford seemed an amiable fellow, quick to make a clever jest. They were only too happy to walk around Cremorne and see all the sights.

When they came upon the acrobats, their entire party fell silent. With a collective holding of their breath, they watched the famous Frenchman, Monsieur Blondin, walk across a suspension rope sixty feet in the air. The many lamps of the park illuminated the very spot in which the tightrope walker would land should he fall.

Fortunately, he didn't. When he made it safely to the second platform and began his descent on a flimsy rope ladder, they all breathed easier again.

"Time for some punch," Radiance's sister said.

"And dancing," Lillian chimed in. He would have to find her a suitable partner unless Lord Foxford would do the honor.

For his part, Edward was eager to take Radiance once again into his arms. Even more ready to be alone with her, but that was unlikely to happen given their chaperone was no longer a distracted housemaid.

He would take what was offered. As a waltz started, they took to the crowded floor, where hundreds of others also circled the merrily lit orchestra stand.

"Is Cremorne everything you hoped?"

"Yes, sir," she said, her green eyes looking up at him from under her auburn lashes. "And more." They whirled around the orchestra house. "Are you enjoying yourself?"

"I have never had a better time," he said. "I mean while at Cremorne." But truthfully, Edward was having a better evening than he could ever recall with any female who wasn't a high-flier. But that declaration might be a tad too candid.

He ought to keep a cool head where the lady was concerned. After all, meeting her sister's husband was a stark reminder that Radiance would be expected to make a match within the upper echelon of her class.

Yet the warmth of her under his hands reminded him that he needn't plan for the future. He should enjoy the time they were having that night and not think of anything more.

"I believe my sister approves of you," she said, surprising him.

He hadn't realized he needed Lady Foxford's approval.

"My sister likes you, too," he countered. It was true that Lillian had already said more than once what a jolly mort she was.

"Does she?"

He nodded and spun her around, then held her closer than perhaps the dance warranted. Her gaze sparkled with interest, making his stomach twinge. *How did Radiance manage to cause that flutter feeling like wings inside him?*

Regardless, she did. And more like a falcon's wings than a butterfly.

The music ended, and he led her from the floor. Lord and Lady Foxford had also been dancing, but Lillian was standing by herself. He ought to have stayed with her.

Edward asked the only other man in their group, "Lord Foxford, would you care to dance with my sister?"

"Oh, no," Lillian protested. "That's quite all right."

But with the ease of a former rake, Lord Foxford took her hand.

"You wound me, Miss Lockwood. Don't disappoint a married man who rarely has the chance to dance with another fair flower."

"Yes, please do," Lady Foxford said. "My husband is an excellent dancer, and I am happy to loan him to you."

Thus, Edward found himself alone with the two Diamond sisters. They couldn't be less alike than if they weren't related. Except for their expressions. They both wore matching ones, which seemed to be taking his measure.

Suddenly, his necktie felt too tight. Edward cleared his throat.

"Have you also been to Vauxhall?" he asked Lady Foxford.

The pretty dark-haired lady blinked. "Do you mean *also* as in *you* have been there and wonder if I, too, have been? Or *also* as in wondering if I have been there as well as here?"

"The latter," he clarified, feeling as if he must stay on his toes.

"Potentially, that is a good question in this social setting. If I had been there and you had as well, then we could compare the two pleasure gardens. However, I do not believe my sister has been to Vauxhall, and I would hate to leave her out of the conversation."

Lady Foxford asked Radiance. "Have you?"

"I haven't."

"And thus," Lady Foxford continued, "it is not a good topic at all since it leaves out the female you are escorting tonight." She finished with a slight shake of her head, as if Edward had greatly disappointed her.

With these rules, he struggled to think of something on which they could all speak.

"It would be acceptable for you to ask my sister if she wished to accompany you to Vauxhall," Lady Foxford added. "Then you could compare the merits of the two gardens together."

"I would enjoy the opportunity to do so," Radiance said.

Edward didn't like to be pressed into anything. On the other hand, if Radiance wished to go to Vauxhall, which wasn't a particularly wise idea given its decline, then he would prefer she went with him than some Johnny-raw or, worse, a slyboots. She needed protecting in these types of places, and he was happy to be her guardian.

"I shall be privileged to take you," he told her. "I suppose it would be most advantageous if you and your husband could come along, too," Edward addressed Lady Foxford.

She wrinkled her nose. "Not my cup of tea. Perhaps our brother and his wife or our other sister, not Lady Brilliance as she is of a tender age, but Lady Hollidge. After all, Foxy and I cannot have all the fun."

Radiance responded with a roll of her eyes. "Shall we go to the banqueting hall next? Or do you wish to dance again?"

"I am entirely at ease, either way," Edward said. As long as he was in her company, he didn't mind what they did. That, in itself, surprised him.

"A very sound response," Lady Foxford said. "Sister, do you wish to dance again?"

"If this is the last opportunity of the evening, then yes, I would like to."

Edward was glad of her answer. He welcomed another chance to hold her in his arms. Thus, as soon as one song ended, he drew her into the crowd as the next one began.

"What about your sister and mine?" Radiance asked.

"Lord Foxford will look after them both." They moved easily together around the floor. It was the second most enjoyable moment of the evening. "You are an excellent dancer," he told her. "A pleasure to—"

A scream rent the air followed by another, and then dancers began to surge toward them, scrambling out of the way of something unseen.

CHAPTER TWENTY-THREE

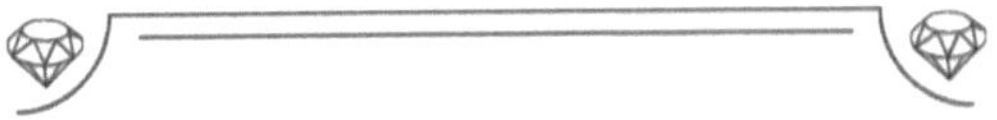

"What on earth?" Lady Radiance wondered.

With the advantage of his height, Edward peered over the heads of those nearby. A horse was racing through the crowd, obviously terrified. Stopping and rearing before running again.

"The deuce!" As the throng parted, Edward tugged Radiance away from the danger and, unfortunately, in the opposite direction to her sister and his. Unable to push against the tide and go the other way, they were sent into the grove of mature trees where the garden's darkness swallowed them.

Edward held her hand tightly.

"Not to worry. We shall make our way around the grove and find our party."

For the time being, however, through no fault of their own, they were by themselves. Why, they might even slip a little farther away without anyone noticing.

In a matter of moments, they were on the other side of the stand of ancient trees and walking into one of the hundreds of secluded lavender bowers. Slowing down, he gently squeezed her hand. Edward intended to take her in his arms.

"I am not the least concerned," Radiance said. "I feel entirely safe when I'm with you."

Blast! He was behaving like the worst rascal.

"I am honored by your trust." He would return her to her sister at once!

To his surprise, Radiance laughed. "That is a morose tone for someone feeling honored."

With that, she halted. "We should take advantage of this opportunity."

Did she mean what he thought?

"We shared something," she began, "that may have been ordinary for you, but for me . . ."

"No!" he blurted, knowing Radiance referred to their kiss. "Not ordinary at all."

With such encouragement, he drew her close, and claimed her upturned mouth under his.

RADIANCE RELAXED, ALTHOUGH her pulse had started to race the moment he pulled her toward him. She tilted her head, rewarded by his mouth more perfectly fitting over hers. In the darkness, her eyes closed while her other senses took over. Edward smelled like simple Pears soap, without a hint of artificial fragrance or cologne. The skin of his jaw was ever so slightly rough on her cheek, as if in need of a shave after a long day.

While the warmth of his body seeped through her lightweight silken summer bodice, she pressed more firmly against him. Almost unwittingly, her hands found their way to his shoulders where she hung on while his tongue took a skilled path between her lips.

"Tongues can fence, if you will," Clarity had once told her when Radiance asked about kissing. At that moment, they were trading stroke for stroke like experienced sword fighters. Moreover, her heart was pounding in her chest like a caged bird at Kew Garden.

Far too soon, Edward lifted his head and rested his forehead against hers.

"Your family may be worried. We should return to them." Yet he didn't release her. Instead, he dropped another kiss lightly on her lips before withdrawing once again.

"And *your* sister, too, may be looking for you," she agreed before outrageously pulling his head back down, demanding a final kiss.

"*Mm,*" she said against his mouth when he delivered what she wanted. *How would she stand not doing this again tomorrow and the day after and the day after that?*

She could kiss him for hours and never grow weary of it. Why, if he offered her his hand in marriage that moment, knowing what she knew of him already, not to mention his ability to make her sizzle, Radiance would reply with a resounding *yes.*

But he simply tucked her hand into the crook of his arm and headed back the way they had come. In less than a minute, they spotted their party of three.

"Thank goodness," Purity said. "We were about to send out Wellington's regiment to recover you."

"Or at least some light cavalry," Foxford said, giving her a quick once-over. Her brother-in-law was a man of the world, and Radiance was certain he knew what they'd been doing.

"Did you see the horse?" Miss Lockwood asked.

"See it? It nearly ran us over," Edward said.

"It was part of the balloonist's act," his sister said. "As soon as it was caught, it was lifted into the sky and drifted away under the balloon."

"Shame, really," Foxford quipped. "I can think of a great many people I would rather see sent flying over the trees than that poor horse."

"No wonder it was trying to escape," Radiance said.

Purity laughed. "At least we are all together again. Refreshments or the shooting gallery?"

Unfortunately, there wasn't another chance to be alone with Edward. If there had been, Radiance would have taken it. Too soon, she had to say goodbye to him and his sister after a wonderful evening.

The best thing—*besides the kissing!*—was that they would see one another at week's end at Purity's home on Belgrave Square. The Foxfords were having a dinner and intimate concert for twenty.

Before Purity had invited Edward, she'd asked Radiance in private if she was amenable. Standing together by a fountain before they all said their farewells, Purity took her arm.

"You seem to be enamored of the man, and I can see why," her sister said kindly. "I am happy to facilitate matters by inviting him to our party."

A minute later, when Edward was asked and agreed to attend without hesitation, Radiance felt a ray of hope. He must be growing a *tendre* for her of equal measure.

IN AN OFF-THE-SHOULDER gown of coppery silk, wearing the golden topaz earbobs she had made for herself, Radiance entered her sister's home with Bri by her side. Her parents had declined to attend, having a prior engagement to dine with old friends.

The instant they stepped into the elegant townhouse on the fashionable square, Bri rushed away with the promise that her own good friend, Lydia, would be there.

Radiance and Purity, who stood greeting guests beside Foxford, looked in the direction their youngest sister had taken.

"I cannot believe that was me a couple years ago," Radiance said.

Purity laughed softly. "You were never quite like Bri. No one is, for that matter. But she will either mature and lose her whimsical manner or mature and stay exactly as she is. I cannot help hoping for the latter."

"That surprises me, Sister," Radiance said, considering Purity's love of civility. Not that Bri was entirely wild, but she was certainly spontaneous, occasionally outspoken, and even impolite but not maliciously so.

However, Purity shrugged. "One of us has to be the black sheep. For a long while, I thought it would be you, what with wanting to work and get your hands dirty."

Radiance smiled. "Don't forget one black sheep in a flock is considered lucky. If there are two of us, then perhaps double the good fortune shall follow."

"Speaking of good fortune, here comes your admirer."

At her sister's words, Radiance's cheeks heated immediately. For one thing, Lord Foxford was listening to their conversation. For another, she wasn't entirely sure of Edward's admiration.

"Now, now," Purity said. "Take a calming breath before he is upon us. You look as if you're going to combust."

Lord Foxford chuckled at his wife's words. "As you did when I declared my intent. As you still do when—"

Purity hushed him with a single word. "Foxy!"

Ignoring their banter and breathing deeply, Radiance turned to meet Edward, dressed impeccably in black with a gold satin necktie that complemented his eyes. Not to mention, her gown. They appeared to be a harmonized couple.

"Good evening, Lady Foxford, Lady Radiance, Lord Foxford," he said, bowing low. "You ladies look astonishingly beautiful tonight, two shimmering gemstones." Yet his gaze rested upon Radiance alone.

She took Edward's proffered arm, and they went together into her sister's drawing room.

"Good thing you rescued me," Radiance said. "My sister and her husband were wavering between praise and quarreling."

"They seem perfectly matched and deeply in love," he said, surprising her that he'd noticed.

"Indeed, I think of them as lovebirds." Just as she could easily imagine herself and Edward.

Purity went a long way to facilitating such a match by partnering them at dinner with Edward on Radiance's left. In the small company of guests, conversation was easy. She and Edward became lost in a private discussion of opals.

"With their supernatural luminescence," Radiance mused, "they seem as if they should belong to fairies."

"You must come by and see the collection I have amassed," he said.

Radiance glanced around, hoping no one had heard the inappropriate invitation. Satisfied the others were all engaged in talk of the concert that would follow the meal, she replied, "I would like that. And to see Monty once more."

Edward laughed. "He has grown on you, has he? I admit, he makes my otherwise empty house seem warm and friendly—or at least furry."

Radiance nearly pointed out there was another way to make his empty house warmer—with a willing wife—but she refrained.

After dinner, they nearly missed the summons to the conservatory, having been spiritedly discussing the age of the earth and Charles Lyell's monumental work, *Principles of Geology*, as everyone who had an interest in rocks did at one time or another.

Throwing about terms, such as *uniformitarianism* and *catastrophism*, Radiance was thrilled to have someone with whom to discuss these issues and to challenge her.

The viscountess Lady Chesley overheard when a group of guests were stalled in the hallway, while those ahead were slowly finding seats around the piano.

"A blasphemy of a topic, indeed," Lady Chesley said. "The exact date of the earth's creation is well known, and that is the end of it. All the digging up of rocks and examining the earth's crust will do you no better than poking around a pile of pebbles at Hastings beach and peeling back a crust of bread!"

Her righteous anger and absolute certainty tickled Radiance's funny bone out of all proportion to what had been said. She started to snicker and couldn't stop.

"Well!" Lady Chesley exclaimed and turned away.

But that wasn't the end of it. Imagining Edward sitting on Hastings beach, his trouser legs rolled up while he examined the pebbles struck Radiance as even funnier.

Apparently, he, too, thought the image amusing. Soon, they were laughing so hard at the viscountess's words, they had to move away down the hall to regain their composure.

Radiance barely noticed when everyone else had gone into the conservatory. However, Edward suddenly sobered. Their gazes locked. Since Radiance knew the house intimately, and he didn't, she took the lead, going a few feet down the hallway. Opening a door on her left, she entered her sister's library with Edward at her back.

A single lamp was lit out of courtesy in case a guest wandered in by mistake, but otherwise, it was obviously not festooned for the party.

Stopping abruptly, Radiance felt Edward's solid figure bump into her. His hands came up immediately to grasp her upper arms.

"Steady," he said. His tone, along with his welcome touch, made her tingle. "Another library. How fortunate," he added with drastic understatement, considering he was already pulling her back against the length of him, plastering her body to his.

With her heart beating like a galloping horse, Radiance closed her eyes and leaned her head on his chest, holding her breath. One of his large hands came up to cradle her breast through the silken fabric of her gown. Gasping softly, she felt her nipple peak under his touch.

His other hand stroked her cheek, before splaying across her exposed collarbone, making goosebumps raise upon her skin. To her increasing delight, he leaned down to drop hot sultry kisses from her jaw to her shoulder where the silk of her gown halted his progress. She wanted to tear it from her body and let him go further.

Perhaps sensing her frustration, he gently—thankfully, without any hint of tearing—tugged at the delicate fabric, exposing her breast to the room's coolness. His hand hadn't even closed over her bare skin when her nipple hardened.

Trying to remember to breathe, Radiance exalted in the sensation of his fingers on her sensitive flesh. No gloves, since they had just finished dining, she could feel the callouses of a man who used his hands. The place between her legs began to throb.

At last, she turned in the circle of his arms, watching his gaze flicker to her naked breasts, relishing the desire she recognized on his face.

"I knew you would be exquisite when undressed," he said.

Before she could speak or even think to be embarrassed, Edward bent low and took her right nipple between his lips, sucking it into his mouth and shocking her to her core.

Radiance moaned softly and sank her fingers into his hair, holding him in place while he teased her. She released him only enough so he could give her other nipple equal attention. With Edward's mouth upon her sensitive skin, her body became molten, and she would vow she was growing damp with wanting more of him.

When he lifted his head, Radiance ran a trembling hand down his cheek. As he finally claimed a kiss, both breathtaking and hungry, her knees weakened.

Could they push a chair against the door to secure it from the inside? She was willing for her first time to be on her sister's library carpet, giving her innocence to this golden-eyed man without any promise or declaration.

But how to tell him?

In fact, she wondered how she would walk out of the room when her legs were weakly quivering, and her woman's core pulsed with an ache only he could soothe.

"Edward," she said his name. He closed his eyes, his jaw tightening with an internal struggle. The gentleman in him was going to win—she knew it, and some part of her was even grateful.

But not the part that desperately wanted him to initiate her into the ways of swiving.

Deciding to listen to her better self, Radiance didn't confess to wanting to be stripped bare and laid upon the Persian rug. Instead, she would tell him how she felt. After all, he might start to think her some light-skirt.

"I find myself thinking of you often," she began.

He took hold of her hand that rested on his face and pressed his mouth to her palm. His kiss was searing and proprietary.

"When you are not nearby, I long to see you." She hoped she didn't sound childishly infatuated. For her feelings were deep and true. "And when you *are* close, I yearn to be alone with you as we are now."

His golden-topaz eyes bore into hers, but he remained silent. She had hoped he felt the same but could not be certain it wasn't wishful thinking. For him, this might be passion, even lust, and nothing more.

Softly, tentatively, with her free hand, Radiance ran her fingers through his hair, directly behind his temple. It was coarser than her own but still soft. Moreover, as she feathered her fingers into the brown waves a second time, she thought it a most intimate act, touching Edward's scalp, knowing underneath was a brain she had come to adore.

In fact, she loved every part of him.

Could she come out and say that?

Before she could confess the truth, he kissed her again. The sensation of his mouth moving across her own felt like coming home from a long journey. There was usually a delightful moment when one entered through one's own front door, caught the accustomed scents of furniture polish and fresh flowers as well as a beloved's perfume, and enjoyed the sound of one's feet on familiar flooring.

In that instant, home was a sanctuary of both the comfortable and the cherished.

Edward's kiss embodied that delightful moment while adding a thrilling aspect, awash in bursts of utter bliss.

When his tongue swept between her lips, she swayed. Perhaps feeling how close she was to collapsing, he pulled her further off-balance and firmly into his arms. Unable to stop herself, she sagged against him, letting her breasts be crushed upon his chest. Her arms snaked up until her fingers clasped behind his head.

"Edward," Radiance breathed into his mouth. "I—"

"*Shh,*" he said.

For a moment, her pride was pricked that he wouldn't let her speak, then she realized there were footsteps in the hallway. Someone was nearly upon them.

CHAPTER TWENTY-FOUR

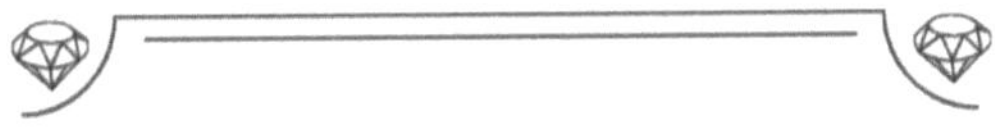

With the swiftness of experience, Edward slid both of her little cap sleeves up her arms before hastening away. Radiance, too, put distance between them, although being alone in the room was enough to ruin her.

Tugging her bodice into place, she knew most assuredly this was what Purity would decree an "improper situation." Should they be discovered, it was the kind of circumstance that destroyed a lady's reputation or forced a man—if he were truly a gentleman—into asking for her hand.

However, instead of coming into the drawing room, whoever it was continued past while Radiance held her hand to her own mouth. Edward remained utterly silent and motionless, head cocked toward the door.

As soon as it was quiet again, she released a sigh.

"You must slip into the conservatory," he said, sounding tense. "Find a secluded place by the windowsill, so when you are discovered, it will be as if you were there all along."

He ran his hands through his hair where her fingers had been. "This was reckless and stupid of me. Unforgiveable, actually."

Entirely worth it, Radiance thought but held her tongue. This was how two people managed to get to know one another. Otherwise, a couple would have to be practically strangers when they arranged to marry.

Would he ask her?

"I shall go first and make certain there is no one lingering about," he said. "Count to thirty and then follow. I shall be hiding while watching the conservatory door, but I won't come in. I shall pretend I felt ill and had to leave. It's the only way. For one look at both of us together, and your sister will know. Probably anyone would know."

Radiance didn't want him to leave her. She didn't want their moment of privacy to come to an end. Yet the magical web of intimacy had been torn asunder, so she nodded.

Perhaps recognizing her forlorn expression, he took a step closer once more and pressed an agonizingly delicious kiss upon her upturned mouth.

Before she could even grab on to him or breathe in his warm scent, he was gone.

What was she supposed to do? Oh yes, count to thirty.

SEATED BEHIND HER worktable at Mr. Bonwit's, Radiance was trying to focus on minute springs to create an intricate *en tremblant* brooch with flower stems of diamonds that would appear to be in motion when the wearer moved. But all she could think of was baring her soul to Edward and how he hadn't said anything in return except words of regret.

True, they'd been interrupted, yet it seemed to her that he hadn't been about to declare himself, anyway. He would rather kiss than speak, prefer to stroke her bare arm or her . . . wrist than tell her she held his heart.

It was worrisome. She was a lady, and a virtuous one at that. Or she always had been, having never let a man bare her breasts or touch her thusly before. Moreover, she wanted to keep her reputation as well as his good regard. At the same time, she wished for them to engage in a deeper association.

In short, Radiance hoped he would soon say she was all he had ever wanted in a wife, or she feared her heart would be sorely wounded.

Wondering whether it would further her goal, as she now saw it, she would accompany him to speak with Lord Exeter, whose office was housed at St. James's Palace. The Lord Chamberlain would know which footman collected the brooch from Garrard's shop, directly from Mr. Minton, as well as from Mr. Neble. Naturally, Edward had promised to collect her.

Thus, on the appointed day, when the clock struck the hour and there was no sign of her geologist, Radiance had the dreadful notion he had forgotten, exactly as he had with the note to Mr. Neble. Except this time, he'd forgotten the woman who had let him take liberties.

It was unforgiveable!

Just when she started storming around her home in high dudgeon, about to summon one of the Diamond carriages from the mews, she heard a cab pull up out front.

"Hurry, Sarah, let us away."

In two shakes, Radiance was standing outside admiring the man climbing out of the cab. Edward Lockwood was a square cove—resolute, intelligent, appealing as Michelangelo's *David*—basically, a dashing dog in a doublet. And she most definitely wanted him for her own.

Edward would never be dull and thus, nor would her life. Of that, she was certain.

Even the cab ride still seemed an exotic treat, almost risqué for its shabbiness compared to her father's private carriage. And with Edward's tiger-gold eyes looking merry that day, she hoped it was because they were together again.

After a moment's shyness upon once more being in his presence, Radiance swallowed her embarrassment, lifted her head, and decided to pretend as though nothing earth-shattering had happened until such time as *he* made mention of it.

In truth, Radiance would abandon the investigation, and her maid, if Edward crooked his finger and told her to go with him . . . anywhere. But he only commented upon the fine weather and occasionally looked out of the carriage window to determine their progress down St. James's Street.

Since St. James's Palace was only a stone's throw from her home, even with the usual traffic, they were there in mere minutes. Radiance rarely had cause to go to the mostly brick building built in the time of Henry VIII. Although a dreadful fire damaged much of the east and south wings at the beginning of the century, it had all been restored by 1813. The Palace's chapel was, of course, the impressive setting of Queen Victoria and Prince Albert's wedding twelve years earlier.

But she and Edward wouldn't be entering any of the regal state rooms. They were simply going through the stone archway, to the Colour Court, which now held royal offices.

Radiance couldn't help halting at the arch to look at the outline of a foot etched on the mottled black and tan granite. Purported to be Henry VIII's, he ordered the engraving so he knew where to set his foot when dismounting from his horse.

She thought it an unlikely story for the particularly bloodthirsty king. Nonetheless, she reached out to touch it. As she did, something grazed her arm.

Hissing with the sudden sharp pain, half thinking a bee had stung her, she turned to glance at Edward, wondering if there was a swarm. The stonework beside him inexplicably crumbled, causing a cloud of granite dust.

"Run!" Edward yelled.

While she tried to determine what was happening, he rushed her forcefully under the archway and through the first open doorway. His momentum carried them both onto the old plank floor where she landed with him on top of her.

"*Oof!*" she exhaled.

He had knocked all the air from her lungs. *Had he gone mad?* Moreover, Sarah was yelling something, and as Radiance looked over Edward's shoulder, her maid rushed in, stopping to stare at the tangled heap of legs and arms.

Why was Sarah yelling? Was she hurt?

"What in blue blazes is going on?" Radiance demanded, staring up into Edward's beloved face.

In other circumstances, she might have enjoyed the unfamiliar feeling of his muscular body atop her own, but not while her arm still stung nor while Sarah was sobbing and making a commotion.

Edward raised himself up on his hands and stared down at her. She sucked in a breath at the look on his face. *Disbelief, fear, relief.*

"A bullet went right by me," Sarah cried. "And by you, m'lady."

"A bullet?" Radiance echoed.

Edward still gazed into her eyes. "Someone was shooting at us."

With those terrifying, unfathomable words, he rolled off her, leaving Radiance bereft of his warmth and his protection.

After scrambling to his feet, he reached down his hand, which she took. Yet when he tugged her to stand, she couldn't help crying out in pain.

"Dear God!" Edward exclaimed. "You are hurt."

"More shocked than anything," she said. Yet when she drew her fingers back, her pale purple glove was stained with blood. *Again!*

"You are wounded!" he exclaimed.

"Hardly that," Radiance protested, although her knees felt weak. There was more blood than what had come from her temple during the previous incident. Either she was becoming terribly prone to accidents and in dire need of a toadstone, or someone had actually tried to hurt her. *Twice!*

"Is there an infirmary on the premises?" Edward asked a liveried footman, who had materialized as if by magic from somewhere farther inside the building. Probably the rumpus had called his attention to visitors.

"Yes, sir. We have a doctor and two nurses on staff."

"We are here to see the Lord Chamberlain," Edward explained, but he was still staring at her, concern in his golden-brown eyes. "Is he nearby?"

"Yes, sir," the footman repeated. "I mean, no, sir. Normally, yes, but he was called to Buckingham Palace. The Master of the Royal Household is here, though, sir."

Radiance simply wanted to sit, and her expression must have shown it.

"Sarah, take your mistress to the infirmary and get her wound dressed." He hurried for the still-open door.

"Where are you going?" Radiance asked, fear making her stomach clench at the thought of him going outside into danger.

"To take a look around. I shall come find you."

"Edward . . ." she began, but he disappeared from view.

CHAPTER TWENTY-FIVE

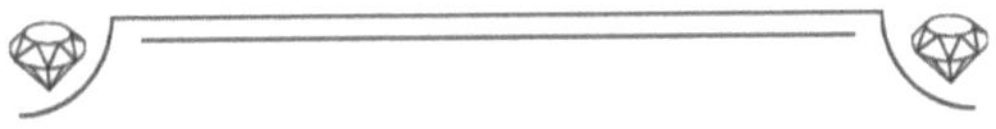

As expected, there wasn't anyone standing outside St. James's Palace holding a gun. Still, Edward searched the area in front of the courtyard along Pall Mall Street and then back the other way, along Cleveland Row.

Nothing and no one looked suspicious.

As sure as he breathed, the shooting was because of their investigation. Moreover, he suspected the prior assault, when Radiance was shoved to the ground, was also related.

After a few minutes, he returned to St. James's and found his way to the infirmary where Radiance was chatting with Sarah who, for once, was not reading.

"How do you feel?" he asked, relief pouring over him for the second time—first when he felt her warm and breathing under him on the floor and now, seeing her perfectly healthy-looking visage. Yet he wouldn't forget that it could have been a fatal shot to her back.

"I am fine. A poorer marksman could not be found. I'm as lucky as the Queen in that regard," she added, making a poorly timed reference to the many failed assassination attempts. "Only think how Her Majesty has been kept safe through six attempts upon her life. In her case, it must be divine intervention. In my case, plain, old-fashioned good fortune."

"I am not sure that nutter-pate who smacked the Queen's forehead with his cane should be lumped in with those who shot at her, but I take your meaning. She has kept up a brave face through it all, as are you at this very minute."

She smiled, then gave a little shrug. "It really was nothing. My second scrape in a fortnight. Imagine that."

Edward was imagining it, and he didn't like where his thoughts were taking him. Eventually, the luck that Radiance was toting so cheerily would run out.

"Did the Queen's physician take care of you?"

"Of course not." She looked embarrassed. "A nurse was very kind, however."

Radiance held up her arm to show him the wrapping just above her elbow. "She cleaned it, which stung, and then dressed it. But truly, it was little more than a scratch, as if I had been too eagerly picking amongst raspberry brambles."

"I did not find the gunman," he confessed.

"I didn't expect you would. Did you?"

"No." He had failed her, and she had expected him to. He wished he had been successful so they could put this behind them.

Radiance rose to her feet. "Regardless, we are here at St. James's, and thus we may as well meet with the Master of the Household."

"No," he blurted before thinking.

She narrowed her eyes. "Mr. Lockwood, do not presume to quell my interest in this, nor exclude me from the search, not after all we've done together."

Stopping abruptly, she glanced at her wide-eyed maid. "I mean, of course, after all that we've *investigated* together."

"But you've been shot, m'lady," the maid pointed out.

Edward nodded at Sarah's sensible words. However, Radiance would have none of them.

"I was shot *at*, perhaps, and merely grazed, for goodness' sake. No harm done at all."

"What do you think your parents will say to that small distinction? Will they be so cavalier with your safety? I think not. I am taking you home at once."

Her gloved hands balled into fists. "This is ludicrous. You, sir, are being overprotective, and I must remind you that it is not your place. Furthermore, we are already securely in the Palace, and I am not bleeding to death. Therefore, it would be entirely remiss of us to give up the opportunity to at least speak with the Master of the Household and, hopefully, discover the footman or footmen in question."

"We are leaving," he insisted.

"No, we are not."

To his amazement, Radiance brushed past him and sailed out the open door. When he hurried to follow, she was striding along the wide hall with her skirts billowing behind her.

He growled in frustration. And then the lady's maid passed him and joined her mistress.

What could he do?

"Hold on, my lady," he called to Radiance's retreating form as she disappeared around a corner.

As it turned out, people were not allowed to simply meander St. James's Palace unaccompanied, and a footman soon corralled them.

"The Lord Chamberlain was expecting us. In his absence, please take us to the Master of the House," she ordered before giving Edward a long, satisfied look and following the footman to the correct office.

"Come in, come in," said a stranger as soon as the footman had mentioned their names.

They were met by a balding man with a thick mustache. Already standing before his polished desk, he moved forward to offer Lady Radiance a deep bow.

"I am Sir Biddulph, my lady."

Then he reached out a hand to shake Edward's.

"I apologize for the Lord Chamberlain's absence, but I hope I may be of assistance. Please take a seat." He was taking Radiance's measure a little more closely than Edward would expect.

Radiance sat where directed. "I had hoped to offer Lord Exeter congratulations from my family on his new appointment."

Edward was surprised at her words, realizing the titled folk knew one another's lateral movements far better than he. Of the latest Lord Chamberlain, he knew only that the man had become a marquess at a frightfully young age due to his father's death, and he was an enthusiastic cricketeer in his younger days.

"But you also have not been in this position long," Radiance continued to the Queen's Master of the House. "Congratulations are in order for you, too, sir."

Sir Biddulph's expression lit up. "The appointment was unforeseen but welcome, my lady." He beamed and then seemed to recall the seriousness of his position. "Before you go into why you wished to speak with the Lord Chamberlain, I understand you met with some mishap when you entered St. James's. A footman told me while you were in our infirmary."

Edward let Radiance explain it, except she didn't. It was all roses and gooseberry jam rather than criminals and bullets. In any case, she soon went back to the question at hand, like a dog gnawing a bone.

"We simply wondered whether you could tell us which footman was entrusted with collecting the Queen's engagement brooch from the Crown Jeweler, Mr. Garrard, and who would have brought the Queen's coronet back from the House of Neble. Or perhaps, they are one and the same."

Even before she finished her long query, the Master of the Household was shaking his head.

"I don't know the answer, I'm afraid. I believe the Crown Jeweler assigns the courier."

Edward exchanged a glance with Radiance. No matter how unintentional, they were being batted from man to man like a shuttlecock. Garrard would have told them if he knew.

He was about to thank the Master of the Household for his time when Radiance leaned forward. Edward's eyes nearly protruded from his head as her décolletage could scarcely contain her fulsome breasts.

"Sir Biddulph," she said, her tone soft and imploring, "we have already spoken with the Crown Jeweler. Would it take up a dreadful amount of your time to find out the identity of those we seek?"

The Master of the Household cleared his throat. "My predecessor, Sir Bowles, was a meticulous record-keeper as well as a man of orderly systems. Why, some people think he is still in this position due to the smooth organization that he left." He shook his head.

"When I took over, I strove to be as scrupulous. I shall peruse the records and, if necessary, speak with the Lord Chamberlain myself. In any case, I shall endeavor to discover the information. What shall I do with it when I find it?"

Edward noticed the man was still looking at Radiance. Probably he was hoping for a return visit from the pretty red-haired lady.

"Please send the information to *my* address," Edward said. Taking his silver card case from his pocket, he flipped open the lid and withdrew one card. "I would most appreciate it."

As he handed this to Sir Biddulph, Radiance turned an arched eyebrow his way. He didn't care. It would be unsafe for her to have the information sent to her parents' home. Next thing he knew, she would try to meet with the footmen without him.

And one thing Edward had decided after this frightening day—she was no longer going to be part of any investigation.

Edward wasn't sure how best to go about dissolving their tightly knit association. Nonetheless, he intended to do it forthwith. Radiance's safety was of utmost importance, infinitely more so than discovering who was skilled enough to create a near-perfect replica of a gemstone and clever enough to do it without getting caught.

In any case, they might never know the answer, nor was it as crucial compared to protecting the Koh-i-Noor from suffering a similar fate. For if it was discovered to be a fake stone sometime after the re-cutting, Edward was certain the blame would fall upon him. After all, he'd been tasked by the Queen herself not only with finding the forger but with keeping the diamond safe.

Yet even above that was his intent to keep Radiance from any further physical harm.

If only she hadn't practically declared herself in love with him at her sister's home. *Him!* He was so blasted ordinary. It pained Edward to think she might feel an ounce of heartache due to the necessity of him cutting her out of his life.

All in all, her recent confession was terrible timing. Undoubtedly, she would consider any distance he put between them being due to how earnestly she'd spoken and conclude that he didn't feel the same way.

To his way of thinking, however, parting company during the foreseeable future was a necessity, despite how his heart had nearly exploded in his chest at her unexpected, wondrous words. At the time, he'd been more intent on kissing her than talking. But afterward, when he'd left the party early to avoid any damage to her reputation, he'd reminded himself that she was an innocent.

In all likelihood, Lady Radiance had simply been caught up in the intense moment or in the general excitement since she'd discovered the fake Hope diamond. Suddenly, she'd been thrust into an adventure and undoubtedly saw him as the crux.

Yet if he understood pretty females at all, having grown up with a sister, then Radiance would recover quickly enough and set her cap at someone else, a far more suitable man, before the week's end.

At least he hoped so. He didn't want her anywhere near him, not at one of his lectures, nor seated across while riding in a cab, nor even at a ball. Not until the shooter was caught.

What if he was never caught? Later that night, Edward couldn't help thinking about such a real possibility as he downed the last of the claret in his glass and gently pushed Monty off his lap before heading up to bed.

If she was no longer associated with him in any way, then Radiance would stay safe.

And he would finally know what it was to be heartbroken.

IN A FEW DAYS, EDWARD received a missive from the Queen's Master of the Household with the name of the footman who had picked up the coronet from Mr. Neble. Sir Biddulph had not as yet tracked down the other one who'd gone to Garrard's and collected the brooch from Mr. Minton.

In the interim, Edward had made no contact with Radiance and half convinced himself she'd gone back to whatever she was doing before she looked at the Hope Diamond in the lecture hall and saw the inexplicable flaw.

More realistically, knowing she was probably awaiting word from him, Edward wrote her the briefest of notes:

Dear Lady Radiance,
I have received a name and will speak with the footman shortly.

He could imagine her head exploding like fireworks on Guy Fawkes' night, so he added:

I will let you know if he has anything of import to add to what we have already learned.
    Yours sincerely,
    Lockwood

CHAPTER TWENTY-SIX

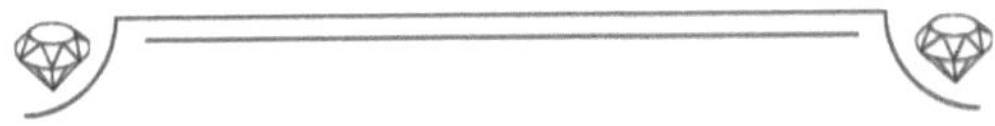

Radiance read the note, turned it over, saw nothing else, turned it back, and read it again.

How dare he?

Edward was shutting her out of the Queen's appointed task. Two things struck her—he still hadn't acknowledged her words of admiration, nor had he shared the footman's name.

The two were linked. He no longer wanted her to be part of the search for the thief because she had stupidly disclosed her feelings. Clearly, Edward didn't return them in kind, and thus thought it best to slip away . . . *like a weasel!*

He had forgotten the freedom and independence her parents afforded her. She could go to Edward's home that instant and demand to remain part of the investigation.

Finding herself pacing her room, Radiance halted, staring at the two windows overlooking the back of her home. A familiar pattern of six large panes over six. Recently, she'd had an idea for a brooch which recreated the same, using table-cut golden topazes in place of flat glass and gold between the gems to mimic the muntins.

Her feet carried her toward one of the windows. Beyond was a small garden, a hedge, and the mews. Edward had stood in the moonlight and said he was impressed by her. Radiance had been sure she could float on clouds.

Curse the man for his perfect kisses and how he had made her feel.
She would make the brooch with beautiful blue spinels so as not to be reminded of his glorious eyes. And if he didn't want to be near her, then she would happily keep her distance. After what she'd said in Purity's library—she could only pray his memory wasn't as good as her own. Horrified, she recalled telling him how she yearned and thought of him all the time. *Like a moonstruck fool!*

Sitting heavily upon her bed, Radiance let abject misery nearly overwhelm her. Knowing that Edward didn't reciprocate her feelings settled like a bag of rocks in her stomach. The last thing she should do was force herself upon him. It would be torturous. Without doubt, her cheeks would heat every time they were near one another, and if she inadvertently gazed at him longingly . . . *the humiliation!*

Allowing him to push her away was easier all around.

But what about the Queen's task? She could not simply abandon it. Moreover, what had been bothering her about their discussion with Mr. Minton had finally come to her in the night. His blunder in saying the wrong Lord Chamberlain's name was important. Just as Sir Biddulph indicated that some people thought his predecessor was still the Master of the Household, what if the thief mistook the wrong Lord Chamberlain?

Why else would Mr. Minton think Breadalbane still held the post, especially if a footman had actually come from Exeter's office?

With that, she decided to pay Mr. Minton another visit, this time by herself. The following day, with Sarah at her side and one of her father's footmen for protection, she entered Newgate, spoke with the warder, and was led into the same small room.

"Oh, it's you," Mr. Minton said when he was brought in.

"How are you faring?" she asked, not taking offense from his lukewarm welcome. Suddenly, she had an inspired idea. "Would you like me to visit your wife? Perhaps I can offer her some comfort."

Radiance watched him carefully. If he were guilty, he would probably stave her off. He didn't. He sniffed and nodded.

"How kind of you, my lady. Is that why you came?"

"No, sir. I recalled you said Lord Breadalbane was the Lord Chamberlain."

"Isn't he?"

"Lord Exeter took over the post recently."

Mr. Minton shrugged. "Be that as it may, the footman who collected the brooch said he came from the Lord Chamberlain's office, and he had a warrant with Breadalbane's signature."

Radiance puffed out her cheeks, then released them. "Very curious, wouldn't you say?"

He seemed uninterested, staring past her to the wall. "I used to work for Rundell and Bridge, you know. They were never called the Crown Jeweler, as Mr. Garrard is, but they were named the Principal Royal Goldsmiths & Jewelers in 1804, which sounded very fine when I learned that as a youth. I knew I wanted to work for them."

"Yes, sir, a fine jewelry company," she agreed, "but about the footman—"

"It makes sense the Queen would make Mr. Garrard the first official Crown Jeweler since he made her engagement ring. But anyone you ask would say that Rundell and Bridge were also Crown Jewelers, including Mr. Rundell and Mr. Bridge themselves." He stared at his gnarled hands.

Before she could ask the important question again, he added, "Before them, the Royal Jeweler was Philip Gilbert, although he wasn't called it officially, and before him, it was William Jones of Jefferys and Jones. Which was also where Mr. Gilbert worked but by then it was Jefferys, Jones, and Gilbert."

He nodded his head as he sorted it out to his own satisfaction, although Radiance was growing frustrated and confused. Then he added, "You know, the jewelers' community in London is a small one."

"Yes, I've heard. So, Mr. Garrard gave you the brooch to work on, and Lord Exeter's footman collected it from you?"

"Don't be daft, my lady. Lord Breadalbane's footman, as I said."

"That is impossible," she said. "He is no longer the Lord Chamberlain of the Household."

"Nevertheless," Mr. Minton said, utterly unconcerned. He shrugged again. "Bridges and Rundell were a force when I started there. They once made twenty-two of the most exquisite little snuff-boxes, a thousand guineas a piece, for diplomats after the Congress of Vienna."

"Did they?" she asked, deciding she would have to let him ramble on.

"That was my first year with them. But they are better known for creating the Irish Crown Jewels."

"Yes, I know," she said, having read about most of the royal jewels over the past year.

"Can you believe the English let nearly four hundred gemstones be taken to make the new Irish Crown Jewels, right from Old King George and Queen Charlotte's own pieces. Now *that* Keeper of the Jewels, as he was called back then, ought to have been beheaded."

Radiance wouldn't ask, but undoubtedly, Mr. Minton knew that individual, as well.

Regardless, he shook his head emphatically. "I can tell you a story—"

"Please, sir," Radiance interrupted, fearing if she didn't, she would soon be discussing who made the first coronation scepter or some obscure crown belonging to Queen Elizabeth I. "Do you think the warrant from the Lord Chamberlain still exists?"

"Unlikely. Just a scrap of paper that was probably cleared off my worktable." His tone was bitter, and who could blame him?

Then she recalled her gifts. From her right skirt pocket, she withdrew a small paper sack, set it on the table, then added another from her left. Pushing them toward Mr. Minton, Radiance hoped to cheer him, although clearly, he felt betrayed by an industry he had served and loved.

Cautiously, he peered into the first bag, and then a smile broke over his face. He looked a decade younger.

"You remembered," he said, his eyes dancing as he popped a small black licorice Pontefract cake into his mouth. "Then the other must be lokum."

Sure enough, Radiance had stopped at the shop dedicated to Turkish Delight as many were now calling it.

"One last question, sir. When the brooch was in your possession, are you certain the stones were all authentic?"

He was still chewing when he looked at her with clear eyes and nodded. "Absolutely certain, my lady. As sure as I'm sitting here with you."

"Then if the gem was switched, as the Crown Jeweler stated a month later, perhaps the individual who collected it was the thief."

Radiance rose to her feet. More than ever, she wanted the chance to speak with the footman.

"Will you come again?" He shoved a piece of sweet, chewy lokum into his mouth.

She thought there was every chance Mr. Minton would be released, but she hated to give him false hope. Thus, Radiance made the only promise she could.

"I shall return if the warder will let me."

FOR HALF A WEEK, SHE still hoped Edward would contact her. For the remainder of the week, Radiance knew if he did, she would not respond. Regardless, direct correspondence with Sir Biddulph yielded the information that he'd already given Edward.

The footman who collected the coronet from the House of Neble was a man named Bob Draper. A long-time member of Buckingham Palace's staff as was his father before him, no one suspected him of anything. Even Radiance. And she thought she had as good a sense for guilt as she had for innocence.

However, to her amazement, there was no second footman! Neither Mr. Draper nor anyone else had been sent to Garrard's shop since it was assumed the Crown Jeweler would return the brooch to the Queen.

Radiance was granted access to the Duchess of Atholl, Her Majesty's Mistress of the Robes, who had accepted the brooch from a Palace footman. He, in turn, had received it at the west portico from a messenger who said he was sent by Mr. Garrard.

She had milked the pigeon, as her father would say—absolutely failing to learn anything of usefulness. Moreover, she knew Edward had been no more successful.

The blasted geologist—as she now thought of him—could take a leap off London Bridge for all she cared.

"Have you chosen your gown?" her mother asked when Radiance wandered into the drawing room for a cup of tea.

"Whatever for?"

"The charity ball at Syon House for the Shipwrecked Fishermen and Mariners' Royal Benevolent Society."

What a name! What a nuisance! Radiance sat down in a huff.

"Tonight? It had slipped my mind."

"They need more lifeboats," her mother reminded her, "at Lytham, Newhaven, Hornsea, and many other places that, sadly, I have forgotten." Lady Diamond sipped her tea. "Luckily, the Society *hasn't* forgotten, and tonight's charitable event will do them very nicely indeed."

Thus, Radiance was attending her first social event since spilling her secret sentiments to Edward. She was determined to enjoy herself regardless. Moreover, she would try not to watch for him, nor miss him when he didn't show up. After all, it wasn't his world. Geologists didn't regularly go to opulent balls, and he'd said he had no events to attend all year.

Once at Syon House, on the banks of the Thames, however, she was hard pressed to keep her head from swiveling side to side. At least for the first quarter of an hour. Then, as she walked across the marble floor beside her mother, Radiance spied Lord Castille. The viscount nodded in acknowledgment, and she began to think about which of the many gentlemen she would honor with a dance.

"Isn't that your geologist friend?" her mother asked.

Radiance nearly tripped over her own slippers. "Where? No, I doubt it." Her heartbeat sped up immediately, but she refused to even glance in the direction her mother was looking.

To cover her discomfort, Radiance walked boldly toward Lord Castille when she ought to have let him come to her. Her mother hurried to catch up.

"Good evening," he greeted, first to the Countess Diamond and then to Radiance.

After pleasant but brief prattle, she had secured his name on her dance card, and then as was the custom, he moved on to another young lady. But Radiance didn't want to stand still, feeling exposed and dreading her first contact with Edward—if her mother had been correct.

Thus, she approached another man whom she knew and granted him a dance. Lady Diamond had scarcely reached them when Radiance was about to hasten forth again.

"You are eager to arrange your partners tonight," her mother remarked.

"Yes," Radiance muttered, keeping her head down. Another man approached to request the honor of a dance, and she graciously accepted.

As they continued their tour of the room, her mother glanced sideways at her. "I am surprised by that last partner."

"Really," Radiance asked, finally looking up and almost at once seeing Edward a mere ten feet away. Her skin grew clammy under the silk of her dress and her cotton shift. "Why?"

"You once said you disliked that man greatly, not only for how he stared down your décolletage but also trod upon your feet through an entire polka."

Radiance gasped and looked down at the card dangling from her wrist. *Lord Weighland!*

"Mother! Why did you let me?"

"What on earth can you mean? I would no more get in the way of whom you wish to dance with than I would fly about the room with a candle clenched between my teeth. You are behaving strangely tonight. Never mind, here comes Mr. Lockwood."

Radiance froze, catching her breath momentarily and not releasing it as her gaze fell to the floor. She wasn't ready for this, for seeing him again now that her heart was shattered. *Blast!*

Managing to stop herself from smoothing the front of her vibrant green gown with nervousness, fearful she'd leave stains from her damp palms, she took a deep breath to refill her starving lungs. After making certain her expression was serene, with a passable placid smile, she raised her head and looked directly at him.

He was . . . the same. Not an ogre as she'd started to imagine, almost wishing he was. It might have been easier.

Instead, he looked impeccable, as finely dressed as any peer of the realm in a black tailcoat, charcoal trousers and waistcoat, and a dove-gray necktie. His gaze flickered over her from head to toe, making her skin prickle.

"Good evening," they said at the same time.

"My apologies for speaking over you," he said.

Radiance was caught in his golden-brown gaze and had no words beyond sadness or anger.

"What a pleasant surprise," Lady Diamond intervened into the awkward silence.

"Indeed," Radiance snapped, knowing this marked the end of her equanimity for the evening. "What an unanticipated place to encounter *you*, Mr. Lockwood. Of all people."

Her mother gave her a look that Purity had inherited, perfectly expressing her dislike of her daughter's tone and words.

Radiance didn't wish to embarrass her and relented.

"That is, I know a ball is not your usual activity. And tonight shall prove to be a long one." Even longer now that she had to dance with Lord Weighland while keeping her emotions in check over her indifferent geologist.

"You are correct," he said politely. "Usually, you wouldn't find me at such a gala, but I am escorting my sister who has had a taste of society recently and finds it to her liking."

"Whereas you do not?" the countess asked.

"I would prefer to be in my workroom."

"There is a time to study gems and a time to dance," Lady Diamond said. "For what is the point of working if you cannot also enjoy the more amusing parts of life?"

They lapsed into silence. Edward might not be the most polished gentleman, but even he knew he ought to ask Radiance for the honor of a dance.

Lady Diamond tried to encourage him. "I believe my daughter has a few spaces left on her dance card."

His hesitation was devastating. What's more, it was mortifying, not to mention invoking her mother's blatant curiosity. Radiance had no choice but to hand him her card and pencil, glad for their gloves as the slimmest of barriers when their fingers brushed.

As soon as Edward had written in his name, tipped his hat, and walked away, her mother rounded on her.

"What is going on between you and that young man?"

Radiance rolled her eyes. "Obviously nothing. He doesn't even wish to dance with me. I cannot believe you all but bullied him into it."

"I thought he was merely being shy."

"A horse's arse, more like," Radiance muttered.

The countess gave a little shrug. "I do not understand you. Do you like Mr. Lockwood?"

"Mother!"

Lady Diamond rolled her eyes exactly as Radiance had done. "If you want him, then speak plainly."

"I did. To him! And this," she gestured toward his retreating back, "is the result."

"Oh!" Her mother frowned, then looked where the tall geologist had rejoined his sister who was laughing in a group of other guests.

"How strange! It cannot be true that he doesn't reciprocate your admiration. I mean, look at you." Since she and her mother were as alike as two peas in a pod, Radiance couldn't help but offer a genuine smile. Everyone thought the Countess Diamond beautiful, after all.

"But then beyond your looks," her mother continued, "you have a brain, a sense of humor, clever thoughts. And you're simply good fun. What's wrong with the man?"

Radiance sighed. "That's what I have been wondering."

"Dance with him," her mother said.

"I have to," she reminded her. "I accepted his name upon my card."

"Yes, dance with him and be your usual radiant self but be aloof. Not cold, nor strange. Be yourself but without any welcome. You will soon see if he's interested. Maybe he simply likes fox hunting."

"I don't understand," Radiance said. *What had his sporting interests to do with dancing?*

The countess nodded to a passing friend, then spoke again. "Dearest daughter, some men are put off by women who fall too easily. They want to feel as if they've earned your affection. They wish to give chase and catch you, like a tricky fox hunt, rather than have you land in their lap."

"Like a . . . ?" Radiance prompted.

Her mother halted and considered. "Like a luscious dove or a purring cat."

"Very clever," Radiance said. "I see what you mean."

CHAPTER TWENTY-SEVEN

Edward had been reluctant to escort his sister.

"This is a bad idea," he'd said to his mother the day before when summoned.

"Why do you say that? In any case, your private reservations don't matter. I have told you I cannot go with her. If your Aunt Gertie weren't suffering so, but she is. Therefore, it must be you at this late notice."

Edward had gritted his teeth. His aunt was prone to dramatic fits of whatever suited her and loved to inconvenience her sister-in-law. Whether by buying an ugly rubber necklace simply to annoy his mother or making her feel guilty enough to keep his aunt company.

In his gut, he had known Radiance would be there. Moreover, polite behavior dictated he greet her. He previously had thought he could be callous enough to give her a cut direct, a *rumping* as it were. It would have put the nail in the coffin, and he ought to have had the fortitude to do it. For her sake.

However, when faced with her glorious beauty, in an emerald green gown that shimmered when she moved, he'd been compelled to go over and say hello.

Literally, he had been unable to help himself. *What a ninny!*

Yet he hadn't expected her mother to practically force a dance between them. And now, despite wanting to keep Radiance at a safe distance, he spent the evening watching over his sister's virtue and looking forward to the final dance.

He had to watch Radiance dance with what seemed like a hundred other men. The best was when Weighland tripped twice and ended up escorting Radiance from the floor before the dance had ended. Her face was a picture of annoyance.

The worst was watching her dance with Lord Castille, a jovial viscount, known to be looking for a wife, according to Lillian, who was narrating the entire evening for him. Radiance seemed to thoroughly enjoy dancing with him. She also ate supper by his side before dancing a second time as his partner, still looking genuinely happy.

Edward wanted to pop Castille a sneezer so his perfect face was a little less so. A childish fancy, as he never brawled unless attacked.

At long last, he went to claim Radiance. Their dance was a slow waltz. *Of course it was!*

"You look lovely this evening," he said. It was a stupid remark. It implied that sometimes she didn't.

As he deserved, her expression was cool. Moreover, she remained as stiff and distant as it was possible to be while dancing. Somehow, she did it expertly.

She also remained utterly silent. He deserved that, too. Regardless, he enjoyed having her close, and his body reacted accordingly.

"Lilacs," he suddenly blurted, making her actually look at him directly in the eyes for the first time. Her nostrils flared delicately, but still, she said nothing.

"I have only just identified the fragrance you wear."

Her expression was nothing so much as a sickly grimace.

Flaring his fingers across her lower back, he felt Radiance flinch and tried to tamp down his own ardor. He could at least tell her of his meeting with the footman.

"I spoke with a footman named—"

"Draper," she snapped.

He was stunned into momentary silence. When she arched a knowing eyebrow, he felt a surge of annoyance. She wasn't going to go quietly out of the investigation.

"I suppose you already know what he said, too."

She shrugged delicately. "How could I?"

"I don't know how," he groused, "but you do." The meeting had been useless. The footman recalled nothing unusual. The man simply collected the brooch in a velvet and satin box and took it to the Palace. He was an ordinary man, still working for Her Majesty, and so unlikely a criminal even Edward didn't suspect him.

They lapsed into silence once again, and Edward tried to enjoy the end of the dance. It struck him hard that he might never have Radiance Diamond in his arms again and stroked her back before realizing what he was doing. Her suddenly wide green eyes indicated she'd felt his moment of weakness and indulgence.

The devil take him!

When the music ended all too soon, he escorted her back to Lady Diamond, a lovely older version of the woman with whom he'd fallen in love—if he were honest about his feelings.

"Thank you for the dance. I bid you good evening." With his body still throbbing from the sight and scent of Radiance, he gave a shallow bow and walked away.

Edward felt a keen sense of loss. Reclaiming his sister, they rode back to their parents' home with him lost in thought.

"You are morose, Brother."

Lillian's statement brought him out of his reverie. Looking out the window, he'd been trying not to forget a moment of the last dance, wondering if Radiance despised him.

"Could it be you are mooning over a particular gem of a lady?"

Was he? How pointless and immature.

"Don't be ridiculous," he muttered. Before she could delve into his private business, he turned the chessboard, as the saying went. "Did you find any gentleman worthy of *your* affections tonight?"

She sighed. "Not really. I danced with a few new partners. I don't think any of mine were as captivating as your last one was for you."

The devil! His sister was a minx.

Folding his arms, he went back to looking out into the darkness, ignoring her teasing laughter.

A FORTNIGHT PASSED without seeing Radiance again. Garrard was reportedly over in the Netherlands, and the Dutch jewelers would be on their way the following month. And Edward was no closer to determining who might have faked and stolen the Queen's gemstones.

Since this wasn't really his forté, playing at investigating—he tried not to let it consume his entire life. He had lectures to deliver, his new fascination with opals that had caused him to forget the letter to Mr. Neble, and lastly, the book he was writing, which detailed how various gemstones were formed, be they magmatic, metamorphic, pegmatites, or in the earth's mantle.

Monty swatted at Edward's pen while he wrote. When the distraction became too great, he collected his things, took a selection of gemstones from his collection, and headed to the Royal Institution on Albemarle Street. It was one of his favorite lecture halls. He was nearly an hour early, but he intended to write some notes for his book, knowing he would get more done without his feline housemate smudging the ink.

In the corridor, deep in discussion with a group of gentlemen, most of whom Edward recognized, was none other than Lady Radiance Diamond.

He stifled a groan. There hadn't been a day out of the past two weeks that he hadn't thought of her. Yet he also had felt relieved, no longer fearing for her safety. And there she was, dressed boldly in violet satin with ruffles and bows and cream-colored lace. If she was hoping to be taken seriously by the science-minded men of the Royal Institution, she was going about it all wrong.

However, if she was hoping to gain *his* attention, she had it. But that was a vain whim. She could be there for any number of reasons. There were other lecturers on the docket, although he wasn't sure of their topics or, for that matter, if any were of interest to someone who liked gems and jewelry.

Except for his own.

Surely, she couldn't be there for his lecture. As Edward passed the group, a number of the men known to him glanced up. Some nodded by way of greeting, while others jovially called out "Lockwood," before directing their attention back to Radiance. She wasn't speaking but listening intently to the learned Mr. Faraday, who had somehow managed to combine his extensive knowledge of chemistry and electromagnetism into a career of dazzling success.

In Faraday's basement laboratory, the man could make glass, or he could make miniature electrical storms. Why, he'd even rotated light using his magnets in some way that Edward could not fathom. Yet strangely, the scientist was most famous in London for his well-attended Christmas lectures over the past twenty-five years. People bought tickets months in advance, and that reminded Edward to put the purchase on his calendar.

A jolt of jealousy shocked him. Despite the difference in their ages, Faraday had Radiance's rapt attention, and in turn, she held that of the rest of the listeners. Willing her to acknowledge him, Edward had nearly given up hope when her gaze flicked up to his as he passed.

Startlingly chilled emeralds stared up at him and then dismissed him before he even had a chance to nod.

However, about forty minutes later, when the audience trickled in, she was among them. Radiance didn't sit in the center as she had before, nor did all her attention focus on the front of the room. Instead, she was deep in discussion with a man who sat beside her. Not the bore from previously, Lord Woolley, but an intelligent-looking chap with dark hair and a strong profile.

The jealousy returned, racing through Edward from head to toe, a most uncomfortable sensation. Distracted, he knocked his papers off the table. Some swirled in the air a moment before they drifted to the floor.

All heads turned, and all eyes were upon him. He couldn't look at Radiance because he knew she would lift a single supercilious eyebrow.

Coughing to hide his embarrassment, Edward crouched to gather his notes. Having stacked them again, he set his oversized satchel containing boxes of gems on the edge of the table and opened it. Monty raised his furry head, meowing furiously.

Laughter erupted within the auditorium. Having expressed his displeasure either at being kept in the satchel or at being disturbed, the cat hopped out onto the table and stretched, obviously having had a good sleep.

Edward shook his head. He'd ignored the unusual heaviness of the bag, thinking he'd brought an extra box of rocks by mistake.

"That's a gem of a cat," called out one of his associates.

"What mine did you dig it up from?" called another.

Edward smiled at the audience and waved a hand congenially, deciding it was better to be unaffected than all hot, bothered, and embarrassed. Nevertheless, he couldn't let Monty roam free. If his cat made it out of the lecture hall and left the Institution onto busy Albemarle Street in the heart of Mayfair, Edward was likely to lose his house companion.

There was nothing he could do but pick up the errant wanderer who was about to jump down from the table. Monty let out a startled yowl.

Feeling helpless for an instant, Edward wondered whether he could shove the cat back in the bag without looking an utter fool. Radiance unexpectedly came to his rescue.

Rising from her seat, causing the rest of the audience to stand as well, she pushed her way along her row and then descended the central aisle until she was beside him.

"I would offer to take him, but I don't know if he would stay on my lap for an entire lecture. However, I believe with this," and she showed him a long narrow piece of green satin, which he realized had been around her neck and tucked down her décolletage, "you shall be able to restrain your cat."

"Thank you," he said, meaning it wholeheartedly.

A part of him, a very large part of him, wanted to bring her smooth scarf to his nose and breathe deeply. Luckily, he recalled he was in front of his peers and the public, clenching his fingers to stop himself.

"Set Monty on the floor, and I shall hold him," she offered.

Doing as she suggested, Edward watched her bend down and wrap her hands around his cat's chest, like a horse halter. Quickly, he tied the satin piece to Monty's plain leather collar and then, after placing his satchel on the floor, secured the other end to its handle. Since Monty often enjoyed curling up in it, Edward could only hope he would do so again.

"Thank you, my lady," he said softly, trying to catch her eye. Their heads were close. Their gloved fingers brushed in his cat's fur. The temptation to touch her was almost unbearable.

Yet she returned to her seat without another word, which pained him. When the entire audience grew quiet again, he began. As usual, once he started talking about geology, he focused on the information, eager to impart it to those who wanted to know. The two hours passed easily with him holding up samples that he passed through the audience, and then it was over.

At the conclusion, as people shuffled out, Edward kept his head down, packing up his things, unless someone spoke to him, in which case he answered. Each time, he hoped it was Radiance.

When the room had emptied, she was gone.

CHAPTER TWENTY-EIGHT

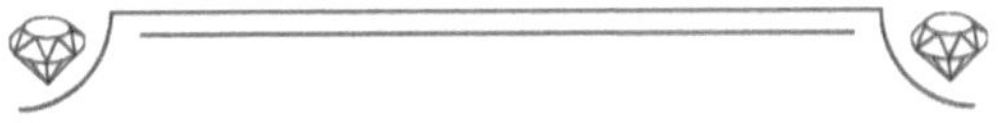

Radiance knew she ought not to contact Edward, but she had to. Nothing had progressed in the investigation for weeks after she'd taken Mr. Minton some sweets and learned of an unnamed footman, who was not really anything of the sort and who could not possibly have been sent by the retired Lord Breadalbane.

That man, probably the forger, was still a frustrating mystery.

But eventually, the Dutch jewelers would come, and she didn't want to miss the cutting of the Koh-i-Noor.

Would the Palace send her an invitation, or did they expect Edward to bring her?

And then there was the curious note, which had recently arrived from Mr. Neble, asking her to stop by his shop. She'd decided it was reason enough to send Edward a missive.

"Sarah, give this to a footman. Make sure it is taken directly to Mr. Lockwood." She handed her maid the folded and sealed page.

"Yes, m'lady."

All she could do was wait. Hopefully, he wasn't too busy to read a missive brought to his door. Any number of things could interrupt the flow of her words to his eyes. Mrs. McSabby might set it down on his worktable, and he might neglect to read it. He might have it in his hand and then think of a passage he intended to write, set it down, and let Monty rest upon it all day.

She paced. Perhaps she should show up unannounced at his home as she had done in the past. When Bri entered the room, Radiance was relieved for the interruption in her endlessly circling thoughts.

Her younger sister plopped down on the sofa and gave a large sigh. "I am beyond dull today. Would you care to take a drive with me through St. James's?"

"I cannot," Radiance told her. "I am awaiting a response."

Bri blinked her lovely blue eyes. "Can't you wait just the same while in a carriage in the park?"

Radiance smiled at her words. "Yes, I could, but then I wouldn't know if I had received an answer."

"Surely, when you get home, the response will be the same whether you are here or not. Perhaps it will even arrive more swiftly if you are not pacing. In fact, you should ignore the very notion of a response, or pretend to, and then it will arrive, as likely as not."

Radiance stared at Bri. Some of what she said sounded like sage advice and the rest, like utter nonsense. That was her sister in a walnut shell.

"Very well. Let us go riding, but I shall drive." Bri was infamous for near misses, and Radiance wished to survive the escapade.

A smile as brilliant as her sister's name broke out on her lovely face. "That is precisely what I wanted. It is so difficult to enjoy one's surroundings and call out to friends when in charge of the horse."

Radiance rolled her eyes. "When you're driving, you are supposed to look where you are going."

"I know. And that is why you are driving."

They were soon out in the fickle sunshine on the single seat of her mother's pony phaeton, and Radiance was ever so glad she'd gone. Bri was correct about friends. They were everywhere. Bri waved and called out and chatted if someone came close by. Radiance, too, saw many she knew from their coming-out parties and from being at the same dances. Diana was out riding with her mother, and they exchanged some pleasant words.

Radiance hadn't relaxed and done anything so frivolous for a while.

It almost seemed fate when Lord Castille came by on his horse, looking extremely attractive due to his height and his seat.

"Good day, ladies. This is by far the most beautiful of carriages in all St. James's Park, a bouquet holding the two most exquisite flowers imaginable."

Bri laughed delightedly. "Well met, my lord. And we are happy you didn't say we are like two diamonds of the first water in a brooch."

"Or a ring or a bracelet," Radiance chimed in. All three things had been said already since they'd set out. "And good day to you, my lord."

"A fine one, it is," he said, looking into her eyes. "Made all the better for seeing you."

Her cheeks warmed. "Thank you," she said softly. "It seems everyone is out."

Lord Castille shrugged, showing off his shoulders. "I see only you and your sister."

Radiance knew if Edward didn't exist, John Castille would have already captured her heart. Lately, they had been having two dances at every ball, and she had let him escort her the past three weeks. People were growing used to seeing them together, and she found his company to be pleasant as well as attentive. Not once had he walked past her without noticing her presence, nor forgotten a promise he'd made.

And she had willed herself to stop making comparisons beyond that.

"Tomorrow night," he said, "my mother and I shall collect you. I am looking forward to another festive evening."

"As am I," she said. And she meant it. Their time together had been joyful interludes during which she stopped thinking about Edward—almost—and even felt her heart beginning to mend.

"A Christmas wedding would be wonderful," Bri said with a dreamy tone wafting on the sweet mid-summer air.

Radiance's smile froze upon her face. Her sister's predictable unpredictability had often been the source of embarrassment. In no way was she ready for a marriage proposal from Lord Castille. How she wished she was, although she couldn't deny a growing fondness for the tall man with the kind eyes.

To his credit, he didn't choke as though his necktie were too tight. In fact, he winked at Radiance before responding, "Who doesn't love Christmas nuptials? But either way, it's a grand time of year."

Phew! Radiance thought he'd handled that well.

"I shan't keep you two lovely flowers any longer," he said. With a nod, he moved on.

Radiance rounded upon Bri. "Honestly, Sister, what were you thinking?"

"About what?" Bri asked, and her expression was as guileless as her mind.

"I know you mean well, but if you haven't figured this out for yourself, then let me tell you. You must never put a man on the spot regarding marriage, nor an engagement for that matter, nor ever asking if they hold someone in high regard. It is simply not done."

After a moment with a furrowed brow, Bri nodded. "I see. It could cause embarrassment, especially if the person did not intend marriage. Thank you for letting me know."

Then after a pause, she added, "Wasn't it jolly lucky, then, that the handsome Lord Castille seems to regard you very highly?"

It was impossible to be angry at Bri. She never intended to insult and rarely even noticed an offense.

As if Radiance's day weren't sufficiently on pins and needles, Bri jabbed her elbow into her ribs.

"*Ooph!*" Radiance rounded on her. "What did you do that for?"

Bri pointed. "Isn't that your geologist friend?"

Radiance's head whipped around. Sure enough, Edward Lockwood was walking determinedly through the park, making his way amid the multitude of horseback riders and carriages.

"Mr. Lockwood," she called out without hesitation, and then nearly clamped her hand over her mouth. Bri was a bad influence.

After glancing to see who had hailed him, he strode over with a satchel in one hand and books under his arm.

"How did you know where to find us?" Bri asked.

Whereas Radiance was momentarily flummoxed that the stars had aligned so perfectly as to deliver him to her side when either of them could be anywhere in London, her sister seemed to think it had happened by design.

"I beg your pardon?" he asked, craning his neck to look past Radiance to Bri, who leaned forward enthusiastically.

"Aren't you here to speak with Ray?" Bri asked.

"Sister, I believe the man has come from a library or lecture hall, given the material he is holding." She turned to Edward. "In any case, I am glad we have run into one another. Did you receive my missive?"

If he had and was in fact out for a stroll or had forgotten its contents already, she would be most disappointed.

"No, I have been at King's College all day."

At least he wasn't dodging her, which would be a dastardly thing to do.

"A good thing we didn't go to Hyde Park," Bri said. "We would have missed you and Lord Castille and so many others. Sometimes these things work out for the best. Such as my spying someone who looks like my friend. Is that Lady Martine?"

Radiance ignored her and leaned toward Edward. "I wish to speak with you on a matter of some importance."

"Do you?" He glanced at her younger sister who, far from being all ears, was peering in the opposite direction.

"That *is* Lady Martine! Such a pretty name, don't you think?" Bri climbed out of the open carriage's low side, even before she finished speaking.

"Where are you going?" Radiance asked, trying to grasp her sister's sleeve. "You cannot simply wander off. Bri, come back!" Too late, her sister had trotted off the path and onto the grass to clasp hands with another young lady amidst shrieks of happy recognition.

Satisfied that there was a woman of a matronly age and demeanor talking with them, Radiance returned her attention to Edward.

Standing beside the carriage, he was windswept, his hat was askew, and his necktie was crooked. Yet her heart was dancing a fast waltz at the sight of him.

Having told herself it was only for the Queen's sake, Radiance had sent him a note that day, even though he hadn't contacted her before or since his lecture at the Royal Institution. A lecture she ought not to have attended, but she'd yearned to see him, plain and simple.

Moreover, it *had* soothed her craving. While she hadn't intended to speak with him, she'd been glad to help with Monty.

Encountering him at Syon House had been a mixture of bitter and sweet. But she hadn't let her heart rush away with false hope, despite her mother's advice. Moreover, Lord Castille's company that same evening, and in the weeks since, had somewhat eased her heartache. She was doing her best to give the amiable viscount a chance to win her over since other avenues had closed.

But here was one of the other avenues . . . looking directly at her.

"You're not talking, Lady Radiance. You're staring," Edward pointed out.

"I paid a second visit to Mr. Minton," she blurted, hoping to impress him.

"I know. You are not the only one who has both ears and eyes open."

Her cheeks warmed. "And do you know what he told me?"

"I do."

Radiance detected a smug look on Edward's otherwise attractive face.

"Then shouldn't someone find this *other* footman? An imposter, I warrant, or a former employee who kept his livery or his insignia perhaps *after* having his employment terminated."

"Thanks to your discussion with the Queen's Mistress of the Robes, the Palace is combing over records to see if that is the case."

She puffed out her cheeks and blew a breath of exasperation.

"We are no closer to solving this puzzle. Are we?" She had to ask. For all she knew, Edward had discovered the identity of the thief.

"You must simply let this slide from your thoughts and go about your former life."

Shocked, Radiance lifted her head. "Why?"

He sighed. "You know why."

Because he didn't want to be near a woman who was infatuated with him.

"I know why, but I assure you that is all in the past."

A deep frown appeared on Edward's normally smooth forehead.

"Is it? How so?"

"I do not have to explain myself further."

"Indeed, you do."

"Fine and dandy!" She would not allow him to think her a desperate sap. "I have recently formed an attachment and am expecting a proposal of marriage by year's end."

Why not? She thoroughly enjoyed John Castille's company.

The furrowed brow cleared immediately, and his glorious golden-brown eyes widened.

"I hadn't heard. Then congratulations are in order, or nearly so, and at that time, I shall offer them to you and to your betrothed."

Radiance didn't like his easy acquiescence regarding her having a future fiancé.

"So, you see, you can relax and—"

Edward shook his head and interrupted. "You think *he* can protect you from stray bullets, do you?"

"I beg your pardon?" She'd had no idea he was still thinking of that silly scrape. "I suppose he can. He was a soldier."

"Was he?" Edward's tone was doubtful. "And if you continue in the investigation, has he agreed to guard you every moment of the day from a jewel thief who doesn't want you to solve a crime?"

Radiance opened her mouth, then shut it again. *Would any man do such a thing?* Follow her around like a servant or a docile pup?

"I suppose he would if I asked. I hadn't thought to do so."

"Then how can you say the danger is all in the past? How am I supposed to relax my guard?"

She was confounded. "*Your* guard? Do you mean you are concerned over my safety?"

He stared at her as if she were a thick-headed dunce.

"Is that not what we are discussing?" he demanded.

Oh dear!

She would have vowed they were having a discussion about how he didn't return her deep affections and, thus, didn't want her near him. She needed to reconsider everything.

"Yes, of course."

"Then as I made clear before, it would be preferable if you simply left the investigating to me," he said.

There wasn't much she could do on her own at this juncture.

"At least, I would like to attend the next meeting regarding the Koh-i-Noor. That is partly what my note was about, which I sent to you earlier today."

He sighed. "That is out of the question. No one shall invite you, and I will not bring you. And I must insist you cease sticking your nose into anything further to do with the forged stones. Will you heed me?" His gaze bore into hers.

Radiance might have if he hadn't put it so rudely.

"I suppose I won't heed you," she said, lifting her chin.

"Is your soon-to-be fiancé the man I have lately seen accompanying you? Or the one who brought you to my lecture?"

She recalled her brother's kind sponsorship of a visit to the Royal Institution.

"Possibly not," she said vaguely. Let him think she had more than one suitor. "I am speaking of Lord Castille."

"He wouldn't have been able to accompany you to the meeting anyway," Edward said, his voice as hard as steel. "He would have been useless and have to wait outside."

"In the path of the bullets," she added tightly.

"Yes," he agreed without a modicum of humor. "As your personal shield." His tone was plainly irritated.

Before he stopped speaking to her all together, she had better get to the heart of the matter.

"Having come to this utter standstill, what will we tell Her Majesty and His Royal Highness?"

THAT WAS A BLOODY GOOD question. And Edward wished he had an answer. He also wished he hadn't learned of Radiance's attachment to Castille. It felt as though he'd been kicked in the stomach. And strangely, it was more painful than the knife slice he'd endured half a year earlier in a dark and lonely place in British Ceylon.

"Perhaps there is still time to come up with an answer." *Any answer*, he thought to himself.

She didn't appear satisfied, but he didn't want to drag her back into danger by discussing the forged jewels any longer. Seeing her out and about, enjoying a summer day with her sister—not to mention looking so breathtakingly lovely he wanted to shield his eyes—Edward was determined to keep her safely away from anything nefarious that had happened in the past.

"I believe the best I can do is to ensure the Koh-i-Noor doesn't suffer the same fate."

Not only would it sting to be outsmarted, but the recriminations would be numerous and terrible.

"That hardly seems a satisfactory response," Radiance said. "On a possibly unrelated matter, I have received an invitation from Mr. Neble. He wishes to speak with me again."

She had his full attention, as usual.

"Does he? Whatever for?"

"I haven't the foggiest notion, but I mentioned it in my note to you."

Edward didn't think it could be unrelated as she believed.

"Are you going?" he asked.

"Yes, of course."

"Is your beau going, too?" he shot back, then wished he hadn't.

"I . . . I didn't ask him. I will take Sarah, of course."

Edward didn't hesitate.

"I shall accompany you." He meant to ask or to offer, but it came out as a *fait accompli*.

She stiffened. "I don't think that is necessary. After all, it is a jewelry shop."

"Nevertheless, I shall." Edward had gone down the path now and couldn't withdraw, even if he wanted to, and he didn't.

"Mr. Neble didn't invite *you*," Radiance said, and he detected her stubborn streak, which he was starting to think was about a furlong wide.

"Regardless, perhaps there will be a clue that you'll miss, and I might catch," he offered.

"Unlikely, sir, but I can see your mind is made up. I will meet you there."

He hadn't expected her easy acquiescence nor going separately. In fact, Edward had hoped he could collect Radiance and her maid.

"Very well," he said. "But I caution you not to go inside without me."

Her right eyebrow raised, and Edward wondered if he'd gone too far. Then he reminded her, "And you didn't tell me when."

"Tomorrow at two o'clock."

"What is happening tomorrow?" Lady Brilliance asked, having returned more quietly than she had departed.

"Eavesdropping is not a virtue," Radiance snapped.

Edward cringed at her tone. When her sister's face fell to an expression of dejection, Radiance relented.

"My apologies, dear one. But it is nothing that concerns you, merely more of my interest in gems. Forgive my abruptness."

Already a smile was growing once again upon Lady Brilliance's face. "You are forgiven. Shall we continue, and then I would much welcome a stop at Gunter's."

Radiance glanced again at Edward who nodded.

"Good day, ladies." And he disappeared into the throng in the opposite direction to which they were going.

CHAPTER TWENTY-NINE

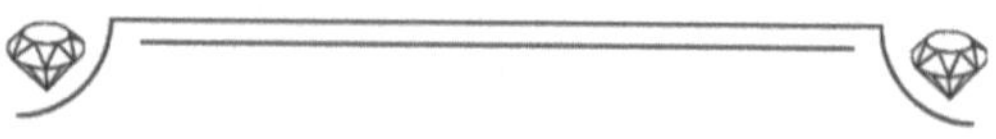

Edward made sure to arrive ten minutes early at the House of Neble. He had a notion Radiance would go inside without him if she got there first. The same clerk greeted him.

"Lady Radiance isn't here, sir. Not yet, although she is expected." The clerk paused, appearing uncomfortable, then he blurted, "But you are not. I don't believe Mr. Neble is prepared to see you today."

"He doesn't see much of anyone, does he?" Edward asked, feeling a little tweaguey at possibly being refused admittance. "While we await Lady Radiance, I wish you to ask Mr. Neble if I may accompany her into his office."

"That's not necessary," the clerk said.

"I assure you it is." Edward didn't care for his insolence.

"I say it isn't, sir, because I know he will refuse you entrance."

"Why do you think that?"

"Because I am the one Mr. Neble asked to write and send the invitation to Lady Radiance. He was adamant only she should come. He will be most irritated to know you are even in the building."

Edward was about to argue when Radiance entered. He didn't have to turn to see her to know it was she. He felt it, and then her heady lilac fragrance enveloped him, making his body tense and his loins tighten.

"Mr. Lockwood, you are most punctual," she declared.

Finally, hoping his loose trousers hid his arousal, he turned. "Sometimes, my lady. Alas, it has done me little good for this clerk informed me I shall not be granted access to Mr. Neble in any case."

"Truly?" She looked at the clerk.

"I am afraid it is true, my lady. Mr. Neble invited you and only you."

"I suppose it is his prerogative," Radiance said. She seemed a little too unconcerned for Edward's liking.

"I suppose you could tell him you insist," Edward suggested.

"But I do not insist," she said, stirring his ire. "However, if I am able, I will tell you what transpires. In any case, there is no need for you to wait here when you have more important work to do at home."

Edward couldn't believe she had dismissed him.

RADIANCE HADN'T MEANT to sound so imperial. And she didn't like the expression Edward currently wore. His handsome face was stern, and she half feared he was going to argue or somehow seek to stop her from seeing Mr. Neble.

With that thought, she hurried to the stairs leading to the old jeweler's office. Sarah, naturally, followed her.

She'd moved so quickly, she had to wait for the clerk to catch up and announce her. Inside his chamber, Mr. Neble and his surroundings were the same.

"Whom have we here?" he asked, leaning forward, peering at her companion.

"My maid, sir. I cannot speak with you alone, as I am sure you understand."

Mr. Neble made a face. "I wish to speak with you on a personal matter. Can I trust your maid?"

Perplexed, Radiance glanced at Sarah, who stared back at her. Her maid had never gossiped, not that she'd caught her, anyway.

What choice did she have?

Continuing to look at Sarah, she said, "Sir, my maid is absolutely discreet. I promise you. If she ever repeats anything you say today, then I will sack her. Will that suffice?"

Sarah's eyes widened.

"I suppose it will have to," Mr. Neble said. Then he rested back in his chair. "I had a good dinner with Mr. Bonwit the other night. He came to my home. Did he tell you?"

Surprised by the initial topic of their chat, she said, "He did not."

"We spoke about you."

Radiance's skin prickled. "About me? Regarding what?"

Mr. Neble remained silent for a few moments. Then he looked down at his hands and spoke softly, "My son died of the grippe. Influenza, if you will."

"I am dreadfully sorry." Radiance wished there was something more useful than those trite words.

Mr. Neble nodded. After another long pause, he looked at her again. "You said that the last time I met you, and I appreciated your sympathy then as I do now. My wife is long dead, and I had only Herbert."

"While I have no children of my own, I have three sisters and a brother," she told him. "I cannot imagine the pain of losing one of them."

"Even worse when you have only the one," he conceded.

"Again, I cannot pretend to know your grief."

He said nothing more for a moment. Adjusting the lamp on either side of his worktable, he asked, "Would you mind coming closer? I would like to clearly see with whom I am dealing."

"Not at all, sir." Radiance rose from her seat and leaned over the table, so the oil lamps lit her features.

Mr. Neble gasped. "Why, you're beautiful!"

"Thank you," she said, returning to her seat.

"My eyesight is not as sharp as it was," he explained.

"I had guessed as much, sir. You have far more lamps than expected for the room."

"They hardly help anymore."

"And your failing sight is the reason you do not let customers engage with you directly. Or anyone, for that matter."

"Correct. I cannot lose my reputation as that will also lose me my business." He squinted at her as he spoke, then leaned forward. "The necklace you're wearing. Did you make it?"

"Yes."

"May I look at it more closely?"

"Of course." While she unhooked the clasp, he donned his two pairs of glasses. When Radiance dropped the necklace onto his outstretched hand, he immediately pulled it up to his face and spent a few silent moments examining it.

At last, he looked at her. "Bonwit has not misplaced his effusive compliments as to your skill."

"I am glad you think so." And she was. The opinion of an older master jeweler like Mr. Neble meant a great deal. He returned her necklace to her.

Finally, Radiance had to ask what had been on her mind since the last visit. "May I ask how you still produce jewelry?"

"With help," he said vaguely. "*Not* using an apprentice, though. My jewelry is all still crafted by a jeweler, here on my premises."

Her heart pinched, realizing the House of Neble would die with him.

"Bonwit is a lucky man to have you," Mr. Neble added.

"I consider myself to be the lucky one."

"You are modest. Even if you only learn from him, he considers you to be a prize. But you are not interested in working for him or being his apprentice, are you?"

"No," she said. "That is most definitely not my goal."

"I hope I haven't insulted you. I know you are an earl's daughter and have no need to earn a living."

"I am not offended, sir." Radiance wondered where this was all going.

"Besides," Mr. Neble added, "he hopes his apprentice shall marry his daughter, isn't that right?"

The two men had obviously enjoyed a deeper conversation than merely how well Radiance could polish a gemstone. "I believe that is Mr. Bonwit's wish."

"Good for him," the old jeweler said. "He is lucky to have a daughter and a future son-in-law who has agreed to keep the Bonwit name above his shop."

The poor man! Radiance wished Mrs. Neble had birthed an entire litter of little Nebles.

"With the help of my two pairs of spectacles," the man continued, unaware of Radiance's distress, "I saw the Koh-i-Noor you drew in its famed armlet, but that showed me only the talent of a sketcher. However, Bonwit told me you have the same innate talent as a jewelry-maker."

She felt her cheeks warm. "That is kind of him."

"Kindness had nothing to do with it, I assure you. He was simply answering my questions." He hesitated. "With your necklace, I have seen your skill for myself. Thus, I have a proposition for you, which I hope you will consider."

She listened carefully and surprised herself by actually considering it a viable option.

"I will let you know after long contemplation, sir."

"Not too long, I hope. I won't last forever," he said gruffly.

"I wish you many more years, sir," she said before taking her leave with Sarah behind her.

As Radiance walked along the narrow landing toward the staircase, another door opened, and a dark-haired man stepped out. He froze at the sight of her, clearly deciding whether to step back and close the door.

Strangely, although she didn't believe she had ever met him, he seemed familiar. It might simply be that he wore the thick apron of many jewelers and metalworkers, marked with tripoli stone for polishing gems and removing scratches in brass. She often incurred the same stains herself and glanced at his ungloved hands to see it upon his fingertips, too.

"Does Mr. Neble know you are here?" he asked without a preliminary greeting.

She realized he must be the one who made the jewelry for the House of Neble, toiling in anonymity. He might even be the one who last cleaned the coronet. Which meant, he might be . . . the forger.

"Good day," she said. "He does. I have just left his presence. He is available if you need to speak with him."

Immediately, the man's face clouded over. "I can think of no reason I would need to speak to *him*," he stated, his tone disparaging.

"Is he not your employer?" she asked mildly. Simply because Mr. Neble was old and losing his sight, it didn't mean he had lost either his design skill or his hard-gained knowledge. Nor should he be spoken of disrespectfully. "Do you not craft jewelry for him, under his direction?"

The assistant looked surprised. After all, no one was supposed to know the older jeweler no longer fashioned the creations that carried his name.

"Is that what he tells people?" the man asked. "I save his aging hide every day, and he lords it over me as if I'm merely his unskilled lackey. Is that right?"

Radiance hadn't meant to cause a problem, and she hastened to smooth it out.

"He didn't speak disparagingly of you at all. I merely assumed, since you wore the garb of a jeweler, that you are one. If you are not, then I apologize for any offense."

He looked her up and down, then his gaze slid to Sarah. Understanding dawned on him that he was dealing with a wealthy lady.

"I am a jeweler and a highly skilled one at that," he boasted. "Are you here to order jewelry? Mr. Neble doesn't normally see his customers upstairs. But then he doesn't *see* much of anything anymore."

His laughter at his own joke struck Radiance as loathsome and petty. Moreover, the fact that she thought she'd met him before was greatly bothersome.

"I might be," she prevaricated, feeling even sorrier for Mr. Neble in losing his only son. "If you create the exquisite jewelry I saw downstairs in the shop, then may I know your name? No artisan of your talent should work in obscurity."

His expression soured. "I have an arrangement with Mr. Neble, a regrettable one. My name cannot be used here. The jewelry I make is to be considered as his own. For this, he doesn't pay me well enough, I assure you."

His bitter tone indicated his dissatisfaction, and Radiance thought it clear why they kept this man hidden away from customers. He seemed eager to disclose the irksome arrangement and destroy Mr. Neble's reputation.

Perhaps he felt himself so slighted that he had decided to forge a few royal jewels to puff himself up. Maybe he thought no one would ever know. And if he had, then he truly was a talented lapidary.

Then she had an idea. "If you made something for me privately," she suggested, "then it would be truly one of a kind. The price is unimportant if you can make me something truly spectacular, and you would benefit by gaining additional clients amongst my friends."

His eyes bulged. He probably had to weigh the potential income she might bring him against the steady work he had at the House of Neble as its only jeweler. And then there was the pride of an artist to add to the scales—something she well understood.

Watching his interest grow, she added the final bait. "Then all you need do is let your name and your reputation grow upon your own merits. Why, within a few months, you could quit working here and have your own name emblazoned over a doorway."

It seemed the promise of fame piqued his interest.

"I shall not tell you today, not here. But I am at your service, my lady." He even sketched a low bow, going from his earlier unpleasant demeanor to excessive obsequiousness, like a newly hired butler in his first position as head of household.

"I am, in fact, in need of a large tiara for a special occasion," Radiance quickly invented, "and I would like some impressive gems to go into it. Unusual, large precious stones if you understand. Cost is of no concern, naturally. I hope you can help me."

He nodded. "I would be pleased to do so. I can get anything you need."

Anything she needed. *How convenient!*

"Then I am exceedingly fortunate to have run into you. I was going to give Mr. Neble my business, but I would rather work directly with you now that I know you are the talent behind the House of Neble." She handed him her card. "Please let me know when you can come by."

She was so excited by the discovery of this unknown jeweler, who had the means and perhaps the motive, she hurried downstairs hoping to find Edward still there.

He hadn't left, for which Radiance was grateful. Perhaps it was merely curiosity that had kept him in the shop waiting for her. Or maybe he'd become so engrossed in being surrounded by gems, he'd lost all track of time. Holding a stone in his hand and deep in discussion with the shop clerk, he didn't notice when she returned.

"You see it's the trace amounts of chromium that cause the alexandrite to be grass green," Edward explained.

"It is assuredly red, sir," said the clerk.

"Take it to the window," Edward instructed, returning the gem to the clerk.

The man did as instructed, holding it out to the sun's rays. Luckily, the London sky was cooperating and cloudless. Radiance smiled when the clerk gasped.

"Truly," he said, lifting the alexandrite into the air and holding it toward the window. "Yes, it changes in the blink of an eye, as if the stone is winking at me."

"I am ready to leave," Radiance said, and both men looked up.

Edward had that expression upon his face, as if he were far away in his thoughts. He was a scientist at heart who became engrossed in whatever interested him. Some would say he was absent-minded, but she considered him to be the opposite—overly concentrating on one thing to the detriment of all other things, especially if the other thing happened to be a female who adored him.

"Will you tell me why Mr. Neble wished to speak with you?" Edward asked after they'd stepped outside.

Radiance hesitated. "I cannot break his confidence." The old jeweler had opened his heart and confided in her. Moreover, it wouldn't be a good example to disclose anything with Sarah close by.

In the end, she didn't want to tell Edward about Mr. Neble's proposition, at least not until she had made a decision. And even then, it didn't involve him in the least.

As to her discovery of the jeweler upstairs, she could not recall conversing with an oilier individual, although she was still unsure why the man seemed familiar. Regardless, Edward would become protective again, even though she intended to meet the suspicious jeweler only in the safety of her home.

"Would you like us to drop you at your home?" she asked.

Edward stiffened before glancing at Sarah, who was all eyes and ears after her unusual adventure.

"No, thank you. I may not keep a carriage in Town, but I do not need to beg a ride in your father's conveyance. I am sure he doesn't lend it to you in order that you take on passengers. I shall make my own way. Thank you."

With that, he offered a quick, shallow bow before turning from her.

"I am sorry you wasted a trip here and an hour of your day," she said to his ramrod straight back.

Glancing over his shoulder, he said, "It wasn't wasted, I assure you."

CHAPTER THIRTY

What had the secretive meeting been about? Edward was brimming with curiosity. Radiance had been wrong, though. Any opportunity to see and speak with her was time well spent. He couldn't deny he had been happy to run into her at the park as well.

What's more, he missed their easy banter.

Regardless, he had to get back to work. As the day progressed and his resilience to remain focused strengthened, he managed some concentrated hours. Eventually, parched and irritable for no reason, he poured himself a cup of the cold coffee he'd neglected.

With Monty in his usual place on the table, Edward sat beside him and sighed.

"I am unsettled," he told the cat before draining the cup.

He couldn't help making a face at what he tasted. "And I am a fool for not drinking my coffee when it is piping hot." He was a fool for more than that. His life had been turned upside down since meeting Lady Radiance. Yet instead of the turmoil making him long for his old existence, he wanted to follow where this new journey might lead. One with her.

But the danger still existed, and now she was interested in a viscount. His chances were growing slimmer by the day.

"What shall I do?" he asked Monty.

"Talking to the cat now, are you? Has it come to this?"

His sister's entrance jarred him to standing. A second later, he recalled they'd had a dinner engagement for that evening.

"Dinner!" he exclaimed.

"You forgot," Lillian said, her face falling.

"I didn't." *The devil take him!* He couldn't lie to her. "Maybe I did, but I am glad you're here."

"Upon most any evening, you could come home and have a meal with me and Mother and Father, too. They would be equally glad for your company."

"They haven't invited me since the party," he said, monstrously glad they hadn't. A family meal at his parent's residence lasted an interminable number of hours.

"That's because they knew you would forget to come."

"Hm." He hadn't realized he was getting a reputation for absentmindedness.

"I would not. That's absurd."

His sister raised both eyebrows, reminding him of a certain radiant gem.

"I wonder on what we shall dine," Lillian said, taking a seat and stroking Monty under the chin.

"As do I," he said.

She laughed, which he appreciated because he was being a terrible host.

"You ought to have some inkling," she admonished. "What if your cook has made nothing at all?"

"Doubtless, there will be something. Tell me about your life at present while I set my things in order, and then we can go into the salon."

"If you promise to listen to me while you do."

"I always listen," he said, then smiled at her very grown-up expression. She looked like their mother at her most exasperated. "I suppose I could do better."

"Is that why you are no longer escorting Lady Radiance? I very much enjoyed her company."

He stopped with one hand in the bag of gems. "I was never . . . that is, we didn't . . . never mind."

"People do not enjoy being forgotten or neglected, Brother."

He continued to put everything away and ignored her. After all, it had nothing to do with him being forgetful and everything to do with Radiance's safety. In fact, far from forgetting, he couldn't get the lovely lady out of his mind.

Eventually, he decided to tell his sister the unfortunate news.

"Besides, the lady has formed an attachment since last the three of us were together."

"It must be with that dapper Lord Castille," Lillian surmised. "But how would you know that? Are you certain? Because I have heard nothing of this, nor have I read about it in the newspaper."

"She told me so herself, which I believe is more reliable than gossip."

His sister shook her head. "More's the pity. I would have dearly liked her for a sister-in-law. If only you hadn't dallied and spent more time gazing at rocks than at her."

"Lillian," he warned. "Let us wish her happiness and move on."

Mrs. McSabby chose that moment to enter, of which he was exceedingly glad.

"Roast lamb tonight, Miss Lockwood, and Yorkshire pudding and peas with mint sauce, just the way you like."

"Then you didn't forget," his sister said.

His housekeeper, traitor that she was, reared back.

"Your brother might not recall his own family, but as head of staff here, I would never forget when a guest is expected. That would be a dereliction of duty, miss."

"Yet you let people into my house," Edward grumbled, "without announcing them."

"I am not *people*," Lillian said. "I'm your sister."

"I wasn't talking about you," he assured her before turning back to his housekeeper, who seemed more like his mother some days. "In any case, I suppose you came in because dinner is ready."

"It is, sir," Mrs. McSabby said. They followed her into the small salon he used for dining, with a modest round table now set for two, although it could hold six at a pinch.

Edward was surprised how many times Lillian managed to bring up Radiance in the next two hours. She'd seen her at a ball. She'd admired her gown and wondered if it would be appropriate to pay a visit and ask for the name of her modiste. She had bumped into her on Oxford Street. And more than once, she mentioned Lord Castille in the same breath, as if Radiance and the viscount were always together.

It was sickening! He could barely eat the lamb. His own Lady Succulent Lambchop was lost to him.

Finally, after Lillian had enjoyed a large portion of trifle and sherry in the drawing room before the hearth, she was ready to depart. Edward packed her into their father's carriage in which she had come and sent her home.

His house seemed cavernously empty afterward, even though Monty was in an amiable mood, curled up on the drawing room sofa.

Edward didn't feel like working, which was surprising. Thus, grabbing his coat and hat, he went out. Although he'd once lied to Chippens about a fictitious social club for geologists, once in a blue moon, Edward did enjoy the camaraderie of his fellow scientists at the Athenaeum Club.

They might not have card tables, scantily clad light-skirts, or the quantity of titled whelps eager to wager on every thought that came into their head as the well-known gentlemen's clubs had. But his organization had an excellent chef and barman, a cozy dining area, multiple libraries in which members read journals and discussed them at length, and one in which they had to maintain silence.

He'd gained acceptance after being elected to the club by the esteemed William Buckland, whom Edward knew from the Ordnance Geological Survey of which they both were involved, directing geologists and surveyors to head out over the entire island of Britain.

Ensconced with his own kind, he relaxed, ordered a glass of claret, and wandered into the dining room. At that hour, many had finished eating and were simply relaxing. Mr. Sebastian Garrard was there, as he often was, with his brother.

"Join us," the Crown Jeweler said, "or at least join me, as Robert was just going home to his wife."

After the departure of the younger jeweler, Garrard asked, "What brings you out at this hour?"

"It's not exactly late," Edward pointed out as his wine glass was set before him.

"No, but I rarely see you here at any time of day. I understand you're working on a book."

"Indeed I am."

Kindly, Garrard asked him questions for the next half hour, allowing him to discuss what was dear to his heart. While attempting to keep the debate of the religious aspects out of it and let others decide whether it was blasphemy to suggest an older earth than the Bible indicated, Edward concentrated only on what he could see with his own eyes, the stratigraphic record, as it were. And most particularly, he was interested in the forces that created so-called precious and semi-precious gems.

Surprisingly, after they had both switched to brandy, Garrard asked about Radiance. Edward noted a pang in the vicinity of his heart. He had the oddest notion that she was actually far dearer to him than his projects, even more so than his written opus.

"I understand she works alongside Mr. Bonwit," the Crown Jeweler said.

"How did you find out?" Edward asked.

Mr. Garrard shrugged. "You know how small our community is."

And Edward knew he wouldn't learn more about how, but tongues were wagging.

"Bonwit says she's rather skilled," Mr. Garrard continued. "Have you seen her work?"

Edward gripped his glass more tightly. "Why, I'm not sure." Perhaps he had seen her jewelry and simply hadn't known it. He ought to have at least asked her to show him something. *What a dolt!*

"Then you cannot speak personally to her skill."

What was Garrard getting at? "She has no intention of seeking employment," he told the master jeweler. "Not that I know of, anyway."

Garrard merely nodded. "Did you know I only returned from Amsterdam last week? I met with Mr. Coster. He is sending not one but two of his finest jewelers to my workshop. We're inviting the Duke of Wellington to make the first cut.'"

Edward nearly choked on a sip of French brandy.

"But Wellington is eighty if he's a day."

"He is eighty-three, but that's no matter. Many consider that India was the making of our 'Iron Duke,' and the Koh-i-Noor represents India. Besides, he cannot hurt it. The Dutch polishers will see to that. The Koh-i-Noor will be encased in lead with only a small plane visible, and the scaif will be positioned so Wellington can do only the most minute of polishing. And you shall be overseeing it, too."

Edward startled, but Garrard didn't notice.

"Will you both be at the next meeting to greet the polishers?" The Crown Jeweler was back to speaking about Radiance.

"I don't know if the lady will attend," Edward said truthfully.

"Really?" Garrard seemed surprised they weren't joined at the hip. "Then at the initial cutting ceremony, surely. It's set for the seventeenth of July. I imagine she would enjoy a first-hand view of the proceedings, even more than you. Your interest lies more in the rough than the cut gem, does it not?"

Edward nodded. It would be an historic occasion, and one which would leave the Koh-i-Noor vulnerable through the entire process.

WHILE OUT RIDING WITH Lord Castille, Radiance had missed Mr. Neble's mysterious jeweler, but the man had left his card. And his name—Peter Sully. Immediately, she sent word to his abode across the river in Clapham. His Netherford Road address indicated a residence of enterprising middle-class comfort. Not nearly in the league of Edward or Mr. Bonwit, yet neither was he dwelling amongst the poor.

Within hours, Mr. Sully had agreed to come to her home the following day for a consultation and bring with him an assortment of his best stones. The anticipation stopped her from eating. *Would he bring the Queen's sapphire and emerald?*

With her sister Bri apprised of her need for privacy and their parents out, Radiance donned all her best jewelry, and even some of her mother's. Mr. Sully needed to know she wasn't wasting his time. Once they were sequestered in the drawing room, with Sarah seated at one end, Radiance could hardly wait to see what the jeweler had brought.

First, he showed her some drawings he'd made of tiaras. They were well drawn, as she expected, having seen his jewelry at the House of Neble. However, when he unfolded a piece of velvet, she was disappointed to see ordinary gemstones, a medium-sized diamond, two small sapphires, and a pretty ruby, as well as some matched sets of garnets and a half dozen pearls.

"I am sorry, Mr. Sully. While I think this design," she pointed to a random sketch, "is precisely what I desire, these gems won't do at all. I can find their ilk all up and down Bond Street or Oxford Street. There is nothing remarkable here." Disappointment dripped from her voice as she added, "I guess you are not in the class of jewelers I had hoped."

His features hardened. "I can get you something finer, but you would have to give me payment in advance before I make the tiara. Is there something you've seen in particular that you like?"

"I know you will think me vain, yet I have been to a ball in which the Queen wore a coronet." She described the one she knew had already lost a genuine stone. "The way the gems were set and the size of them would be perfect for *my* tiara. Anything else, I fear, would look too small."

Would she go too far if she were to sketch it out for him? Radiance didn't want him to comprehend the extent of her knowledge. She waited, trying to be patient and keeping a look of expectancy upon her face. At the same time, she touched her mother's ruby necklace, nestled above her own décolletage. Beneath it hung the single diamond pendant all the sisters received on their sixteenth birthday.

He watched the play of her fingers, as she knew he would. "I know of two gemstones you would especially like, but they are extremely costly."

Two! Although her heart was beating fast, she waved her hand nonchalantly. "As I said before, that is of no consequence. When can I see them? Today?"

He startled at her enthusiasm, and she tried to temper it lest he become suspicious.

"I am eager," she explained, "because there is an upcoming ball at which I wish to dazzle a certain nobleman—in two weeks. Can you create the piece by then? Otherwise, I have no use for it."

His eyes widened. "For the right sum, yes, I could. If you bring a bank note—only from the Bank of England, mind you. None of the provincial banks—for this amount," he wrote down an astonishing sum, "then I shall get you the best stones."

Her father was going to be most displeased if she actually spent such a fortune on a tiara—or worse, lost it altogether.

Mr. Sully could take the money and disappear to the Continent, living like a king for two years at the least.

"I am intrigued by what kind of gems could command such a cost," she said. "I must see them at the time that I pay. If I don't like what I see, then I don't have to buy them. Do you agree?"

If he already had the stones in his possession, as she suspected, then this offer would work. If Mr. Sully had to purchase the expensive gems, then he was going to deny her conditions.

After a moment, however, he agreed. Her plan, which was more of a loose strategy with more holes than Belgian lace, seemed to be working.

"But I cannot bring the stones here," he said. "You must go to them."

Radiance shook her head. Not a fool, she had no intention of going to some quiet spot and getting her throat slit. After all, no one even knew that Mr. Sully worked for Mr. Neble.

"Hear me out, my lady. The gems are in a safe place, and I am unwilling to parade them around the streets."

"Surely, coming here to Piccadilly is hardly *parading* them," she protested.

"I can take no chances," he insisted. "Have you heard of the jewelry exchanges in Houndsditch?"

In fact, she had. They were a legitimate place for jewelers to buy and sell gems, as well as all manner of gold and silver. But since Houndsditch was no place for a lady, she merely blinked at him.

"No. I have never heard of it."

"If you want your tiara made with two spectacular stones that you cannot get elsewhere, stones cut by my own hand, mind you, then you must meet me in Houndsditch tomorrow."

"Impossible. It would have to be the day after. I cannot get the bank note so quickly." In truth, she needed time to contact Edward before she dared meet with Mr. Sully.

"Then I cannot help you." He rose to his feet and looked around the room, taking in her parents' good taste in furnishings. "*Tomorrow*, my lady. Or the gemstones will go to someone else."

She shot to her feet, unwilling to let the Queen's jewels slip through her fingers.

"Very well. Tomorrow. Give me the address, and I will meet you there."

Mr. Sully bowed as if he were the one bending to her wishes. "Perhaps you can get the money in coin." He chuckled at his own jest since even if she had such at hand, the weight of the coins would be impossible for her to carry.

After writing the address beneath the large sum in a neat scrawl, the opposite of Edward's wild one, Mr. Sully gave her further directions on finding the entrance, which she committed to memory.

Finally, he added, "Rap three times on the third door." And he handed her the scrap of paper.

"Three times," Radiance repeated, looking at the address. Then she sent him a wide-eyed look. "I cannot wait to have a tiara that is the envy of all my friends. They shall all demand to know its creator."

He smiled, baring his teeth and reminding her of an unfriendly dog. She shivered.

"Perhaps, my lady, with your patronage, I shall be able to come out of the shadows and quit my employment at the House of Neble. That would be my fervent wish."

Radiance nodded. "Then I shall see you tomorrow."

CHAPTER THIRTY-ONE

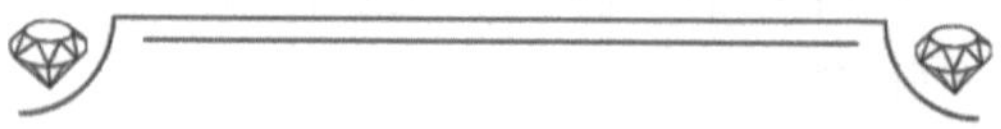

Radiance couldn't do it alone. No matter that Edward had brushed her off like lint from his sleeve and she'd returned the favor in kind. She had to contact him. Again! And with little time to waste, she sent for one of her father's carriages as soon as Mr. Sully's cab disappeared from her doorstep.

While the horses were being harnessed, Radiance hurried upstairs to remove most of her jewelry and make any changes to her appearance. Meeting with Mr. Sully was one thing, but having Edward see her was quite another.

"It's been a long time since we've been here, m'lady," Sarah pointed out after descending from the carriage and approaching Edward's front door.

Radiance wasn't sure of her welcome. She cleared her throat and nodded to Sarah, who lifted and let loose the heavy door knocker. Once, twice, thrice. They looked at one another.

"They must all be out, m'lady."

"Blast!" Radiance exclaimed. It had been hard enough to swallow her pride and come knocking upon Edward's door. Yet knowing she was in the suds over her head, she had done so.

Faced with him being absent from his home, she couldn't deny the crushing disappointment. Most certainly it was because of her desire to do her duty to Crown and country. It couldn't be because she'd wasted precious time making sure she looked her best in a peach-cream-and-navy tartan day dress of the softest, lightest cotton.

But she had been anticipating seeing his golden-topaz eyes take her in.

Drat and double drat!

"Let us try once more," she suggested to Sarah, who raised and lowered the knocker again.

Suddenly, the door flew open. It was Mrs. McSabby.

"Oh, m'lady. My apologies. I was in the back and wasn't sure I heard the knocker. I thought the master would answer in any case, as he often does." She stood back so Radiance could enter. "It's a good thing you're here. Mr. Lockwood is in a right state, and no mistake."

Alarmed, Radiance asked, "Is he well?"

Mrs. McSabby sighed. "I fear he isn't. He's not sleeping nor eating properly. Just working on his rocks and his book, which is also about rocks, I believe. Too many rocks, I say. He's going to end up with rocks in his head and a painful *ulcus* from neglecting his health!"

With those ominous words, the housekeeper turned heel, leaving them in the front hall like the most negligent head of staff Radiance could possibly imagine.

Sarah exclaimed aloud, "Blimey!"

"Well said," Radiance agreed. "But I believe we've at least been invited in. Would you like to go to the kitchen for a cup of tea? You said they had very good biscuits."

"Yes, m'lady." Sarah wandered off, already drawing her latest reading material from her pocket.

Radiance didn't hesitate. She followed behind her maid but stopped at Edward's study. Knowing she was being rude, she tapped softly, then pushed open the door.

Edward's back was to her—his bare, magnificently sculpted back—and it bore a long, raised, horizontal scar that disappeared around his ribcage to the front of him. He seemed to be applying an unguent to its puckered edges by trying to look at his reflection in a window pane.

"Blimey!" she echoed Sarah.

Edward whirled around. "What the devil!"

Radiance was not the type to gasp or faint, but she did bite her lip. His chest was splendid, if such a word applied. Set off by broad shoulders and muscled arms, his torso tapered down to a narrow waist that was hidden by the top of his worsted wool trousers.

In the middle of all the maleness were pale tawny nipples, set wide, and a dusting of hair. Smooth, yet rippling muscles over his stomach caught her attention before it returned to his scar.

Edward snatched up his shirt from the nearby table and yanked it over his head before fastening two of the four buttons. He glanced around wildly.

"Where is my necktie?"

Radiance wasn't sure whether he was asking her or perhaps Monty, who was stretched out on the table in the sunshine.

In any case, he flipped up his collar at his throat and left it.

"Lady Radiance," he greeted sharply while tucking his shirt into his waistband and pulling the boxcloth braces up over his shoulders. "To what do I owe the *pleasure*?"

"My sincere apologies for barging in. Mrs. McSabby didn't say you were in a state of undress."

"She probably didn't know. Besides, *she* would have knocked, and I would have put on my shirt in private."

"I did tap upon your door." Radiance was extremely glad he hadn't heard her. If she never saw it again, she wouldn't forget his naked body or the scar.

Could she ask him about it? Purity would say no, but Clarity would say he might wish to speak of it. Unburdening himself so could ease his mind and make him happy.

"I suppose you're wondering about my disfigurement."

"Your what?" she asked. Radiance hadn't seen anything that would be . . . "Do you refer to your scar?"

"Naturally."

"Hardly a disfigurement, sir. If you wish to tell me, then I should be interested to learn its origin."

"How I received it is not interesting at all. I can assure you. It was a stupid mistake on my part. You know that I occasionally venture to where the gemstones are mined. I was in Ceylon, to be exact."

"How exciting," she murmured.

He nodded. "It was. It's thrilling to see the stones coming out of the ground or being extracted from the water. To me, they are more beautiful when having the dirt washed off them just after they've been sifted from the earth than when they are set in gold or silver."

"I do not doubt there is a moment of intense exhilaration upon seeing a stone freshly mined, but I disagree about its beauty," Radiance said. "I have seen many uncut gemstones, and they were universally dull and without shine. I like to see how light glimmers through a jewel."

Edward nodded. "I understand, and Sir Brewster would agree. But there is a moment of intense satisfaction when a gemstone, unrecognized at first, is discovered in a basket of ordinary rocks."

"In the rough, as they say," Radiance said. "I would like to see that for myself. But you haven't told me yet what caused the scar you bear."

Edward approached the table and absently stroked Monty's head.

"People become animals over certain issues," he said, "such as wealth or jealousy."

His eyes flickered to her face.

"And gemstones?" she prompted.

He nodded. "Gemstones represent wealth, do they not? The person who wanted them was jealous that I had them and needed the money they represented. In the darkness while I slept, naively thinking myself safely guarded by my guide, my hut was broken into. I awakened during the ransacking, and the thief didn't take kindly to my suggestion that he put my gemstones back where he found them. We fought, and I was left with this. It has nearly healed, but today, it was bothering me, feeling tight and itchy."

"You were treating it with something," she surmised.

"Yes. Mrs. McSabby disregarded my wishes to leave it alone when I returned home with an angry-looking red wound. She secured a military doctor who produced a useful balm. I keep it here in the workroom, so I won't forget to use it."

He paused and pursed his lips with annoyance. "And now you know all my secrets."

She doubted that.

"Why do you call yourself naïve? How could you know you would be robbed?"

"I hired a native when I should have kept my eyes open or hired a fellow Englishman. Even a mercenary would have been more loyal."

"And thus, you lost your bounty."

To her surprise, Edward's handsome face broke out into a smile, familiarly lopsided with a single dimple, making her heart clench. He turned away, going to a bureau that had many drawers. Opening one, he withdrew a velvet pouch and brought it over to her.

"Hold out your hand," he directed.

With a small shiver running up her spine, Radiance did. He emptied the contents onto her palm. Two uncut sapphires, an uncut ruby, and three uncut emeralds.

She gasped.

"I did *not* lose my bounty. The thief turned on me, managed a single impressive slice, and then I dispatched him."

"How?" She was staring at his mouth while he told his tale, but she was thinking of his impressive physique now hidden by his white shirt.

"With my fists," Edward said, "until I could reach my pistol. When I brandished it, he ran away."

She imagined him in a fight for his life, alone in the darkness, and felt ill. And to learn he carried a pistol made him seem far different from the mild geologist she thought she knew.

"I am glad you didn't lose them." *Or your life,* she added silently.

Radiance closed her fingers over the stones for a second. When he held the bag open, she funneled them back inside.

"I do like a happy ending," she quipped, trying to lighten the moment and ease her own belated concern for his well-being.

"And I like to keep what's mine," he said, holding her gaze.

She cleared her throat, realizing she hadn't told him why she was there, and he'd been too polite to ask.

Also, she noted the effects of what Mrs. McSabby had mentioned. He had circles under those striking eyes of his, and fatigue hollowed his cheeks.

"I say, sir, are you well?"

"Yes," he said tightly. "Perfectly."

"Sleeping soundly, are you? And eating proper meals?" Radiance looked around, immediately spying not one but two platters containing uneaten food, one a sandwich and one a slice of meat pie.

"Neither is of your concern," he said.

"I suppose not. As long as your distraction isn't due to some turn of events with the jewel thief or the Koh-i-Noor."

"Then you may rest at ease, my lady. Any distraction I may be experiencing is over my work and my book."

"I hope the latter is coming along smoothly."

He looked as if he wished he hadn't said anything. Finally, he nodded stiffly.

"How wonderful," she said, wishing he would soften toward her again. "I shall certainly buy a copy and read it cover to cover."

"That's all very well, and I shall gift a copy to you and your husband as a wedding gift. However, I believe you haven't stated your purpose for barging in."

So much for him being too polite. He had run with the notion of Lord Castille becoming her fiancé like an Epsom Downs Derby horse toward the finishing line.

"Do you know a jeweler named Sully?" she asked.

"No, but then, I am not in the jeweler's community as much as you are. Who is he?"

"I am telling you this in confidence. *He* is the one standing in for Mr. Neble and making his jewelry. Moreover, Mr. Sully wants me to meet him in Houndsditch tomorrow at one of the jewelry markets."

She lifted her chin as soon as he started to shake his head. "I intend to go."

"Not without me," he said.

"Exactly what I hoped you would say." Radiance released a sigh of relief. "I have been accused occasionally of impulsiveness, which I prefer to think of it as spontaneity. Yet I am neither foolish, nor rash, and I have no wish to disappear without a trace in some teeming marketplace east of the city."

"You are sensible, and for that, I am grateful."

Radiance wondered at such a statement. "Are you? Why?"

His cheeks flushed. "Naturally, I don't wish for anything to happen to you, nor to anyone of my acquaintance."

She had hoped for more but stopped her foolish thinking.

"I cannot simply take you with me to meet Mr. Sully," she explained. "I doubt I will learn what I hope to if you are standing beside me, glaring as you are now. However, if you will accompany me discreetly, I will feel immensely better knowing you are merely a shout away."

"Have you ever been to any of the Houndsditch markets?"

"I have not," she confessed, knowing only that they existed to sell all manner of goods. The market at Petticoat Lane sold used and new clothing, Moses Square was known for its second-hand hats, shoes, and stockings, and Cutler Street sold everything else, including items for the soldiers and sailors, workmen's tools, and even musical instruments.

Her mother had once taken Clarity and Purity, as well as two footmen for protection, to peruse the gowns of both Indian silk and satin. They came home with Persian shawls and some excellent pieces of lace that was quickly dispatched to their modiste to be added to their gowns for the Season. Radiance had been too young to go, and she'd never been allowed near Houndsditch.

Naturally, as her interest in jewelry grew, she'd become aware that there were markets selling much more than silk and shawls. Not only did they carry finished jewelry but also raw stones. Mr. Bonwit regularly went to purchase these.

Nevertheless, none of these markets were the type of place an earl's daughter went willy-nilly, being neither a tidy Mayfair shop, nor one of the fashionable arcades or bazaars in London proper.

Apparently, Edward had been to Houndsditch. "It is so busy at certain times," he said, "your shriek for help would not be heard."

She shivered. "In that case, I am glad for your assistance and company."

"I assume you have a name and an address. Within a stone's throw between Bevis Marks and Cutler Streets, there are many jewelry markets. I can think of five off the top of my head. At which one are you to meet? Barnet's? Mendez's? Levy's on Moses Square, perhaps?"

"No, sir, none of those. It is Fogg's to the right of the Orange Market, if you are coming from the direction of St. Mary Axe."

He smiled at her words. "Listen to you, sounding like an East-End moll. I am certain you have never been near the Orange Market, nor traveled the street of St. Mary Axe."

"No, but those were Mr. Sully's directions. I shall collect you—"

Again, he shook his head. "I would not recommend taking the earl's carriage there with his crest emblazoned. In the blink of an eye, you might lose your father's fine tackle, or even his horses. I will collect you and Sarah. What time are you supposed to meet the jeweler?"

"Tomorrow, at eleven."

CHAPTER THIRTY-TWO

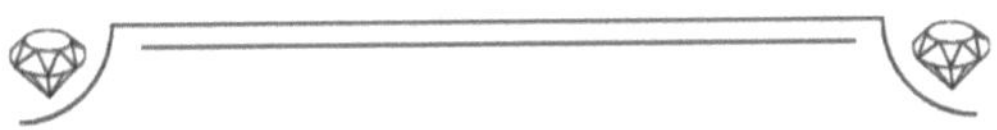

Edward directed the cab driver to the Diamond home, beyond pleased that Radiance had confided in him instead of going to Houndsditch by herself. That morning in his workroom, he could still catch scent of her lilac perfume—a most intoxicating fragrance. He couldn't deny he'd been happy to have her in his home once again, stroking his cat's lazy body, wishing he could have her fingers on him as easily.

Brushing aside such wicked thoughts—*the woman was practically engaged, after all*—he descended the carriage with a request for the driver to await him.

Expecting Radiance's reaction to his disguise—ill-fitting, secondhand clothing, a false beard, spectacles, and a floppy hat—it was the Diamonds' butler who first raised an eyebrow, peering down his nose as if he might slam the door.

"It is I, Mr. Lockwood," Edward said, feeling foolish.

Their butler had no chance to do more than heave a sigh, indicating he had seen it all while in his position, and stepped back to allow him entrance.

Radiance must have been ready and waiting in the drawing room, for he heard her speak a moment later.

"Mr. Lockwood," she called out to him in greeting before coming into the foyer. She wore a vivid red dress as he'd requested, so he could more easily keep an eye on her. She'd added a matching hat and ruby mantle.

He would vow his heart faltered, then sped up at the sight of her—a delicious-looking treat he wanted to taste more than he wanted his next breath.

"Oh!" Taking a step back, Radiance looked him up and down. With a pretty tilt of her head, she asked, "It is you, isn't it, sir?"

"Yes. If you are ready, then let us go." His face was already itching from Mrs. McSabby's rye paste that held on the beard made of trimmed horse's mane, oddly coarse but realistic, nonetheless. Hide glue, the alternative, had given him pause in case it didn't come off with hot water and soap, whereas Mrs. McSabby assured him her concoction would leave little to no damage.

After helping Radiance and the equally astonished maid swiftly into the hansom cab, he let the lady's barrage of questions fly, explaining that his disguise was necessary.

"I have no idea who this Sully person is, but he might know me on sight as someone with whom the Queen and Prince Consort have consulted. If he is the forger, that could put you in danger."

And then he began his own interrogation. "Tell me what you know about him."

Edward was amazed to learn how she'd chanced upon the jeweler outside Mr. Neble's office, managing to manipulate him into a discussion at her home. He was immensely proud of her.

"You've put yourself back in danger," he said.

"Mr. Sully showed no sign of recognition," she vowed. "Thus, he cannot have shot at me or pushed me into a wall."

Edward wasn't satisfied. "Perhaps I can go in your place, as your humble servant, without your even needing to leave the carriage."

"Mr. Sully was most particular that I come alone with the payment."

"I imagine he was."

She shrugged. "It is no matter. You are here—or at least *this* version of you. I assume you intend to blend in with the regular buyers and merchants."

"I shall remain a mere three paces from you."

Soon, they descended from the carriage on Duke Street, including Sarah, who appeared a little nervous.

"I don't half feel as if I'm in a mystery," the maid declared.

"She must stay with you at all times," Edward ordered. Although not more than a slip of a maid, the two of them together would be less easily targeted should there be any nefarious souls about. And that there were such, he was certain.

"Smell it," Radiance said. "The aroma from the Orange Market is like sweet perfume. It's glorious, isn't it?"

Edward wanted her to stop speaking to him and put a little distance between them. To that end, he nodded and disappeared into the crowd as they'd discussed in the cab.

Radiance and her maid walked along Duke Street toward a tavern with the name of *Fogg* painted over the doorway. Naturally, at that hour, it was closed. But as instructed, she went to the entrance beside it, crossed the white-painted step, and entered the jewelry mart.

Edward's heart beat a steady tattoo as he tried to stroll casually when everything inside him wanted to run like a stiff wind. About thirty excruciatingly long seconds after she entered, he approached the same door. It was ever-so-slightly ajar, a welcoming, friendly indication that belied the ruthless dealings he knew went on in these markets.

A gentle push caused the door to swing easily open, and he was in a long hallway, its floor covered by cleanly swept oilcloth. The hall was empty. Edward hurried along the passage to another door, this one neither welcoming nor open. Disconcertingly covered in dark reddish-brown baize, he pushed it, meeting a little resistance that was simply due to its heaviness.

Beyond it was a far shorter hall and a third entirely regular door in one of the walls, looking for all the world as if it would lead him into a respectable parlor or salon. When he tried to turn the handle and enter, however, it didn't budge. Then he recalled the instructions Radiance had imparted.

He tapped three times. The door swung open by an invisible hand of someone stationed directly behind it, giving him entrance into an expansive room, both long and wide. Despite its size, the jewelry market was cramped, being packed with buyers and sellers, mostly men. The women he did see were obviously of a lower class than his lady by both their garb and manner.

"A penn'orth?" offered a seedy man, situated two feet from the door beside a tub of pickled vegetables, which gave off a distinctively briny aroma. The vendor quickly scooped some onto a saucer and held this out to Edward.

Shaking his head, he scooted around him. Then his heart sank. Through the tobacco smoke that hung in the air, Edward estimated there were at least two hundred souls, wandering up and down the two rows of tables that stretched the length of the room. Worse, the curtains adorning the two large windows at one end, while drawn back to let in the light, were a rich red, thus casting a ruddy glow over the entire place.

Radiance was already lost to him, and he set out to find her.

Plunging into the fray, he couldn't help noticing the wares covering the broad tables as he hurried past. This jewelry market was the wealthiest and largest one he'd ever seen, not only in Houndsditch but in all Britain. He couldn't even detect the color of the tablecloths under the piles of gold and silver chains, gold platters and jugs, and heaps of silver spoons.

Naturally, there was jewelry everywhere Edward's gaze landed—rings in bowls and spread on velvet, bracelets glittering with rare topazes and lapis lazuli accents, crosses studded with pearls and rubies, gem-crusted tiaras, coronets to fit any lady's head whether she preferred emeralds, sapphires, or both, and lockets adorned with pearlescent opals.

Opals! The latter might have snagged his attention and caused him to stop were he not desperate to lay eyes upon Radiance once more. Compared to her, everything in the room was worthless.

Thus, he pushed farther into the throng. Scanning right and left, listening to the hum that occasionally rose to a din as people haggled over prices, Edward tramped upon some toes just as his own were trod upon.

Suddenly, a ringleted, dark-eyed woman adorned in gold chains across her ample breasts and thick gold hoops in her ears stepped in front of him.

"What are you looking for?" she asked without preamble.

He nearly told her—*a red-clad lady*.

"Nothing in particular. I will know it when I see it."

"You are new here," she said.

He wondered in the crowd how she could tell. Hopefully his beard wasn't falling off.

"Today seems to be a day for newcomers," she added.

His ears perked up, and he followed the path of her gaze toward the far end. A skylight in the roof illuminated a snug posting-house bar with glasses stacked tidily at one end and a number of people drinking.

He couldn't see Radiance but assumed she had gone in the direction the dark beauty indicated.

RADIANCE DIDN'T KNOW what she had expected, but it wasn't the chaos she encountered. As soon as she'd knocked thrice upon the door and been given admittance, Mr. Sully had greeted her, whisked her past an enthusiastic pickle-seller of all people, and deep inside the crowded market.

"I didn't know you would bring a companion," he muttered, startling her momentarily into thinking he knew about Edward. Then she realized to whom he referred.

"My lady's maid is a necessity when I am out in public," she told him, although she couldn't think what use Sarah, silently watching, could be at that moment. Perhaps if one of Radiance's ribbons came untied . . .

Surveying her surroundings, she noticed men, both shabbily and finely dressed, all of them smoking cigars, and some gaudy women picking through the contents of the trays on each table as if the jewels were no more costly than raspberries.

There were enough earrings sparkling with diamonds for every lady in Britain. And of course, the favorite of most gentlemen, watches in gold and silver were laid out in neat rows upon nearly every table.

No one seemed to mind when someone passed a pearl to a neighbor or tried on a diamond ring. People walked away from the tables, surging around Radiance in eddies, some going toward the windows where the light was better.

None of the vendors seemed the least bit ruffled when their wares disappeared momentarily. Unlike the jewelry stores in the heart of London, where the clerks kept their eyes on every single customer no matter how finely dressed, these good-natured sellers evidently didn't fear being robbed.

"This way," Mr. Sully said, a hand under her elbow, hurrying her along.

But her glance continued to dart hither and yon. While anyone could pick up anything and examine it, no matter how large the gold goblet or how small the ring, there was an order to the proceedings.

Radiance reconsidered her initial impression. People were buying and putting away their purchases in cases and bags in an orderly fashion. These would go to jewelry shops and stores featuring fine furnishings to be sold at quadruple the price.

When she slowed, he tugged her into motion again.

"These other sellers don't have what you're looking for."

She wished Mr. Sully would allow her to see more of the glittering jewelry. But it was what lay beside all these worked pieces that made her suddenly halt—unset gemstones, some uncut. They were heaped in the corners of trays like almonds or cherry pits or contained in wooden and ivory pillboxes. Edward would be like a child in a sweetshop, and she suddenly doubted whether she would ever see him again.

"Come along, my lady. The stall at the end is our destination."

In a short time, she was at the far end of the long room barely able to see behind her through the smoky haze. With no idea whether Edward was nearby, she had to keep her wits about her.

"Mendelson," Mr. Sully greeted a man in a dark suit with a curly beard. "This is the lady I told you about."

The seller looked her up and down. "You are lucky to be here," he said.

It was an odd way of greeting, but this wasn't a private ball with social niceties.

"I shall not know until after I leave whether I was lucky or unlucky," Radiance pointed out, causing the two men to eye one another. "Are you the owner of the jewels for my tiara?" she asked the bearded one.

He hesitated. "Sometimes, it is hard to truly imagine anyone has ownership of a gemstone. They come from the earth. Perhaps no one owns them."

Mr. Sully coughed and cleared his throat, and then the other man, Mr. Mendelson as she recalled, made a wry face.

"He is the owner." He hooked a thumb at Mr. Sully. "I am holding on to them because I was going to sell them for him if possible. Indeed, I may have a buyer later today."

She doubted the coincidence. The man was trying to increase the already exorbitant price.

"If I may take a look, then—" Radiance began as someone bumped into her from behind. It wasn't the first time she'd been jostled. Looking around, unfortunately, she still didn't see Edward.

"Not here," Mr. Mendelson said. "There is a room for private transactions. Come."

He led the way, and Mr. Sully gestured for her to follow, along with Sarah, before he took up the rear. They went toward a bar stacked with glasses on its glossy, polished surface. Behind it was a goodly supply of liquor.

Given the hour, Radiance was surprised to see men lined up and partaking of some fiery-looking liquid, perhaps brandy. On the bar's other side, a man dressed all in black leaned against the counter, chatting with customers, sliding glasses of liquor to those who asked and paid, while also surveying the room.

As they drew closer, he nodded to Mr. Mendelson, who went to a door just beside the bar. The stranger's dark eyes roved over Radiance from head to toe, unsettling her, but he said nothing.

"Who was that?" she asked Mr. Sully once they'd entered a small dark chamber with a square table and four chairs.

"That was Mr. Fogg. He owns the tavern next door *and* the market."

Gracious! The man must be as rich as Croesus. Yet he was serving liquor like a common barman.

Gesturing for her to take a seat and extending the same offer to Sarah, Mr. Mendelson drew back the curtains on two windows. The midday sunlight streamed in. Then finally, he drew out a small sack from his pocket. She wondered how he could have hoped to sell the stones if they weren't on display.

"You wanted something large and unusual, my lady," Mr. Sully said. "You won't find any like these elsewhere."

Mr. Mendelson let two gems roll out of the pouch and onto the table's green leather inset.

She gasped, knowing at once what she was looking at—Queen Victoria's two stolen jewels.

CHAPTER THIRTY-THREE

A large sapphire from Prince Albert's wedding gift brooch and the missing emerald from the Queen's coronet sparkled in the sunlight.

Beside her, Sarah exclaimed, "Aren't they spectacular?"

"Indeed, they are," Radiance agreed, barely stopping herself from reaching out and touching. Instead, she kept her hands in her lap, her fingers tightly gripping her reticule. "Where did you get them?"

Her question was met with silence. And then Mr. Sully said, "Why do you care? You will be the envy of every lady when I set these in a tiara, with diamonds you can choose today."

"You said you had cut them yourself," she reminded him. He had certainly cut some *exactly* like them, a green tourmaline and the blue spinel for which poor Mr. Minton was blamed.

Thus, Mr. Sully might have shot at her, she realized. Moreover, at any moment, he could recall she was the same female entering St. James's Palace with Edward, who may have been the actual target.

"That would indicate you purchased the uncut stones yourself. Might I know the country of origin or the story behind each, so I may tell any admirers?"

Mr. Sully scowled. "That is of no matter. I purchased the uncut stones here in London."

What should she do? Radiance would have to give Mr. Sully the bank note she had tucked inside her reticule. And then all she could do was wait. She might have a tiara with the Queen's jewels by the end of the following week.

More likely, given his history, he would give her a tiara containing two more forgeries, and the royal jewels would be lost to her and possibly to the Queen forever. She had to take them with her.

"I have changed my mind about wanting a tiara. I would simply like to purchase the two jewels." Having said that, she gave in to her earlier impulse and scooped them both off the smooth, worn leather inset.

Both men jumped.

"Impossible!" Mr. Sully said while she clutched them tightly in her fist. "What would *you* do with them?"

Radiance rose to her feet, hoping to display a little of her mother's composure, grace, and iron-willed fortitude.

"That is not *your* business, sir," she said, trying to sound imperial and unchallengeable. "Rather than pay you to work with these stones, I shall buy them as they are."

She held her breath. Perhaps Mr. Sully would go along with it. Or perhaps he'd sold them to others a few times already, yet never delivered the true stones. Suddenly, she had a thought.

"How do I know they are real gemstones?"

"Real?" Mr. Mendelson repeated, aghast. "What can you mean? They are not glass! You are in a jewelry exchange, and we sell noble metals and genuine gemstones. Are you questioning the integrity of Fogg's? Of all Houndsditch?"

As he raised his voice, his face turned alarmingly red. Radiance had a feeling she had committed a dreadful *faux pas*.

For his part, Mr. Sully had gone over all ashen. "They *are* genuine stones," he insisted softly. "Why would you think otherwise?"

Would Mr. Mendelson support Mr. Sully if he knew the truth about the latter's actions?

"I meant only that you wouldn't be the first men of business to try to fool a simple woman."

"*Simple* woman!" Sarah exclaimed.

A dreadful time for her maid to have found her tongue. Radiance hushed her.

"However, I will take the risk and buy them today." Surely the Queen would ensure Radiance got her father's money back.

Mr. Mendelson frowned. "You are implying a risk that does not exist. I examined them myself when Mr. Sully brought them to me to sell. Now you are questioning my knowledge!"

"I did not intend to," she said, wondering how quickly she could get out of the room with the stones.

"Intended or not," the man fumed. "*Are they real?* What a question! You have even insulted all the other buyers. Do you think all those men out there would be foolish enough to buy fake stones?"

"Then why haven't they sold in three months?" she snapped.

Radiance would have clapped her own hand over her mouth if she'd had a free one, but one held the proof that Mr. Sully was the forger and the other, her reticule.

Mr. Sully narrowed his eyes. "How would you know how long ago I gave Mr. Mendelson the gems to sell?"

How would she know that? In fact, she only knew how long ago the second forgery had been discovered. She gritted her teeth.

"I think she is a trouble-maker," Mr. Mendelson declared, looking directly at her. "You are hoping to get a better price by questioning the integrity of our goods, but that won't work here. The reputation of Fogg's is impeccable."

"I am not questioning the integrity of Fogg's," she insisted. "I came to buy *these* gems, and I shall buy them."

Mr. Mendelson looked at Mr. Sully. "What is the price? If it is good, you should sell to her and get rid of her quickly. If I can get you more, even with my percentage, then I will advise you not to sell to this one." He gestured with his chin.

Mr. Sully turned his back to her, speaking into the ear of the market vendor so she couldn't hear his words. But she watched Mr. Mendelson's eyebrows raise. Then the man eyed Radiance carefully.

"You had an agreement. Mr. Sully is a jeweler, an artist. I have seen his work. He is *not* a seller of gems. You said he could create a piece for you that would ensure his reputation."

"I want the gemstones," she insisted. "When I decide how I want them set, then I'll return to him to make the piece. But I don't think they are right for the tiara."

"I am only selling them to you for the tiara," Mr. Sully protested. "And that piece will make my name. My work is impeccable, and that's what I want people to learn." He lifted his chin.

Then why on earth had he done the forgery in the first place? she wondered. By its nature, the act was one of anonymity.

"On the other hand," Mr. Mendelson began while twisting his beard, "I think you should let this lady buy them for the amount you told me. It is a fair price."

Mr. Mendelson ought to have said an *outrageous* price. By his admission, he couldn't get more for them, or he would have tried. She was paying a queen's ransom, indeed.

However, instead of agreeing to the deal, Mr. Sully switched tactics.

"Let me polish them for you." He leaned over the table, his hand outstretched. "They will shine like fire and glitter like the sun."

"No, they are fine as they are." She would not relinquish them to him for a second lest he somehow switch them for others. Backing toward the door, Radiance wished her maid would get up and hurry to join her. "Come along," she directed Sarah.

"I will bring them to you tomorrow," he insisted. "And surely, you wish for me to write out a receipt."

"Neither is necessary. I will take them now, and I have no need of a receipt."

He rounded the table. "They are mine to sell as I wish, and I do not wish to sell them to you."

"Easy," Mr. Mendelson said. "You said you wanted to sell them."

She had her fingers wrapped around the handle, trying to get the door open.

"I have changed my mind. She has insulted me and you and even Mr. Fogg."

"She has," Mr. Mendelson agreed, and they both moved toward her.

Shrieking, she yanked open the door, colliding with Mr. Fogg on the other side.

"Well, now, what have we here?"

"She was trying to leave without paying," Mr. Sully declared behind her.

Mr. Fogg scowled. "We don't allow such mischief here."

"It's a lie," she declared, although she had done precisely that in her haste.

"He is telling the truth," Mr. Mendelson said. "She has the gems *and* the money."

"Release her," said a familiar voice. *Edward, at last!*

Dragging her by her upper arm in a half circle to face her disguised geologist, Mr. Fogg surveyed the newcomer. "And who might you be?"

Edward didn't answer, merely crossing his arms. "Release her. She has done nothing wrong."

"I asked you a question," Mr. Fogg said, although he did as Edward demanded, letting go his hold on her arm.

She took a step toward him, and he reached out a hand, hauling her to his side.

"I've never seen either one of you in my marketplace before," Mr. Fogg said.

Mr. Mendelson, who seemed to enjoy being in the center of it, declared, "She is a troublemaker so he probably is, too."

With the scene drawing observers, men and a few women formed a circle around them. Sarah, wide-eyed and pale, scooted closer. To Radiance, it seemed as if they were soldiers in an enemy stronghold. *How far could they run before the crowd took them down to the floorboards and stomped them to death?* For the general mood of the room had shifted from convivial to suspicious and angry rather swiftly.

"Let me escort the lady and her maid out of here," Edward said.

Mr. Fogg shook his head. "It would seem she owes these men some money." The crowd murmured their disapproval.

"I do, but only because they startled me." She pointed at Mr. Sully. "He was trying to renege on a sale."

Members of the throng gave a small gasp, and she guessed going back on one's word was also frowned upon. While she'd caused the briefest of distractions, she managed to drop the two stones into her reticule and retrieve the bank note. It might be their only means of escape.

Mr. Fogg glanced at Mr. Sully. "I've seen you here before. You are a jeweler, not a vendor."

"That's correct. I came to Mr. Mendelson to sell some gemstones."

"Why didn't you sell them yourself?"

His cheeks stained red, and he stammered a reply. "Ah . . . well . . . his reputation preceded him."

Even Mr. Mendelson seemed surprised by that, but Mr. Sully appeared fed up.

"What does any of this matter?" he demanded. "I don't want *her* money. I want my jewels back."

"Why?" Mr. Fogg asked. "Is the sum fair, Mr. Mendelson?"

"Very," the man answered, twisting his beard with such vigor Radiance feared it might need some of Edward's horsehair and glue to repair it.

Mr. Fogg addressed Mr. Sully again. "Then why don't you wish to sell to this lady?"

Radiance couldn't believe how quickly the tables had turned. Taking advantage of this, she held out the bank note toward Mr. Fogg. She wanted him to see the large amount.

"This is what I owe him." It would go a long way to giving her credibility amongst the crowd.

The marketplace owner's eyes widened at the sum.

"You would be a fool not take it," he said to Mr. Sully. "Why won't you?"

Mr. Sully hesitated, looking uncomfortable. "I keep my own counsel."

In the next instant, he hurried forward and grabbed Radiance's arm, holding her hand high in the air.

Radiance yelped as he nearly lifted her off her feet and caused her shoulder to twinge painfully. He stared at her empty palm.

"I want my jewels. Where are they?"

"They are *not* your jewels," she said.

Releasing her, Mr. Sully swiped for her satin bag, but Edward grabbed his arm. In some fashion she didn't understand, he suddenly had trapped it behind the jeweler's own back. *Bravo!*

CHAPTER THIRTY-FOUR

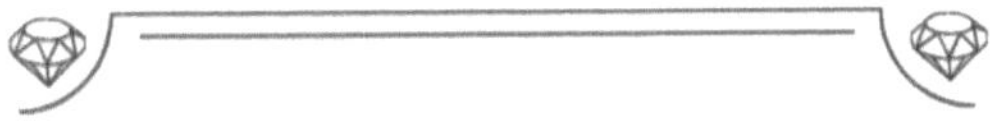

Edward decided it was time to end this lark before someone became injured.

"Are you sure they are the ones?" he asked Radiance since he had yet to lay eyes upon the stones.

"I am certain."

Her belief was good enough for him. Edward addressed the man who had the demeanor of being in charge of this entire operation.

"Mr. Fogg, are you? I understand the reputation of your market is most important to you."

"Yes," he said. "Have you been to Levy's or Mendez's markets? They are like flea-swaps compared to my establishment."

"I have been to them, and you are correct. Thus, I think you would wish to know that you have a forger and a thief in your midst."

The crowd gasped, drowning out Mr. Fogg's expletive.

Radiance tensed beside him, but Edward thought their best chance was exposing the true criminal.

"Mr. Sully was responsible for forging and replacing two gems previously located in Queen Victoria's royal jewelry. Show him," he said to Radiance.

Opening her reticule, she withdrew the two stones, showing them to Mr. Fogg.

"They are not Mr. Sully's to sell," she said, "and the Queen has charged us with retrieving them."

In the blink of an eye, Sully grabbed for the gems with his free hand, snatching one while sending the other one flying. Radiance was knocked to the ground in the process.

Releasing Sully, Edward reached down and pulled her up, knowing the crush of people could surge forward at any moment and injure her.

However, as soon as she was on her feet, in her most commanding tone which he'd come to admire, she ordered, "Get the jewels, Edward!"

Surprised to hear his name from her lips, regardless, he did her bidding. Leaving her with Sarah, he ran in the direction of the exit. The crowd had slowed Sully without meaning to, and Edward spotted his retreating form. Before the jeweler could reach the first of the three doors, Edward tackled him to the floor, knocking the wind out of him. The man lay momentarily stunned.

Kneeling atop him, thinking Sully might do something desperate, such as swallow the stone, Edward pulled his gun out of his pocket and pressed it to the forger's temple.

"Put the stone down."

The jeweler did as he was told and quickly! Tucking the sapphire and the gun away, Edward pulled Sully's arms behind his back and looked for something to secure them.

"A heavy chain if you will," he asked a nearby vendor. And for those who hadn't heard the discourse at the other end of the room, Edward added, "This man is a thief."

In the marketplace, that was anathema, and soon, he had the cooperation of those around him. Using a proffered gold chain, Edward tied Sully's hands together. Another chain went around his feet.

Satisfied the man was incapacitated, Edward addressed the crowd.

"Will someone send for a constable?" Then he left Sully on the floor while he returned to make sure Radiance was unharmed.

In fact, she was still searching for the other jewel, which had skittered amongst the hundreds of feet.

"I have it," called a soft voice, but it didn't belong to Radiance.

The dark-haired woman who'd addressed Edward earlier now held it aloft. Ignoring everyone else, she approached him.

"Is this the stone you seek?"

Previously, while searching for Radiance, he hadn't appreciated the view provided by the beauty's low velvet neckline. But now, as she thrust herself close, it was all he could see.

However, when she offered the emerald to him, Radiance stepped to his side.

"That is the one. Thank you." Smoothly, she relieved the woman of it and dropped it into her reticule. "I think our business is concluded here, sir, don't you?"

She was positively sparkling with her accomplishment. In the meantime, Fogg and the man with the curly beard were having heated words, probably the former blaming the latter for allowing all this trouble into his market.

"We must wait for the police to arrive," Edward said, but his relief at the caper's end had him making a jest. "Unless you think we should make room for Sully in a cab and take him to jail ourselves."

"I tell you, sir," she began, "I almost want to take him directly to the Palace and present him to the Queen and Prince Consort ourselves."

"I imagine you would, but you'll get the credit. Don't worry." With that, he withdrew the sapphire from his pocket and gave it to her.

Radiance rolled her eyes. "*Pish!* I don't care about the recognition." She put the gem in her reticule with the other one. "I am simply excited to see how happy Queen Victoria shall be. With all the responsibility upon her shoulders, she deserves the return of her jewels and the knowledge that the forger has been captured."

"I agree wholeheartedly." Ridiculously, he wanted to take Radiance into the circle of his arms. "I am beyond proud of you for having solved this crime against her."

Radiance beamed with happiness. And then he heard the sound of rattles and running feet and knew the police had arrived.

"If I'm not mistaken," Edward said, "Minton will be set free."

"He must be, although how Mr. Sully got his hands on the wedding brooch at Garrard's shop is still a mystery. I suppose he will confess everything." Then she shook her head. "Poor Mr. Neble! What ill fortune to have hired a thief, even a talented one, to be his hidden hands."

They walked toward the other end of the market to meet the policemen, some holding their truncheons, some their noisy rattles.

"He's a skilled jeweler but a terrible thief. If he wanted the money, he could have stayed in the shadows and let Mendelson sell the stones for a good price."

"He wanted me to believe he had cut them. I suppose, since he cut the fakes, he thought it nearly the same thing. Moreover, he seemed to care more about the fame I could bring him for creating a singular piece for me to wear than the money, although that was exorbitant, too."

"He'll have plenty of notoriety now," Edward told her. "As for Mr. Neble, he will have to hire another pair of skilled hands."

After they explained everything to the constable in charge, there was further delay when the gold chains binding Sully had to be switched for common steel. And then there was the moment Radiance was asked to hand over the jewels.

"I think not, sir," she said.

"It's highly irregular for us to let you hold on to the stolen goods," the constable pointed out.

Radiance glanced at Edward, who nodded.

"This man, although disguised, is the eminent geologist, Mr. Lockwood. Perhaps you have heard of him?"

"I am sorry to say I have not."

"Well, how strange," she added, sounding affronted on Edward's behalf.

He would have laughed if it weren't all so serious. Moreover, his cheeks were starting to feel sore from the glue, and he wasn't sure he could even crack a smile.

"Then perhaps you have heard of my father," Radiance tried again. "The Earl Diamond."

"Yes, m'lady," the constable said. "*Him*, I have heard of."

Radiance turned to Edward. "My father is generous with his support to the city's underprivileged and also to the policemen's widows' fund."

She addressed the constable once again. "Then you must agree that these jewels are better in my safe-keeping as we are going directly to Buckingham Palace, rather than with you and the thief to Scotland Yard. Although you are welcome to send two of your men to protect us," she added.

"Yes, m'lady."

Thus, with the blink of the lovely lady's eye, Edward found himself being escorted to the Palace like a dignitary with police riding on the outside, their truncheons across their knees.

"I cannot dawdle too long," she said from the safety of the constable's carriage.

And precisely when Edward was feeling satisfied with the day's proceedings, thinking with the danger eradicated and the forger in custody, he might ask Radiance to take up where they'd left off, she volunteered some disturbing information.

"I am going to a dinner and dance with Lord Castille this evening. And I need time to get ready."

Suddenly, the day had turned into a dismally disappointing affair.

RADIANCE AND EDWARD had an impromptu audience with the Queen and received her sincere gratitude.

"I am sure anyone who had the opportunity would have done the same, Your Majesty," Radiance assured Her Majesty. "And I could not have succeeded if Mr. Lockwood hadn't been there to apprehend the thief."

The Queen examined Edward's oddly bearded face and smiled.

After making certain that Mr. Minton would be speedily released, she bid Edward good day on the steps of the Palace and hastened home. Actually, he had gone a little quiet from the moment she'd mentioned Lord Castille while remaining utterly polite for the rest of the time they were together. If he had shown some sign of interest in renewing their own brief entanglement, then she might have had reservations regarding continuing to keep company with the viscount.

For in truth, she still had dreams of being in Edward's arms again.

As she changed for the evening's event, she gave herself a stern talking to, albeit a silent one since Sarah was assisting her. She must not be unfair to Lord Castille. He was a good man and openly declared his admiration. Moreover, apart from Edward, he was the only one of the many suitors she'd had since coming out into society who interested her enough to encourage his advances.

If Edward Lockwood had never existed, she thought she would be content with John Castille. Perhaps not wholly satisfied, but enough to believe she could make a life with him. They had enjoyed a number of happy occasions, not only at balls and dinners but also at a concert, two plays, and riding in Hyde Park.

He seemed equally captivated by her and willing to be exclusive until they made a decision.

Yet that evening, on the dance floor, looking up at John, she was devastated to find herself in the same predicament as she had been weeks earlier—missing Edward dreadfully. And all because she'd spent a few hours in his company. She could not credit her own feelings that persisted in finding John lacking.

Frankly, she was being ridiculous!

Determined to overcome her own immature tendencies—for that could be the only reason to want what she could not have—Radiance tried to be extra attentive at the ball.

Nevertheless, the next day, waking up late after getting home in the wee hours, her first thoughts were of Edward and how impressed she'd been by his actions at the jewelry market.

Staring at her canopy overhead, Radiance hoped Mr. Minton, if not already free, soon would be. As for Mr. Sully, he would be jailed for a long time. If his sentence was similar to those who had attempted to assassinate their popular Queen, then he would probably be transported to Australia.

She wondered if he would remain a jeweler as he had been for—

Mr. Neble! Radiance sat upright, her heart pounding before she scurried from the bed, reached for her dressing gown, and then yanked the bellpull summoning Sarah.

The poor man would know nothing about Mr. Sully's arrest. He would spend the day wondering where his jeweler was.

After attending to her morning ministrations, Radiance and Sarah set out for the House of Neble on Saffron Hill. She'd never told Edward or anyone about her private conversation with the elderly jeweler. Regarding Mr. Neble, she had been mulling over his offer, but she wasn't yet ready to accept his proposal.

Regardless, she could help him with his sudden lack of a skilled pair of hands.

"Mr. Neble will see you now," the clerk informed her minutes after she'd asked him to announce her. He didn't even escort her up the stairs but let her make her own way, with her maid following.

A tap on the door and she was inside and seated, brimming with excitement.

Mr. Neble looked wretched. "I am in a dreadful spot, my lady. Deep in the suds. My jeweler has gone missing."

"Yes, sir, I am aware of that, which is why I came to see you."

"Aware of it?" he asked. Then his face lit with joy. "You have decided to come work here with me."

"I am not ready to be your hands, sir. I would hate to disappoint you, which would surely happen as I have more to learn. I would also hate to dishonor the House of Neble."

"*Bah!* There will be nothing to dishonor. Mr. Sully, my jeweler, was a rare find. When he came in looking for work, he was already highly skilled yet desperate enough to join my firm in complete anonymity as I required."

"I believe you can have that again, although it is not truly necessary, is it? As long as you are the director of the House of Neble, what does it matter if you don't craft each piece yourself?"

Before Mr. Neble could protest, she added, "The jeweler Mr. Minton would be an excellent choice. He is not as young as Mr. Sully, but he is honest and extremely skilled."

"Nonsense! He is a forger in jail."

"No, sir. Mr. Sully was the forger. And now *he* is in jail."

Mr. Neble was momentarily speechless. Then he shook his head. "I am astounded."

In a few minutes, after she explained, he agreed to let her bring Mr. Minton to see him. She even had him half convinced to stop trying to fool people, too.

If he did, then he could once more be down in the shop chatting with customers, which he'd always enjoyed, as well as meeting with other jewelers who currently thought him a curmudgeonly hermit.

Yet he had one last concern. "Then everyone will know I am nearly blind."

"You will be nearly blind in any case, whether people know or not, but far freer, sir."

Letting him think on that, she and Sarah left to find the whereabouts of Mr. Minton.

CHAPTER THIRTY-FIVE

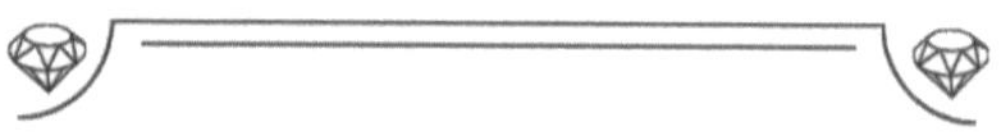

With an invitation to the Koh-i-Noor's preliminary cutting, Radiance didn't have to stand outside Garrard's with the crowd of onlookers. On July 17, she joined a small group inside the first-floor workroom, which had been specially redesigned for the project.

Naturally, Edward was there. Somehow, he wasn't late, nor in disarray. Despite it being the first time she'd seen him since the steps of Buckingham Palace, they did little more than nod at one another.

Radiance found it nearly impossible to believe he'd once had his tongue in her mouth, but perhaps she was too naïve to know that might be commonplace among adults in the heat of the moment.

When the spectators began to cheer, she peered out the window beside which she and Sarah stood. The crowd's roar of approval heralded the arrival of the Duke of Wellington. The popular old soldier came by himself on his beloved horse, and the Londoners parted for him. He dismounted at Garrard's door and entered.

In no time at all, and with little hesitation, the Duke moved the diamond into place with the scaif revolving too fast to see, thanks to the new Maudslay, Sons, & Field steam engine powering the grinder.

As he polished the first facet, there was no sound in the room beyond the engine. When the Duke stepped away, however, those who'd assembled to watch—including Sebastian and Robert Garrard, the Dutch diamond cutters from Coster's in Amsterdam, Mr. Voorzanger and Mr. Feder, Edward, Radiance, and Sarah—all clapped.

This time, Sarah had requested not to remain in the carriage. Her applause was loudest of all.

"Blimey!" she exclaimed, causing the Duke to turn to her and wink.

Then Wellington left, remounted his old white horse, and rode away to the thunderous cheers of the throng on Haymarket Street.

Edward remained, but after a few minutes, Radiance and Sarah left for home. He didn't seem to notice her departure.

Before she knew it, her life went back to normal, exactly as it was before she knocked on Edward's door and told him he was in possession of a fake Hope Diamond. Except now she had a steady suitor in John Castille.

There was no further cause to run into Edward unless she went to a lecture. And in order to halt her obsession with the man, Radiance refused to scrutinize the schedules in the newspaper of the Royal Polytechnic Institution, the Royal Institution, or even the Geological Survey and Museum of Practical Geology to see if he was presenting something that interested her.

Two months later, however, and a mere week after she'd done the unthinkable by telling John they must stop keeping company, Radiance received a missive addressed to her in Edward's messy scrawl. Taking it from the silver salver Mr. Dunley held out, she clasped it to her bosom and hurried upstairs.

Why was he writing? Tamping down her silly fantasies, Radiance sat on the end of her bed, broke the plain red seal, and unfolded the single sheet.

Dear Lady Radiance,

The Koh-i-Noor has been successfully cut and will be presented to the committee by the Crown Jeweler at Buckingham Palace on Thursday in the Yellow Drawing Room. Three o'clock sharp. I hope you will attend.
Yours,
Lockwood

Hers! She sighed and reread it. At least he had said he hoped she would attend. That was something surely signifying he held her in some regard above other women. *Didn't it?*

Then she tossed the paper down and fell back onto the bed. Infuriating man that he was, why did she yearn for him? Of course, she would go to the ceremony if only to be in his company once again. Not to mention seeing the diamond now that it was finished.

Thus, on Thursday, she descended from her father's carriage with Brilliance this time since Sarah had come down with a catarrh. Unsightly phlegm had no place at the Palace. Instead, home in bed with a mustard plaster on her chest and a penny dreadful in her hand, her maid was not suffering a bit.

"But Bri is not a suitable companion," Radiance had protested that morning. More of a hindrance, she thought privately, not sure what unintended mischief her younger sister might get up to. "Can't you accompany me, Mother?"

"Take your sister. She will behave herself. No wandering off, Bri, dear. Do you promise?"

And with that less-than-satisfactory instruction, Radiance was forced to have Brilliance come along with her.

"I'm monstrously excited," Bri crowed. "To think I shall be in the Palace and not in the same room every young lady goes to for her presentation, either." She clapped her hands.

Radiance couldn't help smiling. She'd felt just as thrilled when Edward took her the first time.

Soon, however, it was made clear that Bri had to remain in the wide hallway on a gold satin divan, her entrance barred to the drawing room.

"Sorry, dear sister, but this won't take too long." Bri waved her away, nearly as pleased to be in the beautiful gallery.

Radiance saw most of the same faces, except sadly, the Duke of Wellington had passed away a week earlier and was lying in state. She greeted the Museum Director and the Lord Chamberlain, the two Dutch jewelers who spoke little English, and Mr. Rathmond, who offered her a hawklike stare, and . . . Edward. *Except he wasn't present.*

Mr. Garrard escorted her to a chair. "Where is our mutual friend?" he asked her as if she had any clue. "We cannot begin without him."

Radiance shook her head. "I promise you I have no idea."

"More's the pity!" he exclaimed, staring at the door.

"Let us get on with it," Mr. Rathmond insisted. "The tardy geologist will have to look at it another time."

"Agreed," said the Lord Chamberlain. "I have other places to be."

Mr. Garrard grew more perturbed. To give Edward time to arrive, Radiance decided to strike up a conversation.

"The newspapers turned the cutting into quite an exciting event, as if the entire polishing would be done in that first moment and by the Duke's own hand rather than taking weeks."

They all paused to think of the deceased soldier. Soon after making the first cut, he'd expired in his beloved Walmer Castle in Kent.

"I read it, too," Mr. Garrard said. "'A single slip of the cutter's hand,' and all that drama. Neither I, nor these men," he nodded to the silent Dutchmen, "were about to make such a slip, nor take our attention off the diamond for even a second."

Then he frowned. "Anyway, I believe it brought the Iron Duke joy to be there that day. And now let's hope the diamond brings joy to Her Majesty and the Prince Consort."

"Are they coming here? Now?" Radiance asked.

"No," Mr. Garrard said. "They are in Aberdeen, enjoying the peace at Balmoral before renovations start on it again next year, but they are returning shortly."

Radiance was disappointed she wouldn't see the Queen's reaction to the Koh-i-Noor's new shape. And Bri, in the hallway, would certainly not be pleased at being deprived of Queen Victoria, even if all Her Majesty had done was pass her by.

Mr. Garrard began to pace when suddenly the door flew open, and Edward rushed in. Stopping in his tracks, he glanced around, realized he was the object of everyone's attention, and whipped off his hat to run his fingers through his hair.

"My apologies," he said, and nothing more.

Radiance rolled her eyes. He ought to have taken a moment to straighten his necktie and tug his sleeves down. What's more, his jacket was buttoned up askew, leaving one side longer, and she could see a little of his shirttail hanging down the side of his trousers.

Radiance knew he had become caught up in his work, forgotten what time it was, and had made a mad dash to dress and hail a cab.

Still, he sent her a warm smile, sending the usual spark sizzling down her body. She smiled back at him. It was so very good to lay eyes upon him again.

"Lockwood, you are a scoundrel to make us all wait," Mr. Garrard said, while looking relieved.

"My sincere apologies," Edward said. "Some unpredicted . . . *uh* . . . distractions . . . that is, these particular distractions distracted me."

Radiance would wager gems were involved, and if not for Mrs. McSabby, he probably wouldn't be there at all.

"We have saved the Koh-i-Noor's unveiling for your expert eyes," Mr. Garrard said before taking his seat at the head of the table. Edward found an empty place at the other end, opposite Radiance. Their gazes met for an instant.

Mr. Rathmond scooted forward in his chair, and Radiance, too, could hardly wait to see what the Dutch had done. However, when she glanced at him, she flinched, realizing he was the one who reminded her of Mr. Sully. Or more precisely, Mr. Rathmond had been the man whom Mr. Sully had brought to mind.

Studying him now, she thought it was the color of his eyes and the shape of his nose and chin. Not that they were twins, but Mr. Rathmond's features, even the same black hair, was uncanny.

When he noticed her continuing to stare at him, he looked away, and she regretted her rudeness. Besides, they were there to see the Koh-i-Noor.

At Mr. Garrard's behest, one of the Dutch jewelers opened a stark wooden box set inconspicuously upon the edge of the table before him. From this, he withdrew a velvet pouch. Needles of anticipation pricked Radiance's skin, and she shivered.

When he flipped the pouch inside out to let the diamond remain nestled, a collective gasp sounded. Even indoors, with only the light of the chandelier over the table, the Koh-i-Noor finally shone like the mountain of light for which it was named. She could hardly credit it was the same stone.

The change was so significant, both in size and shape, that Radiance truly wouldn't have known it was the diamond with which they'd started. Some of the others around the table had been following the progress all along. Thus, its new brilliant cut shape was no surprise. But she saw the Lord Chamberlain frown, and Mr. Rathmond actually groaned.

"Eight-thousand pounds," the gem dealer exclaimed, "spent from our country's coffers, and it looks like it has shrunk from a boulder to a pebble."

It wasn't that bad, although Radiance had been unaware of the staggering cost.

"What is the current carat weight?" she asked, noticing Edward was staring at her. She could almost believe he was as hungry for the sight of her as she had been for him.

"It started at 190 carats," Mr. Garrard said, "and is now," he coughed, "105, I believe, give or take."

"Give or take," Mr. Rathmond muttered. "Looks like take, to me."

"But it's much improved," Radiance pointed out, looking at the shallow oval brilliant cut.

At Mr. Garrard's behest, Mr. Voorzanger passed the Koh-i-Noor around the table so everyone could take a closer look. It went swiftly from hand to hand. Radiance swallowed hard as she held it, thinking of its long history and the many rulers who'd worn it. All male, until Queen Victoria.

She passed it to Mr. Rathmond, knowing she would never hold it again. When it was Edward's turn, he donned magnifying glasses and gave it careful scrutiny. She loved the way his hair fell over his forehead when he did.

Finally, the diamond was back in its pouch.

"Thank you, Meneer Voorzanger, Meneer Fedder," Mr. Garrard said. "You have cut it to everyone's satisfaction, and I can vouch for the fact that the Queen will be overjoyed. It is spectacular!"

With that brief commendation, the Royal Keeper of the Jewels took the velvet bundle from the Dutch jeweler's hand. Not bothering with the wooden box, to Radiance's astonishment, he seemed to drop the velvet pouch onto his lap and out of sight.

CHAPTER THIRTY-SIX

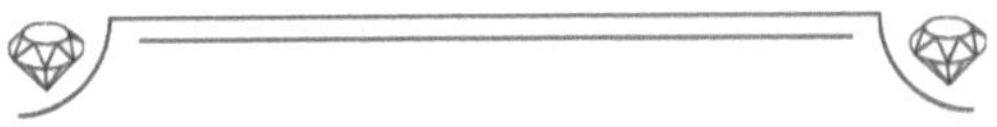

Edward wished he hadn't come late, leaving him off-kilter and allowing Rathmond to have the seat beside Radiance. If she so much as flinched or the man's legs seemed to move, Edward would reach across the table and throttle him.

Regardless, he had done what the royal couple had asked. He'd authenticated the stone to his satisfaction before it was once more ensconced in velvet and out of his reach.

Definitely smaller but far more beautiful, he hoped it would remain the genuine Koh-i-Noor for the rest of its existence.

Thinking the meeting had concluded, Edward was surprised when Mr. Garrard addressed him further.

"The Queen and the Prince Consort have instructed me to give the Koh-i-Nor to you for safekeeping."

The gasps this time were even louder than when Mr. Voorzanger had unveiled the diamond, the loudest of which was from Edward.

"That's preposterous," he said.

"Indeed. It's absurd," said the Lord Chamberlain.

"Nonetheless," the Crown Jeweler continued, "Mr. Lockwood is to keep it in his possession until Prince Albert and Queen Victoria return. That was their wish. It shall be a mere two days at the most. Possibly three. I shall send word in that time for you to bring it to the Palace."

Edward swallowed. "Surely, the stone would be better kept here by a guard or at the Tower."

"That's what I suggested," Mr. Garrard agreed, "but Prince Albert, advised by Mr. Hope, says you are to be trusted above all. You do not covet the gem, you are not a jeweler who wishes to make his own mark upon it for posterity, and you have the knowledge to know at all times that it is the true stone, the very one which I shall hand you in a moment."

Edward nodded as if it were the sanest decision in the world, although he was almost lightheaded with the responsibility of it.

"Keep it safe, and you shall be hailed a hero," the Crown Jeweler added. The implication of how he would be condemned should he fail was left unspoken.

"Very well," Edward conceded, glancing at Radiance who appeared equally surprised with her gorgeous green eyes watching him. "I suppose no one will know I have it, in any case."

"No one outside this room," Garrard reminded him sharply.

Edward looked around at the others. A small number of honest men, he hoped. And Radiance, who now rose to her feet causing the rest of them to do the same.

In a few minutes, everyone dissipated like mist in the morning, including his red-headed lady-friend of late, who sadly was no longer *his* lady nor, it would seem by her quick exit, even *his* friend.

All at once, while he watched her pretty figure disappear, letting his gaze linger upon the last sway of her skirts through the doorway, Edward decided it was time to remedy the situation that was plaguing his heart, distracting him from his writing—and from most everything else in life.

He had almost missed the meeting because of his obsession. This constant desire for the lady had to be quelled by way of making her his wife.

After all, hadn't he determined that Radiance Diamond was ideal for him?

Besides, there he was in the same room as the most famous diamond in the world, and all he could think about was hastening into the gallery just beyond, hoping to catch another glimpse of the most extraordinary Diamond in the world—the most beautiful, clever one, too.

He must correct the present course in order to ensure a better future. The only future he wanted. That very night, too, if he was able. Having begun to follow her social engagements as reported in *The Times*, he'd seen the list of those attending an exclusive ball. All he had to do was obtain a last-minute invitation.

How could he do that?

And even if he could, he had to convince Radiance to renege on any agreement she had made with Castille. Edward clenched his fists. Even the man's name was annoying—so romantically foreign, despite being solidly British and from the ordinary countryside of West Surry, if Edward's private research was correct. Albeit in a massive country manor with a sparkling silver spoon stuck up his arse.

"Why are you standing here scowling like a fiend when you are about to complete the most important service for the Crown that you could ever imagine?" Garrard was beside him, looking at the empty doorway, too, presumably to see at what Edward was staring.

"I was merely wool-gathering upon other matters."

"This isn't the time, Lockwood! When you showed up late, I thought I would have to send the Queen's best after you."

Edward couldn't tell the Crown Jeweler that he'd lost track of time while drinking coffee and perusing the newspaper for information on his lady-love.

Lady-love! A much more accurate description than *lady-friend*, to be sure.

But he had to give Garrard all his attention at that moment. Dragging his gaze to the Crown Jeweler's, he asked, "Why am I being put to such an outrageous, ill-conceived service? That is the question."

From his pocket, Garrard withdrew the velvet pouch.

"Because, as I told the others, you are trusted. Besides, you know how to handle yourself in a fix." He reached out and patted Edward's side, almost precisely where his wound had healed.

"How did you know about that?" he asked, shocked.

"The servants' grapevine, of course. If your staff knows something personal about you, then everyone's staff knows." Garrard chuckled.

Edward didn't see the humor in living under a microscope, the same he used to study rocks in even more detail than with his magnifying glasses.

"I am not Daniel Mendoza," he muttered, although he did admire the fighter from Whitechapel, who a century earlier had used an almost scientific technique, knowing where to punch to do the most damage. Mendoza had become a professor in the art of self-defense and had written *The Art of Boxing*.

If Edward could get Radiance out of his head and into his bed, he, too, might finish his own blasted book.

"Maybe not Mendoza," Garrard agreed, "but I've heard you attend a boxing club in Town."

"More of the servants' grapevine?" Edward asked.

Garrard simply shrugged. "In truth, no. I heard that from someone at the Athenaeum Club. Many of the members are on the scrawny side, wouldn't you say?"

Garrard was correct in his estimation of the scientific community. It had more than its share of whey-faced spindles who looked as if a strong wind might send them tumbling into the Thames.

"Naturally," the Crown Jeweler continued, "the fact that you cut a more muscular figure begets some talking and some jealousy."

Edward had no idea he was the discussion of any such gossip.

"Thus, on the basis of a fight in India's Port of Goa and my exercising my body, I am considered the best person to guard the Koh-i-Noor?"

"Hardly that. Prince Albert appreciates your other skills, which I've already mentioned. Your ability to protect yourself and how you defended Lady Radiance and retrieved the royal jewels from that thief are simply a bonus. Besides, nothing will happen to the diamond. After all, you and the lady have handled the forger already."

So why did Edward have the impression something fishy was happening?

Before he could question further, Garrard thrust the velvet pouch toward him, and Edward had no choice but to raise his hand and take it.

"Very well. Two days, you say?"

"Maybe three at the most," Garrard said. "I shall contact you."

Edward had an idea. "I say, I don't suppose you have an invitation to the ball at Marlborough House tonight." Seeing how Garrard had a royal appointment, it was possible. Probable, in fact, and confirmed when the man smiled widely.

Outside, when Edward hailed a hackney, he wondered what the driver would think if the man knew the cargo he carried. Edward's pocket seemed to have grown exceedingly heavy. He wouldn't slide his hand into it, unreasonably fearing the Koh-i-Noor would be hot to the touch.

Knowing how preposterous his thoughts, yet he almost believed the diamond was sending out a beacon, as steady as a lighthouse, to let everyone know its location.

Regardless of his new charge, like an unexpected infant dropped on his doorstep, Edward intended to go to the ball that evening. With Garrard promising his name would be on the list, all Edward had to do was change his clothing and somehow pass interminable hours before the fashionable starting time of eight o'clock.

And then he would confront Radiance on her own territory, using reason to convince her of their suitability or coercion with another kiss if necessary.

His plan was a sound one. At least, that's what he told himself over a glass of wine while he dressed, undressed, and dressed again. Things that he'd never paid attention to before, like his appearance, seemed of utmost importance. His hair, for one thing, wouldn't behave. It insisted on flopping around, curling up in patches, and generally being unruly. His best necktie looked as though it had been tied by a monkey. And his shoes had street dust on them rather than a well-tended shine.

Never had he more regretted not employing a gentleman servant to assist him in his toilette. It took him hours before he deemed himself even halfway satisfactory, and still, he needed to determine a secure place for the diamond before he went out gallivanting like a troubadour lover.

However, after wandering around his home for another thirty minutes with the velvet pouch in his hand, Edward couldn't begin to imagine what that place might be. The back of his armoire, under his bed, perhaps a box in the attic, he even considered digging a hole in the backyard like a blasted pirate. He knew one thing—putting the Koh-i-Noor anywhere in his work room amongst his other stones would be a disaster. It was the first place a thief would search.

Although, if their investigation had been correct, then the thief had already been caught. Therefore, he couldn't imagine why he was expecting trouble to find him, nor anyone to know he had such a prize in his home.

In the end, he slid the pouch once again deep into his pocket. If he was not going to stay home and guard it, which he simply could not do—not with Radiance out there growing more attached to Castille—then the diamond would be safest kept upon his person.

CHAPTER THIRTY-SEVEN

Radiance hardly had the will to go to the Marlborough House ball, no matter having promised her friend that she would attend. In fact, Diana's mother, Mrs. Stepney, was acting as chaperone to them both, and it would be the height of rudeness to beg off at this late hour.

Thus, she let Sarah dress her hair, fasten her stays, and help her into an elegant gown of the palest blue satin. Lastly, she donned her favorite earrings, the golden topaz ones. All the while, she recalled watching Edward during the meeting and feeling the same intense longing she'd always felt for him.

He had closed off any possible association between them. Yet whenever they met, he treated her as if she commanded his admiration. He was a riddle.

A mere seven days earlier, she'd confessed to Lord Castille the impossibility of a union between them. Breaking it off with John hadn't been difficult except in trying not to hurt him. In truth, he'd been surprised more than anything as she'd given him no indication that she could not and would not fall head over heels in love. In truth, she had hoped to do so.

If she read his features correctly, it wasn't only surprise he felt. She'd wounded him right in the heart of his pride. Should he appear at the ball, she could well imagine him rubbing her nose in his desirability by allowing other women to fawn over him. And they undoubtedly would. He was a good catch, as well as any she could wish for. But he wasn't Edward.

She had no hope her geologist would come, although she did feel hopeful, oddly enough. As a Diamond, a family with a long history that included triumph and tragedy, Radiance had been taught to persevere. Moreover, she wasn't going to give up on finding a mate altogether. At this particular time, however, she simply couldn't bear being with the viscount or any other man who wasn't Edward Lockwood.

Meanwhile, Radiance would support Diana as her friend searched for love, and she would certainly dance at the ball if any gentleman asked her. It was better than staying home and hiding under her bed clothes.

When Mrs. Stepney and Diana collected Radiance at her home, she decided to be as cheerful as a titmouse so as not to spoil their evening. Once they arrived at the Pall Mall entrance and alighted from the Stepneys' carriage outside the symmetrically pleasing three-story structure of brick with white granite accents, Radiance thought she was already doing quite well at pretending.

Her smile didn't slip when they entered the former home of Queen Adelaide, now being used by the Museum of Manufactures to house its collections. That night, not only would she dance, she would wander the special inventions that were dear to the Prince Consort's heart.

Depositing their mantles in the cloak room, they went into the flamboyant baroque ballroom with its stunning black-and-white tiled floor. There was nothing else quite like it in London.

While Radiance was accepting a few gentlemen's signatures on her card, John chose that moment to arrive. He wasn't alone.

Striding into the room, drawing notice due to his height, Lord Castille escorted Lady Lucinda, with her raven-black hair and shimmery pale-pink gown. They were a stunning couple.

Radiance couldn't wear that color without feeling ugly, which she'd always thought a bitter shame since she adored pink. Moreover, all three of her sisters looked divine in even the palest shade of rose due to having hair the color of Lucinda's.

Lady Chetney, Lucinda's mother, strolled in behind them, looking like a cat that had swallowed the cheery little bird Radiance was trying so hard to mimic.

Having known the viscount would be snapped up the moment she released him, Radiance ought not to be surprised in the least. Still, it was strange to see him arrive with another woman when they had been exclusively arriving and departing together for many weeks.

Apparently, the entire room full of people thought it noteworthy as well. Radiance would swear a hush came over the other guests and that every pair of eyes glanced from him to her and back again.

Blast!

The mistake was her own. She ought to have stayed away from society and let John step out first. If she hadn't been there, then the *ton* would have had at least a single evening to adjust to seeing him with another woman.

Instead, they believed they were witnessing a betrayal on the scale of Othello's misguided notion that Desdemona cuckolded him.

At that instant, John, Lady Lucinda, and her mother all caught sight of Radiance standing stock still watching them. Another murmur whispered across the room as if the guests expected some sort of confrontation.

And then Edward blocked her view of the unfolding scene.

Edward!

Dressed as finely as any nobleman in charcoal gray with a rich blue waistcoat and black necktie, he was a mere four feet away and approaching.

What was he doing at Marlborough House?

"Good evening, my lady." Then he greeted her companions somewhat disinterestedly before giving her his attention again, even as Diana's mother was still returning his greeting. "May I have the honor of a dance?"

"Yes." Radiance didn't hesitate.

Reaching for the little card in the reticule dangling from her wrist, she couldn't take her gaze off him. He might be an apparition conjured by her own ardent desire.

Edward gave her a lopsided grin that tugged at her fluttering insides and made her knees weaken at the same time. With her gaze fixed upon his mouth, she handed him the card.

"Do you have a pencil?" he asked.

She handed one to him. Amazingly, he wrote "Lockwood" on her card large and carelessly—with his name going across a few lines, over another man's name, and hopelessly smudging her card. Radiance didn't mind in the least.

Yet he glanced down as he gave it back to her, hastily trying to tidy it by rubbing his thumb and fingers across the mess. His white gloves now had black fingertips. It was classically Edward Lockwood behavior. *Adorable!*

She gestured to his glove with her own blue lace-clad hand.

The deuce!" he exclaimed. Diana and her mother moved a step away.

Stripping off the offending glove, he shoved it into his pocket.

Oh dear, she thought, wondering if there was a way to procure him another. Or whether it was best he removed both. Purity would have known what to do.

"I hope this won't cause you to renege on our dance," he said. "I chose the one before dinner as I wish to talk with you at length."

She glanced at the card again. A sappy smile stuck itself on her face and wouldn't be displaced no matter how she tried to calm her emotions.

"We could take a promenade around the room," she suggested, "if you don't wish to wait to speak with me. After all, it is practically like having hundreds of chaperones."

He glanced around, then offered her his arm. After nodding to her friend and Mrs. Stepney, Radiance let him lead her away.

"I hope this doesn't cause you any problems," he added as they tried to walk through the crowd.

"I don't take your meaning, sir."

"Between you and Castille," Edward explained. "Although I suppose that is a bold lie because I truly do not give two figs whether the man is inconvenienced or annoyed. Not even a single fig!"

Obviously, he hadn't seen John enter.

"I see," she said, and nothing more.

Edward had to release her arm more than once as they moved through the throng, not yet able to converse. Radiance had been to even larger events than this one, but it was overly attended for the size of the room, causing a feeling of decidedly cramped quarters.

Tired of looking at the back of his head as he forged a path, Radiance had two choices—wait until dinner to find out what he wished to say or take matters into her own hands. It was an easy decision.

Having more experience at a ball than he had, she tugged on his sleeve, making him halt.

"Do you see over there?" She pointed up to the gallery where only a few were standing, and he followed with his gaze.

"On the balcony, we can observe the other guests," Radiance told him. "And while we shall also be watched, we can speak without being overheard. If you cross to the left, you'll find the staircase in the hallway."

He didn't hesitate, heading the way she directed. Edward Lockwood was an enigmatic blend—a man of intellect and action, both distracted and focused. At that moment, with him intent on reaching the gallery, she could barely keep up with him.

Briefly, they were alone in the hallway and upon the stairs lined with paintings depicting resounding French defeat at the hands of Lord Marlborough, and then they arrived on the balcony, just as three other guests vacated it. For a moment, despite the possibility that hundreds of eyes could be upon them, they had a measure of privacy, as long as they stood apart.

Edward looked her up and down. If it were anyone else, she would say he was insolent. But his scrutiny made her skin tighten and heat sluice through her like warm mulled wine.

"You look as lovely as ever. Ravishing, I would say."

"Please do," she teased.

His dimple showed. "Absolutely ravishing. And particularly kissable."

Her heart skipped a beat. She wholeheartedly wished they were in a position to kiss. Glancing down at the ballroom, Radiance noticed Diana wave at her, and she waved back, hoping her cheeks weren't bright pink from his comments and her wicked thoughts.

"I brought up your beau, Castille, because I do not want him to be such any longer."

She was still looking at Diana as his words filtered into her brain. His meaning was unclear. Finally, she turned to him.

"I beg your pardon, sir."

"When you call me 'sir,' in that proper manner, it is exceedingly enticing. You make the blood sizzle in my veins."

If she hadn't been looking at him, Radiance would think she was speaking with someone else. This didn't sound like her disinterested scientist.

"Sizzle?" She could hardly swallow or catch her breath.

"Yes," he said. "Where is he, anyway? Why isn't Castille by your side?"

Truly, he hadn't seen John's entrance.

"Lord Castille and I are no longer keeping company."

She would never forget Edward's myriad expressions from shock to delight.

"Why, that's stupendous!" he said. "It makes everything so much easier. I don't have to have a man-to-man chat with him and suggest he relinquish you."

She was flummoxed. "And why would you do that?"

"Because obviously you belong with me. I thought you cared for Castille, but if you are no longer together, then I shall put forth my own suit." He cocked his head. "Unless you loved him deeply and had your heart broken, in which case, it may take a little longer to win you over."

Radiance didn't know where to start with his open declaration except with the truth.

"Lord Castille did not break my heart, nor did I love him deeply. Not at all, in fact."

"That's grand," Edward said, giving a quick clap of his hands, calling attention to the one glove again. They both looked at it for a moment.

With relief washing over her that her dream of a future with this intriguing man might possibly come true, she felt a bubble of mirth rise up. Thus, when Edward started to laugh, she joined in.

"I am an outlandish creature in some ways," he said. "Not worthy of a lady, but I shall endeavor to make you happy."

"You already have. You do," she confessed. "I broke it off with Lord Castille because my heart was set upon a certain geologist, no matter how little he seemed to care for me in return."

Again, Edward's countenance came over surprised. "Why on earth would you think I didn't care for you? Especially after the kisses we shared."

"Because you abruptly wanted nothing to do with me in terms of a social nature."

"I thought you were an intelligent female," he said with a shake of his head. "Did you really not comprehend my wish to keep you far from the investigation due to the danger it could bring?"

He reached for her hand with his bare one, and although she knew they could be seen, she did not pull away.

"When the bullet grazed you *after* the previous incident with the ruffian knocking you down, I felt rather desperate. How could I keep you safe? Short of guarding you with my pistol drawn, I knew pushing you away was the only option. It seemed to have worked, except it made me extremely unhappy."

"For a while, I thought I ought to push harder to be a part of your world in order to regain your interest," she told him. "I confess it stung to have been so easily overthrown when I thought we were moving toward something special."

He shook his head. "Not easily overthrown at all. I have become a shell of my former self, at least according to Mrs. McSabby."

They shared a smile.

"But when the crime was solved, and so impressively by you," he added, "I believed I was too late. My sister told me how often you have been in Castille's company. At first, I thought I should leave you be. After all, the man is a viscount."

She waved away such nonsense over a title.

"However, when I saw you again this morning . . ."

"Yes?" she prompted.

"I simply could not let the most precious Diamond I have ever seen or touched slip through my fingers. Not without a fight."

He took hold of her hand. Radiance dismissed the momentary fear over her stellar reputation. It was being shredded that very moment, but while gazing into Edward's eyes, she simply didn't care.

"Lady Radiance Diamond, will you marry me?"

CHAPTER THIRTY-EIGHT

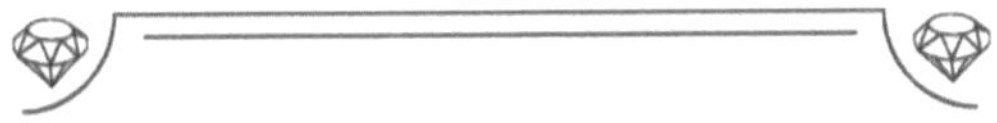

Edward could have knocked her over with a feather. As tears welled in Radiance's eyes at the impossible turn of events, she didn't protest when he pulled her into his arms. Vaguely, she heard a murmur from the room below, but she didn't stop him when he tilted up her chin.

"Will you? Or did I make a damnable misstep? I should have waited some appropriate amount of time between your breaking it off with Castille, is that it? Or at the very least, approached your father for permission before putting the question to you directly?"

"I think you have done just fine," she said. "Yes, I will marry you."

With that, Edward leaned down and kissed her.

Gasps, a few cheers, and some exclamations of outrage rose up from the other guests. Perhaps even a shriek or two. When the kiss ended, they turned to look down at the throng, as if on a stage.

"This wonderful lady has agreed to marry me," Edward called out.

His words engendered a general buzz of merriment. And then the entire assembly began to clap.

Radiance could think of nothing better to do than wave at their well-wishers. She spotted John off to the side, looking none too pleased, but at least he had Lady Lucinda beside him in her pretty pink.

She wished him the best and then thought of him no longer.

"Will you dance with me?" Edward asked.

"Yes."

They disappeared from the general view. And as they reached the top of the stairs, for a few moments, they were hidden completely.

"That kiss was too quick," he said and pulled her close once more.

She slid her hands up and around his neck. "It was. I suggest you kiss me again."

"And I suggest you kiss me back."

Gladly, she pressed herself against him as his hands, gloved and ungloved, roamed her body, easily felt through her fine silk gown. His caresses made her think of warm honey and scorching flames, of soft flower petals and the hard muscles of his frame.

When his mouth slanted across hers, she tilted her head to fit their lips more perfectly.

And then, curiously, she noticed something hard pressing against her hip. Being well-read and having two older sisters, Radiance was fairly sure she knew what was happening. Edward's manhood was growing tumescent as his passions flared. It was exciting beyond measure.

"I can feel your desire for me," she whispered when he drew back.

He paused, then nuzzled his lips along her throat, making her pulse beat a wild tattoo, knowing they had to stop in a moment and return to the ballroom.

"Actually," he said against her skin, "that's the Koh-i-Noor in my pocket. But I assure you I am desperately aroused."

The Koh-i-Noor!

She yelped before she could stop herself, even as he kissed his way back up her neck.

The Queen's diamond was digging into her hip bone. *How? Why?*

"What do you mean?" she asked when he didn't explain himself.

And then his tongue touched her ear, making her shiver before his lips closed over her earlobe.

A second later, Edward coughed and put his hand up. He couldn't speak for spluttering.

"Are you well?" she asked, her hands resting below his shoulders as she tried to look into his face.

Finally, he nodded. "I nearly swallowed your earbob."

She reached up to touch her bare lobe just as he spat out her topaz earring onto the palm of his hand.

"My apologies!" he said. "I got carried away. It's a little damp, I'm afraid."

"You must be careful." Radiance wanted to throttle him. He could have asphyxiated directly after asking her to marry him! "That is precisely what I was always warning you about."

"Did you?" he asked astounded. "Choking on earbobs? I don't think I've ever heard you mention it."

"Not that, but your general lack of awareness. You are forgetful and absent-minded." Having lost her heart to him ages ago, she wanted a long marriage but feared he would get himself wounded again, perhaps on his next trip to the jungle, or shot here in London, or perhaps cause his own demise through carelessness.

"Am I?" He ran a hand through his hair, appearing nonplussed.

Radiance nearly shrieked with exasperation.

But then he grinned, looking so winsome, she laughed. "You are a ninny!"

"As long as you are willing to put up with me," Edward said, "then I don't mind going through life as a ninny."

He blew on the earring before returning it to her.

"Shall I put it on for you?" he asked. "We cannot return into the public eye with you missing one. People will think we were kissing." By his tone, he didn't truly care what people thought.

"I can do it," she declared, rolling her eyes. Radiance slid the smooth gold wire easily through her ear, recalling the day she'd had her lobes pierced, feeling then like a grown woman despite being only ten years of age.

That was nothing compared to having the man she loved express his own admiration in return. Now, she considered herself an adult.

"Only a madman would carry that diamond in his pocket," she said as they descended the stairs.

"Precisely," he agreed. "No one would suspect me of being such an individual."

As soon as they reentered the ballroom, Diana came up to them.

"Congratulations! You provided unforeseen entertainment this evening."

"Did we?" Radiance glanced around. She was lucky they had conducted their conversation in plain sight—except for the stairwell. In a way, being visible had saved them from dishonor and becoming outcasts.

"Yes! You are the talk of the ball, and it has barely begun."

Radiance glanced at Edward, wondering if he comprehended what this meant in her world. They were all but formally engaged. It would be in the morning's papers, and he had better show up at his earliest convenience on her family's doorstep.

He shrugged slightly and offered her an endearing smile.

"You still have to dance with other partners tonight," Diana reminded her.

"I know." But she didn't want to. She wanted to disappear with Edward and explore their newly declared bond. As the music started, however, she let her partner escort her to the dance floor.

WHEN IT WAS FINALLY his turn to claim the lady he loved, Edward left his recent partner as swiftly as possible. He knew he wore a foolish smile, but he could not wipe it away. He'd expected a difficult night, perhaps having to grovel to Radiance or argue his case while somehow disparaging the all-but perfect Lord Castille.

Instead, it had turned out to be far too easy. As smooth as the silk Radiance wore, Edward had found himself the victor of the lady's heart.

Looking around for his prize, he saw an extraordinary sight—*Mrs. McSabby in Marlborough House!*

And she was standing with a uniformed constable.

Edward sprinted toward his housekeeper. "Is something amiss?"

His usually unflappable housekeeper was decidedly agitated as she nodded and looked to the constable to explain.

"Mr. Lockwood, is it?" the man asked.

"Yes. What has transpired?"

"You've had a break-in, sir."

"Were you hurt?" Edward asked Mrs. McSabby.

"No, sir."

Edward shoved his hand into his pocket, taking comfort in touching the most precious royal jewel.

"Left an awful mess, though," Mrs. McSabby said, sounding more annoyed than frightened.

Edward sighed. There would be no delightful dance or dinner with Radiance that night.

"Give me five minutes, and I shall join you outside."

Even as the pair left, both walking slowly, gazing around them at the finery of the people and the residence, Edward turned to search for Radiance. She was already approaching.

"When the music started without you appearing, I knew something was wrong. Was that Mrs. McSabby?"

"Yes. My home has been burgled. I must leave."

She touched his arm. Her green eyes were dark and worried as they looked into his. Suddenly, her eyes widened. "The Koh-i-Noor! If you hadn't brought it with you . . ."

"Exactly what I was thinking. I had believed we'd solved that crime already." He was starting to doubt it. Moreover, as an outrageous plan developed in his mind, he had a notion he wouldn't be able to keep it safe without her help.

"Can you come to my home tomorrow?"

She hesitated. "Actually, I had thought you would come to mine."

Edward frowned, his thoughts already on his treasured workroom full of his life's work. He had to leave and make sure every window in his home wasn't shattered and his front door splintered off its hinges. He couldn't picture any of his maids staving off an intruder. Again, he reprimanded himself for not hiring a manservant.

At his hesitation, her cheeks pinkened. "To speak with my father, sir."

Oh! He had been bent upon planning that very thing before the sight of Mrs. McSabby had knocked his good intentions out of his head.

"Of course, and I shall be there first thing. I imagine word spreads quickly through the *ton*."

"Indeed, it does." She appeared relieved, and he was glad she had reminded him not to let her down. But that wouldn't solve his problem. "Then would you come with me tonight?"

"Words fail me," she said softly.

"It is important. We have work to do for the Queen."

"How can I possibly? What should I tell Diana and her mother?"

"Mrs. McSabby is waiting outside with a constable. Surely, the two of them will be adequate chaperones for an engaged couple."

"We're not exactly that. Not officially."

Edward had never felt more committed to anything or anyone. "As far as I am concerned, as well as this entire gathering of good people, we are. Won't that do?"

"Yes," she said quickly.

"Good. Now that we are engaged, will you accompany me and my housekeeper and the constable to my home?"

Again, she didn't hesitate. "Will you await me here, or shall I meet you outside?"

He couldn't help admiring her gumption. "To keep lips from flapping like bird wings in a stiff wind, I'll depart now and wait by the carriage."

He hoped she didn't change her mind. But five minutes later, just the time it took for her to explain to her friend— *how she could explain, Edward couldn't imagine*—then retrieve her coat from the maid in the entry way and change out of her dancing slippers, Radiance greeted the constable and Mrs. McSabby. Soon, they were all riding in a police coach together.

It wasn't long before Edward viewed the damage. Not as bad as he had feared. A window had been opened, not smashed, but his workroom looked as though a hurricane had passed through it.

"Gracious," Radiance said beside him.

"It's not only in here, sir," Mrs. McSabby chimed in. "The burglar went all over—into the drawing room and upstairs to your bedchamber. When I came out of the kitchen, the only room he didn't enter, the front door was open wide. Anyone could have walked in."

"What can you do, Sergeant?" Edward asked, thinking he knew the answer.

"If you can give us a list of what was stolen, we can at least be on the lookout for your items being sold. There are places in the East End that are regular marketplaces for stolen goods."

"I shall see what I can come up with," Edward told him. "Thank you for bringing my housekeeper and alerting me."

"Very well, sir. I shall bid you and your wife a good evening."

The constable left while Edward was still taking in his words and staring at Radiance.

"Your wife!" Mrs. McSabby exclaimed. "What cheek! Assuming because this nice young lady came home with you at night . . . Well, I mean . . . Oh, heavens!"

"Not to worry, Mrs. McSabby," Edward said. "The constable is nearly correct, albeit a little premature. Lady Radiance and I are engaged to be married."

Mrs. McSabby was silenced with surprise. She rounded on Radiance.

"You are going to marry Mr. Lockwood?" Her hands went to her generous hips. "Are you certain?"

"Mrs. McSabby!" Edward muttered. *What was the woman trying to do?*

"I am sure," Radiance said. "He's a dear man who is also clever."

Edward wanted to hug her.

However, Mrs. McSabby wasn't finished. "Yes, but he is as like as not to forget which house to come home to. What if he takes your child out in the world and leaves it somewhere while he goes about digging up his rocks?"

"Then I shall keep a close eye upon our child," Radiance said, making him want to howl with happiness at the idea of their offspring. A little red-headed boy or girl with his soon-to-be wife's amazing green eyes. "Anyway, shall we examine the damage?" she asked.

As Edward expected, the only damage was due to the speed and carelessness with which the thief searched for the diamond—and undoubtedly, that was his intended purpose. Drawers were pulled out with their contents scattered, cupboards opened, rugs tossed aside, and all his gemstones and geodes and opals were strewn about the room. But they hadn't been taken. In the drawing room, his cushions were ripped open and his rugs overturned.

"The brutes!" Mrs. McSabby said, flipping each cushion to hide the worst of the tears.

Edward wanted to speak with Radiance alone. "You said my bedroom was in equal disarray, didn't you?"

"Yes," his housekeeper said.

"Will you concentrate your attentions on righting it for my use tonight while Lady Radiance and I begin tidying my workroom? I know you're not one for sorting rocks."

"Yes, sir." She headed for the stairs. Then stopped. "What a shame you had to come home early, m'lady. You look so lovely. Like a princess. It was the only proper ball I've ever seen, and even my old eyes could see you were the most beautiful woman in that room. Mr. Lockwood is a lucky man, and we shall be glad to have you under this roof."

She sniffed after her sentimental speech and added, "I can only pray the master doesn't cock it all up." She left before he could defend himself.

"What a sweet thing for her to say." Radiance appeared bemused.

"Her compliments always seem to come at my expense," Edward griped, making Radiance laugh.

He would vow the sound vibrated through him from head to toe, making his body tingle. In the next instant, he realized they were alone. Not even the useless Sarah nearby, ignoring them.

Edward grabbed his lady's hand and yanked her close.

"How long are the engagements in your rarefied world?"

She placed her hands on his chest and looked up at him.

"A few months of torture is expected."

He groaned, for she was right. It would be torture. At that moment, he wanted nothing more than to take her upstairs to his bedroom.

Which, according to Mrs. McSabby, had been turned topsy-turvy.

"I forgot the intruder momentarily and even why I asked you here."

"You mean you didn't invite me to your home in order to kiss me senseless?"

"I didn't actually. But let's do that first."

Without waiting any longer, he claimed her satin lips. As soon as their mouths touched, he felt her relax against him, thoroughly enjoying the feeling of her soft breasts squashing delightfully onto the front of him. His hands moved of their own accord, sliding down her back and past the tiny pleats at her waist until they snagged hold of her plump buttocks, hidden under many layers of flounces and skirts and petticoats, one cheek in each of his greedy palms.

Heat lanced his groin—already the torture had begun of knowing she would be his someday while having to wait for the ultimate satisfaction.

Feeling her heart beating as fast as his own, he pressed his tongue to the seam of her lips, desperate for entry, which she allowed. Like giving a drowning man a lifeline. He wanted so much more, but he would gladly take what she gave, ravaging her mouth the way he wanted to explore her luscious body, imagining how he would pleasure her when she was his wife.

He didn't know how long they kissed. Lost in the essence of Radiance, her delicate fragrance filled his head, and her sweet softness tormented him.

"Heavens!" Mrs. McSabby exclaimed, and Edward jumped back.

"My apologies to you both," his housekeeper said.

Monty was also in the open doorway, perhaps having gone into hiding when the stranger had ransacked his home.

"I was tidying your room when I thought how early you had come home, before the fancy midnight supper, and I wondered if you were needing something to eat."

"I had a fine dinner earlier," Radiance said. "But perhaps a glass of wine."

Edward recollected the task at hand and what lay ahead. "No wine, Mrs. McSabby. Tea, please, for the lady and coffee for me. And some of that lemon ginger cake you served yesterday."

"Yes, sir."

Radiance's curious glance offered him little choice but to explain. First, he withdrew the Koh-i-Noor from his pocket. It was wrapped in a simple square of velvet, which he quickly removed before holding it out to her.

"Take it," he commanded.

She visibly shivered. Reaching out, she bit her lower lip in anticipation, and Edward wanted to sink his own teeth into her plump lip while she wore that same expression of awe. In the next instant, she gazed down at it on her palm.

"I cannot believe how much it is improved in appearance. And yet, something of its ancient origin and magnificence has been lost."

"I haven't even looked at it again, but I understand what you mean. Regardless the smaller, more customary shape will make it easier for you to create a fake."

Her gaze snapped to his, and he thought she would drop the stone. Then she closed her fingers around it and gave him her full attention.

CHAPTER THIRTY-NINE

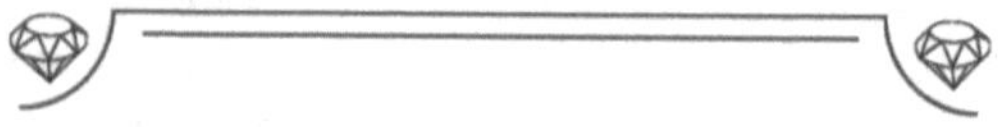

Radiance wasn't sure she'd heard Edward correctly. "What are you saying?"

"There is no other way to keep it safe."

"Impossible!" she declared.

"Not with your skill. Listen to my reasoning. If the Koh-i-Noor is in danger, then what better way to safeguard it than to create a forgery as a decoy?"

"And then what?" she demanded.

"When the Queen and Prince Consort return from Scotland, we shall give them the genuine Koh-i-Noor. Meanwhile, the thief shall have time to steal the fake and reveal himself."

"Mr. Sully is in jail," she pointed out.

He glanced around them at the disarray. "And now we know he wasn't working alone."

"Did you not think Mr. Sully reminded you of someone else we know? Both in his features and the color of his eyes and hair."

Edward frowned. Then his eyes widened. "The ankle-rubber!"

She startled. "Is that truly all you recall of Mr. Rathmond?"

He looked down at her. "Well, yes, I suppose it is. I wasn't thrilled to think of him taking liberties. I didn't even like him sitting next to you again today. In any case, he was in the meeting, watching Garrard give me the Koh-i-Noor."

"Mr. Rathmond came to see me once at Bonwit's."

Edward's expression was shocked. "You never told me!"

"No," she agreed. "We weren't . . . that is, at the time, you and I were not as close as we are now. Besides, the next time I saw you, I learned you had forgotten to send our letter to Mr. Neble."

"My negligence drove everything else from your sensible mind, I suppose."

"Yes," she agreed. "In any case, he frightened me with his questions and a certain menacing manner. He even suggested the Queen had no right to rule India. I ended up running out of the store."

Gently, he pulled her close. "I wish you had told me."

She sighed in his arms, relishing being held against his warmth, feeling his strong heartbeat—and knowing it beat for her.

"He is a possible suspect, don't you think?"

"Even if you are correct, it is not as though I can knock upon Rathmond's door, point my finger, and accuse him of ransacking my home."

She sighed, rested a moment longer in the comfort of his arms, and then pushed away. In the midst of the mess of Edward's workroom, Radiance placed the Koh-i-Noor in an empty space on the table. After lighting his table lamp, he dragged two chairs from across the room where they lay on their sides.

They both sat and stared at the jewel.

"It *is* more beautiful now," she said, "where before it was impressive only for its sheer size. I would almost swear it isn't the same stone."

"I think the Dutch did a remarkable job," Edward agreed, "although it seems Sir Brewster was correct after all, regarding the amount that would need to be cut to remove its flaws and improve the refraction. I didn't think the size would diminish quite so vastly. In any case, its regular, symmetrical brilliant cut makes what I am suggesting easier."

Edward rose again. "Let me show you something."

He went toward his cabinet before realizing its contents were all around his feet. She tried to see what he was retrieving as he searched through one pile and then another while Monty wove his way through the mess, complaining loudly.

"Move off," Edward ordered his cat. And then, "Thank God it's here!" When he turned, he had something in his closed right hand.

"Open your hand, palm up," he directed.

"What now?" she asked. He could place the Dresden or the Nassak diamond in her hand, and she would hardly be any more surprised than by what had already occurred. Still, she did as he directed and presented him with her palm.

With his own hand yet tightly closed, he hovered over hers before releasing a large stone. She gasped. It appeared to be a diamond, clearer than the original Koh-i-Noor but close to it in size.

"Is it real?" she asked. "A diamond, I mean."

"You tell me," he challenged. "Examine it."

If it were truly a diamond, then it was superior, due to having both the magnitude *and* the clarity the Koh-i-Noor lacked before the Dutch cut it.

Studying it, Radiance held it close to the table lamp, then asked for his magnifying spectacles, which he also found on the floor and handed to her. Donning them, she peered at it again.

"I am no geologist," she said, "but I believe this is not a diamond."

"It isn't. It's a white topaz. How did you know?"

"Its refraction is . . . how can I describe it . . . *simpler* than a diamond's. It produces only a pale gray sparkle," she added, "whereas a diamond shines with all the colors of the rainbow."

"My clever fiancée," he said, and her gaze lifted to his.

"Say it again," she demanded.

His tempting mouth turned into his adorably lopsided grin, and his dimple appeared. "Fiancée," he said.

"I do like the sound of that," she admitted, before looking again at the gem. "Is it yours?"

"Yes, one of my favorite, earliest finds. I want you to cut it to look like the newly improved Koh-i-Noor."

"Me?" Radiance now had a lump in her throat as big as the gemstone in her hand.

"Who else?" he asked. "Right now, for nearly two days, we shall have the Koh-i-Noor in our possession."

"Not even two full days—" she began.

"And nights," he added. "Plenty of time."

She nearly laughed at his assertion, reminding him, "It took the Coster jewelers over thirty days."

"Thirty-eight, to be exact. But they were making magic, or supposed to be. Although they didn't do what they promised, did they? Lopping off over eighty carats." He shook his head. "But you won't be trying to polish a diamond, only copy one."

She finally took her gaze off the topaz and looked at him.

"You are serious, aren't you? But we are committing a criminal offense, surely."

"If the thief tries to take it or, God forbid, succeeds in stealing it, then we will be saving the most important royal jewel of our era."

"And if no one tries to take it, then we shall have produced an illegal forgery and appear to be thieves ourselves."

"We shall happily but discreetly return the Koh-i-Noor at that time."

She shook her head. "How can I do this, here? Now?"

Edward shrugged. This time, he simply lifted a piece of cloth from the other table in the room.

"A lapidary's mill," she said, wishing she would wake up because she was suddenly frightened this was real, and he was relying upon her.

"How fortunate the intruder didn't break it," Edward said. "He also didn't mistake my prized topaz for a diamond, which means he knows his gemstones."

"Therefore, he will know this to be a fake," she pointed out.

But Edward shook his head. "We only need him to be fooled long enough to snatch it. When he does, he shall be apprehended red-handed." He gathered a few things as he circled the room.

"Emery and rottenstone," he said placing pots of both before her.

"I prefer to call it by its other name, tripoli," Radiance said, feeling chilled. She was very pleased when Mrs. McSabby returned with the tea and coffee service.

"Regardless," Edward said, "I have everything you will need to make a perfect replication of the new Koh-i-Noor."

"I don't know if I can." After all, she could barely breathe.

"Of all my worries," Edward said, "that is not one of them. I know you have the skill. Mrs. McSabby shall keep you well nourished, and I will be right here sorting out my workroom and offering support in any way I can."

Again, she shook her head. "I cannot stay here all night and tomorrow."

"Send word to your parents. And of course, Sarah must come stay as well."

"This is madness!" she insisted, but she was beginning to be a little excited by the prospect of such a challenge. Taking off her evening mantle, she tossed it over the back of her chair.

"It won't be as difficult as you expect," he promised. "The topaz is not as hard as a diamond, nor even a sapphire."

"I know," she said softly, before sipping the tea. "An eight on the Mohs scale." She had polished a topaz many times. "I suppose you think it's like butter."

"Well, maybe not that easy," he admitted, "but at least you don't have to figure out the planes yourself. Simply copy what the Dutch have done."

"Simply copy!" Radiance rolled her eyes. Taking in a deep breath, she noted how Edward's golden gaze was drawn to and lingered upon the rise and fall of her breasts. Immediately, she felt another type of excitement and wondered how she would concentrate with him nearby.

"I will give it my best attempt. And while my parents won't be missing me until two in the morning at the earliest, I would like to send word within the hour. What am I allowed to tell them?"

Soon, having dispatched a letter back to Piccadilly and fortified with tea and cake, Radiance began to work.

"It is a shame to lose your glorious white topaz," she said while preparing the mill. "I know it is extremely rare."

"Not lost," he mused. "Merely altered and by your hands. The stone will make a fine brooch for my wife."

This made her head feel hot and her body tingle. She wished she was already married to Edward and could skip the waiting in between.

"Discipline," she muttered under her breath. First, she must help the Queen.

Hours later, just about the time she would be going home from the ball, she had to stop.

"Dancing at this hour is one thing, but my hands are trembling. I need to take a short break," Radiance confessed.

Edward had consulted on the progress of the forgery whenever she'd asked his opinion. And after much improving the state of his workroom, he had alternated between pouring them both endless cups from the pots Mrs. McSabby replenished and keeping Radiance company by reading aloud from one of the books she wished she owned.

By half past one, he, too, seemed to be flagging.

"Very well. A few hours rest should do you the world of good. And me, as well."

Nodding, she rose to her feet and didn't protest when he put an arm around her waist when they left the room. Together, they climbed the stairs, stopping outside the guest chamber where Sarah already waited.

Her maid had arrived hours earlier, but having her sit and watch the proceedings seemed pointless, and thus, Radiance had sent her up to bed.

"You did remarkably well tonight," Edward praised her. "As always, you have impressed me."

In truth, she'd started slowly, hesitantly, but as her confidence had grown, she'd begun to cut the facets more quickly.

"As the hours went by, it became easier," Radiance agreed, feeling proud. Recalling why they were doing such a rash plan, she asked, "You don't think the thief will come back tonight, do you?"

"I don't. He has already ravaged my home once this evening."

"And where will you keep it? The real one?" she asked, leaning back with exhaustion against the bedroom door.

Radiance could scarcely believe she was spending the night in Edward's house, but upon hearing the circumstances, her parents had given their permission, written a congratulatory note upon being apprised of her engagement, and sent Sarah to ensure nothing indecorous went on.

"I intend to put the Koh-i-Noor directly under my pillow," he said, "along with my pistol." Then he cocked his head. "Would I be entirely too rakish if I kissed you?"

"Not entirely," she said. Frankly, it had been a difficult night, working in close quarters with this handsome man she adored, who made every part of her body spark with life.

Instead of drawing her close, he pressed her back against the door. Gasping softly at the exciting sensation of his hard body against her curves, she wrapped her hands behind his neck.

Edward's eyes shone brilliantly golden in the light of the sconce beside them. They were twin beacons of warmth and passion, of happy times ahead, of being together by a flickering hearth-fire, or welcoming babies into the world.

And at that moment, she wished he could truly make her his own.

"All I can think about is having you beside me in my bed," he whispered.

With his thoughts echoing hers, she closed her eyes and enjoyed the instant his firm lips pressed her own. A moment later, his hands cupped her breasts. When his thumbs brushed her nipples in a teasing sweep, she felt them stiffen. Her knees began to tremble.

"I wish," she began when he broke the kiss to let them both draw in long breaths.

"As do I," he said, leaning his forehead against hers.

Radiance had a dreadful thought, but he was not bound by the same limitations as she was. "You won't . . . satisfy yourself elsewhere, will you? I wouldn't like that either before marriage or afterward."

Drawing back, his body started to shake. He was laughing! *At her?* she wondered. *Was her request too outrageous?* Both her sisters' as well as her brother's marriages were faithful. Of that, she had no doubt. But she had within her circle of friends some unhappy ladies who knew—as did everyone around them—that their husbands thought nothing of taking a mistress.

"You don't have to worry," he said. "I apologize for how it struck me as humorous. But why would I want to? You must know you are extraordinary in mind and body. Truly, a diamond of—"

"Don't," she said.

He smiled. "I am sure you have heard it before. But as a geologist, I am more qualified than anyone to say you are a diamond of the—"

"Surely, with your extensive knowledge, you can say something original."

"Very well. You are a diamond from the deepest stratum of the earth, with the utmost clarity, like a still crystalline lake. If women were measured in carbon, then you would contain 99.95 percent."

Radiance couldn't help smiling at his silly and dear compliment.

Suddenly, he sobered. "I can tell you something else I hope you have never heard from a man before. I love you with every atom of my being."

Her smile faltered, and she found it difficult to swallow as tears pricked her eyes. She must be extraordinarily tired for his words to make her feel so weepy.

"I am glad to hear you say so. I thought it unladylike to be the first to speak the words—too forward, as my dear Purity might say. But you have entirely captured my heart, George Edward Lockwood. I love you."

He scooped her close again. "Then it is probably acceptable for us to spend the night together in one bed."

"I think not," she returned, knowing he was teasing by his crooked grin. "Sadly, not acceptable at all."

She found the door handle behind her back and gripped it, anchoring herself because she would most likely give in if he weren't speaking in jest.

"Kiss me again," she demanded, "and then I shall retire."

He did, making her tired toes curl in her slippers before she managed to push the door open. Radiance backed into the room with a last glimpse of her fiancé's beloved face.

CHAPTER FORTY

Outside Lord Diamond's home, Edward helped Radiance from the carriage, followed by her maid. Fittingly for what they'd been up to in creating a monstrous forgery, Sarah was reading *Wagner, the Wehr-Wolf*. He was sorely looking forward to the day Radiance became his wife and they no longer had need of her shadow.

"Thirty-three crown facets, twenty-three pavilion facets," Radiance said, not for the first time, "and eight planes around the culet."

"It looked perfect," he reminded her. Except the diamond was now a white topaz. "And you finished early because you are a genius."

Scotland Yard had been put on notice and given what had happened in Houndsditch and because Edward had mentioned the Queen and the Koh-i-Noor, they sent a detail of their finest to hide in his shrubbery, in his neighbors' houses, and even in the ancient planetrees in the Berkeley Square's central gardens.

After a single conspiratorial glance, he'd left the fake in plain sight on a bed of velvet in a wooden container on his workroom table. Moreover, at Radiance's urging, rather than carrying the Koh-i-Noor on his person, he'd found the perfect hiding place. Even she'd agreed it was.

All they needed to do was wait until Mr. Garrard summoned them to Buckingham Palace. Then, the diamond would undoubtedly gain new life as a brooch, a pendant, or in a tiara for it was still magnificently sized and now would outshine most others.

"I hope the thief strikes again today. For I would hate to have to present the forgery to the Queen," Radiance said.

"I agree," Edward said. "That would be difficult."

"As well as treasonous," she added.

Indeed, one wasn't allowed to lie to one's sovereign. And he was fairly certain their unorthodox behavior would be seen as an egregious lie.

And then they entered Radiance's home together to face her parents.

In very short order, Edward found himself sequestered with Lord Diamond. A series of questions ensued, during which he assured the earl he could support a wife and children while keeping Radiance in a style that would be comfortable, although perhaps not as luxurious as what she was used to.

That part was a decided understatement. Edward hoped he understood his soon-to-be wife well enough to know she would not wilt nor lose her shine because of a less prestigious address and fewer servants at her disposal. They had a meeting of the hearts and minds, which had only grown stronger over the past twenty-four hours.

Having passed the earl's examination, Edward accompanied Lord Diamond to the drawing room for a chat with Lady Diamond and Radiance. Their meeting was no less intense as the countess questioned him on any number of topics to do with children—"have plenty to keep you young"—purchasing a country home—"very much advised to get out of the sticky, late-summer heat and to see your offspring gamboling like lambs," and dinner parties— "throw as many as you can afford because they will keep your staff busy, your home always at its best for show, and your friends and family close."

"As to the latter, let us start tonight," the countess said.

Radiance yawned behind her hand, obviously tired from her long endeavor, but at his questioning look, she nodded.

"How fun!" said Lady Brilliance, who had just wandered in carrying a violin and bow.

"Do you play?" he asked politely.

"No," she said and mysteriously left it at that before plopping herself down beside her mother.

Edward didn't see the problem in enjoying a dinner with his future in-laws until he realized that Lady Diamond wanted *him* to throw the party at his home. In that case, he begged a stay of execution.

"Until tomorrow evening," he suggested. "In order that Lady Radiance may rest."

"Then we shall be there at seven tomorrow," the countess agreed.

"Yes," he said, still trying to sound enthusiastic. "I look forward to it."

DINING WITH ONE'S fiancée was better than dining with any other woman. Of that, Edward had no doubt. However, hosting a dinner for her *and* her parents *and* her younger sister, who seemed ready to say anything that came to mind, was more terrifying than being attacked in the jungle by a knife-wielding thief. Of that, he also had no doubt.

When they were finally alone, as he had been granted a few minutes to take leave of his fiancée, Radiance suggested Edward invite his own family, too. He had put his foot down.

"My dining salon is not large enough. We shall be cramped as it is. After we marry, I intend to move my workroom. You must choose a new table and chairs, and we will host properly in our dining room. Besides, if it is any consolation, my parents will invite yours to dine next week.

I can practically hear my mother shouting with joy already. She will adore having you as a daughter-in-law."

Radiance had beamed her approval by way of a heart-stoppingly beautiful smile, and then he'd kissed her behind a large potted palm in the Diamonds' drawing room.

How on earth had he gained her love? He could almost believe she didn't know what she was getting into by marrying him.

"If you want an attentive, fawning doormat, then I am not your man," Edward confessed. "Similarly, I am not known for my flowery speech or witty turn of phrase."

"I don't care about any of that," she promised, "as long as you are passionate about me, at least as much as your gems and geodes."

"That I can promise for the rest of our lives."

"Then I don't need any fawning," she assured him.

He tilted her chin up and held it in place for another kiss.

"Well, maybe a little fawning," she admitted.

"'*The diamonds of a most praisèd water doth appear to make the world twice rich,*'" he whispered against her lips.

She reared back. "You did not just say that trite phrase, did you? Except in an Elizabethan tongue."

He chuckled. "If you won't let me say it straight from Chambers' Encyclopedia, the way every other man in London says it, then I must quote Shakespeare's *Pericles*."

"That was Cerimon's line, not Pericles'," she teased him, "and I thought you just said you weren't one for flowery speech."

"I have nearly depleted my entire repertoire," he confessed, having felt the urge to brush up on all the best sayings regarding gemstones. "'*If heaven would make me such another world, Of one entire and perfect chrysolite!*' I had to wait a long time to find a woman who knew what a chrysolite is before I could heap such praise," he added, earning another smile from Radiance's perfect lips.

He couldn't help dropping a third kiss upon them.

When he drew back, she bit her lip, making his insides dance. Then a flash of recollection crossed her lovely face.

"In return, I can praise you. *Methought all his senses were lock'd in his eyes as jewels in crystal,'* for I do very much adore your eyes, Mr. Lockwood. And that was *Love's Labour's Lost*, by the way."

He nodded, beyond grateful to have been given a second chance when he least expected it. "I adore you with every molecule and facet of my being. I shall endeavor to make you happy for the rest of our lives, and I want to give you boundless pleasure in our bed."

She gasped softly, appearing eager to experience it.

"Or on a table," he added, teasing her. "Or on a rug by the hearth."

She laughed. "Not flowery but very passionate."

His mouth claimed hers one final time. He was certain he'd pressed his luck, and her father would storm in and toss him to the street. Yet when she parted her lips for him, he delved in.

Afterward, Edward raced home to tell Mrs. McSabby to prepare for the onslaught of guests the following evening.

Then, fortune shone upon him like a diamond in sunlight. Just before midnight, while he was already abed, he heard the *thwack, thwack, thwack* of police rattles, loud and large, the size of a man's shoe. The policemen surrounding his home for the night watch were twirling their noise-makers, indicating they had caught an intruder.

Grabbing his dressing gown, Edward darted down the stairs, meeting Mrs. McSabby in the hallway.

"Lord, sir, I fear I'll be killed in my bed one of these nights."

"Never fear, good woman. The police are all around us." He strode into his workroom.

After lighting a lamp, he surveyed his surroundings. The container was open, the velvet was lying on the tabletop, and the fake diamond was gone. The rattles sounded again, and he went outside in his slippers.

With a policeman holding each of his arms, Rathmond struggled.

Edward was not surprised by the perpetrator's identity. He and Radiance had realized in the long hours while she crafted the fake that the gem dealer was the only one from the committee who could possibly have a reason.

While the police were slipping their lead-filled rattles and their truncheons into the specially designed, swallow-tail pockets of their coats, Edward asked him, "You are connected to Sully, are you not?"

But Rathmond remained mulishly silent.

"No matter. It will all come out in court," Edward promised him, "and you shall undoubtedly join him in Australia."

"He had this on him, just as you predicted," the constable in charge said, showing Edward Radiance's forgery. "I shall have to take it with me, sir. I was in trouble last time for not bringing those Houndsditch gemstones to the Yard."

"As you wish," Edward said. Then he stared into Rathmond's eyes as he added, "In any case, it's a fake. The real one is safe."

The gem dealer's eyes widened before his mouth flattened into a line of disgust.

"Although I would like it back at the court's convenience, as the stone belongs to me."

In fact, Edward realized he cherished the white topaz Radiance had worked on more than any other gemstone he owned.

Thanking the constable for his night's work, he wandered back indoors and went to bed. After all, he would have a long day come morning.

The following afternoon, Edward could almost smell success in the air. His small staff had dusted, swept, and polished every surface, brought in fresh flowers, beaten the drawing room rug, and all but repainted the house's interior. Even his staircase banister was gleaming with thick polish.

Delicious aromas were emanating from his kitchen, too, indicating his cook was doing her part. And as far as he knew, Mrs. McSabby was handling her role perfectly, making all in readiness for when his guests would arrive at seven.

Until she ran into his workroom at six o'clock.

"The wine is sour, sir. Sour as vinegar. I should have known something was up when it wasn't Mr. Wright's normal lad delivering the cask."

Edward dropped his pen as two thoughts came to mind. The first he asked at once. "How do you know the wine is sour?"

Her cheeks reddened. "Well, sir. I have to taste it, don't I?"

"Do you?" he asked.

"I often do, sir. Cook, as well, just a sip to make sure."

"What about the scullery maid?" Edward asked, thinking it a wonder there was ever any wine left in the house. "Is she having a tipple, too?"

"Oh, no, sir." His housekeeper chuckled as if the notion were absurd. "Besides, she probably wouldn't know the good stuff from the bad."

His second thought circled back into his mind. "Aren't all the wine merchants closed at this hour?"

"I believe so, sir."

He tried to quell his rising panic. One could not have an earl and a countess and their two daughters over without any wine to offer. And then the answer came to him.

"I shall rush over to the Athenaeum Club. The manager was especially pleased when I helped him purchase an inexpensive sapphire for his daughter's engagement ring. He will sell me a cask, even without a license. I am certain of it."

"Very good, sir."

Thus, he hastened into a cab and returned less than an hour later with the problem solved.

Yet Mrs. McSabby tried to corner him as he started upstairs.

"Our guests are nearly on our doorstep," he reminded her. "Is your matter important enough that I am forced to greet them in this frock coat, dirty collar, and with my hair standing on end?"

"No, sir." She smiled. "I am pleased you're sprucing up. It can wait till later."

Sprucing up, he muttered to himself. He had done well enough so far to capture the heart of a beautiful lady. Still, he took the stairs two at a time and made sure he looked his best when the Diamonds arrived.

A few hours later, Edward thought himself the most fortunate of men. Mrs. McSabby had created a welcoming environment. She knew how to swiftly take his guests' coats and offer them the hard-won wine. Even though the meal was served in his modest-sized salon, his cook had outdone herself with a seven-course feast such as he'd heard the Queen dined on at state dinners—from creamy pottage through an elegant dessert.

Moreover, Lord and Lady Diamond were kind and warm, and Edward could openly praise Radiance on her amazing skill since her family was aware of what she'd done.

"Your permission for her to stay here to work that night and the following day saved the Queen's diamond," he said, bursting with pride. "I only wish I had Lady Radiance's magnificent forgery to show you."

"May we see the Koh-i-Noor?" Lady Brilliance asked.

Radiance's green gaze shot to his, halting the words on his lips. He was going to say no, not wanting to tempt fate by bringing it out into the open. Yet his lady appeared excited at the prospect of sharing something so special with her family.

Into the hesitation, Lady Brilliance added, "I didn't mean you had to interrupt the meal, sir. After the pudding course would do nicely."

"As you wish," he agreed.

Edward tried not to let the evening's success inflate his pride, but how many of Radiance's suitors had been able to show off a royal jewel to their prospective in-laws? Thus, after inviting them all into his drawing room, he went to the hiding place he and Radiance had chosen upon considering the particular qualities of what they were trying to conceal.

Hiding in plain sight, they had agreed. Opening the small door on the right of his sideboard, he drew out the mirrored tray of glassware and set it on the low table in front of his guests who'd taken seats on the sofa and chairs.

"Lady Radiance may do the honors and pick it out," he said.

She peered down into the glasses while her sister put her head close, black hair against red, and gave an excited clap.

"Oh, that's very clever, sir," Lady Brilliance exclaimed. "I vow it is invisible, for I cannot see it at all."

He waited until Radiance looked up at him, her expression perplexed. "Nor can I."

Both Lord and Lady Diamond leaned forward.

"I would wager my favorite horse those glasses are empty," the earl said.

Edward felt the skin on his neck prickle. At last, he, too, peered into each of the six crystal glasses.

Well, the devil take him!

CHAPTER FORTY-ONE

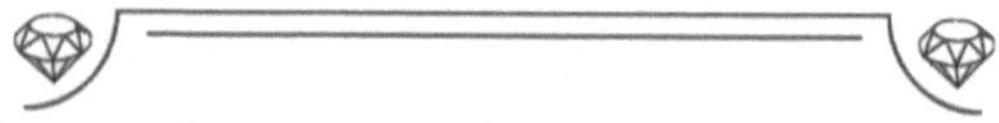

To Radiance's extreme consternation, Edward raised his head and looked into her eyes. His own were filled with disbelief. Then he began to lift each glass, turning it over before putting it back onto the tray.

Together, they stared at the upturned glassware.

"I am desperately hoping you moved the Koh-i-Noor," she said, glad her parents and sister were remaining silent.

"I didn't," he said, his tone choked, as though someone had his fingers around Edward's neck.

Not caring about propriety, she rose to her feet and placed a hand upon his arm.

"Perhaps you did and you forgot. You know how you can be."

He muttered something under his breath. When he opened his eyes, Edward's tawny golden gaze bore into hers.

"I assure you I did not move it. I am also certain I am going to prison for a long time."

Radiance gasped. "That's not fair. We were only—"

"*I* was only." He put both his hands upon her shoulders. "You had nothing to do with this. Do you understand me?"

She did. He was sacrificing himself to save her. It was noble but most likely unnecessary.

"As an earl's daughter, I will be viewed with leniency. In fact, perhaps I should take all the blame. The Queen would never put me in jail."

"I don't understand," Bri's voice sliced through the growing tension. "Why is Her Majesty going to put anyone in jail?"

Her mother and father rose, too. "Let's keep cool heads," the earl said.

"Yes," her mother agreed. "The Queen is a reasonable woman and a mother. She won't put my daughter in jail for trying to help."

"Maybe not," Edward said, addressing her father. "Nevertheless, she might ruin your family as punishment. She could take your title and lands. I shall not have the Diamonds brought so low that you have wealth only in your name. I cannot let you risk it."

Her father crossed his arms. "I doubt it shall come to that." Yet he didn't sound as unconcerned as Radiance had hoped. And if the Queen could punish her family, she could hardly imagine what Her Majesty might do to Edward.

"I cannot let you take all the blame," she said, "regardless of the consequences."

"But I should," he insisted. "It was my plan that has gone awry."

"I was the one who created the forgery," she reminded him.

He barely hesitated. "We cannot announce our engagement."

Her heart squeezed. "Are you reneging on your proposal of marriage?"

"I most definitely am. We must not be associated at this moment, or I shall not be able to save you. After all, more than a few people know you can cut a gemstone."

"Then it is foolish to pretend you somehow did it yourself," she said.

He sighed. "You are being unreasonable."

"And you are being unrealistic. No one will believe you suddenly became a crack lapidary."

"Perhaps we should leave Mr. Lockwood to search his home," her father said.

"Agreed," Edward said. "I am terribly sorry for how this evening has ended."

Bri, who'd been lifting the glasses and peering under each one, spoke into the charged atmosphere.

"Why not ask your staff, sir? Whenever I have lost something, that's what I do. It has proven most fruitful."

Before anyone could respond to that sage advice, Edward darted from the room. Radiance didn't think her family would mind if she followed.

"I'll return directly," she told them, hastening after him.

Darting through the open drawing room door, she would fight for her engagement and upcoming marriage. Although neither were as important as keeping her heart from splintering into a million shards like a badly cut gemstone—yet if she couldn't have Edward, she would have no use for it at all.

Following the sound of his footfalls along the passageway into the kitchen, she found him already calling for Mrs. McSabby.

It was his corpulent cook, with her head of gray curls escaping her bleached white cap, who answered, "She'll be in directly, sir."

Trundling slowly to the bottom of the backstairs, the woman yelled, "McSabby!" in a voice that would be heard by the neighbors.

Radiance laid her hand on Edward's arm to let him know she was there. He startled, turned, and met her gaze. Her insides quaked at his look of utter distress. They were in the soup, and she couldn't set aside the fearful notion that their happy future was slipping away.

Yet hearing footsteps rushing down the servants' stairs, she let a little hope seep in. Perhaps the housekeeper had come across the diamond while dusting and moved it to what she assumed was a safer spot.

Mrs. McSabby practically fell down the last step in her haste. Rounding upon the cook, she demanded, "Is the house on fire?"

The cook simply nodded toward the kitchens' visitors.

"Oh!" Mrs. McSabby exclaimed. "I would've come back to the drawing room, sir, to see if your guests needed anything. I only popped upstairs for a minute. Good evening, again, m'lady."

"Good evening, again, Mrs. McSabby. Mr. Lockwood is searching for something."

"When isn't he, m'lady?" the housekeeper said, as if sharing a joke with her.

Edward stiffened. Radiance feared it was not the right time for teasing.

"You make it sound as if I have misplaced a glove," he ground out. "Rather than discovering a large diamond has gone missing!" He ended his statement by threading his fingers into the hair on either side of his head and making fists as if he intended to yank it all out right then and there.

Yet when Mrs. McSabby's expression lightened, Radiance was sure everything would be well.

"Is that what has you in a tweague?" Edward's housekeeper asked, her hands on her hips.

"Yes. Precisely." Edward lowered his arms. "Tell me you have seen it."

"Of course, I've seen it, sir. It was one of your stranger misplacements, too."

Radiance's stomach twinged, and she watched Edward close his eyes a moment, whispering something—perhaps a message of gratitude.

"I've found sapphires in the dining salon," Mrs. McSabby said, "and giant geodes left for me to trip over in the upstairs hall, but never before have I found a diamond in a drinking glass."

"How did you find it?" Radiance couldn't help asking.

Mrs. McSabby stood straighter. "I am a good housekeeper, m'lady. My maids and I clean as we should. Although even for Mr. Lockwood, it was a strange place to forget something."

"I should have told you," Edward said, his tone hollow, "and warned you *not* to touch it. I didn't misplace it, by the way. I put it there on purpose."

Mrs. McSabby shook her head. "No need to be nettled and up in the boughs, sir. I have the diamond right here." She reached into her apron pocket. An expression of doubt came over her flushed face.

Radiance's stomach fell again. But then the housekeeper reached into her other one and smiled before drawing out the stone and handing it to Edward.

Edward's expression, as if he were going to laugh and cry at the same time, mirrored Radiance's turbulent emotions. Stepping forward, she hugged Mrs. McSabby.

"Thank you," she said, "for keeping it safe."

"Yes," Edward agreed. "But why didn't you tell me what you'd found."

"You were out, sir, getting the wine," Mrs. McSabby said, "as I was doing a last sweep of the drawing room. And I went to tell you upon your return, but you were in a hurry to get dressed for your company." She sent Radiance a kind look. "I admit, ever since I found out you and your family were coming, I've been running around like a chicken what's had its head chopped clean off. Not a usual evening at all, m'lady."

Then Mrs. McSabby's mouth dropped as she stared at Edward. "*You* are the host, sir. And you've gone and left Lord and Lady Diamond and that pretty little miss by themselves all this time. What will they think?"

"They probably think I have been carted off to Newgate. But you are correct. We had best return to them immediately. Please bring some of your fine macaroons. If we haven't driven our guests out with neglect, then I shall pour them each a glass of port."

In the hallway, Radiance momentarily sagged against him, taking comfort from his strength, and then pushed herself away.

"I admit to a few minutes of sheer terror. But my parents have been polite long enough."

With that, they returned to the drawing room to find Monty had been playing host and was now on Bri's lap.

"Is everything settled?" her mother asked. "Did you find the Koh-i-Noor?"

"Was I correct about the staff being helpful?" Bri asked.

Her father crossed his legs and leaned back. "Are we having brandy or port?"

Radiance answered all the questions on Edward's behalf while he poured the port. When they each held a glass, half filled with the ruby liquid, he spoke.

"A disaster averted. Soon, the diamond shall be back with its rightful owner." He placed it on the table in front of her family. "But tonight, we can enjoy it along with this sweet *Oporto*."

In turn, her father, then her mother, and finally Bri held the diamond.

"It is much improved from the one we saw at the Great Exhibition," her mother said. "I remember Ray being disappointed in the extreme. And to think, now you've had a hand in saving it."

Bri handed it to Radiance. She was nearly as thrilled as her family to take a good long look at the Koh-i-Noor. While copying it, she had spent all her time fixated on the white topaz, looking at it through the magnifying spectacles in order to find the best cleavage. All the while, she'd had this marvelous stone set to the side, referencing it only for its angles.

This marvelous stone. This . . .

With her heartbeat quickening, she held it up to the light of Edward's chandelier, a lamp burning with the new paraffin fuel. Radiance's heart jumped into her throat and stuck there.

"I need your magnifying spectacles," she said. It came out as a whispery croak. Without waiting, she ran from the room and along the passage to his workroom.

By the time she'd donned a pair and examined the stone closely, she felt him behind her.

"What's wrong?"

She didn't want to tell him. *But what choice did she have?*

"It's a fake."

Edward didn't grab for it or mistrust her. Instead, calmly, he asked, "*A* fake or *your* fake?"

"Not mine."

"I see," he said. "Actually, I don't see at all. But for a moment, I thought we had let Rathmond steal the real one."

"That would be a blessing," she said. "Then it would be safely at Scotland Yard."

"Indeed." He still sounded too calm, and it was scaring her.

Mrs. McSabby came in. "I took the macaroons to your guests," she said in a scolding tone, "and they were alone. Again!"

"We seem to be in the suds once more," Radiance explained when Edward said nothing.

"Sir?" the housekeeper asked. "Was it my fault?"

Managing with great restraint not to snap at her, although Radiance could see the tension etched upon his face, Edward shrugged.

"Not at all," he said. "Somehow, while the Koh-i-Noor was in my care, it seemed to have been switched for a forgery."

Mrs. McSabby gasped. "That was the Queen's Indian diamond," she said, her voice having dropped to a terrified whisper. "You shall be executed."

Radiance shook her head. "He won't, Mrs. McSabby. This isn't a hanging offense."

His housekeeper shuddered. "Then he'll be sent to Australia with all the other convicts, to broil in the sun or be eaten by saber-tooth crocodiles."

Radiance wondered where Mrs. McSabby got her facts. Before she could soothe her, Edward spoke up.

"Unlikely," he said, which by the look on the housekeeper's face did nothing to quell the woman's fears.

Radiance spoke up. "Mr. Lockwood will set it all right again."

He eyed her sharply, but she nodded with encouragement. With her upbringing, she believed the staff should always think their employer able to fix any problem to maintain the tranquility of the household. That was how one kept their loyalty and devotion, simply by offering it in return.

"Regardless," Edward said, "I promise you that the responsibility begins and ends with me. And now, I had best bid my guests good night."

Radiance watched him turn heel and nearly leave without her. She would get used to his singular focus and not take it personally. At least, she prayed she would have the chance to become accustomed to his ways.

At the last moment, he halted and gestured for her to precede him. Once in the hallway, however, she pressed her hands to his chest to keep him from moving.

"You must let me go with you to the Palace, as before, when we went together to face Mr. Hope."

Ignoring her, he set her to the side as if she were no more than a reedy twig.

She chased him into the drawing room.

"It will be better if I am there."

"No," he said sharply, then glanced at Lord and Lady Diamond, perhaps just recalling they were in his drawing room. He softened his tone. "It would be better if I explained my foolish plan to them by myself."

"But I think—" she began, desperately wanting to help in case Mrs. McSabby's dire prediction of jail or deportation came true.

"Radiance," her father interrupted. "Let Mr. Lockwood deal with this as he sees fit. If your assistance is required, I am sure he will let you know." Then he lifted his glass in the air, toasted to all their health, and drank down the last drop.

Her mother looked as if she might contend otherwise, although she sipped to the toast as well. And Bri looked utterly unbothered, petting the cat and sending her sister a warm smile before adding, "These things have a way of working out."

Radiance wanted to argue with all of them, even her sister for her naïvely cheerful attitude. Everything did *not* have a way of working out. *Not at all! Not without help.* She had only just got Edward back, and that had been bloody difficult.

Radiance had no intention of losing him again!

CHAPTER FORTY-TWO

Edward half expected Radiance to show up uninvited at Buckingham Palace. That would be a disaster. He didn't know how he would protect her from the royal couple's wrath, but it would be impossible if she were there.

For that matter, he didn't know how he was going to protect himself.

Swallowing against the dryness that had plagued his throat all morning, he made his way through the original west wing. Having received word that Her Majesty and His Royal Highness had returned from Scotland, he'd requested an audience. Within two hours, during which he'd paced like a fiend, he'd received a summons to the Throne Room of all places.

Naturally, Edward had bypassed Garrard entirely, not wanting the Crown Jeweler blamed for putting his trust in the wrong man.

Unlike the previous visit, there would be no hopeful Queen and pleasant Prince Consort telling him how grateful they were for his service.

Upon being left alone in the Throne Room by a footman, Edward strolled the chamber. It was very . . . red, as much of the royal decorating was. And gold. Massive red walls stretched up to a gilded ceiling from which sparkling crystal chandeliers, four of them, were suspended. Only the carpet in palest of golden weave, the white marble fireplace, and the wall of windows looking out over the central courtyard broke up the sea of crimson.

Even the huge mirrors on either side of the fireplace, as well as the overmantel mirror, reflected the thick red wallpaper, the window hangings, and the throne canopy. It was beginning to remind him of a butcher's shop.

He started to pace again. Even if it had been permissible to take a seat, he couldn't have as there were none. Except for the throne. Naturally, this, too, was red velvet with gilded wood. He approached it, glancing at himself in the large mirror, startled to see he wasn't a pale shell of himself.

Despite not sleeping, and a general sense of dread, he counted himself a fortunate man. He had won the heart of Lady Radiance Diamond, and that was something he could take to his grave . . . or to Australia.

With the eye of a scientist, he examined the seat of the ruler of all Britannia and India. The throne had been built in the same year Victoria became queen in 1837. Topped with a carved gild crown, under it were her initials, *VR*— for *Victoria Regina*—very prettily engraved in a squiggly fashion. They reminded him of gold filagree, which he knew Radiance had studied and mastered.

Underneath the fancy letters was a row of equally gilded emblems. He bent closer, then straightened. The rose for England, the thistle for Scotland, and the Shamrock for Ireland. Nothing for Wales, he noted, nor for India.

He wondered whether a master wood carver would be invited to add a few more emblems to it. And if so, what would be the symbol for India?

Probably the blasted Koh-i-Noor!

Edward was starting to think it cursed, even as the latest forgery *rested heavily in his pocket.*

While he was admiring the rest of the throne's carvings, its oak and laurel leaves, a hidden door covered in wallpaper to the left behind the throne's gold-fringed canopy opened.

Seeing the Queen's face, Edward would prefer to be underground in an African diamond mine scrabbling in the dirt with his bare hands. In that instant, it wasn't her and the Prince Consort's anger he feared as much as their disappointment.

Directly behind Queen Victoria came the Prince Consort, and behind him, Radiance.

Edward did a double-take. "Lady Radiance?"

"Your geologist is by such a large measure besotted," the Queen said to the stunning redhead who came to a halt to one side of the throne, "that he forgot to greet his Queen first and foremost."

Edward tried to reconcile the fact that his lady-love was at the Palace when he had hoped she was safely in her Piccadilly home.

"I apologize, Your Majesty," he said, coming to stand directly before the Queen and bowing low. He waited a long moment.

"You may rise, Mr. Lockwood. But do not forget the courtesy due my husband."

"Of course not, Your Majesty." Edward bowed to Prince Albert next. "I am glad to see you well, Your Highness."

"And *now* you may greet Lord Diamond's daughter," Queen Victoria added in a teasing tone.

However, when he went to bow to Radiance, she rushed forward to curtsy at the same time.

"I would not feel comfortable if you bowed to me in this setting," she said, "unless I may return the greeting."

"You are above me in station," he reminded her.

"I don't believe I am, sir."

While Edward enjoyed a good riddle, this wasn't the time nor place for one.

"I do not understand," he said, his head spinning to see everyone looking placid. "Why are you here?" It struck him that she had gone ahead of him to confess.

"Your Majesty, whatever Lady Radiance has said, she is *not* to blame. It is entirely my fault the diamond was stolen."

"Is that so?" the Queen asked, taking a seat on her throne. "Husband, what do you make of this?"

"I don't believe we should tease our favorite geologist a single minute," Prince Albert said.

"Agreed," Queen Victoria said. "Let Lady Radiance tell him."

"You never had the genuine Koh-i-Noor, sir."

He would not unman himself by fainting, but for a second, he was lightheaded with relief.

"Mr. Garrard had the diamond the entire time," she explained.

And then a spark of anger shot through him. "Then I was used as bait." He looked at Her Majesty, and said, "My home was broken into twice."

The Queen had the grace to blush. "We knew you could handle anything that occurred. We never dreamed you would go to such measures as those which Lady Radiance has described."

Prince Albert added, "And although you were unaware, we had already requested your house be under surveillance by Scotland Yard."

"I am flabbergasted," Edward said, "and utterly thrilled to learn this."

"There is more good news," Radiance said.

"I am not sure I can handle anything more."

The royal couple chuckled before Queen Victoria said, "I am honoring your service and sacrifice with a barony."

"Isn't that grand, sir?" Radiance asked.

Edward wouldn't disappoint her or the Queen by saying he didn't give a fig about becoming Lord Lockwood. Only because it occurred to him that his wife would now continue to be addressed as a lady. Lady Lockwood. It sounded very good.

"I am grateful and honored, Your Majesty." He knew enough about etiquette to bow extraordinarily low.

Then he recalled Radiance's words of a few minutes earlier. "That's what you meant about our stations."

She smiled softly. "It never mattered to me anyway."

"Young love," the Queen said. "They remind me of us, Husband."

"They do," the Prince Consort agreed.

Edward couldn't wait to leave the Throne Room and soundly kiss Radiance.

THEY DIDN'T EVEN GET out of the Palace, only as far as the landing of the Grand Staircase, before Edward pulled her into an embrace. Ignoring the footman who halted ahead of them, Radiance let him kiss her. It wasn't a mere passing peck, either, but a full-on-the-mouth kiss, making her insides turn to jelly and her knees buckle.

Could she sit on the stairs of Buckingham Palace?

Luckily, his strong arms held her steady.

"How did you know?" he asked.

"I didn't. I came to throw myself on Her Majesty's mercy, only to find out I didn't need to."

He shook his head. "How did neither of us notice we weren't holding a diamond?"

Radiance had pondered that astonishing fact ever since Prince Albert had told her.

"For my part, I was concentrating on your white topaz. I couldn't make a mistake, knowing you had no other. I didn't even study the supposed Koh-i-Noor with the magnification glasses. Why would I? I was concerned only that the forgery be the right shape to fool the thief into taking it."

"I never looked closely after Garrard foisted it upon me," Edward admitted. "The Dutch had presented it, so why would I think he slipped me a different stone?"

"The Crown Jeweler is a tricky man," she said.

"I confess I was more interested in asking him to help me gain admission to the ball and planning what I would say to you than I was in the diamond. Until you pressed against it, I had all but forgotten I even carried it. You are far more important to me than any gem."

Radiance initiated the next kiss. After all, the footman was giving them privacy by keeping his back to them. She might as well take advantage of the situation. *Who knew when next she would be alone with her fiancé?*

"The whole dastardly episode is behind us," Edward said. "And I don't even care about the motivation of Sully and Rathmond or how they are related."

"Half brothers," Radiance told him, having learned it from the royal couple. "That's why Mr. Sully struck me as familiar. It's their eyes and mouths," she mused. "I vow their faces are as alike as two peas."

"And did Mr. Sully *also* rub your ankle?" Edward asked, tilting his head in that way she loved.

Radiance laughed, feeling so lighthearted now that the entire mystery was concluded. "He didn't. To be fair, though, I didn't give him a chance."

"I should hope not. No man had better put a finger on your ankle or anywhere else for that matter, not while I still draw breath."

"The same goes for any female's fingers upon you," she reminded him.

"Of course not," he said, dismissing the notion. "I think we should go directly to your parents and tell them the news, and then to mine. My mother will be thrilled to have a baron in the family."

And she was, but even more so to welcome an earl's daughter.

Two months later, Bri got her wish for a Christmas wedding. Radiance became Lady Lockwood and moved all her belongings to Berkeley Square. As promised, Edward vacated the dining room, giving them space to accommodate both their families at one seating. However, it soon became apparent they should think about moving to a larger house so there would be room for each to have a workroom, as well as plenty of space for a nursery.

One morning in January, she came across her husband motionless, staring out the window. She simply watched him, admiring Edward's profile and the breadth of his shoulders. Eventually, however, she wanted to see his golden eyes.

"Lord Lockwood."

He didn't turn, nor even acknowledge her. She was used to this and took no offense. She even accepted that Mrs. McSabby might be correct in thinking Edward could easily wander into the wrong home if he were lost in thought.

She waited. Another minute passed. Monty circled her legs wanting her to stroke him, which she did. And then, she addressed her husband again.

This time, he turned.

"Lady Lockwood!" He sounded surprised. "How long have you been standing there?"

"Not too long," she said. "How long have you been looking out the window?"

"Looking out the . . ." He stopped. "No, I wasn't. I mean, obviously, I was, but I wasn't seeing anything."

"You were doing nothing, then?"

"Of course not! I was working on a passage for my book. Some days, I fear I'll be an old man when I complete it."

She nearly laughed. "You're not exactly ancient." Seven years older than herself, he was not about to run out of time.

His expression softened. "I am *not* ancient. But I am eager to do and learn many things beyond what I've already done and know."

They were similarly minded. Still, she had yet to tell him about Neble's offer. And now that she was a married woman, she wondered if he would try to restrict her.

"I completely understand," she said. He, more than anyone, knew how she pushed herself beyond the limitations of what was expected. "Naturally, for my situation, the boundaries are narrower than yours, and thus, my endeavors may be smaller."

He shrugged. "I do not see why they should be. I enjoy traveling. You can travel with me. We shall plan a trip for the spring. I intend to keep learning, and I imagine, given your attendance at lectures, that you do, too. I admire your curiosity."

With this encouragement, she couldn't make herself ask his permission to become the head of the House of Neble, so she didn't. Instead, she smiled at him.

"This instant, I am curious as to whether you would like to take a nap with me."

His expression was priceless. It was two in the afternoon, after all. But Radiance considered their time spent in the bedroom to be as enlightening as any lecture she'd ever attended.

She didn't have to ask twice. In two steps, he grabbed her hand and ran for the stairs.

EPILOGUE

To Radiance's amazement, front and center in the window of Asprey's on Bond Street, known for its tasteful decorations, furnishings, knick-knacks, and jewelry was a pyramid of dainty, black jewel boxes, all with their lids open. Upon the blue satin of each interior sat a Koh-i-Noor replica.

Wisely, the fakes appeared like the original, irregularly cut, lumpy stone that last displayed at the exhibition, and thus, with no possibility one could be used in exchange for the current brilliant cut diamond.

With Sarah, she went in and purchased one just for fun to give to her mother. As for herself, she still had her own cherished replica she'd made from Edward's gorgeous white topaz. On the eve of their wedding, he'd presented it to her as a brooch, and currently, it was pinned to her winter wool mantle.

And then she went along to the House of Neble to see how Mr. Minton was doing as the primary jeweler. Beyond that, Radiance was ready to tell Mr. Neble her decision regarding the business proposal he'd made months earlier.

"My answer is yes," she told the old jeweler when seated across from him in his room full of lamps. "I will be honored to take over the House of Neble and handle the day-to-day management, and I vow to keep its name as requested. What's more, I will study your designs and make sure we continue to create your signature pieces."

The jeweler bowed his head momentarily over his steepled fingers. When he raised it, he looked directly into her eyes. "You have relieved me of much worry. It will be almost as though I still have family to carry on my name. I know it is the vanity of an old man—"

"I don't see it that way at all. Neble is the name of this fine establishment because you have built it up from nothing. I completely understand why you would want that to remain the same."

"And you won't feel as though you are working in the shadows? As if you would like to see the name *Diamond* etched in the sign above the door? It is a very good name for a jewelry store."

Radiance laughed. "In a way, sir, women are used to working anonymously or behind the scenes, as it were. Regardless, you may not have heard, but I am no longer a Diamond. I married Mr. Lockwood a fortnight ago."

He nodded, appearing unsurprised. "My vision may be cloudy, but even I could see the two of you made a fine couple. It is a pleasure to share a mutual interest with one's spouse, is it not?"

"Yes, sir."

Then he cocked his head. "I am a little surprised you are not away on a honeymoon trip. In my day, that's what Mrs. Neble and I did."

"We shall do so, sir. My husband is still making preparations for a long voyage, in fact. We are going to Brazil so I can see actual diamond mines for myself. We shall be away for a few months."

"Jolly good," he said. "I shall be ready by then, I think."

"Ready, sir?"

"To step down. I am looking forward to putting my feet up and letting you take over."

Her heart beat a little more swiftly, imagining returning to the shop once she was its owner and manager—and even one of its jewelers.

"At that time, sir, I shall buy you a new ottoman for your comfort, as long as you promise to be available for consultations when I need assistance."

BY DINNER TIME, RADIANCE could hardly wait for Edward to come out of the small upstairs chamber he now used as his workroom. In fact, she gave up waiting. When she felt as if she'd been patient long enough, letting him work without distraction, she intruded upon his lair, a place she tried hard to stay out of.

Not that he minded, but they usually ended up in a horizontal position on one of his worktables. It was the most peculiar and inconvenient place to become extremely aroused.

His head was bowed over a pad of paper and next to him were three small stones.

As usual, he was so focused, he didn't even hear her enter. She crept toward him, determined to place a kiss upon the back of his neck, although his hair was currently covering it. She would blow gently to uncover his skin and then quickly drop a kiss.

She did both, laughing when he startled and dropped his pen. In the next instant, however, he had hold of her arm, pushed his chair away from the table, and tugged her onto his lap.

"Are you trying to steal my gemstones, Wife?"

"Perhaps." She perused the colorful jewels. "I could make a bracelet."

"Would you take my precious work into Bonwit's and turn it into something useless?"

"Useless?" She shook her head, knowing he was teasing. He always exclaimed with fascination over the intricate designs she could now make. "I shall not be going to Bonwit's much longer."

He grinned. "True. Soon, we shall be sailing out of Liverpool. Exciting, isn't it? I cannot wait to show you South America."

"I am beyond ready to sail away with you," she told him. Her trunk was already packed. It had been packed, unpacked, and repacked while she made sure she had what she wanted for the long voyage and overland trek. "However, that's not what I meant. Edward, do you mind having a wife who works?"

"If I did, then I married the wrong one, don't you think? If you don't mind having a husband who works instead of enjoys living off the rents of his tenants, then I don't mind having a wife who makes jewelry. Although I recall you once snapped at the term *work*."

"That's true. At first, I thought it unseemly for me to be anything but an amateur. Now, however, I have changed my mind." Still, she could hardly speak the words for the excitement fluttering in the pit of her stomach. Life was grand and everything good seemed to be ahead of her.

Threading her fingers behind his neck, she pulled him closer for a kiss.

"Lady Lockwood is feeling frisky, is that it? *Before* dinner?"

She giggled, but he claimed her lips, growling softly when she parted them for his exploration. However, when his tongue slid alongside hers, she nearly forgot what she had been going to tell him. And as his teeth sank gently into her lower lip, tugging at it, her most sensitive place reacted.

The next instant, she felt his fingers drawing up her skirts. If he continued, then they would be caught *in flagrante delicto* by Mrs. McSabby—*again!*—when their housekeeper came to announce their dinner was ready.

With that thought, she pushed against his chest.

"Edward!"

He leaned his forehead against hers. "Do you know how much I adore you? As soon as you're near I want to devour you."

His nearness was making her eyes cross, so she squeezed them closed and laughed.

"I can only hope you adore me as much as I do you, but I have something to tell you."

"Do you?" He leaned back. "Then why didn't you say so?"

"Because you are such a dash-fire man, you distract me from my purpose."

"Which is?" He let his finger trace her nipple under the satin bodice of her gown.

Radiance felt it harden, and the other one joined it for good measure. Maybe they would skip dinner and go upstairs. They could always eat later. That seemed an excellent idea as he leaned down to nibble the soft skin at her throat. She arched back to give him access while still talking.

"Which is that I am going to own the House of Neble."

"Are you?" he asked against her neck, before nipping at her skin making her shiver all over.

"Yes. And I am going to run it."

"Will you?" he asked as his tongue took a little trip down the column of her throat to her collar bone.

She sighed. "Yes. What's more, I intend to be one of its principal jewelers."

"You should be the primary jeweler," he said, pushing down the décolletage of her gown and cupping one of her bare breasts.

Gripping his shoulders with both hands, she lay her head back upon the table, giving him room to suck her nipple into his mouth and roll it, easing the tension she was feeling.

Except it didn't. His mouth upon her breast sent a hot tingling sensation straight between her legs.

"Edward!"

"Yes!" he agreed. In another moment, she was once more on her feet, yanking up the neckline of her dress and letting him take her hand in his. They ran for the door and then for the stairs.

"Dinner," Mrs. McSabby called from the hallway, and Radiance was thrilled they had escaped past her.

"Keep it warm," Edward called down to her.

Radiance knew she should be embarrassed, but surely a newlywed couple were allowed to feast upon one another as often as they fed on their cook's offerings.

In their bedroom, they came together like two gemstones in the perfect setting. He eased into her gently, but their lovemaking was bright and rich—like rubies in the sunshine.

With their passion played out, when the powerful storm of their climaxes had rushed through them, shaking and shattering, leaving them damp and spent, Edward rolled over onto his back.

"Ow! What the devil!"

Reaching under him, he withdrew the fake glass Koh-i-Noor she'd bought earlier and had been examining before she'd changed for dinner. He held it up in the air.

"Thank God!" Edward said. "I thought Monty had left us another mouse."

He started to laugh, and Radiance couldn't help joining in.

"I already have one gorgeous Diamond in my bed," he declared, tossing the worthless piece over his shoulder. Taking hold of her hand and bringing it to his lips, he added, "I most certainly do not need another."

Finis

ABOUT THE AUTHOR

USA Today bestselling author Sydney Jane Baily writes historical romance set in Victorian England, late 19th-century America, the Middle Ages, the Georgian era, and the Regency period. She believes in happily-ever-after stories, engaging characters, and passionate romance.

Born and raised in California, she has traveled the world, spending a lot of exceedingly happy time in the U.K. where her extended family resides, eating fish and chips, drinking shandy, and snacking on Maltesers and Cadbury bars. Sydney currently lives in New England with her family—human, canine, and feline.

At her website, SydneyJaneBaily.com, you can learn more about her books, sign up for her newsletter (and get a free book), and contact her. She loves to hear from her readers.